The Demon Spell,
The Vampire Maid, and
The Land of the Hibiscus Blossom

Hume Nisbet

**The Demon Spell, The Vampire Maid, and
The Land of the Hibiscus Blossom**

Contact:
BibliotechPress@gmail.com

The present edition is a reproduction of 1900 publication of this work. Minor typographical errors may have been corrected without note, however, for an authentic reading experience the Spelling, punctuation, and capitalization have been retained from the original text.

ISBN: 978-1-61895-084-0

CONTENTS

The Demon Spell

It was about the time when spiritualism was all the craze in England, and no party was reckoned complete without a spirit-rapping seance being included amongst the other entertainments.

One night I had been invited to the house of a friend, who was a great believer in the manifestations from the unseen world, and who had asked for my special edification a well—known trance medium. 'A pretty as well as heaven-gifted girl, whom you will be sure to like, I know' he said as he asked me.

I did not believe in the return of spirits, yet, thinking to be amused, consented to attend at the hour appointed. At that time I had just returned from a long sojourn abroad, and was in a very delicate state of health, easily impressed by outward influences, and nervous to a most extraordinary extent.

To the hour appointed I found myself at my friend's house, and was then introduced to the sitters who had assembled to witness the phenomena. Some were strangers like myself to the rules of the table, others who were adepts took their places at once in the order to which they had in former meetings attended. The trance medium had not yet arrived, and while waiting upon her coming we sat down and opened the seance with a hymn.

We had just furnished(sic) the second verse when the door opened and the medium glided in, and took her place on a vacant set by my side, joining in with the others in the last verse, after which we all sat motionless with our hands resting upon the table, waiting upon the first manifestation from the unseen world.

Now, although I thought all this performance very ridiculous, there was something in the silence and the dim light, for the gas had been turned low down, and the room seemed filled with shadows; something about the fragile figure at my side, with her drooping head, which thrilled me with a curious sense of fear and icy horror such as I had never felt before.

I am not by nature imaginative or inclined to superstition, but, from the moment that young girl had entered the room, I felt as if a hand had been laid upon my heart, a cold iron hand, that was compressing it, and causing it to stop throbbing. My sense of hearing also had grown more acute and sensitive, so that the beating of the watch in my vest pocket sounded like the thumping of a quartz-crushing machine, and the measured breathing of those about me as loud and nerve-disturbing as the snorting of a steam engine.

Only when I turned to look upon the trance medium did I

become soothed; then it seemed as if a cold-air wave had passed through my brain, subduing, for the time-being, those awful sounds.

'She is possessed,' whispered my host on the other side of me. 'Wait, and she will speak presently, and tell us whom we have got beside us.'

As we sat and waited the table moved several times under our hands, while knockings at intervals took place in the table and all round the room, a most weird and blood-curdling, yet ridiculous performance, which made me feel half inclined to run out with fear, and half inclined to sit still and laugh; on the whole, I think, however, that horror had the more complete possession of me.

Presently she raised her head and laid her hand upon mine, beginning to speak in a strange monotonous, far away voice, 'This is my first visit since I passed from earth-life, and you have called me here.'

I shivered as her hand touched mine, but had not strength to withdraw it from her light, soft grasp.

'I am what you would call a lost soul; that is, I am in the lowest sphere. Last week I was in the body, but met my death down Whitechapel way. I was what you call an unfortunate, aye, unfortunate enough. Shall I tell you how it happened?'

The medium's eyes were closed, and whether it was my distorted imagination or not, she appeared to have grown older and decidedly debauched-looking since she sat down, or rather as if a light, filmy mask of degrading and soddened vice had replaced the former delicate features.

No one spoke, and the trance medium continued: 'I had been out all that day and without any luck or food, so that I was dragging my wearied body along through the slush and mud for it had been wet all day, and I was drenched to the skin, and miserable, ah, ten thousand times more wretched than I am now, for the earth is a far worse hell for such as I than our hell here.

'I had importuned several passers by as I went along that night, but none of them spoke to me, for work had been scarce all this winter, and I suppose I did not look so tempting as I have been; only once a man answered me, a dark-faced, middle-sized man, with a soft voice, and much better dressed than my usual companions.

'He asked me where I was going, and then left me, putting a coin into my hand, for which I thanked him. Being just in time for the last public-house, I hurried up, but on going to the bar and looking at my hand, I found it to be a curious foreign coin, with outlandish figures on it, which the landlord would not take, so

2

I went out again to the dark fog and rain without my drink after all.

'There was no use going any further that night. I turned up the court where my lodgings were, intending to go home and get a sleep, since I could get no food, when I felt something touch me softly from behind like as if someone had caught hold of my shawl; then I stopped and turned about to see who it was.

'I was alone, and with no one near me, nothing but fog and the half light from the court lamp. Yet I felt as if something had got hold of me, though I could not see what it was, and that it was gathering about me.

'I tried to scream out, but could not, as this unseen grasp closed upon my throat and choked me, and then I fell down and for a moment forgot everything.

'Next moment I woke up, outside my own poor mutilated body, and stood watching the fell work going on—as you see it now.'

Yes I saw it all as the medium ceased speaking, a mangled corpse lying on a muddy pavement, and a demoniac, dark, pock-marked face bending over it, with the lean claws outspread, and the dense fog instead of a body, like the half formed incarnation of muscles.

'That is what did it, and you will know it again.' she said, 'I have come for you to find it.'

'Is he an Englishman?' I gasped, as the vision faded away and the room once more became definite.

'It is neither man nor woman, but it lives as I do, it is with me now and may be with you to-night, still if you will have me instead of it, I can keep it back, only you must wish for me with all your might.'

The seance was now becoming too horrible, and by general consent our host turned up the gas, and then I saw for the first time the medium, now relieved from her evil possession, a beautiful girl of about nineteen, with I think the most glorious brown eyes I had ever before looked into.

'Do you believe what you have been speaking about?' I asked her as we were sitting talking together.

'What was that?'

'About the murdered woman.'

'I don't know anything at all. Only that I have been sitting at the table. I never know what my trances are.' Was she speaking the truth? Her dark eyes looked truth, so that I could not doubt her. That night when I went to my lodgings I must confess that it was some time before I could make up my mind to go to bed. I was decidedly upset and nervous, and wished that I had never, gone to

3

this spirit meeting, making a mental vow, as I threw off my clothes and hastily got into bed, that it was the last unholy gathering I would ever attend.

For the first time in my life I could not put out the gas, I felt as if the room was filled with ghosts, as if this pair of ghastly spectres, the murderer and his victim, had accompanied me home, and were at that moment disputing the possession of me, so instead, I pulled the bedclothes over my head, it being a cold night, and went that fashion off to sleep.

Twelve o'clock! and the anniversary of the day that Christ was born. Yes, I heard it striking from the street spire and counted the strokes, slowly tolled out, listening to the echoes from other steeples, after this one had ceased, as I lay awake in that gas-lit room, feeling as if I was not alone this Christmas morn.

Thus, while I was trying to think what had made me wake so suddenly, I seemed to hear a far off echo cry 'Come to me.' At the same time the bedclothes were slowly pulled from the bed, and left in a confused mass on the floor.

'Is that you, Polly?' I cried, remembering the spirit seance, and the name by which the spirit had announced herself when she took possession.

Three distinct knocks resounded on the bedpost at my ear, the signal for 'Yes.'

'Can you speak to me?'

'Yes,' an echo rather than a voice replied, while I felt my flesh creeping, yet strove to be brave.

'Can I see you?'

'No!'

'Feel you?'

Instantly the feeling of a light cold hand touched my brow and passed over my face.

'In God's name what do you want?'

'To save the girl I was in tonight. It is after her and will kill her if you do not come quickly.'

In an instant I was out of the bed, and tumbling my clothes on any way, horrified through it all, yet feeling as if Polly were helping me to dress. There was a Kandian dagger on my table which I had brought from Ceylon, an old dagger which I had bought for its antiquity and design, and this I snatched up as I left the room, with that light unseen hand leading me out of the house and along the deserted snow-covered streets.

I did not know where the trance medium lived, but I followed where that light grasp led me through the wild, blinding snow-drift, round corners and through short cuts, with my head down and the flakes falling thickly about me, until at last I arrived at a silent square and in front of a house which by some instinct, I knew that I must enter.

Over by the other side of the street I saw a man standing looking up to a dimly-lighted window, but I could not see him very distinctly and I did not pay much attention to him at the time, but rushed instead up the front steps and into the house, that unseen hand still pulling me forward.

How that door opened, or if it did open I could not say, I only know that I got in, as we get into places in a dream, and up the inner stairs, I passed into a bedroom where the light was burning dimly.

It was her bedroom, and she was struggling in the thug-like grasp of those same demon claws, and the rest of it drifting away to nothingness.

I saw it all at a glance, her half-naked form, with the disarranged bedclothes, as the unformed demon of muscles clutched that delicate throat, and then I was at it like a fury with my Kandian dagger, slashing crossways at those cruel claws and that evil face, while blood streaks followed the course of my knife, making ugly stains, until at last it ceased struggling and disappeared like a horrid nightmare, as the half-strangled girl, now released from that fell grip, woke up the house with her screams, while from her releasing hand dropped a strange coin, which I took possession of.

Thus I left her, feeling that my work was done, going downstairs as I had come up, without impediment or even seemingly, in the slightest degree, attracting the attention of the other inmates of the house, who rushed in their nightdresses towards the bedroom from whence the screams were issuing.

Into the street again, with that coin in one hand and my dagger in the other I rushed, and then I remembered the man whom I had seen looking up at the window. Was he there still? Yes, but on the ground in a confused black mass amongst the white snow as if he had been struck down.

I went over to where he lay and looked at him. Was he dead? Yes. I turned him round and saw that his throat was gashed from ear to ear, and all over his face—the same dark, pallid, pock-marked evil face, and claw-like hands, I saw the dark slashes of my Kandian dagger, while the soft white snow around him was stained with crimson life pools, and as I looked I heard the clock strike one, while from the distance sounded the chant of the coming waits, then I turned and fled blindly into the darkness.

THE END

The Vampire Maid

It was the exact kind of abode that I had been looking after for weeks, for I was in that condition of mind when absolute renunciation of society was a necessity. I had become diffident of myself, and wearied of my kind. A strange unrest was in my blood; a barren dearth in my brains. Familiar objects and faces had grown distasteful to me. I wanted to be alone.

This is the mood which comes upon every sensitive and artistic mind when the possessor has been overworked or living too long in one groove. It is Nature's hint for him to seek pastures new; the sign that a retreat has become needful.

If he does not yield, he breaks down and becomes whimsical and hypochondriacal, as well as hypercritical. It is always a bad sign when a man becomes over-critical and censorious about his own or other people's work, for it means that he is losing the vital portions of work, freshness and enthusiasm.

Before I arrived at the dismal stage of criticism I hastily packed up my knapsack, and taking the train to Westmorland, I began my tramp in search of solitude, bracing air and romantic surroundings.

Many places I came upon during that early summer wandering that appeared to have almost the required conditions, yet some petty drawback prevented me from deciding. Sometimes it was the scenery that I did not take kindly to. At other places I took sudden antipathies to the landlady or landlord, and felt I would abhor them before a week was spent under their charge. Other places which might have suited me I could not have, as they did not want a lodger. Fate was driving me to this Cottage on the Moor, and no one can resist destiny.

One day I found myself on a wide and pathless moor near the sea. I had slept the night before at a small hamlet, but that was already eight miles in my rear, and since I had turned my back upon it I had not seen any signs of humanity; I was alone with a fair sky above me, a balmy ozone-filled wind blowing over the stony and heather-clad mounds, and nothing to disturb my meditations.

How far the moor stretched I had no knowledge; I only knew that by keeping in a straight line I would come to the ocean cliffs, then perhaps after a time arrive at some fishing village.

I had provisions in my knapsack, and being young did not fear a night under the stars. I was inhaling the delicious summer

6

air and once more getting back the vigour and happiness I had lost; my city-dried brains were again becoming juicy.

Thus hour after hour slid past me, with the paces, until I had covered about fifteen miles since morning, when I saw before me in the distance a solitary stone-built cottage with roughly slated roof. 'I'll camp there if possible,' I said to myself as I quickened my steps towards it.

To one in search of a quiet, free life, nothing could have possibly been more suitable than this cottage. It stood on the edge of lofty cliffs, with its front door facing the moor and the back-yard wall overlooking the ocean. The sound of the dancing waves struck upon my ears like a lullaby as I drew near; how they would thunder when the autumn gales came on and the seabirds fled shrieking to the shelter of the sedges.

A small garden spread in front, surrounded by a dry-stone wall just high enough for one to lean lazily upon when inclined. This garden was a flame of colour, scarlet predominating, with those other soft shades that cultivated poppies take on in their blooming, for this was all that the garden grew.

As I approached, taking notice of this singular assortment of poppies, and the orderly cleanness of the windows, the front door opened and a woman appeared who impressed me at once favourably as she leisurely came along the pathway to the gate, and drew it back as if to welcome me.

She was of middle age, and when young must have been remarkably good-looking. She was tall and still shapely, with smooth clear skin, regular features and a calm expression that at once gave me a sensation of rest.

To my inquiries she said that she could give me both a sitting and bedroom, and invited me inside to see them. As I looked at her smooth black hair, and cool brown eyes, I felt that I would not be too particular about the accomodation. With such a landlady, I was sure to find what I was after here.

The rooms surpassed my expectation, dainty white curtains and bedding with the perfume of lavender about them, a sitting-room homely yet cosy without being crowded. With a sigh of infinite relief I flung down my knapsack and clinched the bargain.

She was a widow with one daughter, whom I did not see the first day, as she was unwell and confined to her own room, but on the next day she was somewhat better, and then we met.

The fare was simple, yet it suited me exactly for the time, delicious milk and butter with home-made scones, fresh eggs and bacon; after a hearty tea I went early to bed in a condition of perfect content with my quarters.

Yet happy and tired out as I was I had by no means a

comfortable night. This I put down to the strange bed. I slept certainly, but my sleep was filled with dreams so that I woke late and unrefreshed; a good walk on the moor, however, restored me, and I returned with a fine appetite for breakfast.

Certain conditions of mind, with aggravating circumstances, are required before even a young man can fall in love at first sight, as Shakespeare has shown in his Romeo and Juliet. In the city, where many fair faces passed me every hour, I had remained like a stoic, yet no sooner did I enter the cottage after that morning walk than I succumbed instantly before the weird charms of my landlady's daughter, Ariadne Brunnell.

She was somewhat better this morning and able to meet me at breakfast, for we had our meals together while I was their lodger. Ariadne was not beautiful in the strictly classical sense, her complexion being too lividly white and her expression too set to be quite pleasant at first sight; yet, as her mother had informed me, she had been ill for some time, which accounted for that defect. Her features were not regular, her hair and eyes seemed too black with that strangely white skin, and her lips too red for any except the decadent harmonies of an Aubrey Beardsley.

Yet my fantastic dreams of the preceding night, with my morning walk, had prepared me to be enthralled by this modern poster-like invalid.

The loneliness of the moor, with the singing of the ocean, had gripped my heart with a wistful longing. The incongruity of those flaunting and evanescent poppy flowers, dashing the giddy tints in the face of that sober heath, touched me with a shiver as I approached the cottage, and lastly that weird embodiment of startling contrasts completed my subjugation.

She rose from her chair as her mother introduced her, and smiled while she held out her hand. I clasped that soft snowflake, and as I did so a faint thrill tingled over me and rested on my heart, stopping for the moment its beating.

This contact seemed also to have affected her as it did me; a clear flush, like a white flame, lighted up her face, so that it glowed as if an alabaster lamp had been lit; her black eyes became softer and more humid as our glances crossed, and her scarlet lips grew moist. She was a living woman now, while before she had seemed half a corpse.

She permitted her white slender hand to remain in mine longer than most people do at an introduction, and then she slowly withdrew it, still regarding me with steadfast eyes for a second or two afterwards.

Fathomless velvety eyes these were, yet before they were shifted from mine they appeared to have absorbed all my

8

willpower and made me her abject slave. They looked like deep dark pools of clear water, yet they filled me with fire and deprived me of strength. I sank into my chair almost as languidly as I had risen from my bed that morning.

Yet I made a good breakfast, and although she hardly tasted anything, this strange girl rose much refreshed and with a slight glow of colour on her cheeks, which improved her so greatly that she appeared younger and almost beautiful.

I had come here seeking solitude, but since I had seen Ariadne it seemed as if I had come for her only. She was not very lively; indeed, thinking back, I cannot recall any spontaneous remark of hers; she answered my questions by monosyllables and left me to lead in words; yet she was insinuating and appeared to lead my thoughts in her direction and speak to me with her eyes. I cannot describe her minutely, I only know that from the first glance and touch she gave me I was bewitched and could think of nothing else.

It was a rapid, distracting, and devouring infatuation that possessed me; all day long I followed her about like a dog, every night I dreamed of that white glowing face, those steadfast black eyes, those moist scarlet lips, and each morning I rose more languid than I had been the day before. Sometimes I dreamt that she was kissing me with those red lips, while I shivered at the contact of her silky black tresses as they covered my throat; sometimes that we were floating in the air, her arms about me and her long hair enveloping us both like an inky cloud, while I lay supine and helpless.

She went with me after breakfast on that first day to the moor, and before we came back I had spoken my love and received her assent. I held her in my arms and had taken her kisses in answer to mine, nor did I think it strange that all this had happened so quickly. She was mine, or rather I was hers, without a pause. I told her it was fate that had sent me to her, for I had no doubts about my love, and she replied that I had restored her to life.

Acting upon Ariadne's advice, and also from a natural shyness, I did not inform her mother how quickly matters had progressed between us, yet although we both acted as circumspectly as possible, I had no doubt Mrs Brunnell could see how engrossed we were in each other. Lovers are not unlike ostriches in their modes of concealment. I was not afraid of asking Mrs Brunnell for her daughter, for she already showed her partiality towards me, and had bestowed upon me some confidences regarding her own position in life, and I therefore knew that, so far as social position was concerned, there could be no real objection to our marriage. They lived in this lonely spot for the sake of their health, and kept no servant because they could not get any to take service so far away from other humanity. My coming had been opportune and welcome to both mother and daughter.

For the sake of decorum, however, I resolved to delay my confession for a week or two and trust to some favourable opportunity of doing it discreetly.

Meantime Ariadne and I passed our time in a thoroughly idle and lotus-eating style. Each night I retired to bed meditating starting work next day, each morning I rose languid from those disturbing dreams with no thought for anything outside my love. She grew stronger every day, while I appeared to be taking her place as the invalid, yet I was more frantically in love than ever, and only happy when with her. She was my lone-star, my only joy—my life.

We did not go great distances, for I liked best to lie on the dry heath and watch her glowing face and intsense eyes while I listened to the surging of the distant waves. It was love made me lazy, I thought, for unless a man has all he longs for beside him, he is apt to copy the domestic cat and bask in the sunshine.

I had been enchanted quickly. My disenchantment came as rapidly, although it was long before the poison left my blood.

One night, about a couple of weeks after my coming to the cottage, I had returned after a delicious moonlight walk with Ariadne. The night was warm and the moon at the full, therefore I left my bedroom window open to let in what little air there was.

I was more than usually fagged out, so that I had only strength enough to remove my boots and coat before I flung myself wearily on the coverlet and fell almost instantly asleep without tasting the nightcap draught that was constantly placed on the table, and which I had always drained thirstily.

I had a ghastly dream this night. I thought I saw a monster bat, with the face and tresses of Ariadne, fly into the open window and fasten its white teeth and scarlet lips on my arm. I tried to beat the horror away, but could not, for I seemed chained down and thralled also with drowsy delight as the beast sucked my blood with a gruesome rapture.

I looked out dreamily and saw a line of dead bodies of young men lying on the floor, each with a red mark on their arms, on the same part where the vampire was then sucking me, and I remembered having seen and wondered at such a mark on my own arm for the past fortnight. In a flash I understood the reason for my strange weakness, and at the same moment a sudden prick of pain roused me from my dreamy pleasure.

The vampire in her eagerness had bitten a little too deeply that night, unaware that I had not tasted the drugged draught. As I woke I saw her fully revealed by the midnight moon, with her black tresses flowing loosely, and with her red lips glued to my arm. With a shriek of horror I dashed her backwards, getting one last glimpse of her savage eyes, glowing white face and blood-stained red lips; then I rushed out to the night, moved on by my fear and hatred, nor did I pause in my mad flight until I had left miles between me and that accursed Cottage on the Moor.

THE END

The Land of the Hibiscus Blossom

Preface

LAST year, while travelling over Australasia collecting material for a work then being prepared, I thought to score a point for my firm while up in Northern Queensland by visiting that as yet considerably dark island, New Guinea.

The Melbourne editor and agent at once consented to my proposal, and considered, with me, that it would be of great advantage to the work if I could make my notes and sketches from the savages and their land direct, if I thought it was worth risking my life for; but was it after all worth the risk?

In Australia, New Guinea is a name to inspire fear and trembling; they are much nearer to the dreaded cannibals, and hear more of their deeds of atrocity than we in England are and do. Tales of death from fever to those who luckily escape the spears and poisoned arrows float down monthly.

"God help you if you go to that fever-stricken land," wrote a Victorian friend, by way of farewell.

I considered it worth the risk, and as I had in former years lived with the cannibals of New Zealand, besides having had some distant relations wolfed amongst them in the good old days, I did not feel quite the same shrinking as a new chum might.

It was rather amusing to hear the sad forebodings of casual friends whom I picked up as I progressed towards my destination; the nearer I drew to it, the sadder became the gloomy farewells.

"You are too plump to escape the natives."

"Just the temperament to catch the fever quickly." And so on.

I made friends at Thursday Island, and was fortunate enough to find the mail-steamer going, not only to Moresby, but round the coast as far as Teste Island; so Mr. Vivian Bowden, the plucky manager of the enterprising firm of Messrs. Burns, Philip, and Co., made up his mind to take a little holiday and accompany me on the voyage round the British part of the island.

I am indebted to his kindness in many ways; not less to his great patience, allowing me to use their vessel pretty much as I liked, but in giving me time to take as many sketches as I wished, besides introducing me to the genial and generous traders throughout the islands of the Torres Straits, and where they had ventured to establish stations in New Guinea.

I met with no mishaps from natives, nor did I catch the fever. Everywhere I was cordially received and overpowered with kindness: by the Governor, his Excellency Sir John Douglas, the missionaries, white and coloured, the traders, and those splendid man-eaters, the natives; so that now I can hardly know which to admire or regret the most, since fate has forced me to say "adieu."

I mixed with the traders and listened to their thrilling tales night after night; I went amongst the natives, who gave me presents, looked wonderingly upon my sketches, and treated me like a friend and brother, acting with scrupulous honesty, and feeling my arms and legs with apparent pleasure, but without desire.

The Kanaka teachers whom I met astonished me, without exception, by their patience under no ordinary sufferings and their Christian heroism; they had come to the land to lay down their lives, and went with contented faces about their daily sacrifices.

With the missionaries it was the same, Protestant and Catholic; it was not only a question of giving up the necessities of civilization, but the yielding up of their lives.

To write a story about New Guinea and introduce fictitious characters I found to be one of the most distasteful tasks I have ever attempted, as the number of white men who have as yet been there are so few that they are all known, with their characteristics, as well as the names of the islands, with their differences of outline, which lie about the coast.

Again, when I tried to work out my characters, the men I had known came up so vividly before me that I found it next to impossible to resist describing some peculiarity when building up my heroes.

Therefore, if any one is inclined to take umbrage, or fancy himself to be the person I describe, because in some points he may trace a resemblance, I trust he will exonerate me entirely as he reads, and believe me when I tell him that "It is not you I mean."

There are no such characters in reality as Niggeree, Carolina Joe, General Flagcroucher, or Professor Killmann—remember that always as you read; they are entirely imaginary characters, or, rather, embodied principles of what might influence the future of this great island, if lawlessness was allowed to run riot and religion and order were not in the majority.

Yet I will, however, admit that there was a Toto at Hula. He may be known to those who have been there, particularly to those who may have been unjustly blamed for his iniquities.

Regarding the geographical correctness of locality, however,

13

the truth of colouring, and the habits and customs of the people, I have been most rigid, and never for a moment permitted myself a licence; also I do not think that I have exaggerated the murders. If the incidents did not happen while I was there, that they have taken place, and are taking place weekly, a glance at the Government records of massacres and atrocities will convince any one; so that, although I escaped hurtless, it might have been otherwise I will at once admit.

Besides my own observations, I was indebted while in the Papuan Gulf for much information from Mr. Andrew Golchi, botanist and naturalist at Port Moresby, who placed his diaries and experiences of ten years at my disposal; Mr. Cuthbertson and party of surveyors; Mr. Bruce and the young missionary, Mr. Savage, at Murray Island; Father Virgirce at Yule Island; Messrs. Gerise and Moresby, of York Island; Mr. Kissick, of Teste Island; and Mr. A. Morton, Curator of the Museum, Hobart, a New Guinea traveller; besides many of the native teachers and traders with whom I sojourned.

His Excellency Sir John Douglas and his representative, Mr. Milman, at Thursday Island, also gave me the benefit of their experiences, and authenticated the sketches and notes which I had taken.

The Rev. Mr. and Mrs. Lawes I only saw for a few minutes at Port Moresby, as they had just returned from a coasting cruise; but when I reached England I had the benefit of many hints and suggestions from the Rev. James Chalmers, whom I met in London; also a very great amount of valuable information from my lately-gained friend, the Rev. Dr. S. Macfarlane, LL.D., whose long experience in the South Seas and New Guinea fully warrants the trust which I place in his criticisms.

Details of the discovery of two important rivers since I left the Papuan coast I received from my friend James Burns—to whom I beg to dedicate my story—Mr. Theodore Burns being the explorer, for particulars of which discovery see note on New Rivers.

I admire the missionaries, as I admire the traders, when I can place myself on their different platforms and look as they do; they are working faithfully and well in their different ways to civilize the savages. Yet this is not a missionary tale, but the words of one who believes as Professor John Ruskin believes, that what the savage gains from religion and civilization is not equivalent to his own benefits when left alone.

On the whole, I think we civilized savages murder as much and as atrociously as the so-called savages do in dark lands, even though we may not eat our victims; and, aside from this evil, I fancy that they are happier in their simplicity than we are with our vaunted civilization.

Still, since we have souls to be redeemed, and if the penalty of ignorance is damnation, then it is the duty of the missionary to enlighten the dark races, and ours as Christians, to help them to our utmost in their noble work.

Looking on the savages of New Guinea from a material standpoint, I think that they are much more comfortable as they now are than are our English poor—indeed, than many of our English middle-classes—who are fighting so madly for an existence, while they, the natives, bask away luxuriously on their coral-fringed and sunny strands.

Professor John Ruskin, the philanthropist and friend of mankind in general, wrote to me on my arrival in England, saying, "I hope you intend to print some record of the kindness of the native race, whom I suppose our Christianity will now soon extinguish with gunpowder and brandy."

I have endeavoured to give a faithful record of the natives and their kindness, when not abused, towards strangers; and I trust to be able to tell further, at some future time, of their traits. As yet I can vouch that I never saw a native of New Guinea touch intoxicants; they are simple in their diet and drink, and have no more taken to our firewater than they have taken to our other habits. But how long it will be before they lose their simplicity, become converts, and finally are extinguished, is but a question of time.

We who are the favoured ones of earth teach the naked races how to dress themselves before we bury them. It is the legend of the devil and Adam being constantly enacted under the specious title, Civilization.

THE AUTHOR

Chapter I
An Island in the Torres Straits

A DARK night, as nights are in the tropics before the moon rises, in spite of those dense clusters of stars which stain, like milk-splashes, the intense blue-black of that vault above, or the more isolated worlds which hang, as if they were electric globes let down by invisible wires, from that vast ceiling, whose extremity the eye cannot reach!

Very bright those irregularly hung lamps; very close-set, and sparkling, those clusters of gems beyond, very filmy the milk-stains upon that blue—black roof; but the space is too mighty to be illuminated even by those myriad lights, their effulgence is sucked up by the miles of atmosphere, and so on the shores, and in the jungle, darkness grapples with form and wins the battle; the eye looking up becomes dazed with that studded diamond vault and blinded to all beneath.

It is an island within that great barrier reef, which extends from above Keppel Bay to Cape York, and along the Torres Straits to the Papuan Gulf, making eternal summer and calm seas—one of those islands raised by the insect creators of continents, who are for ever working, regardless of time; one of the many formed, or in process of formation, which greet the anxious glance of the mariner every few miles of his dangerous navigation through those uncertain waters upon which the sun warmly smiles, and shows in the varied shades of delicious green, the spots to be avoided; and, in the threads of amethyst, the narrow passages to trust for safety. There are no charts to guide the mariner as yet, only the sharp eyes and the steady head; for woe to the unlucky master who pins his faith to a chart, when his vessel sails within these reefs.

This island has been long established as a place of call for vessels going pearl-fishing, bêche-de-mer, or copra collecting, and is inhabited by a tribe of blacks who give hospitality and work to the traders who have settled amongst them, and who feed them and teach them the refinements of civilization, in return for hospitality and assistance in their business.

The island is well protected from rough seas by the great coral wall which lies about two miles to westward, and is guarded from the near approach of uninvited visitors by hummocks and sharp-edged fringes which are covered at low-tide and surround the smooth sand-shore, layer within layer, with fathomless depths of ocean between, until the innermost fringe is passed. Then a long spread of shallow water has to be waded over, before dry land is reached, so that the trader, as he sits in his bungalow with his friendly servant-hosts behind him, need only wait and finish his pipe, if the visitor chances to be one of those interfering personages, until the unwary vessel safely runs and sticks against the protecting reef-walls, when he sallies forth to rescue the wrecked crew and claim the wreckage according to the very just and proper law of flotsam.

On this dark night there were several small stranger vessels lying about alongside Carolina Joe's own craft. (Carolina Joe was the title this protector of these friendly natives bore amongst his friends and admirers.) As these vessels were all safely at anchorage, we must conclude that they had been here before, and did not come for hostile purpose.

Neat little craft, rocking under the starlight, and breaking the reflection of the sparkles below with their hulls and hull-shadows, but with nothing definite as regards outline or proportion.

On shore—along the dark strips of sand discernible only because of the more intense shadow of the palm and croton groves behind and the jet-like reflecting blackness of the water lapping softly against dead shells and broken fragments of coral—a heavy breath breaking upon the silence along with a faint cocoa-nut odour, apprises one of a native gliding past. The sand is smooth, and hard, and pleasant to the bare feet where it is not covered with those spider-spiked shells; and from the shallow parts you step upon a smooth warm plain, for the night is still too young for the heavy dews to cool the ground; thence into the copse, guided by the faint red glow from the drying-house. This gleam comes through the crevices of the corrugated iron sides of the shed, or further on from the hut, where the king and his family wait awake for the orders of their friend and master, the trader, and where they silently squat and smoke. The red fire from their pipes, and the sombre glow from their neglected log alone break upon the blackness of the night.

It is all quiet and indefinite until a splash of oars, from the rocking boats, breaks in upon the repose, a gentle splashing of paddles used by dextrous hands, and the huts are deserted, while the lonely shore is peopled as if by magic.

They are landing something from the boats, and, without a word spoken, the object is taken out, lifted by two indistinct forms, and carried forward, while the canoe drifts back again as the crowd disappear into the general dark envelopment of night, and once more all is still.

Chapter II
Captain Cook's Telescope

"THIS yer telescope, mates, belonged to Capting Cook."

"Coudn't ha' believed it?"

"No, there's not a many as can."

Carolina Joe, as host, was exhibiting the curiosities of his bungalow to the brother traders, who were now sharing his hospitality for the night, some on their way to New Guinea, some to the islands and stations scattered over Torres Straits, devoted to pearl-fishing, copra or bêche-de—mer collecting, bird or curio hunting, &c.

The etceteras of their profession included various modes of making money, which may appear in the course of their conversations, and so need not be here explained.

Joe held in his brown paws a large copper and canvas-bound telescope, much battered, though hardly of ancient enough pattern to have done service in the Endeavour; yet, as these honest old sailors, who formerly scoured the seas and now bask their declining days under the cocoanuts, are proverbial for their rigid adherence to facts, it might have been Cook's.

"This is how it happened, mates: ye all remember the Polly going on the reefs half a mile from here?"

"That night you lighted the fires at the wrong place, you old beach—coomber," observed, in a very gruff voice, a swarthy young man, from a corner where he sat panikin in hand, almost doubled up from the remains of the malaria fever.

"That was the night, Nig! only you're all out about the fires, I knowst nothink what-some-ever about these yer fires; the natives had a wake on that night, and I was sound asleep until they called me up next morning, and no one can say that I didn't do my duty as a man; I saved the crew, as ye all know, and lent them my boat Daisy to carry them to Thursday Island."

"That's true, Joe, the same smack that you afterwards sold the French missionary with, and which they have christened Pope Pius; and you say you are a good catholic."

"I am a darned freethinker, as all the world knows; I've got all the books on it in that yer chest along o' my revolver and 'munition, and I only did my duty by that yer Daisy. Didn't these missionary chaps want to get to Yule Island after they were refused permits to land on New Guinea, and didn't they see the cursed smack afore they bought her? that was fair and square dealing, wasn't it? Did they ever ax me one question as to her age, or state of repair? and didn't they offer me right away 8ol. for her, and no questions axed, and was I going to be a darned old fool and tell them she was rotten? Not likely, boys; Carolina Joe wasn't raised in old Virginia to come it that way; besides, didn't I get the boys to paint it all neat over inside and out without being axed in the bargain?"

Joe paused a moment, flourishing Captain Cook's relic in his right hand and his empty panikin in the other, and glaring savagely in the direction of the doubled-up "Nig," who only smiled quietly, without replying.

"That's all correct, Joe; you did, even before they saw her, as soon as you heard they wanted a boat," cried out a very slender, gentlemanly young fellow dressed in spotless white, with an aristocratic and clean-cut face, who had twice filled his can from the bottle while Joe was speaking—"but go on about the telescope."

Joe swaggered over to the deal plank which did service for a table, emptied about half a bottle of whisky into his panikin, drank it straight away without winking, and, drawing the hairy back of his hand across his grizzly beard, went over through the soft sand to his former place beside his sea-chest, and continued:—

"Wall, along o' the other articles in that er wreck (and precious little there war, for all the trouble as I took over it)."

"What trouble, Joe?" asked the young man, filling up for the fourth time, and emptying the bottle as he inquired.

"Landing it on the safest reef in course; didn't I watch her all that cursed arternoon a-coming on afore the wind with the infernal moon—soon blowing in my teeth, and not a drop o' liquor to keep the ague back."

"Oh you did, did you?"

"Of course a man's got to keep his eyes about him, or them niggers allays bungle business, an' not a wink o' sleep that night I got, thinking they'd get off after all."

"But I thought you were fast asleep that night," observed Nig softly.

"Asleep, who do you think could plant the fires right if I fell asleep?"

A general grin passed round the company, as one little girlish-looking man, with bright blue eyes and fair moustache, drew with his knife corkscrew the corks from three more bottles of whisky, while the others held out their panikins for him to fill up, and then they settled down to listen, and light their pipes.

"Cartainly Queen Ine is purty smart, and can do most

anything I teach her to do, but it's best to superintend delicate work oneself."

"Quite right, Joe! Quite right," responded, in a thin voice, Captain Allan Collins, with his head on one side; he wore it thus, not from choice or habit, but from necessity, having had it nearly severed at one time by natives, the same cause which produced his piping voice.

"But about that telescope, Joe; how do you know it to have been Cook's?" asked the youth with the clean-cut features.

"Because after we got that wreck broken up, I found it amongst the coral under her hull, and because his name war written on it; of course, mates, it warn't very plain, yet I could just make it out, though the friction had wore off the date. I could just make out the letters, 'COOK,' a way he had o' spellin' his name, I believe."

"Not an uncommon way of spelling cook. Might it not have belonged to some ship's cook—?"

This from the youth with an air of innocence, upon which the others laughed.

"Ship's cook! When did ye ever hear of a cook with a telescope like this?"

"It certainly would be superfluous furniture to cart about, but let's see it; is the name still on it?"

"Wall, you see, Queen Ine is fond o' polishing up brass work, and I guess that's how it wore off, but it was there when we fust had it, wasn't it, 'Spears'?"

"Oh, yes! right under where the canvas now is, we covered it so to preserve it," responded Spears, from his chin.

"After it was gone," murmured Nig sadly, puffing out a little smoke from his nearly finished pipe.

Chapter III
In the Bungalow

CAROLINA JOE'S abode, where this little convivial gathering of friends were now seated, was built after the style of the native houses upon the islands; a hut with posts and rafters of bamboo, lathed with split cane, walls and roof thatched with fronds of the bamboo and tattered fringes of the banana, a sloping roof with the ragged ends of the thatch hanging down between the bars of split cane, walls hung at odd places with tortoiseshells

20

strung together and ready for transport, native curios, spears, shields, and ornaments, all there for sale purposes, yet giving the interior a most picturesque appearance. A rough form had been made by "Spears," formerly a ship's carpenter, but who now represented the handy man of the island, a table likewise made from a roughly sawn board, and which, with three sea-chests, comprised the furniture of the bungalow—that is with the exception of the bamboo couches; with these the place was plentifully supplied, three sides of the room being taken up with them; broad springy couches, each capable of accommodating six or eight people, and where Joe was wont to loll and smoke during the days when there was no drink in the locker, for on these balmy islands whisky does not come every day in the week, nor even once in the month. Sometimes months passed before the ordered case arrived, and when it did turn up, one day was sufficient to empty it, the rest of the long interval having to be spun out with cocoa-nut milk. To-night Joe was merry, for three long-delayed cases had arrived all at once, so that the result meant a glorious orgie while they lasted.

The bungalow had been raised on the sands which served for floor and carpet, soft fine dry sand into which the feet sank deeply; like all native houses the door-way served to admit fresh air and light, so that while by day the sun glared outside, and beat upon the sea shores until they felt nearly red hot, or slanted in long white rays between the fronds of palms, here there was always a cool and constant twilight.

A pleasant home to rest in, amid tropic heats, in spite of the multitudinous life which swarmed and throve amidst that tawny coloured thatch; scorpions, centipedes, spiders and snakes—one gets used to all that as one gets used to mosquitoes, and soon forgets the dangers and discomforts; but upon the stranger, the flop-flap of the poisonous snake moving about at nights after mice and vermin inside the sleeping quarters, has a disturbing effect. The thud of the large centipede, as it drops from the roof upon your face or shoulders is apt to cause a shudder, while the sight of a huge hairy-limbed tarantula lazily moving towards you, not many feet off, does not conduce to speedy repose, any more than the buzzing and stinging of the myriad mosquitoes will do; yet to all these discomforts time brings the cure, and after all it is astonishing how little trouble there is about even misery when one gets used to it.

A pair of tight boots, or the parting with a dear friend, shape in alike by degrees.

This night the mosquitoes swarmed in myriads; spotted fiends bred in the mangroves and making night musical with their revengeful ditties; in the soft sands one being pricked in the foot never felt sure whether it was the bite of a centipede or the sharp edge of a shell; from the slender rafters heavy webs swung undisturbed, the whole only faintly lighted by the single tallow-candle which flared in the night breeze and overflowed the square sides of the empty gin-bottle which served as a candlestick. But those assembled were long accustomed to sights like this; indeed this represented Elysium after the close cabins of their little vessels, and they spread out their scantily clad limbs with an air of unaccustomed comfort.

A ruddy illumination of bronzed faces, bare arms and legs, and exposed chests, as they sat there gradually getting mellow and disconnected in their articulation, while fresh corks were drawn, and young cocoanuts emptied of their fluid.

These young cocoanuts are only used for the milk, which serves instead of water to quench thirst or dilute spirits, although on nights like this, and in such company, like the water used in the punch-brew of the "Noctes" club, one cocoanut went much further than a bottle of "Tappit Hen."

The apartment was about eighteen feet by twelve, so that the company sat close and the single candle served to make objects discernible while at the same time flinging heavy shadows behind and above.

Spears and Danby (the youth with the aristocratic features) half reclined upon one of the couches in the shady side of the room, dangling their naked limbs, with their pijamas rolled up to the thighs for the sake of wading freely, and dipping their feet into the soft loose sand which they caught up between their toes and scattered about while they drank and smoked.

By the plank-table, and crouched together leaning his bare brown arms against it, sat "Nig," or Niggeree, as the natives called him; sallow, thin, and looking undersized and weary, from the after prostration of the fever he had gone through, that wasting fever caught at Port Moresby: to-night he appeared to be about twenty-six; a weak young man, speaking in a low dejected tone, and with great effort; he was clean shaven, with regular features and eyes black and filmy; he only spoke when addressed or when chaffing Joe, and then said as little as he could as if finding the attempt too much for his strength; his pipe had gone out and he did not attempt to light it afresh, and when he lifted his can to his lips he merely tasted the contents, and put it down again with a contortion as if it was medicine.

Near him, on one of the sea-chests, sat Captain Allan Collins, with his head on one side, displaying a long thin neck, and sharing the seat with the German engineer, Hans Helfich; while on

22

the ground amongst and half buried in the sand squatted the short and burly figure of that old sea—dog, Captain MacAndrews, master of the little reef-steamer Thunder, which now lay to leeward of the island.

The group here gathered together, and unconsciously striking up picturesque attitudes within this native-built hut, might well have been taken for a pirate crew holding their nightly orgies ashore under the wind-shaken flame of this candle— perhaps in drawing the picture it would be better to substitute a flaring torch for the flickering candle, only that this was a hut built of easily-ignited material instead of being a sea—rover's cave, while the gentlemen assembled were only honest traders and idlers out for an adventure instead of being bold buccaneers, so perhaps it is as well in this case to adhere to strict facts, prosy though they be.

Niggeree being nearest the candle, caught upon his swarthy, if wan, neck and chest, the strongest glare, and as he had turned to speak to Hector, the young man with the fresh girlish face, his profile was completely in shadow, as were his lower limbs and left shoulder, a trifle brown where the skin shone out, with an edge of dingy yellow undershirt torn open at the neck for air.

Hector stood still drawing corks, but tasting only from the half—cocoanut, which he had made a cup of, for while he diligently filled out for the others, as strong as they desired, he took his cocoa-milk unadulterated, as Joe took his spirits.

The light shone full upon Hector, and revealed a fair young face, which the sun had only slightly reddened, and a breast white as a child's flesh below the abrupt line made by the shirt when buttoned; a golden moustache, and limpid blue eyes, where truth might have dwelt serene; his voice soft and caressing, his manner deprecating, as if he felt an intruder, and his age seemingly about twenty-one. As he replied to "Nig's" dejected question with a few earnest words, as if his soul spoke through his lips, a stranger might wonder at so much innocence wandering so far from home; but none of the company seemed surprised. In reality he was twenty-nine, and if the shirt had been thrown a little wider, discoloured blue blotches would have revealed where the spear or bullet had pierced; also the table cast too heavy a shadow over the bare lower limbs to reveal the many scars there. Hector, with the girl's face and small body, had fought his way into respect with these rough traders of the Torres Straits, while the man-eating savages of the Fly River paid as much attention to his tender words as to a pistol-shot.

Joe, as master of the premises, was monopolizing the conversation, and no small portion of the grog. As a rule, he was said to be equal to a case of whisky or brandy by himself at one square sitting, and wild stories were afloat as to how long he had continued to consume this daily case before he began to see snakes about. When three parts of the case, i.e. six bottles, had been safely stowed away, they said he was getting good company. But, as has been stated, he had had a long spell of enforced abstinence, and now, although only the contents of a case and a half had gone the round, he was already getting disconnected in his reminiscences.

"I was reared in Virginia, boys, and all our family were Federals. Would you like to hear how I lost my mother?—"

Captain Allan Collins was remarking to Hans Helfich and the burly MacAndrews, whose clustering grey curls surrounded the upper portion of a head and beard which might have served as the model for Achilles as it gleamed out in half-tones against the intensity of the shadow behind, that although admiring Niggeree's principles in general, he considered him a little too quick with his Winchester and cutlas, while the Irish mate of the Thunder was engaged amidst the tobacco fog singing an Irish legend entitled "Brian on the Moor;" so that no one replied, or expressed the slightest curiosity about the maternal affliction which had befallen their host.

"My mother, boys, was the natural but unacknowledged wife of the late General Jackson; so that I, being her only child, oughter ha' been his heir—"

"I don't approve of shooting the moment a native pokes his head down the gangway," said Captain Collins; "Nig does. Give them time to declare themselves, and after that, fire or don't fire, as the case may be."

The mosquitoes were being driven out by degrees as the atmosphere became loaded with tobacco-smoke; still the Irish legend was chaunted behind the veil, while no one paid any attention except to his own voice.

"Wall, it was just afore the war that the Injuns came down and scalped the whole twelve on 'em, leaving me, in a manner, an orphan."

"What twelve?" asked Danby, the aristocratic-featured youth, simply.

"What twelve did you think, ye blasted fool? not the twelve apostles, surely?"

"Well, how could I know unless you tell me?"

"My poor brothers and sisters, of course, along with their dam, fought, Jeruselam! but they did sell their blessed lives dear, yet it warnt no use."

"But I thought you were the only child and heir of General Jackson?"

Joe stood for a moment dazed, as if he had lost something, while he passed his hand over his brow and threw back his grizzly hair, then with a drunken laugh he picked it up,—

"Don't you know Amerikay's the place for divorces cheap? and could my mother not marry again if she liked, and have twenty children if she blarned well liked to? What's to prevent her, I want to know—?"

"I don't often shoot," said Captain Collins, "but when I shoot, I kill; and, take my word on it, that's about the only way to get respect from the natives of New Guinea."

Chapter IV
Queen Ine

"KILLMANN! Who says he didn't shoot? Ax the natives? I tell ye what, when he was up that 'ere coast, if he saw a man walking along the sands with a fine mop on him and some beads which he thought would look well amongst his curios, he thought no more of putting up his rifle and potting that native, than he did o' bringing down a bird of but then I always did say that he was like Nig there, just a little too reachy."

Captain Allan Collins was having the best of it, for he had got an audience while Joe had dropped upon the sands nearly helpless, with hardly voice enough left even to blaspheme.

"Ten o'clock, boys, and Carolina Joe as drunk as Tam o' Shanter; time we were all aboard if we mean to be up to time to-morrow morning," said a voice from the fog as it parted and revealed a figure about five foot eight, slim built and gentlemanly, with an olive tinted face and close—clipped black beard.

"All right, Bowman, I'm ready," responded Danby, getting up as calmly as if no whisky had crossed his clean-cut lips, although the boy had been supplied twice every round.

At the same moment the burly sea model of Achilles struggled to his feet, as did the others.

"Get up, Orphan Jackson," said Danby, giving the prostrate Joe a heavy slap with his bare foot, "here comes your father-in-law, with two of your royal brothers, and you haven't shown us Queen Ine and the last batch of pie-bald twins yet."

Carolina Joe, who had not lain above five minutes, rose as if he had been sleeping twelve hours, and apparently shook the drink-stupor as easily from him as a man might shake the night mists away in the early morning, while at the same moment an old native appeared in the doorway attired in a soldier's faded red coat minus the buttons, a tall white hat, and by way of under garb, a blue rag tied round his waist; he was white-bearded, grey-skinned, and bleary-eyed, and as he stood in the dim light of the guttering candle looked like a mummy dressed for a masquerade, while close behind him appeared two stalwart young blacks, bearing between them the third case of drink.

"What's in that case, Bowman?" inquired Joe, in a surly tone.

"Gin, Joe!" answered Bowman. "It's all we have now left aboard."

"It'll do," growled Joe. "Break the thing up and let us taste it."

Little Hector, ever ready with his sharp knife, stooped to prise open the case, while Joe continued, turning to the ancient king,—

"Where's the women, Primrose?"

"All gone sleep, Joe."

"An' Queen Ine?"

"Waiting down by beach."

"Fetch her, I've promised to show her to my mates, d'ye hear! an' don't forget the kids."

"She say you too dam drunk, and she no come to-night," said the king solemnly.

"You go down and tell her I want her, an' no humbug."

"All right!" replied his majesty, stalking out with an offended air as if at not being honoured enough.

"Here!" bawled out Joe, who seemed to know what the matter was.

The king returned, and stood solemnly waiting with his two sons behind him.

"Boys, this yer is my father-in-law, and the king of this island, and these yer are two of the princes, so if ye've got a stick o' baccy to give him, give it without more ado, and let him fetch his daughter."

Bowman and Danby pulled out some sticks of trader's tobacco, and bestowed them upon his majesty, who in return gave them his paw to shake, and then went out to fetch in the rebellious spouse of their host.

Meanwhile the case of gin was opened, one of the bottles produced, and uncorked, while Joe, now once more sober and genial, drank a parting peg along with his friends; he took a full measure to himself, but was economical as regards the measure of his friends.

"You've had nigh enough o' my grog, mates, this bout; I'll keep the rest for a nightcap arter you're aboard, for the Lord only knows when the next lot will come to hand."

Joe had reached that rebounding stage, which often succeeds the generosity of the drunkard.

"I suppose you want to have a good old spree with your father-in-law to-night, Joe," said Bowman, laughing over the meanness of the trader.

"No fears, I don't encourage drinkin' on this yer island, I give them tobacco, but not a drop o' grog, that's too precious."

Queen Ine appeared at this moment with her month-old twins, sullen, and being pushed forward by her father.

"My wife, mates, and the two last kids."

"Hallo! Joe, they are the same as last lot, one half caste and one pure black," cried Danby, looking over them, while the mother stood with sullen brows, and casting ominous glances towards her lord and master.

"That's the curious part on it, boys, Queen Ine always fetches twins, and always that way, one black and one white."

Queen Ine was a magnificent specimen of womanhood, tall, black as coal, upright, and, where exposed, with flesh as firm as marble; she was attired in the loose blue single shirt-gown which the missionaries give to the native women as a token of civilization. It was fastened at the shoulders and open in the neck, the rest falling in the graceful clinging folds with which sculptors drape their goddesses; she now stood half—shrouded in that rank mist through which the expiring candle shot up irregular flashes, that barely reached her, with that sullen look upon her heavily-bent brows and that lurid gleam in her dark eyes, while beside her, like a showman at a fair exhibiting the points of a leopard, hung the half-intoxicated ruler of her life, with his dirty, torn, red shirt open to the waist, his ragged patched trousers, and his bestial expression as he laid his heavy brown hairy arm across that satin-lustred jet-black shrinking shoulder; for he had half torn her gown from her as she stood passively but sternly under his coarse caresses. The two tokens of her own degradation were lying against her breasts, and were held carelessly up with one strong, lovely-modelled arm. She appeared to represent an ebony statue of indignant Nature, protesting mutely against that bestiality of so-called civilization, which degrades where it cannot slay.

Her father, like an ape, and her two brothers ranged beside her emotionless, seemed to be sunk to the level of her white husband, but she stood like a ruined queen.

"That's the sort of woman for a sailor, boys; I can leave her to look after this island when I'm away, and not one dare disobey; look on these arms, why, she could fell an ox with her club."

Queen Ine stood passive and scowling as he lifted her disengaged bare arm to show it to his friends, and as he let it go it dropped limply by her side, while his drunken friends pinched the firm flesh, and praised her up according to their lights. The candle leapt up wildly, before it sent its flame to air, and showed the whole scene with an intense flame, which did not even screen the bloated tarantula on the rafters: then, as they turned with one impulse to stagger out to the stars and freshness of the night, the degradation of the picture was mercifully blotted out, and Joe was left in darkness, with his case of gin and the woman who called him master.

Chapter V
Bêche-De-Mer Working

IT is impossible to lie in bed after the sun rises in the tropics (no matter how late one goes to sleep), but pleasure ineffable to get up as the light appears and before the stars are quite quenched by the approaching flood of light.

Next morning the scene on the beach was a busy one, natives thronging in their canoes, laden with water-casks and fruit for the vessels about to sail, little boys and girls tumbling about the waves, or trying to fish with their pronged fish-spears, women with their infants sitting on the sands, and a constant passing to and fro of dark semi-nude figures, or sunburnt seamen.

Behind the slueing cluster of smacks lay the more massive, if less picturesque, outline of the little steamer Thunder, with her black sides and heavy Dutch-built stern, and her painted funnels emitting their gaseous vapours, which became discoloured as they were wafted towards that opal space overhead, and spread in filmy melting clouds upon the otherwise cloudless sky.

The natives had been awake and working even while the stars were still lustrous, under the direction of King Primrose, and his stern-browed daughter, Queen Ine; but the master lay grunting and tossing on his bamboo couch in that uneasy after-slumber which ever precedes the awakening from the dreamless lethargy of the drunkard.

Joe was right about the mother of his children; whether she loved or hated him was a matter of little consequence, so that she kept the islanders in good order. This she did with a devotion and energy which might well be the zealous outcome of love; the natives obeyed her orders with alacrity and without a murmur; even her father, as he took up his position of august dignity on the sands, was fain to skip nimbly out of her way, as with club in hand, and gown tucked up, she swiftly passed from group to group of the workers.

A constant chattering went on as they laboured, but Queen Ine only muttered a word now and again, or lifted her club threateningly over some skulker, yet none appeared to wait upon its descent, for when she drew near they bent down instantly, with the obsequity of slaves to pick up the bag or cask they had been inclined to pass before, and energetically rushed to the spring or boat waiting to receive it.

Her six children were on the sands under the charge of an old black woman, and at times when they came near her, or clung to her skirts, she caught them impatiently by the arm, and flung them from her as if they were puppies or kittens, and when she did so they ran back to the old nurse, but never cried, as English children would have done, over their rebuff and fall.

Six children, all naked, and of assorted sizes, four boys and two girls; three of the boys were of a rich deep brown, while the other boy and the two girls were copper tinted, a shade or two lighter than the sun-tanned skin of their father.

Pretty children, who rolled over one another in the bright cool dawn, half-buried at times in the grey sand, like young leopard pups—three pairs of twins, with the month old ones lying alone mutely on their backs, and seeming to look at the wonderful pearly-toned immensity above; the aged nurse with close grizzled hair sat heedless of all around, preparing some yams which she held upon a flat canoe-shaped wooden basin and put, when peeled, into an earthenware pot.

Not far from the aged one, a fire was burning on the beach, and one or two girls sitting round it, also cutting up yams, taro, and hard bananas, with their platters and pots beside them. On one side a woman crouched with her hands over her face and her head bent, rocking backwards and forwards and moaning piteously, at which no one appeared to pay any attention, although the eyes of the others looked bleary as if with weeping.

There had been a death in the village the day before, and the others had done their lamenting; this one, however, having been at the other side of the island, had only just arrived to hear the sad news, and now alone sat weeping.

It was the custom for every one to do a stated amount of lamenting, so she was only performing her duty, while the others went on calmly with their daily work and chattered amongst themselves as the glorious light grew more intense and rosy behind the dark thicket of crotons, and inside some shady hut in the village over within that dark thicket, some heart lay moaning, yet not according to custom.

The bêche-de-mer prepared weeks before against the coming of this little trading-steamer Thunder, had been mostly transferred on board, with the water casks filled from the spring and emptied into the ship's iron tanks, before the sun lifted its dazzling disc above the crotons; it was all subdued and silvery, a coral island done in soft grey tones, with the exception of the rose-madder gleam eastward over by the rocks, crotons, and palm-tops, and the different dingies had landed their human freights of blacks and whites, who now mingled together on the sands as the canoes and dingies hobnobbed on the waters.

Five minutes more the sun would be in possession, and that comparative hush banished for the day. Joe came down from his bungalow, unwashed and dry-mouthed, cursing the light and d——g all the eyes which that light was bathing, and the world in general as he staggered towards his guests of the night previous, attired as he lay down in his ragged bepatched pants and buttonless dingy red flannel shirt, while Queen Ine stood waiting silently with her subjects for his further orders, and, as she waited, suckling one of the twins which she had snatched up from the ground at the sight of her husband; it was the black baby she had taken up, the other lay still looking up at the sky, his mouth stuffed with one end of a cowrie shell.

"——my eyes," observed Joe in husky tones as he came up, "have ye got all the cargo aboard?"

"All aboard, Joe, but what about that other lot you said you had?" answered and inquired Bowman, who stood attired in a gay suit of pijamas rolled up to the thighs and armpits, while young Danby, with his pale, thin, aristocratic face, calmly sucked at his briar-wood pipe, attired in a waistband of Turkey red alone, his slender limbs and body gleaming whitely amongst the sunburnt and black surroundings.

"You'll have to come for it over to the other island; it ain't much out of your way, and I'll go with you arter we've got summut to drink and eat. What have ye got aboard?"

"Fresh mutton, a keg of brandy, and a good king-fish caught this morning," replied Bowman.

"That'll do, it's a long time since I tasted anything fresh," grunted Joe; "but have ye no whisky?"

"Not a drop; but you can bring one of your own bottles; we left you half a case last night, besides the gin."

"I'm keeping that as a medicine against accidents; Queen Ine might be bad, or the kids, so we'll just do with your brandy."

"As you will," responded Bowman, who knew his man. "Fetch your own dingey and go aboard; I want to see what Collins and Hector have got before we start, so go aboard and we'll follow you."

"All right," said Joe. Then turning to where his wife stood with her black baby, he said, "Look ye here, Queen Ine, I'm going away for a couple of days, so you'll see to the island while I'm away."

Queen Ine nodded silently.

"An' don't have any humbug or laziness. The cargo in the smoke-house will be ready when the sun goes down. Get that other lot over yere" (he pointed to a black mound lying a little distance from them on the sands, at which she again nodded) "put in to-night, it'll be about ready by the time I get back."

Joe did not waste time kissing, as he turned his back on his spouse and prepared to step into the dingey, which he shoved off.

"An' look ye here, wench," he shouted, resting on his oars with one foot on the gunwale, "send Sam over to the island with Fairy to bring me home again; he'd better start at once as the wind is fair."

Queen Ine once more acknowledged with a bend of her sombre head that she understood, and walked straightway towards the croton thicket, as Joe, now having shoved his boat into deep water, sat down, with both oars dipping into the blue-grey waters and his back against the steamer towards which he was bound; while Bowman and Danby turned into their own boat, which their Malay boys were now pushing along by the shallow sands.

A second more and the sea will be gleaming quick-silver; the palm—fronds still heavy with the dews, which lie like hoar-frost upon the broad, umbrella-like leaves of the undergrowth and grasses, hang limply down underneath the refreshing weight; the spiders' webs which swing, hammock-fashion, from branch to branch, are like filagree work in dull white metal. All the shadows are purple with the vapours of the earth that steal upwards and blanch the local tints of green, the flowers scarlet and blue upon the shrubs and creepers, are drooping like half-closed lids. There is an air of slumber over all; on the cool grey sands, where the tinted and spiked shells are lying unheeded, are lovely shapes and prismatic splashes of pure and broken colours, like the fresh setting of a palette in a shady studio; the sea, without glitter enough to make a shadow, lies a subtle gradation of blue-grey to bleached fawn, the rocks and exposed brown edges of the reefs are inane grey, with hardly a break; the natives round their fires, some distance off, seem to pose silent and motionless, as natives do, waiting for that intense second to elapse, and then the Lord of Day has risen.

First a gleam of scarlet upon the bare upper branches of the bone-like croton-trees, and a dash of glittering bronze running down the core and quivering ribbons of the top palm branches as they seem to shake off their sleep and stretch upwards, like arms thrown out while wakers yawn; then over the thicket, towards which Queen Ine slowly paces, the golden rim appears, burning the outer edges and seeming to shrivel them downwards, as he flings mellow fire upon the edges of ringed trunks and dew-drenched leaves.

Now the paroquettes and cockatoos begin to wake up and flutter in that light-bath, and the sands blush till they glow like the petals of delicate roses. Then, with the gaiety of the gathering sunbeams, Rest seems to fly and all becomes laughter and motion; the ocean is swarming with ripples and golden threads, and the boulders and shells become filled with detail.

Joe, a dark spot upon the even sea, seems to be sucked into that universal lustre, and is soon absorbed from sight. The Thunder still holds her own, as a shadow, but her propeller, idly thrashing the water, appears as if it were turning up silver, and the smacks, as they dance about, to become nautilus shells; deep purple streaks border those rosy flushes, growing to gold, and the head of the mourner beside the yam-peelers is lifted up to greet the penetrating ray, for she has finished her task of lamentation and now laughs, with the tears still hanging like diamonds to her dark cheeks.

Queen Ine pauses in her walk as she reaches the inky mound of half dry bêche-de-mer, and fumbles amongst it for a moment with the hand that does not hold the baby, turning over the under layer of damp slugs so that the sun may also finish his work, and as she stoops, a sun-shaft strikes within her eyelids and turns the dark eyes to a blood-red glare; then she raises up her square, strong shoulders and looks at it for a moment while it beats softly against her heaving breasts, and with a full breath of satisfaction, her stern features somewhat relax, while she clutches the child a little tighter, and passes on.

Half way to the thicket a figure stands in the shallow water gazing fixedly upon the distant sea; Queen Ine, as she sees him, deviates from her course and walks towards him, but he pays no attention to the splashes that she sends up on either side of her as she impatiently beats the water down with her hasty feet; he stands motionless with his face sea-ward and his back upon her.

A weird figure, clad only in a tattered and faded blue cotton shirt, with the arms torn from it and the extremities fluttering like banana leaves when wind-tossed and tattered.

"Hafid," she says sternly, laying her hand upon his shoulder, and then he turns round and faces her, and the two look at one another without speaking.

His hair is falling loosely and wildly about his neck, straight black hair, streaked with white, and all in a tangle, that makes it almost appear wavy, his fine mournful features, the features of a very young man; but his large brown eyes are filmy, and look vacantly at her, while his hands hang meaninglessly down his sides. He has beautiful features and delicately rounded limbs, yet they are scratched all over, as if he had rushed through a prickly jungle; an eastern face, such as we may see in Ceylon or India, with the pathetic languor of a love-sick woman.

As she regards him, her stern, gloomy features become wonderfully soft and tender, while his express nothing in return, except melancholy, as he slowly lifts up one arm and points to sea, muttering some words which she does not understand; then she holds her black baby out to him, which he takes mechanically, and as she turns he follows, like a dog, still carrying the baby, upon which he looks with gaze as vacant as the milk—satisfied infant regards the sky above.

Chapter VI
The "Sunflower"

NIGGEREE feels a good deal better this morning; one of the peculiarities of the fever he is slowly fighting down is that one day you feel as if it had left entirely, and rise without a trace of the helpless lassitude or ague which seems to be devouring your flesh and bones; then, as you are joking upon the subject, and wondering that you could ever feel so low-spirited, the pluck flies from you, and you sink back sick and faint, or ice-cold and shaking, till every bone rattles, while the perspiration pours like rain from you. No one can tell exactly when he has got rid of it, or when it has seized upon him; a strong, burly man in less than a week may be reduced to skin and bone.

Last night Niggeree could not do more than sip his grog, and for a week before that he had tasted neither food or drink, but to-day, as he springs lightly from his close cabin, when he expected to crawl, to greet that blushing dawn, he finds himself gifted with an appetite both for food and drink, drink particularly, and nothing in the locker to satisfy the tardy craving.

"Confound it all," mutters the Greek, as he prepared to pull off his shirt so as to enjoy his morning ablutions, "if I only had been like this last night ashore, I could have enjoyed myself and no mistake."

As he doffed his garment, a sallow, hollow and high-cheeked Malay sailor came over to him from the bows with a bucket and line, which he tossed over the side, bringing it up full, and emptying it with a sluugh over his skipper, who stood with bent head and back towards the sailor to receive this primitive shower-bath. Again and again he drew up the bucket filled, and poured it over, until Niggeree cried, "enough," after which he joined the other Malay, and went on with their morning work of swabbing the deck.

As it is impossible to take a plunge in these waters on account of the sharks, this is the only plan left to those who cannot, like Joe, dispense with cold water.

"What you have for breakfast this morning, boss?" inquired the Chinaman who did duty as cook on board the Sunflower,—this Niggeree called his little vessel,—approaching his master, who was diligently drying himself.

"No need getting anything for me, I'll go aboard the Thunder and feed."

"All right, boss," and John returned to his post beside the little stove which stood on the deck and served for a galley.

If Niggeree, the Greek master of the Sunflower, appeared to be a weak and undersized man when crouching under the candle-light, a very different figure stood out against the soft grey background of this morning sky. By this time he had attired himself in his striped cotton shirt and white duck pants, and sat on the edge of the water-cask while he slowly filled his black clay pipe with the strongest of negrohead; his black, close-set eyes now looked sharp and bright enough, as he gazed on the shore; a low, square brow, and head well thatched with close-cropped jet-black hair. Not having shaved for the past few days, his chin and upper lip were grizzly and covered with strong dark stubble; a massive chin, with lips thin and firm-clenched, and when he smiled, as he often did, at some idea crossing his mind, it gave him the appearance of a convict smiling upon his jailor. Once he laughed, and muttered something to himself, and then, when his mouth opened, it disclosed teeth jet-black, and almost worn to stumps, which, with the blood—coloured gums and lips, told of the lime and betel chewer. His manner was quiet and sedate, even when alone, and he never raised his voice, even when giving an order, but his boys seemed to be on the alert to bear it as soon as it was uttered. He had a massive neck and square shoulders, with large arms and legs which made the pants seem to be tight. Since the night before he seemed to have expanded twice his size, and as the risen sun kissed him on the cheeks and neck with the same utter want of distinction as he had touched the satiny shoulders of Queen Ine, there was no shade of difference between his colour and that of the bare—chested Malay who was working near to him, only by some instinct one felt that the tawny tint of the one was imparted by the sun, and the other was the gift of ages.

"Fetch round the dingey, Jake," he softly said, and the Malay straightway left his task of polishing the brasswork, and hastened to obey, while Niggeree, with his pipe now filled, struck a match, which he held sailor-fashion in the hollow of his hand against the wind, and having lit, puffed away seriously, looking, as he sat there with bare arms, legs, and chest, and with head covered with a strip of turkey red cloth, not a bad ideal of a ruthless pirate.

His vessel, like himself, lay on the waters quietly, yet as if watchful; the hull low and painted green, sharp as a yacht, and about as trim, differing only from the other craft lying around by its rakish look, it being the swiftest sailor, evidently built more for speed than carrying, a quality which before now Niggeree had found very useful.

In these little schooners, not bigger than ordinary fishing-smacks, and much less than some of the deep-sea herring-boats, traders took their dangerous journeys over the rough waves of the Papuan Gulf; drawing little water, they served best for those narrow passages and shoaly patches of the inside reefs. A deck covered the hold, extending from end to end almost, with the exception of the three or four feet where the berth of the skipper was apportioned off. An awning was raised over part of the midships where, on hot and dry nights, all slept. The berth was used only in wet weather; and when it was raining the crew slept in the hold if it was not over-full. The crew was mostly composed of South Sea Islanders, Malay, or China boys, with the one white man to guide and control them, so that murder was not so much to be wondered at as the faithful adherence of these coloured men to their white master; and, considering the hourly risks ran from natives and other dangers, treachery was rather a phenomenon; and if at times these brave traders were not over scrupulous in their means of attaining their end, still they were, as a rule, easy to please, not hard task-masters, and, without exception, utterly regardless of death.

Joe, in his own coarse way, fed and petted his island employés well, perhaps finding it to his own interest to indulge them as much as possible, while, if punishment had to be inflicted, he left it to his wife or the king to do as they thought best; from motives of selfishness, perhaps, he forbade them intoxicating drink, and never interfered with the teachings or influence of the native teachers, so that as much concord and civilization swayed this island, as on most others subject to the softening influence of the missionary.

With Niggeree, who hitherto had no abiding-place, but traded from station to station, staying a month or two on an island, where he generally ruled recklessly, marrying gaily the most important female of that part and leaving behind him an aroma of terror and respect, the other traders found grave fault. As Collins said, he was too hasty with his Winchester and cutlass, but withal, brave as a lion. He seemed to regard neither God nor man; he had gone to parts as yet unopened to the explorer or missionary, where treachery and man-eating are constantly practised, and from where fearful legends are wafted of massacres and practices all the more horrible because veiled in uncertainty; yet he had always returned to contradict the stories which the natives brought of his death, although he seldom brought his crew intact.

From years of intercourse, he seemed more at home with the savages than he would have been with honest citizens, all their habits and customs had become his own, to which he added other habits, acquired on the coast of Africa and South America, on the Solomons and South Sea Islands, and those far-away isles of Greece from where he originally had drifted.

The Government wanted him very badly, also the representatives of Exeter Hall; but with the guile of his nation he had hitherto evaded the traps they had set for him. "Niggeree," as the natives called him, was a name well known from one end of British New Guinea to the other, a name to send the nude and dusky warriors and their women flying into the bush, yet not one of them would bear testimony against him, what crimes he had committed remaining a secret between his own conscience and their discretion.

Was he thinking of these dark acts as he quietly sat on that water-cask, sending up the white puffs from his black clay pipe with that illuminated warm-toned atmosphere, for he smiled that convict smile which made him look so like a pirate, or was he concocting plans for the future? He was down in his luck at present, for this fever had paralyzed his energies, and he had to lie inactive for weeks, so that it had all been outcome, and no profit, and the exchequer was getting low. He had only a few bags of copra to give in exchange to Bowman for his next three months' supply, and he had not yet succeeded in winning over young Hector to join his fortune. As he suspected Hector to know where gold was to be found easily, in spite of the doubts cast by the colonial public on the nugget he was supposed to have discovered in New Guinea (for that doubt of the gold is not shared by a single person who has been in the land), he wanted to have him near him to find out why the little fellow again sought the shores, and for other reasons he wished him as a partner. Hector hitherto had parried his generous offer of a free passage and a share in his investments, yet to-day Niggeree felt hopeful that he would succeed in his persuasions.

Hector would be useful in many ways, for since his last scrape with the Queensland Government, when he, to be able to return, had been forced to become naturalized, he wanted a British subject to advise him, now that he was under the power of the commissioner, and Hector had a cool head, and might steer him safely out of many perils, and perhaps be the scapegoat if ever the necessity arose to have one.

Yesterday he was despondent and hopeless, any man might have wrung his nose with impunity, but to-day he felt the master, and smiled as he looked towards the canoes and boats; so, having finished his pipe, and the boat lying alongside with one of the South Sea Islanders at the oar, and the Malay holding the rope, he sprang to his feet, stretching himself full up, as he gave orders to those left aboard to get the bags ready for transferring, and then he dropped lightly into the dingey, taking the steering oar in his hand, while the others dipped theirs into the transparent deep blue.

A few strokes and they were absorbed, and lost in the intense sun-glare which had shortly before swallowed up that black spot, Joe.

Chapter VII
A Parting Glass

BUSINESS is all arranged now, and the chops, fish, and turtle steaks are set out on the table-cloth of the saloon, or cabin, of the Thunder, while the Singalese steward waits meekly at the door for the masters to take their seats.

Bowman has gone over the copra-bags of Niggeree and the pearl-shells of Collins, and exchanged the provisions which they require for their coming cruise, so that in the transfer, many oaths have been uttered, if not registered amongst the representatives of western culture, and much chattering and skurrying amongst the dusky children of uncultivated Nature, who, with their canoes and the dingies, are still passing between the steamers and the schooners.

Queen Ine has delivered her orders, and now brother Sam with the smack Fairy is rapidly becoming a little speck of white upon that distant sapphire sea, as he speeds away westward to the other station, to await the commands of his brother-in-law.

They all—that is, all the white men on board, Hans, the engineer, with his cockney assistant, and Gallacher, the Irish mate—come down from the poop, and take their seats without distinction. They don't trouble washing themselves, as they have not bothered about washing the deck; Captain MacAndrews, with a splitting headache from the night before, declines taking the head of the table, but sits beside his dirty mate, in a dejected attitude, wrinkling up his Caledonian nose with disgust at the sight of food; Bowman has just administered to him one of his infallible pills. Niggeree sits between Hector and Collins with his quietest air, for he has succeeded in enlisting both, Collins by the promise of a hitherto unknown oyster-field near the mouth of the Fly River, and Hector who has consented because Collins is going. Hector, agreed to go because he had sailed so far with Collins, his own vessel lying at present under repair at Thursday Island.

Joe takes up a lot of room at the foot of the table while Bowman occupies the head, and Danby, now clad in white pants and undershirt, with a gay-coloured sash round his waist, sits on the right-hand side of his friend Bowman.

There are tea and coffee served with brandy instead of milk, and the Singalese grins when he is called to pull a fresh cork, handing a slip of paper to the caller to sign: this mild-featured native of Ceylon is particular about these slips of paper, and always informs the signers of other slips which they have put their mark to before but not yet paid, and when he is reviled, he merely laughs, showing his beautiful teeth, and retires to his sideboard.

Bowman and Danby use their knives and forks, but the others dispense with these articles of super-refined luxury, and taking the chops from their plates in their dirty hands, gnaw them like hungry apes.

Only the captain does not eat; he sits with both hands clutching his grey, tangled, curly locks, and looks at his greasy plate with gloomy preoccupation.

Outside the natives squat on the aft-hatch, catching bits of food thrown to them from the inside, and scrambling laughingly over it; the coloured sailors take their meal at the bows.

Over against where the captain sits, at the back of Danby, a large rat darts out at times, and runs along the bunks with impudent effrontery, its bright eyes glancing at the meat being devoured, as if it could hardly restrain its wish to join in also; a singular mixture of boldness and nervous timidity.

Looking up from his plate, the captain sees the rat and starts, then watches it with a wild eye.

"Is that a rat?" he asks, nudging the mate and pointing to the crevice where it is just disappearing.

"Of course it is; what did you take it to be?" replied the mate, glancing up and then going on with his bone.

"I wasn't quite sure if it was a real one," murmured the afflicted old man, half to himself, as his head sank again over his plate.

A loud laugh followed this murmur, as if the captain had made a joke.

"Thought you had them, I suppose," observed Danby calmly, after the laugh had subsided.

"You'll have them before long, young man, if you dinna put in a peg," said the captain savagely; and rising, he passes out to where the natives are squatting on the hatchway, kicking two of them out of the road, and flinging himself down wearily.

Joe, after breakfast, became more interesting than he was the night before; told of many strange adventures down by the Spanish main, deeds of daring which were all performed personally, some of which had been already related in the lives of Captain Kidd and other bold buccaneers. He evidently had been a very daring pirate in the olden times, before he became virtuous and settled down upon his little island.

Then they found that the water supply was short, and another trip ashore had to be taken, and a rove round the island while the natives fetched the water.

First to the smoke-house, which stood by the sea-shore; here they saw the sheet-iron shed used for the purpose, with the closed doors and ladder reaching up to the loft, where the sea-slugs were laid to smoke, having been first sun-dried—Joe looking in below to see if the wooden fires were all right. They sent out a great cloud of bluish smoke as he peered inside which made all the others fall-to coughing.

This bêche-de-mer, from which they make soup much relished by the Celestials, is prepared for the Chinese market; the fires are fed from below, while the fish are laid upon a bamboo floor with spaces between each spar for the smoke to pass through: about thirty-six hours are required to smoke them thoroughly.

Outside the shed, and lying on their backs, were three large turtles, caught the day before. After a deal of bargaining—for Joe, despite his federal parentage, had all the instincts of his Israelitish ancestors, for although he denied being a Jew, his nose asserted his nationality—Bowman bought them for the ship's use, and another canoe took them aboard.

Then through the thicket—a thicket gorgeous with rare plants and flowers—they passed to the native village, now deserted of all but native pets—pigs, dogs, and tame pelicans—who popped out of the way with ungainly movements as the party looked into the empty huts. The huts were like Joe's bungalow, only sweeter smelling; cool, dark places, which the white glare beating upon the sands outside could not penetrate.

They looked into all the houses excepting one, where the door was fastened, and before which Joe planted himself with a rough delicacy not to be expected from him.

"Not there, mates; ye see the poor critter lost her man yesterday, and I guess she wouldn't like to be disturbed."

On shore they were all resting, and Queen Ine, with her family about her, sat down beside the women; the Hindoo also sat near to her, dipping his hand into the yam dish and feeding one of the twins—the second lot—a little fellow of about sixteen months, who had crept up close to his feeder and watched him, while he gobbled down the yams which the other put into his mouth. He had large brown wondering eyes.

Queen Ine held her head down and looked stolidly at the brown and white babies clinging to each breast as the party passed, while Joe explained how the Hindoo was a maniac whom a trader had left with him at one time as being of no use amongst his crew.

"He had been kidnapped somewhere down there about India, away from his young wife—so a chap who once stopped here a night and understands his lingo tells me," explained Joe. "Taken off for a short voyage, under promise to be sent back soon, then, arter they had him in Amerikay, they shipped him again to Sydney, telling him they were taking him home; and then he got drifted from one ship to another, always thinking he was going home, until he got melancholy like, as these niggers do, and turned as you see. He's no blarmed bit o' good, except to look arter the young ones, only he takes fits and runs off to the woods and stops there all by himself, rushing about till he gets too hungry to hold out longer, when he comes back and stands for hours looking out to sea; not a stroke o' good, and feed extra. I'm now waiting to see if I can get some one to take him off my hands; and if I don't soon, I'll have to knock his brains out, I guess, an' be done with it."

Joe is kind, after his nature, but this poor madman's

40

melancholy makes him miserable, so he wants to have done with it.

The last bottle has been opened on board by the grinning Singalese, and they wish each other joy and a safe voyage.

The Thunder, with Bowman, Danby and Joe aboard, shrieks out her steam whistle, at which the afrighted natives tumble into the blue waters and swim ashore; then the anchor is hauled over the bows, and the propeller swishes the water into white curd as she ploughs through the deep passages of the reefs.

The Sunflower and Coral Sea follow each other with sails set, a fair western monsoon driving them towards New Guinea and the east, and as they recede—the Thunder sailing in the direction taken by the Fairy—assuming the proportions and some of the shape of a little tub as it drifts out of sight slowly. The island falls asleep in the brilliant midday ray once more, and all seems again as it must have been before the white man came to devour and pollute.

Chapter VIII
Hafid and His Little Friend

THERE is not much to do on the island now that the ships have sailed. Some have gone fishing for the sea-slugs, but they will not be back before sundown, so that only the sun-baking mound has to be turned—which is being looked after by two or three old women—and the fires in the smoke-house replenished; this has also been looked after, while most of the islanders lie basking in the hot light, and silence broods over all.

Hafid seems amused with his little friend; at least, like a big dog, he lies passive on his back and lets the child roll about him and do with him as he pleases.

Queen Ine still sits looking on her children, as these natives, male and female, will sit for hours without moving, bareheaded with the sun beating fiercely upon them, languid and indolent until the moment comes for them to be active, and then they can shake it off without an effort.

King Primrose, now relieved from the presence of those whom he wished to impress, had relaxed in his dignity, thrown aside his military jacket and tile-hat, and now lay amongst the dilapidated elders of his tribe, smoking the pipe of peace and comfort, while over them all hung the noonday sun, a small concentrated heat-spot in the midst of that deep ocean of ultramarine, while the sea and earth sweltered, and aerial gases rose so that the rocks and trees seemed to tremble in distance.

After a time Hafid raised himself up, and taking the little fellow upon his shoulders, slowly went towards the narrow foot-path which led through the woods to the village, the only place where anything like shadow was to be found.

On, past the empty houses, and into the deeper intricacies, where the purple shadows lay in longer patches, and the golden sunshine fell irregularly, small spots lying like rain-drops on the dewy shadow—stretches.

With broad green leaves on each side, speckled crotons and tufts of reed-like grass-growth, the greens here were very fresh, and in parts the ground felt damp and cool, while bright spring-like tints lay over the grasses; spotted mosquitoes swarmed over him in dense clouds as Hafid crossed these swampy places, and the quivering haze became denser, the under-shades changing to dusky blue and growing indefinite near the roots of the bushes.

Now and again a gay-plumaged bird flew out of the deep recesses and sought the higher branches, or it might be a chattering flock of square—flying snow-white cockatoos making a little cloud-patch in the open parts of blue sky above the tree-tops; once he nearly trod upon a bright green snake as it lazily crawled across the path and became lost amongst the reeds, but Hafid went on seemingly tireless, with that straight look-out in his melancholy eyes, as if he was seeking for the woman he had lost, while the naked child, perched upon his shoulder like a little brown ape, clutched at the leaves above its head, trying to catch the large gay—coloured butterflies as they circled round him, or the flowers and bright scarlet, white, and blue berries which trembled upon the swinging tendrils.

At last they came to a small recess where they had been often before, where the shadows were very dense, and the ground rose to a sort of bank; in front of them spread a swampy piece of ground with the sun shining full upon it, where butterflies in thousands kept up a perpetual motion and uncertain glitter above the lilies and swamp flowers; while perfect clouds of gnats and mosquitoes swarmed and kept up a drowsy chorus.

Here Hafid lay down with his head on the shady bank and his feet in a sunlit pool of water, and the solitary game of tumble on the part of the boy recommenced.

Savage hordes of hungry tiger-mosquitoes darted upon the lithe naked body and exposed limbs of Hafid, without disturbing either in the slightest degree; lizards large and small, of all shades, darted over the sunny lines, while ants ran about with the important fussy air of city clerks—and all the time the sun rolled along on his daily round, making as he descended the western plains, shadows longer in that tropic retreat.

The boy was tired of his game, and Hafid had fallen asleep, and so the youth looked about him for some other mode of amusement.

Meanwhile, on the sea-shore, work had recommenced, and Queen Ine, putting her children once more under the charge of the old crone, became the active over-seer; the fishing canoes had returned as the sun grew orange-toned in the west, and all hands were required to unload and prepare the slugs for next day's drying.

So from one group to another she sprang, now in the smoke-house, hauling out the dried slugs, now pushing her useless old father out of her road, or superintending the spreading and cutting up of the bêche-de-mer. She did not spare her own lithe body any more than the serfs about her.

All was about over by the time Hafid came to view, this time carrying the child as if asleep in his arms. Queen Ine merely glanced at him as he laid down his little friend beside the other tired-out children, and went on with her work, while Hafid passed over to the sea, wading out a space till the rising tide came over his knees, and watching the crimson sun sinking below the dark belt of purple ocean over beyond the surf-line of the distant reefs.

She had finished, and the labourers slowly left the beach in their family groups, and went towards the village, while with a careful look round to see if all was rightly done, she turned towards her sleeping children, and prepared herself to take them indoors.

The old crone took up the two eldest twins, and after laying them down on one of the bamboo couches, came back for the others, while Queen Ine, meanwhile, had picked up the youngest.

At this moment the old woman uttered a howl that startled the younger woman and made her turn round, wondering what was the matter.

The old woman was holding up a little clenched hand of Hafid's friend, from which she was trying to pluck some bright-tinted berries.

In a moment the apathy of Queen Ine had disappeared, and she became the distracted mother; with a wild cry, which echoed through the woods and startled the sleeping parrots, while it arrested the dragging feet of the villagers, she flung down the infants, and sprang to the side of the unconscious child.

Some wild words were uttered and answered, as she stooped down to smell the mouth all tinted with the bright colour of the berries, while she clutched up the child, and flew backwards and

43

forwards on the sea-shore, uttering screams which became hoarser each repetition. The old woman ran as fast as possible towards the village.

Hafid, meanwhile, stood motionless near the sea-shore up to his knees in water, with the twilight fumes of rosy purple folding him up as with a mantle.

Chapter IX
Hafid Again on the Road Home

IT is vain to attempt to describe the agony of the woman when the child she has brought into the world is passing from it, no matter her condition or nationality, if she be a woman.

Queen Ine was a woman with all the savage instincts of maternity in full force within her—a savage in every emotion, and the dying child was her own flesh, being torn from her by the remorseless enemy Death; a woman without one consolation, for the South Sea Island teacher who tried his best to comfort, had not learnt enough of his lately-taught creed to translate to her those passages whereby the pastor seeks to alieviate the heavy woe.

From her arms the child had not stirred all through the night, and the antidote which the old woman had rushed off to the village to procure, had been administered too late to be of any service against the subtle effect of the poisoned berries. Every three of the little body had cut the heart of the mother; yet, after the first wild madness of the discovery, she became silent, and only the fierce clutching with her hand at her throat or the sullen bloodshot eyes betrayed how much the mother felt.

All her other children were as nothing to her now, only this one lying so still in her lap with its dimming eyes fixed on space. Her own tearless ones were like flame watching each step of the approaching enemy.

Hafid had disappeared before morning, unconscious of the disaster he had brought upon his benefactress; he wandered, as was his wont, over the most unfrequented portions of the island, and as yet no one had sought for him. By-and-by, however, when the child was dead, their wrath would turn to his direction, and he would be hunted down and offered as a victim to their vengeance.

Emir, the native teacher, would not seek to prevent this action of savage vengeance; to him it would seem all right and proper, in spite of his Christianity.

The sun was warming in the west when the end came. On the sea-shore they all sat silent, except the teacher, who did what he thought right under the circumstances, sang his native hymns and read at random from his native testament.

The tribe was assembled waiting on the death, before they began to weep and lament. Death was a very common visitor with them, and was treated by all except those most interested in a very callous manner; there was no use in wasting any time before the right moment arrived.

Children die easy, and so would this one if they had not tried to save him. Their united efforts increased the torture by prolonging it, but now it was all over, and while the mother's hot eyes still look upon the little tawny ashen face and glazing eyes, the limp limbs are becoming stiff and cold.

Then the ceremony of lamenting begins, while the young men with their spears scatter to hunt for the poor unconscious Hafid; they will do their hour of weeping after they have found him.

But Queen Ine does not weep, or take her eyes away from her dead child. The old woman tries to lift it away, but desists at the wild clutch the mother's hands make upon it, and instead, puts the youngest children by turns to the full, throbbing breasts, where she holds them while they drink, for the mother pays no attention.

It is about the hour when Joe should return, and some of those who have done their time of lamenting set about preparing for his coming back, while others hold up their hands to their eyes, shading them from the declining sun, to catch the first sight of him; but Queen Ine orders or threatens them no more.

By-and-by some of the watchers say they see it, and with it the fire—ship, as they call the steamer, and they all begin to bustle about.

There they are together, the Thunder towing the other along in her wake. Joe has been drinking and swearing, and trying to cheat and lie all day, while his child has been suffering the agonies of death.

A little grey speck, which looms up against the grey undersides of the cloud-bank below the mellow sun-circle, growing from the grey blue to black, separates as the golden orb gets behind it; then nearer every moment, until the dark funnels and masters of the two vessels are easily distinguished, as the amber-brown smoke rolls around that orange and dun space, where the great eye of day is rapidly turning bloodshot as it is nearing that clean-cut line of horizon.

It seems hours to the watchers on shore before they can hear the lashing of the monster's iron tail. Then the yelling and curses of the captain and mate, and dropping of the anchor, intermingle with the blood-thirsty yellings of those ashore who

45

cluster round the prisoner Hafid, dragged by the young men from his retreat in the woods.

"There's something up over there, Joe," remarks Bowman to Joe, as he sees to his revolvers being ready, before he drops into the dingey, inside which the nearly intoxicated Joe is sitting waiting.

"I'll soon settle all that once we land," answers Joe easily, and they pull off towards the excited group.

"Eternal Thunder, what's all this about?" yelled Joe, staggering up towards the group where Queen Ine sits with her dead child, and the natives are gesticulating about their prisoner, whom he does not yet see.

He stops and lays a heavy, uncertain grip on the black shoulders of his wife, as he lurches forward and prepares himself to be delivered of a volley of oaths, when something in the face she turns up to him partly sobers him, and then he looks into her lap and knows all about it.

Queen Ine looks into his face mutely for a moment with the agony of a wounded doe, while he stands swaying to and fro, passing his helpless, horny hand over his drink-dazed eyes and through his beard. Then her eyes drop once more, as if she had not found what she sought for in those brutal features; perhaps she did not look for bread, although she did not like the stone.

Meanwhile Bowman and Danby drew near, and, the dead being only a black child, did not display much interest in it.

Then Joe, whose grief found vent in a fresh volley of curses, asked how it happened, and when one of the natives told him, and pointed to the nearly naked Hindoo standing amongst them, all unconscious of his offence and danger, he turned to where Bowman stood and said,—

"I told you as how that blamed nigger would bring me no luck, and now he has done it, and my wench won't be no good for work for the next month. Poor little man! Blast my blooming eyes."

Something like two drops of water gleamed in Joe's bloodshot eyes as he spoke, but he was ashamed of giving way before his friends.

"What are they going to do to the Hindoo?" asked Bowman.

"Kill him, for certain; may be, roast and eat him."

"No, no! we must not let them."

"I can't stop 'em when their blood's up; it's more than my head's worth. Only Queen Ine could do it, and it's not likely she will."

But Queen Ine belied his idea of her; her heart was too full of woe for any thought of vengeance to stay there, for as Joe spoke she lifted up her dead baby in her arms, and going over to where her tribe stood about their captive, cleared a passage, and taking him by the arm, led him over to where Bowman stood, none disputing her right to dispose of the captive.

"You white fellow, take him away in fire-ship," she said, in the best English she could muster, her voice so husky and dry that Bowman had not the heart to refuse.

"Go way when sun rises. No let them kill Hafid, he good fellow; but take him away."

She returned to her seat on the ground, but this time when the old woman approached she took both infants into her arms, and permitted the other to take the dead baby indoors. She did not look at her husband any more, but bent her head over her little ones as they hung at each breast, so that they could not see her face.

"Best take the idiot aboard at once," advised Joe. "I'll come with you; it feels too blasted lonesome to-night on this yer island, and Queen Ine is best by herself."

Joe slunk to the stern after the others, and said no more till he came aboard, when he straightway set to drown his grief in the only way he knew, which no one sought to deny him. Hafid went forward amongst the other coloured men, and appeared pleased to think he was once more on his way over the seas to find his home. And the others, having already had tea before landing, proceeded to fill their pipes, and lighting up, went up the companion-way to the poop to enjoy the evening breeze.

The young horned moon was slowly sinking below the horizon, and the green and rosy short-lived twilight colours were spreading over the sky.

On shore, in front of the fire, they could see the dark figures squatting, or passing to and fro, and loud sounds of weeping were wafted on the balmy air, blowing the aromatic perfume of burning palm-wood and dulse towards them; fresh arrivals dropping in and joining in the funeral service. And at the sight Joe swore a savage oath, and called for more brandy, which the steward brought to him without the usual slip of paper.

But they were too far off, and the night was getting too dark for them to see the figure which crouched all by itself down by the sea-shore amongst the shells.

Her dead child was being buried by her relations and friends, and her other children were asleep in the bungalow, so that she had come down to the sea-beach to be alone.

And the wind sighed round her from the land, while the little wavelets lapped and splashed about the skirts of her cotton gown and over her bare feet, and the world above her became luminous with moist pitying eyes, which she did not see, for her head was buried in the folds of her gown as it rumpled between her knees. The sounds of the weeping fell unheeded on her ear, for she knew that they meant nothing; but a shudder passed over her back, as the gruff intonation of Joe's curses rolled brokenly in from the deck of the steamer upon the returning breezes, and struck her ear.

Chapter X
Hula—A Lover's Quarrel

ALL the names given by the natives of New Guinea are euphony itself—Elevira, Hanuabada, Aroma, Kerepuna, Piramata, &c. The Colonial Government are planning out a city at Port Moresby, i.e. Elevira or Hanuabada, which they propose to call Grenville.

Hula, the native town, on the sea, where the houses stand out from the shore on their tall piles, and the highways are, like the highways of Venice, blue ocean. On shore the Sistu tribe resides, surrounded by orchards and lovely gardens, with the lofty mountains of the mainland soaring up to the clouds and hiding the vast aerial mysteries of the yet unexplored Owen Stanley ranges.

The shore tribes of Hula are hunters and gardeners, bold traders who go westward with their wares in their large trading Lakatoes, as the ancient tribes of Greece traded their merchandise, facing, like them, dangers by sea and land, from robbers, murderers, and pirates, and, like them, they are all warriors as well as workmen.

The sea tribes live by fishing, which they also barter.

Love and war mingle up with their hourly avocations, and they take their pleasures and do their work as the Jews did at the rebuilding of Jerusalem, with one hand on the spade and the other on their spear.

It is a rest-day at Hula, and they are all enjoying the glory of the sun, cooled by the strong sea-breeze, in the way they like best—wrestling, sailing their large and small vessels about, practising with the bow or spear, running races, smoking, telling tales, or making love to the girls who are cutting up the taro, yams, and bananas for the modest mid-day meal.

One youth, who has been the length of Brisbane in the bom-bom or war-sloop, tells the wonders he has seen to a group who listen open—mouthed to some of his tales or laugh incredulously at others. They have all seen a screw-steamer in Hula before, and are partly prepared for the other wonders he tells, the strange sight of houses built one above the other, and bridges crossing large rivers, of horses carrying men, and coaches, but they openly laugh to scorn his description of the trains; there, like the sailor's mother when he told her about the fish that had wings, they drew the line.

"You know the fire-ship that thump-thumps and kicks the water all white, well they have beasts the same, who puff-puff like that, and swallow up hundreds of men as they run up mountains and over the big fields, big snakes who smoke the bau-bau."

A loud burst of incredulous shouts greeted this wonderful tale, so that "Kamo," the narrator, was fain to walk off in a dignified way to console himself as best he could with the society of his future wife, who, by reason of her position as an engaged young lady, was exempt from all work, and now lay on the outside of the circle of yam-preparers basking her dainty limbs in the sun with all the abandonment of perfect idleness.

Kamo, a tall boy of about eighteen, like all the male portion of New Guinea, was perfectly naked, with the exception of the elaborate breast and nose ornaments, earrings, and armlets. His bushy and frizzed hair, standing about two feet all round his smooth, comely face, was adorned with scarlet blossoms, like the wreaths which the ancients were at their love-feasts, dyed of a golden hue by his girl, and with the long-handled comb stuck rakishly on one side—a splendid specimen of uncurbed, fresh young humanity, he strode along the sands, swinging his highly—decorated bau-bau or pipe, in his hand, and looking at the shadow which fell from his handsome limbs with evident satisfaction.

Rea, his young lady, watched his approach with half-sleepy admiration. She had picked him out from many other handsome youths, impressed by the sense of his superior knowledge, and treated him with more consideration than New Guinea girls generally display towards their expectant husbands; but, in spite of her evident awe at his fame as a traveller, she was not inclined to be too amiable, but led him an uncertain dance while he waited his appointed month of probation, it being the custom, after preliminary arrangements are got over, such as satisfying the parents as to means, &c., to put the suitor under trial, that is, the youth has to deliver himself over, body and soul, to the caprices of his intended partner, live in her father's house, and be for ever on his good behaviour.

Kamo was a very wealthy young man, according to these parts. He had much tobacco, and some pearl-shells, with other treasures gleaned in his travels, and so he was greatly respected, and, to use a vulgar expression, thought no small beer of himself.

Rea, his betrothed, was also an heiress, her father being chief of the land tribe, with an orchard all her own since her mother's death; a dainty little girl of sixteen, tattooed to the waist in beautiful designs of blue upon brown, hair cut short and curly (when she is married she will shave it all off), a pert round face, with little nose, full red lips, and teeth only as yet slightly stained with the betel-nut, large brown mischief-loving eyes, small ears, even although the lobes hung down rather far to suit European tastes, yet here it was considered a mark of beauty to have lobes hanging down and weighted with shell earrings.

Her figure was plump, although, compared with the Apollo-like proportions of her lover, somewhat undersized, yet the feet now kicking petulantly at the sands were small and beautifully formed. She had not so many ornaments about her as Kamo had—as here it is the custom of the male, like the gorgeous male birds of Paradise, to look as splendid as possible—her only dress consisting of the "Raumma," or bulky grass petticoat, which fell from her waist to her knees in many folds, giving her a bunchy appearance round the hips, and making her lower limbs appear much less than they really were.

She was gazing at Kamo with indolent admiration as he left the group of unbelievers with that lordly air of his, feeling all the pride of easy possession; but as he came nearer she drew her brows together and the corners of her little mouth down in the manner of a spoilt, petted child, which, when the young man saw, made him slacken his pace, and seemed to take a considerable lot of the swagger out of him.

He ceased to swing his bau-bau, and drew near with a conciliatory air, almost fawning in its humility.

"How much longer have I to wait for you, Kamo, while you tell lies to the men and make them laugh at you?" exclaimed this spoiled beauty in an angry voice.

"I didn't know you wanted me to come, Rea. You know you said you were tired of hearing about the white man's great places, and wanted to sleep."

"Of course I am sick of all these things. Do you think no one except you has been out of Hula?"

Kamo did not answer, being a wise youth, who could afford to wait his time.

"Well, have you nothing to tell me, Kamo, now that you are here?" she inquired, still offended, or pretending to be so, as he took his place beside her on the sands.

"Only that I wish my month was over, and I had you all to myself," replied Kamo, trying to take her hand, which she snatched from him.

"I don't; it's too pleasant to lie about and do nothing all day, and I haven't yet made up my mind whether you are worth working for. Perhaps I'll turn you over like Mea did Rika."

"No, Rea, you would not do that to me, for I know the road to the white man now, and I'd go away and never see Hula again."

"I would not care about that, you may depend, if I sent you from me; there are plenty of fine boys in Hula."

"Would you kill me, Rea?"

"I'll think about it; but you must be more amusing, or I'll not take you."

"I'll do whatever you like, Rea."

"Then carry me through the streets. I want to find out how it feels like, on the beast you call a horse."

Poor Kamo cast a rueful glance round at the other youths and maidens, for he knew how they would jeer at him if he did this, and said,—

"Wouldn't a sail be nicer, Rea? Come, we will go over the sea in my new canoe."

"No, I want a ride, and you must be my horse, and take me all round the village."

Kamo felt he must obey, so with a deep sigh of resignation he put down his bau-bau and put his arms about her to lift her up, when she stopped him.

"Not that way; I want you to go the way you showed us the horses went."

Kamo remembered, with a shudder, how he had run all-fours to illustrate the horse, one night when they were merry, and cursed his vanity when he remembered his pride at being the hero. That was weeks ago, when he first came home and his stories were listened to.

"Well, boy, are you going to do it, or must I go to my father?" cried the maiden, impatiently. And at this dire threat Kamo bent his back meekly, and went on his hands and knees, while Rea, gathering her skirts well around her and taking up the ornamented bau-bau in lieu of a whip, sat down upon him, and hitting him smartly over the shoulders, told him to "Gee up!" as he had said the white man did with his horses.

On went poor Kamo under his loved but not fairy-like load, panting and sweating with the heat of the sun and the exertion and the shame before him, while Rea sat calmly and contented with her new mode of torture.

She did not spare either his back or his shoulders, and he dared not complain. The motion pleased her, and she considered nothing about her horse except a wicked little thrill of pleasure at the thought of this novel mode of tormenting him.

And all the village men and boys left their sports and their

51

talking to watch and laugh at this new spectacle; the old women stood up with their knives in one hand and the half-peeled yam in the other, laughing at the fun, even while they were thinking how soon Rea's reign of tyranny would be over; while the younger maidens forsook the cooking-pots altogether, and followed jeering and laughing at the fool Rea was making of her lover, and wishing the time had come when they could torment a lover also.

The father of Rea also followed, laughing like the rest, but keeping a sharp look-out on the pair, as fathers and mothers in these parts do during courting season.

And in the midst of the yelling and hooting crowd Rea sat unmoved, urging on her unlucky victim with vicious little pinches and kicks, as well as blows from the bamboo-pipe, while he groaned in spirit as he ambled on with shell-cut hands and feet, his hair filled with sand, and the hibiscus blossoms all tumbled about.

"On, beast, on!" shouted Rea, spurring up those jaded limbs until his heart was sore with the exertion, while the crowd of girls flung more sand over him and shouted,—

"Yes, on, you beast!"

How long it might have lasted, who knows—for Rea felt the heroine of the hour, and liked the motion too well for any thought of her victim to enter her curly little head—had not a lucky idea struck the throbbing brain of Kamo of a horse he had once seen throw his rider.

Perhaps it was desperation prompted the idea, for he felt he must sink down with exhaustion if he went on longer, or the sight of a nice soft green mound of grass right before him, or maybe the wicked grin on the ugly face of Toto, who stood at hand in his gay suit of orange and red, leering at the girl bestriding him; but he instantly acted upon it, kicking up his heels in the air at the moment that the smiling Rea was least expecting such a motion, and landing her unhurt, but ignominiously, right in the centre of the grass tuft.

"That is the way the horses do," gasped Kamo, getting up and shaking himself, while all the natives laughed at Rea.

Rea, who had fallen in a most ungraceful attitude, picked herself quickly up, and, first adjusting her raumma, ran up to him with blazing eves.

"And that's what I do, you beast!"

With both hands she slapped him full on each cheek, and walked off towards the gardens, leaving poor Kamo shamefaced and dejected, with smarting cheeks and a growing consciousness that it would have been better if he had played the patient instead of the kicking steed.

Chapter XI

Toto Remembers One of the Christian Virtues, and Forgives

THERE was a wealthier man in Hula than Kamo, albeit not nearly so well liked, yet riches are always treated with some respect amongst savages, as they are with more civilized communities.

Toto was not a pretty man, in spite of his most gorgeous costume as he stood there, grinning at Kamo and leering upon Rea.

A strong-built fellow, with the face of a libertine, mingled with all the cunning of the treacherous savage; his nose resembled the nose of a Tartar, and his eyes were elongated and appeared as if lashless, with a most unpleasant droop at the outer corners; his mouth also was very large and slobbery-looking from the constant habit of betel chewing, and looked like a freshly jagged wound, wide, gaping, and showing the scarlet gums and stumps of blackened tusks behind.

He was the only man dressed in Hula, excepting the freshly-installed South Sea Island teacher, who had lately arrived with his pretty young wife to take the post from which Toto had been deposed.

Toto was the only Papuan who could read and write in Hula; formerly he had been taken in hand by the missionaries and educated to become a teacher amongst his people, almost the first New Guinea native who had been converted.

After his training at Port Moresby, he had been sent down amongst his own kindred and people, to continue the good work; but, alas! Toto had been only half-redeemed when let loose, and soon relapsed into something worse than his original uncultivated state.

Toto, like the other native teachers, had been allowed twenty pounds a year to maintain himself and family—ample means for him amongst his own tribe, where he had his own portion of land, although barely sufficient for the poor strangers, who were compelled to buy everything they required at the prices fixed by the natives and traders. The Papuan being close-fisted and yielding nothing out of charity, these poor South Sea Islanders come with their wives amongst people callous, if not regarding them as intruders. They spend their year's allowance in less than four months, and then half starve the rest of the year, working on bravely and uncomplainingly upon this arid soil, till their wives droop and die, or themselves are murdered and eaten.

Toto was not the man to make a martyr of himself, and being worldly wise, after getting all he could out of the mission-station, a pretty young wife (he had left one at Hula working in his garden while he was being converted), and his first instalment of salary, he took up his position, and cast about for other methods to increase his meagre income.

Under the protection of the missionary he became a power in his own land, while the hymns he sang drew the young boys and girls to his house, which he got built large and commodious. When traders came they applied to Toto, as mediator between them and the tribe, getting him to drive the bargains for them, so that he was paid both ways, deceiving all round, in the feathering of his own nest.

By-and-by, as time went on, Toto learnt that which they, his people, have not yet learnt, the use of money direct; he got to know what these rough sailors wanted besides copra and curios, and by stages became the pander to their vices, turning the mission-house into a place of ungodly riot, under the cloak of his supposed office of assistant teacher, and making the name of Hula vile throughout the land.

He was an unbounded hypocrite, and knew how to fawn and hold the key as well as any keeper of houses of the same description in European towns, without being as yet suspected either by the missionaries or the honest people he was daily betraying, while laying up treasures of iniquity.

The girls he taught by degrees those lessons of duplicity, so that they might hood wink their husbands and parents, and the cunning scoundrel knew by all the instincts of the trained pander whom to approach.

By-and-by, however, rumours reached headquarters, and he was dismissed at once ignominiously from the office which he had defiled, yet not before he had made enough to treat their dismissal with grinning contempt. He had established his name, and had plenty of customers, while the natives could not help respecting his riches, even though they had sprung from their dead honour. Toto could still swagger about in the gay garments which the traders brought to him, and awe his people with his splendours, while his courtyard was seldom empty of visitors.

His South Sea Island spouse had died some time before this, worn down with the hardships of her life amongst these unsympathetic strangers and killed at last by fever and neglect. The wife he had left behind was getting too old for Toto, so some time before Kamo had returned he had been one of the suitors for the hand of Rea.

But in Hula, as throughout all New Guinea, women, although finally bought, are permitted to make their own choice, so that Toto, favourably received by the father for the sake of his wealth, had been rudely dismissed by the wilful young lady, who had a good knowledge of Toto's profession, and hated him accordingly.

Still he leared upon her and made disgusting remarks when he met her alone, and had not given up hopes even after Kamo appeared.

When Kamo came to himself, after his chastisement and the abrupt departure of Rea, the first object that met his moody eyes was the large yellow and red-striped pants of this abhorred, would-be rival.

The colour upon him had the effect of red upon an excitable bull. Slowly his eyes wandered up to the evil, open mouth of the betel—chewing pander, and he fixed upon the opportunity to avenge the insults which Rea had told him about.

The tribe all round were still laughing merrily at the late scene, and Toto, thinking the quarrel meant fresh hopes for him, also swayed from side to side indulging in silent bursts of malicious mirth.

"What are you laughing at, you pig?" shouted Kamo, coming up to within an inch of Toto's sallow Chinese-looking face, and clenching his fist.

Toto could not stop all of a moment, besides he did not think there was any necessity, Kamo was such a boy compared with him.

"At the funny figure you cut on your knees—"

He did not finish his little joke, for Kamo's fist had rattled against his gums, and the men gathered round to separate them, knowing that Kamo was no match for the other; but Toto did not strike back, he had learnt one lesson at Port Moresby, to control his temper.

The leering grin became intensified with the swelling lips, as he wiped the blood away with his gaudy sleeves; but he only nodded his head at Kamo, and said,—

"We'll settle all this by-and-by, Kamo, my boy; you just wait and see." Then he hitched up his trousers, and went down past the crowd towards his own house, while Kamo and the others looked after him, marvelling at his Christian forbearance.

Once, as he nearly reached his door, he looked back and waved his hand towards them; appearing still to be laughing, but with his lips bulged out.

Chapter XII
In the Gardens of Hula—The Reconciliation

REA ran, with burning cheeks and flaming eyes, straight out of the village, shame in her little heart at her discomfiture, and wild hatred for the man who had affronted her, never stopping until she had reached the spring in the woods, over by the gardens, where the women came night and morning to fetch water.

There she flung herself face downwards on the moist grass, tearing it out by handfuls, and howling in her savage passion.

It was a new experience to this spoilt young beauty of Hula to be treated in this way. Of course she knew that after her marriage she would have to work, and submit in some things to her husband; but, before that came to pass, all precedent had proved to her that men were slaves, and that she ought to make the most of her time, as other girls did. It was nothing to torment and hurt her lover; that was what they all had to expect when they went courting, but to be herself humiliated before her people in that way was too much to endure.

"I will give him up at once and for ever," she cried savagely. For ever! The two last weeks had been very pleasant weeks, and there was no one to compare with Kamo in Hula. Perhaps his wanderings amongst white men had spoilt him, for she remembered that Kamo had told her that white men treated their girls differently.

"What fools these white women must be," she thought, "to be tender to their lovers, and let them bully them from the first. Have not all women to suffer after they are married? And it is only right that the men should have their share beforehand."

Kamo had told her that he had seen the men in Brisbane knock down their women and kick them; and she now remembered all these horrors, and wondered if this was only a foretaste of her future if she married him, for in New Guinea the husbands were always kind to their wives, and only fought amongst themselves.

"No, he would never dare go that length, nor will I give him the chance."

As Rea thought over these things she recalled how handsome he looked that morning when he came over to her, and at the prospect of giving him up the fire in her brown eyes became quenched with the tears which welled up from her sore little heart and rolled down her tawny cheeks, and she left off kicking with her toes and tearing out the grass with her hands, and, crossing her bare brown arms under her face, did exactly as a white maiden would have done under the same circumstances, namely, had a hearty crying match, pitying her own sweet self very much, and feeling very desolate, with the wish that she was dead.

"Rea," murmured a soft voice in her ear, which made her leap up, ashamed at being caught crying, to find the wicked face of Toto near her. He had quietly crept up beside her, and sat himself down on a tree-stump by the edge of the spring, and looking as sympathetic as his swollen mouth and evil eyes could allow him to look. "Don't run away, Rea; I saw what Kamo did to you, and got this for taking your part."

He pointed to his cut mouth, and at the sight Rea felt a gentle thrill of satisfaction.

"Did he fight with you about me?"

"He struck me, Rea," answered Toto meekly.

"And did you hurt him much?"

"No, Rea; I did not touch him."

"Why?"

A wealth of scorn was in the question. She knew Toto was a strong man, and had feared that Kamo was hurt in the encounter; but she could not understand a man not striking back. The little savage did not understand the Christian principle of forgiveness, although her heart had already endorsed it towards the recreant Kamo.

"I thought on a better way, whereby you and I together might hurt him much worse," replied Toto, in a soft voice.

"In what way, Toto?"

Rea was on her guard now, and all her anger forgotten.

"I know a man who could take Kamo away from Hula, and give you and me a big present for him; he will soon be here now, before another moon. But you hate Kamo now, don't you, Rea?"

"Yes, yes; but go on, Toto," impatiently answered Rea, stamping her foot.

"And if you will come to my place now and then, when the white fellows come, you may soon have as much money as Kamo has—"

What Rea's reply might have been Toto could not say, and never got the chance of hearing; for, while he tried to meet her glance as she looked steadfastly towards her feet, he gave a sudden cry, which caused the maiden to look up startled, and to find Kamo standing over his prostrate enemy, his club in his hand splashed with blood.

Rea looked upon her lover as he stood there like a young god, his eyes blazing and his nostrils quivering. Then a great timidity and fear crept over her, as he turned his eyes from the half-conscious Toto, who had now sat up trying to collect his scattered senses and clear his eyes from the blood which ran down his forehead and nearly blinded him.

"What was Toto saying to you, Rea?" he demanded fiercely.

Rea breathed once more; he had not heard the infamous proposal.

"Nothing, Kamo."

"Toto doesn't come to say nothing."

Toto by this time had risen to his feet, and stood at a convenient distance from the lovers. He replied for Rea. "I was asking Rea to marry me now she is done with you."

"Ah!" Kamo remembered that he was a sinner, and became limp and dejected at these words. Had she given him up? It seemed a small fault for so hard a punishment, and yet, according to the Hula code of morality, he dare not appeal against it, Rea being still mistress of her own fate.

"Then I had better go," said Kamo, sadly, "since you give me up, Rea; only I'll kill you, Toto, before you can get her."

"Don't go, Kamo; he is telling lies. You know, Kamo, I would not marry him if there was not another man to have, although I don't like you any longer."

"Then tell him to go, if he won't fight me now," said Kamo, sternly.

Toto did not wait to be ordered off the field. He was a big man, but he did not care to contend in battle for Rea or any other woman, and that single taste of Kamo's club seemed to be enough in one day for him.

"Yes, I'll go now, Rea, and will get your answer some other time," said Toto, going off as he spoke. He did not feel at all easy in his mind as to what Rea might tell Kamo, but on the whole trusted to chance. If his little plan were revealed he could always say it was a joke, and accomplish his purpose when his friend Niggeree came, as he expected him before long.

There are cowards in New Guinea as in other portions of the world, and Toto, in spite of his great size and superior education, was a rank craven; he had no taste for the standing accomplishments of his country, and would much rather run away than fight any day. Although not now a model Christian, he still adhered to the tenets of the new creed which he had been taught, and liked peace.

Kamo looked after him, with a scornful smile, as he slunk into the cover like a wounded snake, while Rea, watching her lover out of the corners of her eyes, and mentally comparing the two, decided that after a little penance she would give Kamo one more trial.

There is no need to describe this penance laid upon the unhappy sinner. She made all her conditions hard ones, which he consented to perform to the letter. He was to go that night into the bush, and stay there till morning amongst the ghosts. Kamo did not mind this so much as she thought he would, as a great deal of his early superstitions had been brushed away by his contact with the white people, but he was too cunning to let her know of this, and so pretended to be very frightened, which mollified her greatly.

She did not mention what Toto had told her, for she trusted to her superior wit to defeat his vile projects when the time came; besides, she feared for Kamo if he again met Toto, for she could not believe in one man being frightened at another, it was only the women they ought to fear and respect.

They had both missed dinner by the time peace was made up, and the sun was sending horizontal shafts of gold through the close leafage behind them, while the mosquitoes were coming out in detachments. But when did lovers ever care about dinner? In a few more moments the village women would be coming here to fetch water; already their chattering was borne, like the clatter of cockatoos on the wing, upon the evening winds. The gardens spread behind the umbrageous balustrades like long shady avenues, where these tawny insect-crowded shafts of sunlight were stretching down like golden ropes. Neither Kamo nor Rea had any desire to be seen in their moment of reconciliation or be twitted about their quarrel, so they turned in time into the thicket, as the first company of girls appeared from the village pathway with their water—pots upon their shoulders.

Round the well there was an open space, grass-covered, where the girls lingered to chaff one another, as girls do, or listen to the experiences of the old women. Here, also, the boys wandered about at this hour, to impress the girls with their splendour; for there were great dandies in Hula, who were in the habit of sporting all their property in the form of ornaments, and who here strutted about arm-in-arm, with their bushy heads adorned with flowers and feathers, so that the girls might admire them as they passed.

It is curious how much alike human nature is all over the world, and how youth must assert itself in the spring-time, either with nose ornaments or stiff high collars, just as the young tree puts on its blossom.

It was all the same here in Hula under the down-hanging fronds of the palm-trees as in the streets of London on a summer night, or on a village green in the country, where the maidens and young men foregather under the unlighted lamp-posts or the old oak branches.

The same as will happen in Iceland during the short fierce summer, or on the banks of the Ganges—the same that took place on the banks of the Nile or the canals of Assyria four thousand years ago, and will go on while the world rolls round the sun.

Rea had not been many moments amongst those shady avenues of fruit-trees before she regretted the penance which she had imposed upon Kamo. It was so nice to be out here all alone, away for a little time from her father's watchful eye, although she knew that even now he was hunting after them both; and kisses don't taste so nice before an audience as they do when taken in shady places with no spectator. She felt too the punishment would be hers as much as his, because she would not have him near her to torment; as she meditated she watched with delight his glorious form.

"I'll let you off to-night, Kamo, if you never do anything to annoy me again."

Rea was very tender just now, with the twilight hush upon her; and Kamo's arm, the one round her waist, trembled as he drew her closer beside him and kissed her, which she did not try to stop. Over their heads, between a rift in the papua-tree, the young moon basked upon her back, on a velvet bed of orange-green, while all the garden was steeped in the sombre shapelessness of a low-toned Flemish study—tender and filled with mystery.

Rea's heart was beating down the walls of affectation and reserve, for Kamo grew more her master than she felt she ought to let him be; but it was too sweet to rest passive, and too much effort to resist his caresses. And she had had enough of trouble in asserting her rights already for one day, so for one short twilight hour she permitted him and herself to be happy.

"Ha! so I have found you at last!" cried the deep tones of her parent, as he laid a heavy hand on Kamo's shoulder; and the honeyed dream for that time was over.

Chapter XIII
Towards the Fly River

IT is not a very long run to the New Guinea coast when the wind is fair, although in the Papuan Gulf very violent storms are apt to be experienced. Niggeree, in his Sunflower, led the way, with the Coral Seas keeping as nearly beside him as it was possible, and although the weather was calm inside the reefs and as long as they were in the Straits, there was a deal of tacking to be done to keep to the course.

Still the wind was pretty fair, it being now nearly the middle of the dry season, with an easterly monsoon blowing on their broadsides as they made towards Kiwai, at the mouth of the Fly River.

A patchy sea, very treacherous as to bottom, right on to Bampton Island, yet protected as far as Flinder's Entrance by the great Barrier Reef, which made sailing comparatively easy by day, particularly to so experienced a pilot as Niggeree, who knew every inch of the way.

Niggeree would have liked Hector to have gone with him; but as he had an extra crew of Malays and South Sea Islanders, old hands whom the Greek could manage and trust, it was thought expedient that he should accompany Captain Collins in his schooner, and follow as best they could in the wake of the Sunflower.

So, after they parted from Joe and the Thunder, keeping well to the wind, they sailed along smoothly; the sharp Sunflower, like a fresh young filly, springing a mile or two in advance, to wait while the other schooner, like a more sober old horse, tried to make up.

Over a sea filled with ripples, all emerald and amethyst, with a cloudless sky overhead, and a sun blazing down and making the pitch in the seams bubble up and the iron and brass work feel almost red hot.

Niggeree lay on the deck when not wanted, full in the fiery glare, with bare legs and feet, with stalwart limbs brown as berries, his pipe in his mouth. He was gazing upwards at the bulging sails and cordage, while his Malay boy, who knew the waters almost as well as his master, steered.

On the forecastle lay the Islanders, Malays, and Manilla boys, a little crowd, too many to be required for such a small vessel; but Niggeree knew his business well, and did not take a single man without a purpose, and where he was going he knew well he would require them all.

Arms of all kinds lay scattered about the decks as the men had left them to be polished up—Winchesters and double-barrelled rifles, cutlasses, and revolvers. Beside Niggeree lay a belt with two of Colt's latest improvements and a fifteen-chambered Winchester, while in his left hand he lazily held a freshly-ground cutlass, the keen edge of which he lightly touched with his right

61

thumb, laying it down to remove his pipe when he had to expectorate, which he did without raising his head, and lifting it again with the dreamy tenderness with which women are apt to finger a love relic.

At times he uttered, in a quiet, muffled tone, without removing his pipe, an order which the Malay instantly caught and obeyed, and once, without waiting to see where they were, he sprang, with the agility of a sleeping cat suddenly roused up by a foot treading on her tail, and, running up to the masthead, clung there for a few moments with one arm and one foot round the bare pole, while he motioned with his other hand the direction to the man at the wheel.

They were passing over a green patch of water with only a ship and a half's length of deep blue channel, all crooked and circuitous, where the many-tinted fish could be seen darting about in myriads, and as the sunbeams dived down amongst the cool transparency, lovely shapes, like trees and flowers, could be seen springing up as if carved from emerald, lapis lazuli, or amber, while in front of them leapt and flew the shoals of flying-fish, and all round, like fairy barges, floated the nautilus fleets steering due west.

A scene of light and soul-satisfying beauty and warmth, with that strong yet soft breeze pressing upon the skin like eider-down and tossing the locks aside with velvet flappings. Away in front and east-ward the horizon was a tumbled line of intense blue, with broken fringes of dazzling white; they were nearing the point where the protecting barrier ceased entirely, and where the ocean boiled in fury. There was a cloudless gale outside there, and no mistake—one of those gales most dangerous to sailing craft, where the waves beat up faster and stronger than the wind, giving the steersman hardly a chance to evade the swamping mountains.

As yet it was all right with the calm sea, and the strong blast filled to straining the shortened upper sail, and drove the mist wreathes merrily out of the way.

"Furl sails!" cried Niggeree, coming down from his perch aloft. "Let's know the depth; there ought to be a sand-bank hereabouts where we can anchor."

Some of the men sprang up to the yard and stowed away the canvas as the lead showed satisfactory anchorage, so in another moment the Sunflower was riding safely amongst the coral, while her captain waited upon his consort's approach.

"Hallo, Nig! what's up?" bawled out Collins from his deck when they got within hail.

"Nothing, only it's too rough outside to go on; besides, we'll lose nothing by this half-day at anchor. We can easily reach Mibu to-morrow, while the wind may lull a bit to-night."

"It does look roughish outside," responded Collins. "Have you good anchorage there, mate?"

"Only a sand-patch of a few yards. Try over by the lee of you, there ought to be something there if it hasn't shifted since last voyage."

Collins reefed his solitary spread of canvas, and, letting his vessel drift in the direction Niggeree pointed, watched anxiously as the man threw in the lead and sounded.

A sleepy Manilla man the sounder was, who threw out his line and drew it in again hand over fist in a listless way, singing out in a monotonous drone, as if it had been an old lesson the interest in which he had long since lost.

"Five fathoms!"

"Four fathoms and a quarter!"

"Three fathoms less twain!"

"Two foot, sah!"

This last was jerked out in a surprised tone as the Manilla man looked up suddenly, very wide awake indeed, to meet Hector's laughing blue eyes fixed upon him. They were on the sand-bank safe enough, and had been for the minute and a half while he had been throwing out his line.

"Low tide; you are all right. Drop the anchor, mate," cried the Greek, who had been quietly watching this mishap, knowing well how it would happen.

Collins gave a grunt of relief, and next moment the anchor-chain was rattling through the hawse-hole.

The atmosphere, very clear here, enabled them to see a long way around them. Far away to the northeast they could trace, like a faint stain upon that grey-white lower space, a lofty range of mountains with abrupt summits and edges, like sheets of blotting-paper with the edges frayed and torn, the faint outlines of distant New Guinea.

Nearer at hand and all round were numberless islands, some high, rising with rocky sides, others low and mango-covered. On one small island, about two miles off, they saw a long row of pelicans standing seemingly motionless in the afternoon sun, snow-white against the yellow sand lustre, with scraggy bushes here and there. Behind this patch of sand (the formation of a future island) the larger and older island lay, with a line of smooth water between. A palm-grove waved above the mangroves' outer rim; but, beyond the flocks of sea and land-birds fluttering about, there was no sign of other life.

63

"Did you shoot the whole tribe, Nig?" asked Captain Collins, pointing over to the palms.

"Oh, no," replied the Greek from his deck—there was only about fifty yards between the vessels, so that in that rarefied air they did not require to raise their voices. "I left my young woman with her old father and mother, to keep her company when I was away. I'm going ashore as soon as we have some grub."

"How did it happen?" inquired Hector.

"Well, you see, they were always sulky with me ever since I shot her brother, and never got enough copra ready, so that I knew that they were only waiting a chance to do for me if they could. I had burnt down the village twice, and roasted two or three of the kids left sleeping, but it was no use; I could see every time I came that they meant to do it, but were afeared of my Winchester.

"Well, one night my gal comes to me, and says she, 'Sleep on board to—night, Niggeree.' I axes her 'Why;' so she says, 'Nothing, only the mosquitoes are bad.' I knew that she was telling lies, for you never yet see a native cared a brass button about mosquitoes; you see, she knew the plot, and that her brothers were in it, and didn't want me to be hurt or them either, so I didn't press her just then, but took her straight away on board.

"When we got out of the house, I could see two or three black figures popping about; however, I took no notice of them, but pulled straight on.

"When I gets her into my cabin, I took her square by both shoulders, and says I, 'Now, my gal, what is it? Out with the whole yarn, or I'll blow your head to pieces;' and with that I clapped against her head the barrel of my Colt. Then she drops on her knees, and tells me all about it, asking me not to kill her own relations, which, of course, I promises, so as to hear the whole yarn. They had got her to join them, and steal my firearms, and all she could lay her hands on of the 'munition; but at the last she had repented. I was to be killed that night in her father's house, but now they would know that game was up.

"'What did they take the guns for?' I asked, for I knew they couldn't use them.

"'So that your men might not be able to help you. They mean to board her to-night, and murder them, after they are done with you, and take the ship.'

"'Where are the guns?'

"'I hid them on the west side of the island.'

"'Do they know about where they are?'

"'No; I did it all by myself.'

"'Well, wench, I won't punish you this time, so let's get to bed.'

"I thought there was no good frightening the boys, and there was lots of time before us, so I turned in to get an hour's sleep, she tumbling and tossing about, with now and then a sob, waking me up just when I was going off, or, maybe, it would be her hot arms getting about me, at which I'd give a cuss or two, and fling her off, with a pretty tough smack.

"I must have gone over asleep at last, for I was just in the middle of a nice cheery dream, in which I had got the whole batch of them safely over to Maryborough, and the tin in my pocket, without any questions axed, when I felt her hand on my mouth, and her voice in my ear,—

"'Wake, Niggeree! they are coming off!'

"I gets up to listen, and there, sure enough, they were pushing off the canoes from the shore.

"'Come with me,' I whispered to her, and she followed.

"Then I goes on deck, and telling the boys to keep a sharp look-out, I quietly drops over the offside, the gal following after me, and strikes out for the point furthest from where the canoes were pushing out; the night being pitch dark, I know'd there was no chance of them seeing me, and we both took jolly good care that they didn't hear us.

"Of course there were lots of sharks about, but we had no time to think about them at that time; all I wanted was my Winchester and some rounds.

"Well, we reached the point all right, and, creeping softly through the woods, got to the plant, and I only takes what I think would suit my purpose, and back we goes to the shore.

"I had a little dingey lying in a cove in case I might want it, which no one knew about except myself; so we gets into it, the wench sitting like a mouse, holding the guns and cartridges so as to keep them dry.

"I pulled very gently to the side I had started from, and, making the dingey fast to the anchor-chain, I got up that way, she handing up the articles when I was safe up.

"'Sit where you are,' I whispered soft-like, 'and don't move, whatever you hear.'

"Then I creeps along the deck, till I sees them all very busy at the hatch, unloading my cargo, and handing it down to the other niggers in the canoes; four of my boys I could see, faint like, lying on the deck with their skulls battered in, while up aloft I saw some figures squatting on the yard, and watching the work a-going on. I thought they might be the other boys who had got off, as they sat astride the yard like as if they were used to it, so I made up my mind what to do.

"They were all so busy hauling away at the cargo, and

chattering in the dark, that they did not notice me till I planked myself down beside them, with my back against the mast, and my feet dangling down the hold, my cutlass laid over my knees, and my Winchester careless-like slung across my left arm; but when they did spot me, they jumps double-quick time back in a crowd, and stood gaping on me as if they had seen a ghost.

"'Will we toot, master?' whispered one of my boys from aloft. Then I knew that the wench hadn't taken all the guns, and I felt comfortable.

"'Not just yet; cover them, boys, and wait till I give you the word,' says I, keeping the trail of my eyes all round, to see that none of them got behind me.

"'Well, of all the cussidest bits of cheek, this beats hollow. What were you a-doing down my hold?' says I, sternly looking them all round. I could see them plain enough now, for the sky behind me had begun to lighten, and I knew the old moon was a-going to rise.

"For a while they stood staring, and saying nothing, then by-and-by they plucks up courage, and begins all a jawing together, and a moving nearer, with their clubs up and ready for action.

"'Keep back if ye don't want a bullet in your throats,' says I, and then they sees I had my gun, and back they all goes a second time.

"'Now,' says I, 'just you put every bag back again, and as quick as you can.' They started to haul up the things from the canoes and drop them down the hold as if they had never meant no harm.

"They got three or four bags back and into their places again, when all of a sudden one of my gal's brothers says something, and they pitched down the loads, and makes a rush.

"I was just a waiting for this, and without budging a step, or moving my Winchester, I says, 'Oh, you will have it then!' and—crack! crack!!—the brother and one behind him fell dead on the deck right in front of the others, who fell over the bodies, and rolled about in all directions, some going head over heels down the hold.

"Then the fun began; I'm a pretty safe shot, as you know, but like to save cartridges when I can. Up I jumps, all of a sudden, with my cutlass cutting off a head wherever I saw one, and shouting, 'Come down, boys, and let them have it.'

"It was a busy few minutes after that, for they kept swarming up the sides to help their friends, now lying bleeding like a lot of stuck pigs. My blood was up, and I let them have it; sometimes a shot, or a slash with the cutlass, or a man's brains splashing across my face, as I land him one with the butt end of my gun.

"My boys came down the rigging and joined in cheerily, for these Malays like blood when they once begin, and when there's not much danger about having it, and I bet you they got a treat that night, and so did the sharks when we pitched the carcases overboard next morning; but that was after we got back.

"As soon as the deck was cleared, we got into the boat and tore like devils through the water; I felt drunk, and almost blind, too, with the blood and brains in my eyes.

"Up and down the village we ran, firing the houses, so as to give us more light to do our work, and the moon being now full up though thin—like and worn to half its size, they hadn't a chance to get away. Besides, until we were amongst them, they thought their friends must have won, and were holding a grand corroberrie.

"Whenever I saw a nigger—man, woman or kid—I put it to death. Some of the kids we took up, not being worth a cut, and pitched them into the fires, where they roasted, screeching like wild cats.

"A rare old time, I tell you, mates, that was, with the flames bursting out on all sides, and as hot as hell, while the moon turned thinner as the sky got lighter. It was coming on to daylight before I stopped, with a throat as dry as a cinder, and my pants sticking to my legs with the red glue. There wasn't a white spot on me, for I never stopped while one nigger lived on the island.

"The boys, too, were fagged out, and as we knew no one could leave the island, we thought it best to knock off till daylight, when we could go round and finish off any who might be left, or had run into the woods.

"All this time I had forgotton about the wench, and only minded about her when I got to the ship.

"Down we all staggered, scarce able to move a leg or arm, and pulled slowly back to the Merry Mermaid, that was the schooner I owned, that one the Queensland Government confiscated afore I was naturalized.

"As we came near to the bows, I saw the dingey wasn't there, so concluded she must have rowed after me, and got killed with the rest.

"'Serve her right for her cussed obstinacy,' says I, as I poured myself out a stiff pannikin of rum, passing the bottle over to the lads to help themselves.

"After that I lay down on the deck in a clean place—there warn't many clean spots on it—and tried to get a sleep while the boys were pitching the dead niggers overboard.

"Yet, although I was most dead beat, I couldn't manage to

67

close my eyes, but kept looking up at the stars, as they popped out, one by one, like burnt-out candles afore the light which was getting stronger every minute.

"Perhaps it was the dead bodies as they plunged with a loud splash, one after the other, that set me a thinking on the gal. I'm mostly tender—hearted where women are concerned, and I thought she warn't a bad sort, taking natives all through, and must ha' liked me a bit, or I'd be food for the fishes by that time, so that I began to feel sorry that she hadn't stopped in the dingey that night.

"Things came up that had been between us two, and I missed her badly just then, for I'd have liked another glass of grog, and some one to fill my pipe, being too lazy-like to do it myself, and she was always handy and willing at that sort of thing.

"Then I minded the day I gave her such a welt across the back with the flat of my cutlass, that the mark never left her, or ever will, as long as she lives; when she fell down on the sands and lay for dead, nearly half a day, all for stealing a bit o' baccy out of my tin case, which, as it happened, I found afterwards in my own pocket, having put it there myself, after taking a quid, and some one interrupting at the time. She always had a bad cough after that welt, but she said nothing about it, and, of course, I didn't ever tell her of my mistake, for it don't do to let them think the white fellow can do any wrong; it would make them too conceited.

"Of course I felt perfectly easy in my mind as regards the Government, for there was no one left to tell them about it, and my boys wouldn't blab, being as deep in the mud as I was myself; besides, I wasn't then a British subject.

"'Curse her obstinacy,' at last says I to myself, getting up, and going to the locker where I kept the rum, and then cutting myself a fill of baccy. I drank out of the bottle, for I was too tired to fetch a pannikin, and I didn't want the boys to get any more.

"After taking a good long swig. I feels some better, and lighting my pipe, goes over to see how they were getting along.

"They had chucked all the bodies over, and I could see the bay swarming with black fins, tugging and tearing away at the carcases. None of them had been allowed to sink to the bottom, for I could see three or four fighting over one body, while they tore off long strips from the ribs and bones, and shaking themselves in their hurry to bolt it, and be back again before the others got too much of their meal, while more came up and snapped at it, bringing it with a jerk up half out of the water, so that I could see the bones washed with the salt water, and looking as white as the shark's bellies; every moment white ribs and leg-bones with crimson ribbons fluttering from them turned to the surface.

"A large fellow now and then snatched a whole body from the teeth of the smaller fry and made off with it, shaking it about as a mastiff dog might do with a terrier when he was in a bad temper. I thought on my swim ashore during the night, and felt disgusted at the cruelty of dumb beasts; a kind of a cold disgust as made me shiver and half feel their sharp teeth at my own backbone.

"My men had got all the cargo back into the hold again, and were mopping down the decks from the mess we had made, all the excitement gone out of them, and working away like lambs. They drew up buckets of water, all kinds of pinky colours, from the sea which the sharks were staining, and flung it over the decks, scrubbing along with their mops, and squeegeeing it out of the scuppers. It took a deal of slunging and mopping to get the dried clots rubbed out, or the crusted brains scraped off. They got down on their knees amongst it when they came to the dry bits, and scraped with their jack-knives, while the water ran down the ship's sides almost thick.

"It was a misty morning, and the sun didn't show up till pretty late that day, but the sky was warm-coloured and blushing-like, and as the sea was a dead calm, with only the ground-swell— as always is of a morning—that reddish colour in the sky got casting down darker on the smooth water and bulging towards us, as if the whole ocean was crowded with sharktorn dead bodies all gushing with blood.

"We were in shallow water—about five fathoms—where, on other mornings, you could see the fishes playing about, and the coral, as it is here, at most times; but as I looked over the sides I could see nothing but crimson colour right down, and no bottom.

"I took off my pants, as I always do of a morning, to have a slunge along with the deck, which I needed as much as I ever did; but when the boys drew in the bucket and I saw how red the water was in it, I told them to stash it, and went aft for a fresh pair of pants, letting the blood stop about me as it was, although it was main claggy.

"Well, after my smoke we had some breakfast. My Chinaman then had hid himself at the back of his stove, and never came out till they dropped across him when they were washing, and he was in such a state of fear that he put salt in the tea instead of sugar; and then, after a spell, we went ashore.

"It warn't much of a sight, the village that morning, with the smoke still rising from the white ashes, and here and there a bit of a post smouldering away or a leg or breast half roasted where they had fallen, and still lay steaming, with the smell about the air something between a butcher's killing-yard and a hotel kitchen. Some of the palm-trunks were blackened on the side next to where

69

the houses had been, and the bananas were all shrivelled up—that is, all those near enough—while at every step you either tripped over the headless body of a woman or a man, or else sent some round head rolling like a ball amongst the ashes or between a pair of dead legs.

"My bare feet also would go squash into a pool of blood kept from sinking through the sand by the steeped grass petticoat of some young woman. It was nasty to feel those wet grasses getting between your big and little toes, and clutching at your ankles like snakes; but I turned over the young ones, where they had heads left on them, to see if my gal was amongst them. The young ones mostly fell on their faces when they were shot, and the old ones on their backs; kids fall about anyhow.

"Well, we went the round, and I did not see her anywhere, neither her father or mother. I was mighty easy in my mind at this, for I knew then that she had got them safe away, and was hiding about the bush somewhere. So we started on the hunt straight away.

"First I came upon the dingey in the cove where we had landed the night before together, and then I felt sure that I'd find her near the plant, for she was not very fly, but something like a wild beast that runs always to the same hole. So telling my boys to beat about the other parts, I started by myself to find her and her old 'uns.

"It felt calm-like and holy, walking through the woods in the early morning, now I was content in my mind that she was still alive, and having got away from the red sea and that burnt-down village. The leaves, all wet, brushing my face, felt cool and nice, and I lay down once or twice to have a roll on the wet grass, leaving the place I rolled on when I rose all crushed down and red.

"At last I came upon them sitting—the two old ones dazed-like, and doing nothing—on the wet grass. They were all whitish, like the grass, and covered with dew. Most like they had sat there quiet all night; I think so, for a bush-spider had finished his net-like web, and had gone in to watch, either amongst the old man's wool, where one end of the web was fastened to, or into the bush at the other side of the footpath, over to where it stretched. The web was all heavy and grey with the dew, like the old man's head, so he must have sat still for hours.

"The old woman also looked straight along the road, and never budged, although she must have seen me coming, looking like an old idiot, with dead-lights for eyes. She has always gone about stupid since.

"The wench lay all of a heap at her mother's feet, with her back to me, and the broad welt from the cutlass raised out and whitish against the dark skin. I couldn't make out where her legs, arms or head had got to.

"'Hallo!' says I, funny like, giving her a bit of a kick behind, 'so you're not dead yet?'"

"She gathered herself up very quiet and reluctantly, with eyes all on the stare, and when she saw it was me she kneeled down and kissed my hand, all wet with the dew and bloody from holding the cutlass; kissed it two or three times, so that when she lifted her mouth away it looked as if it had got a blow and was bleeding.

"She's a very good gal, mates, so I made her queen of the desert island, and if she wants another tribe to keep her company when I'm away, why, then she'll have to begin and raise them."

Chapter XIV
The Voyage of the "Thunder"

THE next morning the Thunder left the island, after landing Joe, who had by this time recovered his accustomed flow of spirits. A baby after all to him was not so serious a loss as a firing of bêche-de-mer, and now that Queen Ine was off duty there was the more need for him to exert himself.

He did not grudge the relations their time of lamentation, but they must do it in relays; so before very long he was swaggering about and blaspheming all round, according to his usual routine.

The baby had been buried during the night, thus that bother was got over without trouble to him, and he kept out of Queen Ine's road as much as convenient, and when he had to go indoors he moved as quietly as he could, and swore as seldom as possible. So the mother sat in the shadow or went into the lonely woods and there communed with her own heart, while the unseen angels of God moved about her in their own way, pouring balm upon this wounded heart.

Verily sorrow brings us very near to heaven, and dead fingers lie gently on the soul.

It was about two days' journey to their island, and about twelve hours' from the perfect Island of Darnley.

When Hafid felt the motion of the sea he seemed to rouse up, and moved about the deck with a look of almost cheerful expectancy in his eyes. The next land he would behold must be his own native land, where on the mud-banks he would once more see his wife waiting on his coming, the same as when he left her six years ago, the almond-eyed girl he had courted amongst the tamarinds, with the lips of the damask rose and the even teeth like rows of pearl. Over that dancing plain, with the sunbeams laughing to him, and the eastern breeze singing in his ears.

Mr. Bowman was a kind-hearted man, if a keen trader in his employer's interest, and felt as he looked at Hafid much exercised in his mind what to do with his charge. "However," he thought, "I may be able to leave him with the missionary at Murray Island, who will have a chance of sending him back, or failing that, I'll take him back to Thursday Island and send him in one of the British India packets going south." So he contented himself with that reflection, and went below to the cabin to look with the captain over their charts.

So the day went past, they steaming gently along that tropic ocean, with a sharp look-out for any patches on the way, and by afternoon the lovely-shaped island rose slowly on the horizon, growing from blue haze to purple, and at last taking on the delicious local colours and shapes. Nearer, and native houses came into focus with the palm-groves behind, then the natives were to be seen clustering along the beach and wading about the waters; the point where the mission-house stood boldly against the sky on the edge of the hill, with the upward green slope about it, has an air of infinite peace and rest.

Two boats put off at the same time to welcome them, one with the sails up, running before the wind, belonging to the trader who came to traffic, and the other being steered by the large-bodied, gentle-faced South Sea Island teacher, while four stalwart natives rowed him.

There being no other white resident here except the trader, who was not very particular about dress, Bowman and Danby received them in their airy costume of pajamas.

Hafid with glowing eyes saw the land loom up, then, as the outlines became more defined, the expectant light died out, and a hopeless disappointment dulled the amber, and crept like grey ashes over his delicate features; once again he had been deceived by the white man, for he had no sense of time or space. The dream was over, and for ever; he could wait no longer, so he crawled away to a corner between the boat and the bulwarks at the forecastle, and laid himself down with a gentle sigh.

He shared with Orientals and Africans that curious faculty of being able to die at will. When hope ceases to glow in their breasts, or a superstitious omen tells them that they are to die, it may be the word of the magician or the bone pointed at them, as amongst the Queenslanders—or the lizard running over them, as with the Maori—or the utter weariness of life taking possession, as with the Seedy boys, they can lie down and give up life as easily and methodically as they fall asleep.

Hafid had given up hope, trust in man was dead; the weariness of death was upon him, so he turned his face to the bulwark, and waited quietly on the coming of his fate.

Perhaps it was better to give up before going home, better to have seen his sweetheart as he left her, and as he will always see her throughout eternity; for those who die young, like the absent, grow no older; the dark tresses never grow thin nor the baby lisp deep and full, and as we live in memory here we must so be shaped hereafter.

After business was arranged with the trader, Bowman, Danby, and the captain went ashore with the missionary. Hans, the engineer, not being invited, occupied himself, along with the Hibernian mate and the little Cockney assistant, in abusing the whole crowd. Hans had a fine contempt for any one who slighted him, or, rather, whom he fancied did so.

They went in due form, and were introduced to the native king of the island. All the islands have separate kings; there is an immense quantity of royal blood in the Australian colonies, as well as a vast stock of aristocracy; we meet them knocking about everywhere.

Next they visited the missionary house, a roomy bamboo structure of two apartments, with the large yard behind, where the women cooked and did their work, and having gardens around. Inside, the floor was covered with grass matting, and was beautifully cool and clean. There were no chairs, as the habit is to sit on the floor. The Europeans, not being used to this, sat on the edge of the large bed, near where a young woman lay, nearly wasted to a skeleton with the fever. Her husband sat by her side and held her hand, which he stroked gently, while he read in a low voice from his native testament. She had been lovely at one time, and was still very young, not more than seventeen, but her cheeks had fallen in and her lips were thin and drawn from the white teeth, while her dark eyes looked too large for the thin face, and her long black wavy hair hung down limply and was streaked with grey.

On the ground two young girls sat holding a young infant, also wasted and lifeless-looking—the baby of the fever-stricken and dying girl on the bed.

A tall, comely woman moved lightly about breaking the young cocoa-nuts, and filling the jugs with the milk, all they had to offer the strangers; she was dressed in the usual falling robe of

73

spotted blue, which, as she moved about, showed her full proportions and rounded limbs.

Bowman took out his flask to qualify the fluid she gracefully offered them, and motioned to their guide if he would share, at which he gently shook his head and smiled.

They had no medicine to give the sick girl, so they did what they could to relieve her, read the words of consolation and prayed, placing her future and their own in higher hands with child-like trust.

One look round at this household was enough to convince one of their sincerity and zeal for the cause in which they laboured and without a murmur laid down their lives; abstemious, industrious, and meek, they sacrificed themselves and all that they loved best, living cheerfully in the land of their adoption, knowing that they would never again return to their native homes.

No need to ask how they managed on the twenty pounds a-year; they were now existing on the yams and taro, which they had cultivated, without a taste of bread or animal food until their next allowance came.

Sometimes when very hard up, they appealed to their own countrymen in the Straits, those who were pearl-divers, and who made and spent small fortunes by their dangerous calling, and they never appealed in vain, these reckless sons of the South Seas, who made money hand-over—fist, sending as much as forty pounds at a time to assist their hard-up brothers labouring and starving in the Lord's vineyard; but they never appealed to the mission station for more money, and they never rebelled.

This poor teacher holds the hand of the woman he is losing, whom he loves so dearly; yet both know that when she is dead he will have short time for lamenting her loss, for according to his bond he must choose another wife within six months. He is saying good-bye, and hopes to meet her in heaven, along with the wife who has gone before her, and the women who are to follow, unless he dies first. It is, perhaps, as well that there is neither giving away nor marrying in Heaven.

After a walk through the gardens and along the shore, they put off and pull to the steamer, the missionary coming with them to get some quinine for the sick girl, and bringing with him in return some curios in the shape of spears and necklets.

The sun has just disappeared behind the ocean-line when they jump on board, and the air is filled with the brown lustre, which falls along the deck with a sickly glow, and hardly have they touched the deck before the captain bustles about bullying and cursing all round in mixed Scotch and colonial, to which the mate replies in choice Irish; the coloured men sulk about in detached groups.

There are no ladies present, but that would make little difference when Captain MacAndrews is flying round. A nautical order does not sound like a command, unless it is well interlarded with adjectives, at least it was so with the old school. Now we walk the decks of steam-packets instead of sailing-vessels, and see officers attired in drawing-room costume, addressing Lascars in chow-chow Hindoostanee, while silent, white-clad, turbaned figures glide ghost-like about: but on the Thunder, although the sailors were dark-skinned the blank cartridges were not fired from air-guns, neither would the officers have adorned a drawing—room, for they dressed as they spoke and lived.

Danby laughed gently as the echoes wafted back the strong accents, and said, "Keep your collar on, old man," to the skipper, as he lurched past, at which remark MacAndrews, considering that he had never yet been beheld by mortal man inside such an unnecessary article of furniture, seemed on the verge of blasphemy, and Danby merited the glare which that precise young gentleman received as reply.

"Massa Bowman," said the steward, as he came up to the cabin door, "Hafid going to die."

"What!" said Bowman, startled.

"Yes, he got the devil in him inside, all over sick."

"Where is he?"

"Over there by the boat, very ill."

Bowman and Danby went over to where the Hindoo lay on his back, where the men had found him, quiet and seemingly unconscious of all about him.

"Bring him aft, and let's see what the matter is," said Bowman, turning to the Malay, after touching Hafid with his foot, without, however, getting any response from the prostrate figure.

But none of the coloured men moved to assist, indeed they gave even Bowman a wide berth, as it was a conviction amongst them that he was also doomed from having come in contact with the devil in Hafid.

This will-power is utterly beyond the comprehension of us Westerns, nor can doctors give the complaint a name, sailors say they die out of "pure cussedness." A Maori will count up the days he has to live, inform his friends of the fact, and die up to time; they calmly lie down and die, without an effort. What a gift to be possessed of by the miserable, but we are coarser in fibre, the life holds firmer to its tenement in us barbarians, and so it requires the pistol, knife, or strong poison to accomplish what the Eastern can do without, seemingly, an effort.

Between Danby and Bowman, Hafid was dragged along the deck and laid in a comfortable place under the awning. He made no motion, but let them do as they liked with him, only turning his face from them after he was laid down, and waiting, without a smile, on the coming of the angel who carries the silver shears.

Was he dying of that trouble which we all scoff at now-a-days, or only sulking out of pure cussedness?

Chapter XV
The Storm

A STORM at sea, under a smiling sky, with sweltering decks, seems as great an inconsistency as to see a married couple quarreling; that is, the husband raving like a madman, and the wife looking her most aggravating sweetest.

In the Bay of Biscay it is all in harmony—the slaty sky, driving rain deluging the sheets and making the furious waves appear to smoke as they rise and tumble in the distance steel grey, or break over the decks bottle-green and flecked with foam like the froth driven from the fangs of a mad dog.

We picture misty outlines, all blurred and broken, when the ocean rises up in its wrath not to be driven along and pitched from side to side under the flaming lustre of a tropic sun, which licks up the brine as it recedes after each mad leap, and makes prismatic flashes of the liquid drippings, while the mountains behind and around, snow-crested, are mountains of emerald and sapphire, all shot with molten gold.

Captain Collins and Hector clung to the wheel as the Coral Seas staggered along and shook amongst those tumbling furies.

They were alone on that raging ocean, for the wind had not lessened, and when they dashed together out from the protection of the reefs, no man could attempt to curb the schooners or keep them together. The Sunflower went out of sight ahead like an express train, dropping behind the horizon as if she had suddenly swamped, and leaving her consort to follow as she best could.

They had agreed to meet, if possible, at Uibu, where they would once more find shelter and smooth waters inside the Fly River, Niggeree giving full directions, and leaving behind him a chart of his own making, where all the dangers were marked out, before he started.

That night he had gone alone to the island. Somehow his

little yarn inspired neither Collins nor Hector with any desire to see more closely the scene of that tragedy or the survivors, and they asked no questions about them when he returned the next morning.

At present both men have enough to do, for, with that furious hot gale trying to push them westward and their united efforts to keep her head towards the north, all their strength was required to manage the wheel and keep their feet.

The men clung to whatever they could cling to, all loose articles being firmly lashed before starting; they had nothing to do except wait and battle for life with the sea.

Every moment the green sparkling waves broke over them with a shriek like horrid laughter, and the light little vessel heeled over before that overwhelming strength until the bare yard touched the rising waves on the lee side, hardly having time to right herself before the next swamping mass came down upon her.

But she was light, and water-tight, and the crew being well accustomed to the Papuan waters, although never before so far west, did not suffer much uneasiness. So long as the vessel obeyed the helm and the wheel did not break, all they concerned themselves about was to ease her off as much as they could while keeping their course.

Now and again they saw ahead portions of the waters where it seemed quieter, but on the east side of these quiet places the foam rose up like straight walls, and these places they tried to keep clear of; but as long as the waves rose and fell steadily they felt easy.

Inside some of these pool-like places they saw little islands, some bare strips of yellow sand surrounded by deep blue spaces, with pelicans and other sea-birds backing against the wind or rising with ungainly motion and flapping wings, as if protesting against the unusual commotion which disturbed their mid-day siesta.

On other and larger islands they saw the first approach to fertilization in the shape of scrubby trees and distorted wind-beaten-down branches; yet even there were the strips of golden sunny sands and smooth girdle of blue waters surrounded with that straight, up-spouting wall of snowy foam which fringed the tumbling mountains outside—golden sands and smooth waters where elves might have disported themselves or mermaids might have waited on the coming of the ships, only that orthodox mermaids like the storm-beaten rocks of the North Sea, as elves and fairies like the gas-lit pavements of large cities—this is the condition of Titania's court in this unimaginative nineteenth century.

It was getting on towards night, and still the waves broke as wildly as ever, and not a sign of the Sunflower or of the wind slackening down. The night they dreaded most, for there was no moon, and unless they found an anchorage soon they would have to drive about all in the dark, and take their chance of reefs and shipwreck.

Eagerly they looked ahead, seeing many coral-walled lakes, but without a break in their white walls, and they knew well what an approach to these meant.

Meanwhile, the sun went down all yellow, crimson, and violet, making golden seams run down the sides of those blue waves, like melted metal running out of a half-closed furnace; and when the vessel rose on the crest of a wave, all dripping wet, that metal lustre seemed to bronze over the hull and decks with sharp edges of burnish. Then the twilight spread beyond those solid-looking gigantic masses which appeared when they rolled into the trough of the waves like iron ridges against a lighted-up transparent tinted screen. Then the darkness grew like an opaque green curtain behind a black and rumpled pall. During the night, countless stars glittered like angry eyes within a deep pit. The brave sailors held on, with drooping lids and wearied arms, ever staring ahead and trying to evade those awful walls, now tarnished silver in the blackness, where the howling became horrible shrieks, while around them blazed phosphorescent lights as the waves hissed past them or broke over them emitting flashes and sparkles like unholy corpse-candles.

Chapter XVI
Driven Ashore

MORNING came at last, and Collins and Hector were freed from all anxiety, in the sense that the condemned criminal feels relieved after the judge has pronounced his sentence. Their steering-gear had snapped just as the darkness melted away, and they were now pitching and rolling due west, without the power to alter their course or avoid reefs which might come in their way.

No boat could live on that sea, so that they had just to take their chance of whatever mishap was in the near future.

At present the ocean seemed clear, and presented only a tumbling waste, so now the pair sat sucking away at their

78

saturated pipes, and hanging on to the sides while they lay on the deck and waited.

"Whereabouts do you think we are?" observed Hector, quietly.

"God only knows," responded Collins. "I take it we were near on to Bristow Island when the gear gave way, and now are drifting on to Sabai or the Baxter River; but we'll very soon find out."

The schooner was full before the wind now, going at a furious rate, and so they relapsed into silence, dropping asleep now and then, to be roused up by another sweeping wave, when, after they had cleared the brine out of their eyes, they'd look ahead, and then settle down again to sleep.

The men forward still clung, as they had done all night, and looked towards their masters with apathetic faces.

"Land ahead at last!" suddenly cried Collins, getting up and staring out. "The mainland, or I'm much mistaken."

Yes, there it was, like a low bank of clouds, very flat, and spreading out in front of them; nearer, and they can see the yellow sands with a fringe of white beating against it, and between them and it, in detached places, patches of reef with wide openings between.

"Like as not we shall strike against one of these patches and go to pieces; let's have the boat ready."

The sea was not quite so wild now, and since the vessel had been left to herself the waves broke less frequently over her; she went with the waves and the wind, and rode lighter over the crests, so that they were able to get the dingey ready.

"It's no use, you know, if we strike a patch, but it's our only chance." And they all got up and stood beside the boat ready to spring in if she struck, but they did not loosen the lashings, but waited with knives drawn ready to cut.

The coast was level as far as they could see it, with a thickly-wooded country behind, but no sign of natives.

"A near shave that time," cried Collins, as they darted into one of the openings only a few feet distant from the reef, where the waters beat against it with a thunderous fury. "I think we are pretty safe now, for the rest of the way seems to be sand."

The waves were much quieter inside this partial barrier, and so mixed up with mud and sand that they could not see the bottom or what they were passing over.

"We'll get ashore yet, mate," again cried out Collins, his piping voice almost cheery. "Heave out the line and let's see the depth, and be ready, boys, with the anchor."

A heave or two showed them they were getting into shallow

waters with a good mud bottom, and soon they were near enough to drop the anchor, which, after dragging a few yards, caught fast, and brought them to with a jerk. So far, they were in comparative safety, although far from being comfortable, and could look about them.

The coast appeared completely deserted, for not a native village could be seen, while from where they lay a broad river of nearly a mile wide could be seen emptying itself into the sea, all muddy coloured; the banks of the river were lined with mangrove bushes and low mud banks.

"That ought to be the Baxter River from its appearance," remarked Collins. "If so, we'll tow her into it as soon as the sea settles down, and strike overland and make for the Fly; if Nig has got right, we'll find him somewhere there."

"Our only plan now, while this monsoon lasts; so meantime let's have something to eat and drink."

The storm had spent itself, as they could see, and although still raging away outside, it was growing quieter every moment at their anchorage, so, after making the best breakfast they could, they got the dingey over the side, and, taking their revolvers and rifles with them, rowed into the river, where shortly they discovered a pretty safe landing-place, and making their boat fast to one of the branches, they waded through the soft slime to the firm grass beyond.

"A splendid lair for alligators," observed Hector, as they stood on firm ground once more.

"First-rate! but I'm much more concerned about natives; let's get along cautiously and see if there are any about."

The sun was now full up, and they could see the vessel tugging away at her anchor chain and the two boys they had left in charge squatting upon the deck cleaning and drying their guns, but no signs of either house or canoe anywhere.

Out to sea the billows still rose and fell in irregular dark masses, with the white splashes which marked a hidden reef, but the wind felt softer as it struck against their cheeks. Yes, decidedly, the storm was over, and by mid-day they would be able to tow their little schooner into the calm shelter of the river.

Chapter XVII
Rea's Troubles Begin

TOTO was a comic rogue when he liked to set himself out to amuse people; his large loose mouth gave him a soft appearance, while he could make faces which convulsed the on-lookers; no merry gathering or feast was considered complete without this witty one.

A coward, ah, yes! they all allowed that, but then he made no pretensions to be a hero; he could sing hymns so that they sounded like comic songs, and mimic the missionary to perfection, and tell lies by the yard, but then his were comic lies, and no one ever took offence at his jokes, because people don't like to hit those professors of peace who will not strike back again, and Toto seldom jested unless he knew his man.

He passed in Hula amongst husbands and fathers for an easy-tempered wealthy fool who could not do much harm, and he knew too much about the daughters and wives of some, for them to betray his real character, while at the same time he was by nature discreet where they had entrusted their secrets to him. In New Guinea his profession was unknown; indeed, he was there the originator of his calling, and the natives of Hula were the last to hear how their village was talked of in other parts of the land, just as a husband is ofttimes the latest to hear that which the world is constantly whispering about.

Toto was the very last one to boast about what would have cost him his head.

Since the father of Rea laid his hand on her lover's shoulder in the gardens of Hula, and parted the pair, there had come a change over the spirit of their dreams.

Toto's wealth had long attracted the attention of the father, who wished for nothing so much as to break his engagement with Kamo and take on with the more eligible suitor, yet hitherto he had not dared to interfere with the choice of the maiden, but now that unlucky Kamo had given him the opportunity, he determined to improve upon it, so that while the fond pair were making up their differences under the cocoa-nuts, the stern parent had been holding a consultation with the elders of the tribe, Toto assisting with his sage advice. The result was that the youth was condemned for having affronted the dignity of his chief in the person of his daughter, and the sentence passed that the engagement should come to an end, and parental authority he brought to bear upon the inclination of the maiden if she did not herself see the necessity of asserting her own dignity.

Kamo that night slept in the woods after all, while Rea lay in the house of her father, a tearful prisoner, and alone.

To-night there is to be a feast and a ghost entertainment, for the spirit—men have come into the village, to tell fortunes and to prophecy.

The spirit-men are the guests of good-natured Toto.

This is one of his good qualities; he is very hospitable, and ever ready to place his two-roomed house at the disposal of strangers. All day long the preparations went on, and Toto bustled about getting masks and things ready, while the villagers kept away from the vicinity of the wizards with great awe, and waited on the night with trembling expectancy.

Kamo went about disconsolate, only able to get a look and wan smile from Rea, as she peeped out from under the matting of her father's house. He could only wave his hand in return and pass by, for her father sat in silent, stern state by the foot of the ladder and looked on the young man as if he had been a stranger.

Kamo, having been with the white men, did not place much faith in the predictions of these spirit-teachers or devil-men, but he appreciated the power they possessed, and knew quite well that the result of to-night's predictions would be another bar in his way; he felt convinced that the friends of Toto were not likely to predict anything favourable to his love, and he also surmised that it was by Toto's arranging that the show had been got up.

Nevertheless youth is hopeful, and the present ever better than future benefits; he felt sure that in the bustle of the crowd and in the darkness he might have a chance of whispering a word in Rea's ear, and that was enough to comfort him.

A balmy night towards the close of the dry season! In another week the wind would shift, and the lakatois with their merchandise might be expected home; most of the men had gone west to Moresby, and other places along the coast, so that the population at present consisted principally of women, old men, and boys. Kamo's projected marriage had interfered with his taking part in the expedition, and now he wanders over the sands watching the people as they gather round the fires, placed in front of Toto's house, all anxiously waiting on the opening of the door.

They were, or pretended to be, very much afraid of these devil-men, and although they knew the hideous masks were made of wood and paint, yet the spirits behind transformed the wooden stocks into real monsters for the time.

These natives have no mode or ceremony of religious observances, they believe in a good spirit and a malignant one. The good spirit makes the world fair, and the flowers and fruit to grow, and does good because he cannot do evil. It is only the evil spirit who, by reason of his imperfections, can be moved by prayers and flattery, as a bad man, a tyrant, likes fawning slaves; so they administer to the vanity of the Evil one that he may forego his wicked intentions. They honour the Good by the silence of unuttered respect.

The new moon shines upon the bay with a subdued

radiance, for over her silver horn the filmy mists which betoken a change of weather are gathered; this thin veil the rays scatter, till the whole scene is penetrated by the tender illumination. The houses in the water are ghost-like and seem to hang in the air, the vapours lying heaviest around the posts.

Through the trees Kamo gets crimson and golden glimpses of the fires, with the dark figures moving about and mixing at times with the slender columns of the palms, while long shafts of dim, dust-colour spread from those bright splashes to the sands and water; a glitter of gold is on the over-turned side of the advancing wavelet, where the dust-tinted shafts fall, or a shade of deep red on the tawny limbs of some naked savage, as he stalked across these light gateways, and for an instant blocked them up; while up the tree-trunks and along the branches or drooping fronds run and drip worsted-like threads of vermilion.

They are now beating on their iguana skin drums and sounding their pan-reeds and shell-rattles, so Kamo moves nearer to the crowd, for he knows the show is about to begin.

As he glides behind the trees and takes his observations before advancing, the door opens and the dread priests of the devil make their weird appearance, led on by the large open-mouthed Toto, who takes the part of the comic muse, or clown, dressed with a female petticoat round his waist and his gaytinted trousers underneath, and making uncouth, and I fear to add, rather obscene gestures as he marches in front.

They laugh at Toto, but gaze with fearful expectancy behind him into the shadow of the doorway from which he has emerged, and where now slowly comes a strange diabolical figure with glassy eyes, which catch the red glitter from the flame, and appear to glare with fury upon that assembled crowd.

Kamo sees where the father of Rea is placed amongst the elders of the tribe, while the maiden he loves sits with downcast air on the margin of the circle of young girls.

She has taken her seat very much in the background, so that she sits in the shadow of the other's backs, while behind her grows a thick undergrowth of shrubbery.

Kamo watches his opportunity, and on hands and knees creeps through the long grasses till he gets near enough to her, then putting out a brown arm, he touches her softly in the side, whispering, "Rea."

None of the others hear him, and Rea does not appear startled, she only allows his hand to drop down to her side, and with Kamo's grasp murmuring, "Yes, Kamo!" and then they are both quiet and appear to watch.

The first actor has come forth, and now stands in the full

fire-light, while Toto, feigning great fear, falls flat on his face with his petticoat, as if by accident, over his head, but no one laughs now at the comic fellow, they are watching, eyes and mouth wide open, for what has to come.

The mask is like a monster beast on all fours, shaped something like a gigantic alligator, with feathers and streamers of grasses partly hiding the four feet.

While all eyes were fixed upon it some figures came out of the hut, with false faces and strange dresses, dancing wildly and spinning round the monster, singing a wild chaunt and beating upon their drums. Then from the shadows behind, as if rising from the earth, appeared all dim in the half-light, a great upright form of about fifteen feet high, with a ghastly white face and holes for eyes, which glowed crimson, while from the half-open mouth came puffs of smoke and sparks; it was draped in a mat which fell to the ground like a screen, and hid the performers, who were behind.

When this tall and horrible-looking spectre appeared, the drums ceased their din, and a great silence fell over the crowd, for this was the ghost which prophesied. A hollow rumbling sound first broke upon the silence, suspiciously like two or three men groaning in unison behind, at which the old men shuddered, while the women hid their faces, and then the oracle spoke.

First it praised the eastern monsoon which gave them all health, and blew the traders away on their voyages, then it foretold a rich return when the wind veered and brought them home.

"Meet the men with songs, for they will come in safety when Rea is a wife—"

"Ah!" grunted Kamo, as he heard this ending of the song, clutching at the little hand nervously in the shadow.

"Rea, the daughter of the chief, who will bring much riches to her father, and prosperity to the tribes.

"The tribes who are brothers of Hula.

"They shall swallow the enemy before them as the shark eats up the little fish.

"Rejoice for your men who come back laden to dance at the marriage of Rea.

"Who is the man to marry Rea?

"The wise man of the tribe.

"The rich man of the tribe.

"The good man of the tribe.

"Toto is good, he can buy his wife with many presents.

"He can keep his wife as the daughter of a chief ought to be kept.

"He can—"

"Can he fight for her?" cried out the impulsive Kamo,

springing up from behind the circle of girls, and leaping right in front of the huge ghost, which shrank back a little, while Toto looked up from under his petticoat.

"Ho! men of Hula, there is the son-in-law of a chief for you, a man to look at with a woman's raumma. Toto the wise, who makes money out of your daughters; Toto the good, who has made Hula the cry of Kerepuna and Hanuabada. Bah! he is a fine fellow, but let him keep to the petticoat. She how he fights this brave man of Hula."

And Kamo, with a kick at a certain portion of Toto's person just then presented to the gaze of the tribe, snapped his fingers contemptuously, and stalked into the darkness.

Chapter XVIII
On Board the "Sunflower"

THE Sunflower flew before that east blast like a bird on the wing, while Niggeree, who both knew his boat and the ocean before him, took the wheel, as he always did in moments of emergency, while his men stood ready to work at the ropes.

He passed the shoals and islands on the way, and by night had brought to anchor near a hilly and rocky island which afforded a good shelter, and where he knew of a good sand-bank near to him; here he lay to, and waited, looking out for his consort.

It was with great anxiety he watched, for he had no intention of losing sight of his friends. Hector knew where the gold was to be found, and he wanted Collins to join him in a little pearl-fishing expedition; Collins had both divers and dresses, &c., with him, which Niggeree was not in a position at present to purchase, but he knew the ground, and so the partnership was one of capital and experience, like that contract entered into once between the Jew and the Scotchman, only in this instance it was reversed, the Greek had the experience, and the Scotchman the capital.

After waiting till about midday on the look-out, he once more put to sea, and before sunset brought up safely at Brampton Island.

From here he made for Mibu, and finally resolved to wait at Kiwai till they should join him.

Here he fell upon his old master, Professor Killmann, with whom he had previously explored the eastern coast, and who now hailed the chance of aid, in recovering his vessel which he had been forced to abandon to the natives, and take to the woods.

Professor Killmann had just come from Alligator Island, where he was forced from his vessel, and compelled to walk overland about a hundred and fifty miles through jungle and swamps, living as best he could on the way and fighting as he went along; he presented a deplorable sight, with his legs and feet swollen and covered with sores, his clothes in rags, and his stalwart frame almost reduced to a skeleton, but with spirit unsubdued, and the flames of revenge burning in those deep-sunken dark eyes; here was the man of all men whom Niggeree respected most, for he never spared an enemy, holding men's lives as lightly as the lives of the insects he slaughtered and preserved.

This time, as usual, he entered Kiwai alone, his followers had been slaughtered by the natives, while he himself was wounded in several places.

There were dark tales afloat concerning his actions, and it was said that his name, coupled with that of Niggeree, was enough to send the natives flying in a panic of fear into the jungle; they told how he pitched dynamite charges wantonly into approaching canoes, without waiting to learn their intentions, how he had shot down natives for the sake of their beads, and once when his Chinese cook had asked permission to go ashore to hunt for eggs, he had merely replied, "Go if you like," but that as soon as the poor fellow had been landed, he had given orders to steam away, and leave him behind. They tell how when the cook saw the intention of being abandoned, that he rushed down the shore, and held up his hands, imploring to be taken with them, and that the Professor replied, "Oh, you do want that, do you? hand me my gun, boy," and when the trembling islander handed it, he coolly aimed at his cook and shot him dead, going ashore and bringing the murdered body back again: they say the Custom-house officers at Cooktown wondered where he had got that Chinaman which he carried in a stone jar of spirits amongst his other specimens, and what he was going to do with it when he got home, but he explained the matter to their satisfaction, and as on that return voyage he had a fresh crew, his explanation had to be taken.

It is astonishing how stories are carried about and exaggerated in New Guinea; for instance, an action done at Port Moresby will be related to the actor when he lands at East Cape, the news having gone much quicker than his steamer or schooner can sail, even before a fair wind.

So the reputed actions of Professor Killmann and his trader friend, were whispered in every native village throughout the land, and terror had invested them with the superhuman qualities of devils; most improbable tales were told of their demoniac powers, how the thunder and lightning obeyed them; this was the native version of the dynamite—traps laid for them by the Professor; when he slept on shore, they said, he laid traps in a circle of about half a mile in extent, so that he could not be surprised, dropped lumps of the explosive material amongst groups of natives as they sat on the shore watching his vessel pass by, and laughed when he saw the pieces of humanity shoot up amongst the trees.

But he wrote very nice accounts, for all that, of the natives, and how little trouble they were to him; he related how he wept over the death of a bird of paradise which he had heedlessly shot one morning: they say he was writing this pathetic passage in his diary when he suddenly observed a fine-looking boy pass along the bank with a magnificent headdress on; "Quick, my gun," he cried, starting up and laying down his pen in the hurry thoughtlessly across that pathetic passage.

The next instant the native youth was lying shot through the head, his Malay boy rowing ashore to get the magnificent specimen to add to his other curios. They say the Professor swore very much in his own language when he saw that his pen had made a blot on this beautiful and pathetic passage, for he was very neat and cleanly in his habits when he could be so, and liked to keep his MS. free of dirt.

"The parting was touching, and the regret mutual when I bade adieu to this simple-minded people," so they say the Professor wrote in his notes, and there was regret, the natives say, for they had sworn to roast him alive, and did not like to see him sail away as he had sailed, all alive.

"Will you go with me up the river?" asked Killmann, fixing his glowing eyes on the Greek's dark face, while his own tightly-drawn sallow skin flushed the colour of an amber lamp when lighted.

"Where have you left your crew?"

"I was surprised in the night, when ashore, and five of my boys who held the ship killed before I knew anything about it."

"I suppose they knew too much to come to where you were sleeping?"

"They lay in ambush all night, till I had taken up the traps, and fell upon me as I was getting into my dingey, but, aha! they found that they had made a leetle mistake."

"You blew the batch up?"

"The first batch—yes, they went up like sky-rockets; I waited until they were in a compact mass, and about thirty yards distant, and then threw my charge amongst them; those who were not broken into pieces ran back again to the woods, which enabled us

87

to get into the stream; but, alas! they had some pretty ornaments upon them which I was forced to abandon."

"They had possession of the ship, of course."

"That is so, exactly; we were hailed from the decks by a shower of arrows, one entered my thigh, and the other stuck in my left shoulder, while two of the boys were struck to the heart, still there was more danger in retreating than in advancing, so we held on, and, springing up the side, got amongst them, and then our revolvers did the rest."

"What! you recaptured the ship?"

"On that occasion—ah, yes; but with a sacrifice: my engineer and both firemen were slain, also all but one boy, who, being very badly wounded, I thought it wiser to despatch without more ado, so that I was alone amidst the enemy."

"What did you do next?"

"Exactly what you would have done, my friend. I waited till night, setting up some of the dead men with caps and shirts upon them, and guns in their hands, so that those watching from the bank might think I had my crew.

"I went backwards and forwards, locking up my boxes of specimens as best I could until it grew dusk. I knew they would not come before midnight, so I made all ready. Over the hatchway I placed some small machines which would not do much damage to the vessel, but a good deal to the boarders; then I planted a chain of charges where I thought them likely to step, after which, lashing the helm fairly on, so that the ship would be more likely to keep to the centre of the stream, where the current ran strongest, I cut through the cables, and, letting her drift as best she might, I very gently slipped into the stream, and swam over to the shore where last I saw them."

"Why there?"

"Because they would not expect to see me at that point. I went softly to the thicket, and lay down to watch and listen.

"After a little time I could see the ship moving slowly down the current. I knew they were on the alert, and would before long perceive the change of position; and I was right, for soon they came from a part not far from where I lay, and began to consult. I heard them say we were escaping, so that it would be best to attack at once, and as this was what I expected, and waited for, I was not disappointed. They did not make any noise or blow the conch-shells, so from that I felt sure there were not more than the one tribe implicated, and they did not desire to share their plunder with any neighbours, so I watched them all depart, one canoe after the other, until I could count eight canoes, each loaded with about twenty men. I felt sure that all had departed with the exception of the women, children, and any old men, and that by stealing up to the village I might take my revenge; but, alas! to do so would betray my presence on shore too soon, which I did not wish to do, so I put aside the strong temptation, and proceeded, instead, to follow the course of the river, keeping the canoes and ship in sight.

"I could see them hang off for a while, not understanding the dead silence on board, for they had some experience of me before that morning, and feared a trap being laid for them; however, at last they determined to make a dash for it, for they all raised a loud yell together, and next moment were swarming up the sides.

"It came to pass just as I had planned—the first advancing line trod upon the traps I had laid, for I heard the sharp detonations and the flashing from different points of the vessel, as those coming behind the first line fell backward in their fright into the canoes and water with dull thuds or loud splashes, while the echoes of the woods rang again with the shrill shrieks of those left writhing on board; and so, partly satisfied, I took my departure.

"I kept as much as possible along the banks of the river, walking cautiously till I had got a few miles from the village, then I lay down to await the coming of light, so that I could dry my weapons; my cartridges and dynamite charges were safe enough, as they were all inside indiarubber bags.

"Well, my friend, there is no use going over the details of my lonely march. You know what the land is like—in parts marshy, where the alligators bask themselves—in parts dense and scarcely penetrable, filled with prickly creepers, and ants which drop by myriads as you crawl under the branches, and sting you in a thousand places. My clothes were soon reduced to what you see them; my food the leaves and herbs, as I could find them, with the sun blazing down upon me during the day, and a hundred dangers to be encountered by night, the damps which chill one to the bone and bring on the fever. A fortnight ago I weighed fourteen stone, now I hardly carry eight; but that is nothing, if I can have my revenge, and rescue my specimens."

"Did you pass many villages?"

"A great number; but mostly all deserted and going to ruin; they have been fighting with one another much lately, so that the ground is pretty clear. Sometimes I heard the conches sounding, and at these times I made a détour, keeping well out of sight. Once I saw a furious battle, in which about two hundred lost their lives; the victors walked past my place of concealment, in a line, carrying home the bloody heads on long poles, with portions of the bodies in baskets to cook. At one time I nearly walked into the midst of a great feast before I was aware; the sun was going down and dazzled my eyes so that I could not see, while the wind blowing from me prevented me from smelling the smoke, so that I ran right into the back of the outpost before I knew where I was; but before he could turn round my hand was on his throat and my knife in his heart; I dare not use my gun, as I did not know who might hear me at any time, so I drew the body into the thicket and covered it with leaves, and went on.

"I only once caught a pig, and that I also killed with my knife, and devoured what I wanted raw. However, I have done the journey, and feel well enough to return with you."

"But what of the native teachers, are they not up that length?"

"Yes, they were; but I fear they will be slaughtered and devoured by this time in my stead; yet, if they are not, it does not matter,—they are my friends, and will not speak ill of my actions; besides, they admit the necessity of making an example. You will come with me?"

"Yes, I think I will," murmured Niggeree thoughtfully. "I left a woman up there who will help us; but what will you give me for the job?"

"Fifty pounds when we return, as much loot as you can take from the natives we kill, what females you wish to spare for yourself, the friendship of the missionaries, and a general permit, as soon as we reach Moresby; nay, I will use my influence to get you a good post with the government."

"The money and permit will do; I shall also want forgiveness for some little scrapes in the past. You know the war-sloop is looking out for me at present, and mad with me for that last trick I played upon them."

"Ha! ha! that was a very clever dodge of yours, Niggeree. Tell me about it."

Chapter XIX
Niggeree's Version of His Escapade

THE Professor filled his pipe and leaned back to enjoy the story, while he meditated on his plans; he did not care much for the tale, but he wished to please the Greek and enlist him in his cause, and he knew well that Niggeree liked to hear himself speak of his own exploits.

"You have heard how I got out of that trouble about the copra, Professor?"

"No, my boy, tell it to me."

"Well, it happened in Milne Bay; I had made a station for myself there, and married one of the chief's daughters. I always like to marry where I make a station, for it gives the tribes an interest in me."

"Very true," murmured the Professor, absently.

"We had a big corroberee over that wedding, for I had paid a good price for the gal—two bags of rice, four pounds of tobacco, and a full—grown female pig. She warn't worth it, of course, for these native gals are like logs, they never wake up to a white fellow, no matter how kind he may be to them, and deceive you right afore your blessed eyes; but they know better than put on airs when I am on the job. I only marry them to make the time pass, and get as much work as I can out of my relations."

"Quite right."

"Wall, next morning, arter the marriage, I gets up to have a wash, when who should I run against but the old man, her father, who stood solemnly in my road, and would not move when I run against him.

"I looks at him a moment, and then taking him by the arm turns him about and gives him a hearty kick, saying, 'You go, old bloke, and get some fish for my breakfast,' at which he looked astonished for a bit, and then walked away.

"One of the natives, who saw me kick him, comes up to me and tells me that I was breaking a sacred law, that my father-in-law was waiting for me to salute him, and that next time I met him I must bend my head low and respectful when I passed him.

"'Oh, must I,' says I, 'we'll see about that when the time comes.'

"The old boy brought me the fish, and we had breakfast all together, boiled taro and fried fish, winding up with a puff at the bau-bau, and a chew of the betel.

"That day we all went hunting the Wallabis, you know how it is done, so no use explaining that process, but before night we had bagged about thirty fine fat fellows, and had another great feast.

"I missed my gal once during the feed, and sent a young fellow, whom she had palmed off on me as her brother, to hunt her up; they were both gone considerably longer than I liked to be kept waiting, and when they did come back, all the natives burst out a laughing, but wouldn't tell me what was the joke.

"Next morning I met the old man as before, right in my road, waiting to be saluted; you bet I did salute him, although not exactly us he cared about, after which I again sent him off to fish; then, by way of a warning, I goes over to his hut where the old woman lay, and treated her to a little of my fun.

"As I left the hut I sees one or two natives running up to see what the matter had been; I suppose they had heard her screeching. My gal also was coming out of our hut and behind her the young man I had thought to be her brother; as she came along I saw a couple of sticks of baccy drop out of her Raumua, which the young fellow picked up with his toe and hid.

"'So that's the game, is it,' thought I. 'It isn't a brother you're prigging my baccy for,' and I walks straight up to him and caught him by the arm, shouting out, 'He is not her brother.'

"Then one of the old women comes up trembling and tells me that he was her husband, and that she had committed bigamy when she came to my hut.

"When I heard this I made up my mind to wind up this kind of deceit, so I just took a couple of steps from him, and pulling out my barker, I says, 'I give you a chance for your life while I count five—run while you can.'

"But the darned young fool wouldn't run; he drew himself straight up, and folding his arms, looked on me smiling, he had no weapons or he might ha' done something else.

"'Run,' cried out his wife and the others, but he only smiled, and looked at me without winking a lash.

"'One, two, three, four—'

"I hung on to the last word a bit, for I like pluck, and if he had only turned, I'd have let him go; but there he stood like a target afore me, and my gal, his wife, wringing her hands; I knew that I'd have to fire or they'd think me afraid.

"One more chance.

"'F—I—V—E.'

"I drawled out the letters slowly, and at the last one let go.

"How she did it I cannot say, but when the smoke cleared they were both there as dead as door-nails; the ball had gone through her back and his breast, splitting both hearts with one shot, and they now lay, her arms round his neck with her face down, and him a smiling still at the sun. My pig and rice and baccy had been a swindle.

"The natives didn't say a word, but slunk back to their huts, and left me alone with my smoking revolver and the two dead fools, in the middle of the village.

"I knew after this there would be a rumpus, so I goes down to the shore, and hailing my boys, told them to be ready for sailing when the tide turned. Then I went back to the hut and begun to pack up my traps.

"By-and-by the old man came, and I could see them creep out and tell him what I'd done; his old woman also was jabbering away like an old ape and pointing to where I was, while he lifted up both hands and tore some of his white hair out, after which they all went into the big house to consult.

"Meantime some of my boys came up and carried down my baggage and put them aboard, while I goes over to the door of the big house, and shouts to the old man to come out.

"'You old blackguard, you cheated me,' I said, when the old fellow appeared, holding down his head and looking at the ground. 'I thought the gal was single or I wouldn't have married her, and now it's all your fault if she's dead, so give me back the price I paid for her.'

"He didn't answer very plain, but mumbled something inside the room, at which four young fellows started towards his hut, and came out carrying the two bags of rice and the pig, with the tobacco.

"'That's all correct, says I. 'Put them in the dingey. Now, old man, I am going off now; and as a punishment for your deceit, see that you get me a cargo of copra ready by the time I come back."

"'When will you come?' asked the chief in a low voice.

"'Next moon! and if it's not ready—a full cargo, mind you, I'll burn down your village and take six of your best-looking wenches.'

"'We'll be ready for you, Niggeree,' replied he, and went back to the hut.

"I sailed away at the turn of the tide, for I had some business to get through at Brooker Island, and I thought it best to get out of the road for a bit."

Chapter XX
Niggeree's Version of His Escapade (Continued)

"AT the end of a month I came back to the village, and found a full cargo of copra all ready, and that's how the mistake took place which cost me £85 at Cooktown.

"You see, Professor, Captain Smith had been before me, and had made a bargain with the natives to supply him with all the copra which they could get ready for the next twelvemonth. This arrangement the deceitful savages had never told me about; not, of course, that I took the trouble to ask them, nor would I have paid much heed to what they said, but it just happened to be one of them chances the Government had been waiting on to convict me and get me turned off the land.

"Well, the natives made a bit of a barney about letting me have it. However, after I had set a light to their big house, which

93

the teacher owned was a good deed, as it was there all the mischief was hatched, and run amuck amongst their women—married and single—they gave in, and helped me with the cargo aboard, after which I up sails and away before the sun went down towards Moresby.

"I got rid of the copra to the store there, and was just having a bit of a spree, when in sails Smith with a mighty complaint to the Governor, who straightaway seizes my vessel and takes me in his own schooner over to Cooktown, to be tried for false possession; Smith being the only witness.

"When we got to Cooktown a friend of mine bailed me out, and, knowing Smith's inclinations, I hunted high and low till I came across him, half drunk, in a shanty.

"'Have a drink, Smith?' says I. 'Right you are, mate,' says Smith. So we sat down and had one or two nobblers, till I could see that he was as drunk as an owl. Then I began.

"'Smith, my boy, I'm sorry over that mistake about the copra, and I don't see the use o' going to law when we can settle it between ourselves.'

"'Well, mate,' hiccuped Smith, 'what do you consider settling this hash?'

"'What do you consider a fair price?'

"'Well, I consider sixty pounds none too much.'

"'There's your money, old boy,' says I, counting out the flimsies, which, as he sees to be all right, he takes with a 'Thank ye, Nig.'

"'Now, old man, just you sign this receipt and it's all square, and we'll have another shout.'

"I had a receipt dated back two months, so he signs it, and I felt pleased, and drunk him safely to bed.

"Well, I had a good man to look after me in court, for which I paid £20, and he saw me through it firstclass. The Governor calls on his witness, certain of having me in for a year or two, when no Smith turns up, much to his astonishment.

"'What is all this?' asked the magistrate.

"'Merely that a British subject has been wrongly accused, as this here dockiment will prove,' and he handed my receipt.

"Meantime Smith had been found, and took his stand.

"'Did the prisoner purchase your copra from you, Captain Smith?'

"'Yes,' said Smith, shamefaced, and not liking to look up.

"Then my man made a splendid speech about the rank injustice of the Queensland Government, and making me feel that noble that I wondered if it was me he was describing, or some imaginary person who was called by the same name. The

Opposition papers also took up the case, and made out long leaders about honest traders who were obstructed and badgered by the present Government in their lawful calling. I was taken over to Cooktown in irons, and left it like a successful explorer.

"But for all that, when I went to renew my permit I was denied it, and told that if I remained twenty-four hours on shore after getting my ship ready, that it would be again seized by the Government, and me treated as a pirate.

"'All right, so be it,' said I, snapping my fingers, 'and that for your permit;' and I walked out, found Smith, who didn't show his face to the Governor, and got a passage to Moresby with him."

"How did you raise the eighty pounds, Niggeree?"

"Well, you see, I borrowed it from my Cooktown friend, and won it all back at cards from Smith, and ten more to the good, before we left Cooktown. Smith owned that copra cargo brought him bad luck, for he lost through it the friendship of the Government and £30 as well, and vowed he'd never more try to come between me and my rights.

"When I got to Moresby I assembled my boys, and sailed away to Moto-moto, where I did a little trade; then the wind changed, and I gets eastward to Dinner Island, and so on to Brooker, where I knew I'd be safe, as the natives there have a very bad name.

"Well, after I left Dinner Island I got to another island where I had left some natives, and they tells me that the bom-bom man was after me to hang me. That was the time I made up my mind to play my little trick. I goes over to the mainland in a canoe, after leaving my boys and vessel safely at the outer edge of the island, then I travelled overland till I comes to where they were lying, and, taking a canoe, I boarded.

"'Who are you?' axed the captain.

"'A hunter,' says I, giving one of the hunters' names whom I knew.

"'Do you know this part of the coast?'

"'As well as I do Burke Street.'

"'Have you seen a blackguard called Niggeree?'

"'Yes, captain; I know where to find him.'

"'Will you pilot us to him?'

"'How much will you give me?'

"'Ten pounds."

"'On the job?'

"'After we have found him.'

"'No, it must be now, or I won't go.'

"The captain was one of those mighty, fine-dressed, haughty, soft—headed gentry which the naval service are so chokea-block with. I knew he had too little sense and too much dignity to condescend making a bargain with me, so I took this way of getting up his dander, and the cash out of him beforehand, and I was right; he just frowned majestically upon me and stalked aft to his cabin, sending the steward to pay me the money, as if it had been dirt.

"I guided them all right through the reefs, until we came to the inner side of the island, where my ship lay, and where I knew he'd take some trouble to get out of, and then he says,—

"'Is this the place, pilot?'

"'He was here, sir, last time I saw him; I'll go ashore and inquire.' And the softy let me go.

"I made my road straight over the island, got up my anchor, and, before we sailed, sent a line with a native to take to the haughty naval captain. That's how it happened."

"He vows he will shoot or hang you for the trick," replied the professor.

"He must catch me first," said Niggeree, laughing at his own cleverness.

"Do you know he was very nearly stranded that time after you left?"

"So they told me."

"However, I shall speak well for you when we return from our expedition. When can you start?"

"Well, I am waiting on my consort. If she was in—"

"We shall leave word here that we have gone up the river, and they may follow and help."

"That will do—yes, I'll go when you like."

"To-morrow morning?"

"Yes, to-morrow morning we'll start at daybreak."

Chapter XXI
Hafid Finds His Bride

WITHOUT doubt, General Flag-Croucher was the biggest personage who had yet set military heels upon the coast of New Guinea.

He was not an explorer, although he had once upon a time tried to organize an expedition in England, the purpose of which was to take possession of the land something after the style of William at Hastings, the noble General to be William the

Conqueror, of course. The project had fallen through, as a great many of the General's projects fell to pieces, from lack of the one thing needful—cash.

The General felt that he was born to be a leader of men; he was himself a man of parts and inches. Having served all nations and escaped from many dangers—decorated at different courts, police and otherwise, he looked upon the world as his oyster, a very much alive oyster, which his private necessities made him resolve at all hazards to open as energetically as possible. He did not know anything about either geology, botany, or those little points of learning which an explorer requires to enable him to traverse a new country, but as he emphatically remarked, "Damn it, sir!—a soldier, and a man who has served under one hundred and eighty-five flags, surely don't want knowledge to guide a body of men through the country of an enemy; it's courage, sir!— courage does it, and I flatter myself I have that."

He did flatter himself, very much at most times, when he had the chance, this gallant general.

This was the first spectacle which greeted the eyes of Bowman and Danby after they had anchored at Port Moresby, and been rowed ashore;—a tall, gaunt, high-cheekboned, moustached figure, with small blue-grey eyes, gleaming wildly under a much battered pulp helmet; he stood in position number one, with feet advanced and leaning on his staff, as a leader of armies might appear when reviewing his troops. He was not very well dressed, but then no one dressed much at Moresby except the Governor and his limited staff; the General's costume consisted of a pair of muchpatched breeches, a stained red sash, into which he had stuck an old rusted revolver, a flannel-shirt originally white, now grey from use and lack of soap—the native washer had declined to trust the hero any longer, and he had too much dignity to do his own washing. An old yellow silk jacket completed the outer man. This costume the General had adopted on leaving Brisbane some few months before, and not at present employing a servant, he wisely did not encumber himself with more luggage than he could carry easily, for in hot countries an extra shirt even becomes cumbersome, and the General did not like to be encumbered, so he did not carry an extra shirt.

The Thunder had some of the varied experience of the other vessels in crossing the stormy Gulf of Papua; but having the advantage of steam, had been able to steer a pretty straight course, luck serving the gallant old sea-dog of a skipper in better stead than knowledge.

Poor Hafid found his peace at Murray Island; he had made no further effort to retain life after that disappointment at Darnley,

97

but passed into the sleep of death as a lamp going out without oil, painlessly and quietly, with the steady decrease of light until the final flicker came before the flame expired.

We have all watched the lamp grow dry and the flame diminish as the wick became charred; now we turn it up, gaining but a moment longer, while we read a few lines more,—so they tried to reanimate the soul that was passing out of that hope-dried heart, and thought when they saw the mirage of a smile that he was getting over it.

The flame does not always leap up when it leaves that crusted wick—edge; but in light, as in life, there must always be a last moment when the ambient spirit lets go its grasp of the material.

Hafid went out like the lamp, and had but an instant's re-lighting as the soul went out—that instant of illumination when the senses are supplanted by the outer influences, and revelation takes the place of instinct. To those about him it seemed only to be the stretching-out of arms towards the setting sun and distant palm-fringed strand, the dawn of a pallid flush behind the olive cheeks, and the opening of the mouth as the sigh went forth, while from the deep-set eyes a gleam shone out like a shaft of golden sunshine mingled with amber; then the head fell back on the seaman's jacket they had laid for a pillow, and the opalescent space above became dimly reflected in the glazing eyes.

That instant had given to Hafid all his desires, the woman he loved and the mud-flats of the Ganges;—true, she herself may have forgotten his existence, and, while he held her girl-shape in his outspread arms, may have been toiling from the paddy fields of his successor and her master, dragging her weary load homewards, with the last of the other man's brood clinging to the prematurely withered breasts of this mindless slave.

What mattered the reality, if the vision was radiant which those heaven-lighted eyes beheld? What mattered the pitiless march of time, if the spirit was young and ardent which that flying spirit caught in its passage and bore onwards in its close embrace?

Perhaps, as the woman paused in her homeward walk to change the infant to the other pendulous breast, the hot yellow sun-shaft smote her in the wearied eyes and pierced her dazed brain with a stroke of memory that cast the shards of labour and affliction from her, renewing in that quicker pulse of her sluggish blood the throbs of a day gone by, when her heart beat fast and her shape was round and smooth as satin; perhaps on that shaft of sunlight her soul sped forth to join the other soul not far away.

Who can tell how a life may be filled out in a second, or

eternity accomplished in a glance, as she trudges onward with her load? the dead body of Hafid is not more lifeless than that living burden by the Ganges. Happy each that they can only see love in his eternal youth.

They buried Hafid before they left Murray Island;—he lies in the little mission graveyard under the shadow of the sago palms, where the sea—breezes rustle softly through the long grasses and pensile branches, and leaves droop down; where the sounds of the silky rustlings are blent with the bubbling of the wavelets as they roll gently amongst the lovely shells.

Here, at this island, they were entertained by the missionaries, this being one of the headquarters of the Society. Here they found the natives orderly and docile, their savage traits seemingly subdued, and cleanliness with comfort pervading every hut and bungalow. It was a pleasant sight to see the genial influence of religion here. It was a good memory to carry away, the devotion and brotherhood of the self-exiled men and women who labour here so far from the friends they may never see again.

A bundle of newspapers, more than four months old, was seized with avidity by the young teacher who had at present taken up his quarters at the house upon the hill. He had been forced to leave New Guinea, having caught the fever there; he was just getting over it, but very weak and listless.

Here they saw amongst the black skins, the pallid features of a delicate woman, one of those gentle heroines, who move quietly in their onward path, braving danger which would appall many bold men; enduring troubles which might well break down the strongest mind. She was wasted almost to a shadow by repeated attacks of the malaria; she seemed like one of those bloodless, but refined creations of Orchardson, with eyes and lips alike blanched with the debilitation of that soft but insidious breeze, yet she moved with languid grace to do her duty to the young teacher whose life she had saved, to the husband whose troubles she shared, and she felt the thousand anxieties which only a refined woman can endure amongst savages, even though they are so far reclaimed. Here she lived with none of her own sex of her own colour, with her children about her, bearing her fate as a daily cross.

The white and dark children played and splashed about the clear waters, coral-protected from the sharks who swarmed outside. Both white and dark children swam with equal ease; they were equally shy at the sight of strangers as they were at home in the sea, and the curious part of it all was that the white children spoke the native language fluently and their mother-tongue with considerable difficulty.

99

From Murray Island, with its memories, the Thunder ploughed across the briny furrows, and tossed and tumbled in a most fearful manner upon the storm-beaten ocean; there was nothing which could stand upright, or keep its place when the Thunder was on the roll. From captain to steward they fell about in utter disregard of all the laws of gravity, while the only object that appeared to retain its equilibrium was the solitary rat which they had fattened since leaving port.

This rat nibbled calmly and gleaned a rich harvest, while the plates and cups rattled about him. He had lived upon the best, and grown out of all proportion for the size of the hole which formed his first retreat; now he was compelled to hide in out-of-the-way corners, and dodge the knives and forks which Danby shied at him as they sat opposite one another—the rat clinging to the floor, while Danby clutched at the table. Sometimes the rat, in its endeavours to evade the missile, lost its hold and slid for a yard or two, but not far before recovering its balance. The rat seemed to be the best-fed sailor on board.

The captain called his vessel the "Hummer," as a term of endearment. He always used this pet name when she spun extra furiously round, or as he recovered himself after one of her most forcible thuds; at such moments he would pass his hands over his matted locks to feel if the skull was not fractured, then clearing the mist from his eyes, as he sat upon the floor and held on to the table-leg, "Aint she a little hummer?"

The Thunder did not always go as her captain wished her to go, she did not often obey her propeller, either; but she always went, if not in an orthodox way, in a manner peculiarly all her own.

Through the Papuan Gulf she rocked, upsetting all ideas of propriety as regards the progress of screwguided craft; indeed, upsetting all which could be upset in the material, as well as ideal laws of order. She appeared to have such a contempt for waves, that she could in no other manner express it so well as sitting upon them, and as she was by build a heavy sitter, when she sat down the wave was generally squashed; also, as a rule, when she chose to sit, every object within or upon her had to leap.

One, two, THREE! that is how the little hummer asserted her position and the inferiority of the advancing wave—one, a slight premonitory touch; two, a decided thud, and three, the total collapse of convulsed nature.

Number three was a clash like the colliding of two trains, or the chance meeting of rival stars; but the Thunder seemed to be the least conscious of the accident, for next moment she rose as easily to repeat the motion of contempt, as a ball-room belle might rise to her twentieth invitation. In one sense she strongly resembled the lady in question, inasmuch as when not sitting she was the rest of her time waltzing.

Many were the ghastly legends told of her aquatic feats, the fearful havoc she had made in former trips amongst the property and persons of those who had entrusted their fates to her tender mercies; dark hints of her diabolic powers were not wanting, how she had encountered and overcome difficulties in the form of sandbanks and rocks, which would have wrecked the strongest-built ironclads. Gaps were pointed out even in the great barrier reef as the traces of spots she had butted against and broken through; these might be sailors yarns, of course, and slightly exaggerated truth, yet a general belief prevailed on board from the humble Sudy boy to the Irish mate, that while her present Ajax-looking skipper controlled—or rather yielded to her whims, and stuck faithful to her caprices, wreckage was an impossibility; the reef might be wrecked, but the Thunder never, and all things considered it consoled those aboard for the hourly fractures received.

Through the storm and the gulf they lived, and after three long days and nights of bodily and mental anguish, sighted the lofty mountains of New Guinea.

It was early morning when from the mellow haze the vast proportions upheaved, and the captain exclaimed joyously, yet in a tone of astonishment,—

"New Guinea, by——"

"You didn't expect it to be Africa, did you?" inquired the calm young Danby.

"Where is it?" asked Bowman, getting up from his deck-pillow, yellow-faced and bilious-looking, and rubbing his heavy eyes with his dirty hands—no man could wash or eat, while the Thunder swept the main.

"Over there, about ten miles off."

"Which part do you think it is?" again inquired Bowman.

"Well, it ought to be Moresby by the course and charts; but somehow I don't think it is," answered the captain doubtfully, and scratching his head.

The old Malay at the wheel looked ahead steadily for a moment, and, as he had been to the coast before, they all looked towards him for instruction.

"Mount Yule over there, sir!"

"Good," cried the skipper, merrily, "she's done well. We are only sixty miles out of our course, and she's a little hummer."

Chapter XXII
Yule Island

THEY made Yule Island about ten o'clock. Here they were met by the two French missionaries, Fathers Ambrose and Durand, who, having been denied permission to land on any portion of the mainland, took up their station upon the island, which is divided by only a narrow strip of water from the mainland.

Indeed, it is a wonderful system this law of permits in New Guinea, where three or four people grant, or deny permission to people wishing to land, as they—the three or four representatives of this protective Government—think proper to decide, without chance of appeal or redress. Of course, it is only a moral obligation which makes the simple—minded traders or visitors bend under this very illegal system of justice, and the Governor does not often strain his despotic authority; still that the system prevails is vile as a precedent, and that those Catholic preachers were compelled to resort to stratagems, before they could preach the charity of Christianity, is almost too great a sacrifice in this liberal nineteenth century.

When I say moral obligation I mean that these permits are only farces, which the good temper of the genial traders humours; for what is there to prevent three or four men from landing at any time on the shores of New Guinea, in spite of all the permits issued or refused by any Government? The land is theirs in exactly the same sense as it belongs to the Government or to the missionary, i.e. it belongs to neither.

Father Ambrose, like nearly all Papist missionaries, did not value his life much when he took up his work in this Protestant-abandoned island; he lay down to sleep each night, at first, expecting only to wake in the company of saints and martyrs. He saw that with the old savages the rites of Christianity were idle ceremonies, and that to try to teach them religion was a hopeless task, so he made up his mind to be content with getting a baby baptized now and again, meantime seeking by force of example, till he had learnt their language, to give them some faint notion of the laws of health.

By dint of indomitable perseverance he mastered, in a very short time, their dialect, and then he went amongst them healing their sick and modifying, as far as he best could do, their savage, bloodthirsty customs;—in eight months his mild example, patient forbearance, and ready help had worked almost a reformation on Yule Island and the adjacent mainland occupied by his rivals in the good work.

He did not gain his present influence without danger, hardship, or sacrifice; once, when they made up their minds to slaughter him and his two companions, he mastered them by courage only.

One of the chiefs had received from him payment for some work to be performed; the chief, like most people paid beforehand, thought how he might evade his promise, and appeared before him with a plausible story, thinking it an easy matter to take in the gentle Frenchman.

He told his lie badly and was discovered, upon which Father Ambrose sternly ordered him never to come before him again unless it was to pay his debt.

The chief threatened him with death, at which the missionary only smiled, and passed indoors, leaving the native to go off with vengeance in his heart.

That night Father Ambrose was awakened by yells outside, and getting up he muttered a quiet prayer in the dark.

"Come out, you white pig, and let us see you. We want your head to roast!"

These were the words which he heard as he rose from his knees, and without a pause he opened the door and went out into the moonlight.

Over two hundred naked and armed savages stood in the clear space in front of his palisade, with the chief, his enemy, in front.

A little awe still held them back, for the fire of the white man was known to them, and they did not yet fully gauge the extent of his power. A dark, threatening, howling crowd, with waving arms and clashing spears, while the full moon-rays shone upon their supple, smooth skins and wicker-work shields, casting black shadows on to the ground, dancing shadows, like tangible and contorted figures with grey phantoms above them.

"I am here; what is it you want?"

"Your head, white pig!" shouted the tall chief, advancing swiftly with quivering lance poised above his head.

"Well, come and take it."

The savage paused in a stupor of amazement. Father Ambrose stood quietly but upright, clad only in trousers and shirt, his thin face gleaming pale in the white light, with his shirt taking on silver edges where surfaces of the folds were exposed; his brown beard looked soft and surrounded with a strange lustre, as the rays caught it with a softened shine—a mild, patient head they wanted, like the misty outlines of St. John.

They saw he was unarmed, and, as they looked at his folded hands and meek head, a strange terror ran like a thrill through all. Never had enemy seemed so formidable to them, this passive resistance filled them with feeling as of a supernatural power; surely he must be immortal to wait so quietly, and no spear could pierce him!

"What! Do you think we cannot kill you?" cried out the chief, plucking up some faint show of courage.

"Kill me, if you like."

The words were simply and softly spoken, as by one about to receive his reward; but the effect was instantaneous. With a universal howl of dismay and horror the camp broke up, and the warriors fled back to their village, no man resting till he had covered his head with his wife's rauma.

When the missionary opened his eyes he was alone, with the holy moonlight shining over the weapons, flung down in the hurry of that complete rout, lying in confused masses in front of him. Truly a miracle had been performed, as when the Assyrians fled in the night.

"My hour has not yet come," he sighed, half regretfully, as he knelt down once more to his midnight prayers, while his two brothers, who had stood trembling inside, went quietly out and gathered up the spears and other trophies left behind.

From that day no native sought to hurt him; the life of the man who wished to be killed was sacred, and the respect born of fear grew up into a child of love, when they came to know and benefit by his goodness.

Next day the old chief came with the payment of his debt, to implore the pardon of his friend—came on his knees, with his kneeling warriors behind, asking him to forgive them and stay amongst them. To each man he gave back his weapon, consecrated, and with words of pardon and loving-kindness. Thus peace was won with very little trouble; so Father Ambrose pleasantly informed Mr. Bowman.

The sight of the natives, who came in their canoes, was not reassuring to those on board the steamer—stalwart young men, perfectly nude, who made their catamarans rush through the sunny waves, and the foam hiss from their paddles, while they grunted as they bent their brown backs to the task, and the sinews and muscles moved and swelled—young men who seemed to be without an instinct of fear or caution, as they caught hold of the rope-end hanging over the bulwarks and slung themselves with a single bound on to the deck, where they stood upright and dauntlessly facing the strangers, while the sun-beams glinted on their smooth limbs and shining breasts like burnished copper—young men who came armed with spears, bows and arrows, with mop-heads stuck over with gay feathers and long-handled combs, with cheeks painted with stripes white and black, with sinews of trained athletes, who neither understood fear or displayed astonishment.

They were the friends of the priest, and, trusting him, trusted all whom he appeared friendly with. He told Bowman and Danby, as he sat down to lunch, that they were now perfectly safe, and offered to show them the beauties of the island; so, as soon as they had finished eating, they accepted his kindly offer, and got into his boat, while the natives once more went ahead and around them in their canoes, leading the way.

They found a natural stone landing-place as they drew near the shore, a long causeway of slaty-looking rocks, worn flat, and like steps, leading up from the water's edge into a somewhat dense thicket. On each side of this stone landing-place the mango-bushes grew, and dipped into the deep waters.

Past the landing-place they came to a footpath going through fields of long cane-grass, which closed high above their heads as they passed through it, folding them in so that they had to keep very near to the heels of their guides, and look well to their feet, or they would have been lost entirely, for as they dipped into the hollows this grass grew to the height of ten, twelve, and in parts fifteen feet, of a dry-hay colour, yet strong and fibrous, touching with strong clutches like withes of reeds, and gathering behind them like giant corn-stalks. When they rose to the high places, where the ground was more stony and drained, they could overlook this virgin grass and see the hills: in parts stony, in parts grass—covered, like the ground they traversed, and in detached portions patched with dense jungle, which began and ended abruptly; here the wild boar lay with her litter, and the game-birds hid themselves.

They were passing by the side of a valley cultivated by the natives. Here, as they looked along, they saw gardens of yams, taro, rice, with plantations of banana, sago, betel, and sugar-cane brakes; over against them, on the further ridge of the valley, they could see above the fields and trees the palm-thatched houses of a native village. This was the only village on the island as yet which held out against the benign influence of Father Ambrose. They were coming in, he observed, as he pointed them out; that is, they didn't throw spears now, as they used to do, when strangers passed, or lie in wait with their man-traps, which was a great concession, certainly.

Behind them the sea gleamed like a deep sapphire—that intense blue which seems to engross within its centre all the colours from the paler immensity above, taking in light, and giving out again only the suggestion of fathomless depth and movement.

The little, commonplace, red, white and black painted and varnished Thunder lay upon this lovely indescribable tone of blue, like a child's cheap toy laid upon a widespread sheet of rare spun silk.

Before them, as they walked, they could see the house which the missionary and his brothers had raised, standing upon a little mound in the valley, with the flag fluttering feebly in the soft breeze from its staff—a white flag, with the device of the bleeding heart wrought upon it in red silk by the little sisters of Thursday Island.

"Our mission-house, gentlemen," observed Father Ambrose, with a touch of honest pride in his gentle voice; "beyond there lies the sea on all sides, with the coast of New Guinea to the east. No, you cannot see Mount Yule from here; but from the top of that hill you will see it, also the two villages, who now listen to my words. My little chapel lies down by the seashore, between the villages. It does not do to raise jealousy, gentlemen, so, although it is some distance for me to walk, still it is near to them both. I will take you to see it after you have rested in our little station."

Chapter XXIII
A Hunting Expedition

AFTER a bottle of very harmless, home-brewed beer, qualified afterwards by a glass of the best French brandy which they had yet tasted, they set forth on their tour over the island, accompanied by the two priests, who were armed with very antiquated, barrel-loading fowling-guns—the sort of articles which you load from the top, pouring down small shot and ramming them home with a rod—I dare say about the only relics now to be found outside of an old iron and rag store.

These guns were evidence in themselves of the pacific intentions of the missionaries—warranted to make a great noise and do very little damage.

They met with no success in their search for game that afternoon; once they started a bush turkey, which Danby attempted to stalk, but he found the bird too much for him. The sides of the mountain here were in parts very barren, covered with loose crumbling earth and small stones, and very steep, so that climbing became a very difficult feat. After a while they reached the edge of a thicket, dense and dry-looking, with much dead wood, and hard to get through on account of the confusion of interlacing tendrils, all withered and shrunken. Here they found tracks of the wild boar, with deep, dark intersections, water-worn cuttings, which were completely covered in by closely-woven networks of branches and shrivelled leaves. Here, as they stooped and laboured to get through, the heat was intense and most oppressive in the broken light, while under the feet crunched the dry twigs, and from the blighted-looking leafage and clusters of delicate orchids which battened upon the dry branches, dropped myriads of small yellow ants, covering the exposed portions of the body, and getting under the shirts and up the trousers, while they bit and stung with a maddening sharpness from which there was no getting away; these ants are worst in the dry thickets on the mountain sides and summits.

Father Ambrose smiled apologetically as Bowman and Danby danced about, and used their Saxon with unadulterated and emphatic purity, and when they emerged from this purgatory he energetically set to work brushing off the tiny tormentors from his companions, seemingly unconscious of the legions in possession of his own person.

"Don't they bite you, Father?" asked Bowman, turning to assist the priest, after he had been liberated.

"Yes! a little, just enough to give me a lesson in patience; we require that virtue in our work out here."

Father Ambrose's deep-set, blue eyes had a very far-away look as he said this—a look in which hopeless melancholy was blent with apathetic resignation—yet his lips still wore the set, gentle smile which did duty for contentment.

"Are you getting many converts here?" asked Bowman next.

"I do not try to get converts; I am content if I can civilize them a little more, teach them to bury their dead so that the survivors may not suffer in consequence; and I teach them not to eat their enemies. They are a wise people in many ways, but they have no religion, and will not be taught to believe in spiritual benefits. When I say mass they come and look on; the little prints which I have placed round the walls seem to amuse them, and I believe that unconsciously they get the benefit of my prayers; to attempt more would be to fail. So far I have not laboured in vain, for they come for my advice when in trouble and perplexity, and I do what I can to give them good advice; this is all which I seek to achieve in my life-time."

"Do you intend staying here long?" inquired Danby, irrelevantly.

"I hope to die here, my friend," replied the priest gravely.

"Have you forgotten your own land?"

"Ah, France! No, I can never forget it; but we who are the servants of God have no land on earth, as we have no ties; it is easy for us to be able to make sacrifices, easier than for your ministers who have their wives and children to think about. I wonder sometimes how they can be missionaries with bonds like these holding them back; I think they must be very brave men, much more so than I could be."

"That's a matter of opinion," muttered Bowman grimly, remembering a few other motives which the simple Romanist overlooked.

They were now walking through the fields towards the sea-beach, along which the native villages were built. A slight turn from the pathway brought them to another thicket, differing altogether from the one on the hill; here the parasites were covered with greenery, and the leaves were moist and cool, while the soil felt swampy with the constant drippings.

A dense thicket composed of sugar-cane, partly cultivated, with castor—oil plants shooting up here and there and long lush grasses which bent and fell over with their own weight. They did not penetrate very far, but could see that here lay a rich harvest for the future workers when their time came.

They now passed through the fields towards the native villages, Father Ambrose leading the way with rapid strides, while the others followed as well as they could, guided by the sound of the rustling grass which closed over their heads; frequently he had to shout out to show his direction, for it was all a wild stampede through moving blades. As they went on sometimes the ground rose and the grass became scanter, when they had a passing glimpse of heads in front before they dipped out of sight.

On one of these barren mounds the missionary paused to take breath and allow his companions to get up to him. As they stood he pointed out Mount Yule with its flat table-top, and the island spreading round; the mission-station stood out boldly against the mellow afternoon sky, while beneath them lay the two native villages, Rolto Arriena and Morna Cherne.

"My chapel is just between the two villages, behind that dark clump of trees, and if we make haste we shall be able to see it before the sun goes down."

They all hastened after this, and making a détour by the edge of the cultivated fields, passed through Morna Chorna, with its huts raised amongst the clusters of cocoa-nut palms, and where the natives very gravely welcomed them.

"There has been a death here last night, and they are all mourning, otherwise we might have had some fun."

At the entrance to the village a young native met them with his body ash-smeared, and carrying in his hand a small firebrand which he was blowing hard upon to keep alight, with a most dejected appearance of melancholy. The good priest stopping him asked him a few questions, receiving very hopeless replies, after which he turned round and explained that this was the eldest son of the dead man whom they were mourning for at the village; being the eldest son, his part of the rites consisted of holding lonely night vigils in the forest. At each sundown he left the corpse to pass the hours till daybreak in the woods, and, as all natives dread the darkness, and believe implicitly in ghosts and evil demons, the horror of those lonely hours more than counterbalanced the grief which he might otherwise have felt at his affliction; the firebrand was to light the fire which he said would keep away the ghosts, so that the blowing part was a most important one with him, as all his thoughts were concentrated in the effort to keep it alight, and yet make it last the mile or two of distance between the wood and the village.

Poor boy, I doubt if he felt much for his father, as he left them to go on his lonely watch; what feelings he still retained were evidently expended upon himself.

It is very wonderful how pitiful we all can become when self poises up as the victim, how pathetic we grow over our own miseries, and how we wonder that other people cannot see them in exactly the same light as we do; but fortunately for the unity of the world, and unfortunately for the individual cause, each applicant to pity is so intent upon his own case that he has no time to devote to his neighbour's wrongs, so each atom in the grand whole plan goes on wriggling his own wriggle while maintained in his own circumscribed space by a stern order of economy far beyond human judgment, and the man is of no more account than the sparrow who may drop dead from his perch without, as far as we know, any sentimental self-condolence. This is a truth which man cannot learn in youth, or in age either, if God has answered his cry for "daily bread;" it is only revealed to those who rise up hopeless and lie down wanting, in spite of their everlasting cry, "Our Father!"

Inside the village named Roiro Arrienna they found great preparations going on for the funeral of the old chief; so that with little persuasion Father Ambrose induced the visitors to wait and witness the ceremony.

All night and during the early part of the day, the relatives and friends had spent their strength weeping and lamenting wildly; they did not seem to have any deity to appeal to or reproach in this their hour of grief and woe. The French priest explained that this was the hopeless part of the missionary's work, the futile endeavours to create a faith or the necessity man has to own a greater power beyond his comprehension; what they could see and touch they would credit, but nothing beyond, yet they feared the darkness as children do, and had vague notions about ghosts and evil spirits—the world beyond was a world to regard with horror as something evil.

As they drew near to the hut where the body lay in solemn state, and where a large number of the natives had assembled—the relatives easily to be distinguished by the black ashes with which they were thickly bedaubed—two women and two men came out carrying the nude body between them, supported on bamboo-poles and cross-pieces. The grave had been dug in the centre of the village between two cocoa-nut palms, about two feet in depth, a mere scraping away of the loose sea-sand.

Then the younger son brought out the sleeping-mat of the dead man, and carefully laid it in the bottom of the grave, upon which the body was gently placed, while the outside mourners stood silently watching.

When this portion was finished a lane was made in the crowd, down which the widow with her daughers, rushed with bitter cries, plunging themselves wildly upon the body and tearing out their hair, while a party of young men went slowly round and round the grave chanting an extempore ditty of laudation of the departed one's great deeds and virtues, beating loudly all the time upon drums, while over the scene the ruddy rays of the setting sun slanted between the palms, and made long sombre shadows over the level sands.

"We had better leave them now," whispered Father Ambrose, hastily, making the sign of the cross over the grave, and moving away.

It might have been a warning the good priest meant, or only his sense of delicacy, or perhaps a blending of the two qualities, for as they moved towards the open space, they could not help noticing one or two evil glances directed towards them from the crowd of silent onlookers, while the women were rapidly following the group who had now taken off the widow and her daughters, leaving the men by themselves—always a dangerous sign with savages.

"A lovely sunset, is it not?" observed the priest, as they walked along the sea-shore, which was thickly strewn with many varieties of delicately-coloured and beautifully-shaped shells. "A lovely sunset compensates for much discomfort and danger, yet we must walk quickly if you would see my church before it grows dark. Are your revolvers loaded?"

"Yes," replied the company; "why?"

"Nothing to fear, only do not look round; but see if you can hit that branch over there."

A branch of cotton-tree gleamed out of the dark mass of foliage where he pointed, like a bar of gold with its scarlet blossom intensely red where the sunray caught it, as the priest pointed out the mark. Bowman raising his weapon, took a quick aim, and with the sharp report the flower-clad branch fell at the feet of Danby, who picked it up.

"A very good shot," murmured Father Ambrose, "and quite effective for the present. Now we may get along in peace."

Bowman glanced back as he heard these words, to see a retreating band of natives; evidently the report had frightened them from whatever evil intention they had in view, for a couple of spears lay on the sand.

"Hallo! was it going to be an attack, Father?" cried Bowman, in a startled voice.

"I was half afraid it might have been, as I gathered from a word or two dropped during the ceremony. I think they were beginning to charge one of you with having the evil eye which had caused the death; they are like children, and will not listen to reason, but they know enough to respect the gun of the white man. Yet, had you missed that branch, I fear we would have had to fight."

The cotton-tree branch became at once an object of general interest.

"Yes! to-night they will go back and tell a wonderful tale about the fire-stick that speaks and kills without touching, and to-morrow the tree will be regarded with great awe. We have time just to get a short look at the church, and then home."

They had now reached the little hut, which was dignified by the title of church, and the priest unlocking the door, showed them with a gentle apology the interior: rude log walls, whereon were tacked a few cheap and highly-coloured prints of the Passion, with a couple of rough packing-cases raised up on end to form the altar, covered with a white table-cloth, and two candles stuck upon wooden sticks—a place for thoughtless people to laugh at, yet not even the careless Danby felt inclined to smile, as the poor priest uncovered and entered with bent head.

"They come to look at my pictures, and I pray for them

while they are looking. You will excuse me, gentlemen; just one moment, while I thank God that we have escaped a danger."

He quietly knelt down before the altar with his two brothers, while the others looked round them for a moment, and then with one impulse turned towards the setting sun.

Over between them and that orange and crimson lustre lay the sea-built village of Morna Cherna, now completely deserted, as the two closely—connected villages were allies, and the inhabitants had joined in the funeral ceremonies, and also possibly with the avengers.

A canoe or two lying idle on the sands; some mats and débris of cooking, with cooking utensils scattered about. The houses, built on piles of about four and five feet above water-mark, line both sides of the beach, and form a square at the end, with the ocean outside shivering and glittering as it passes downward from the sun, now seemingly dipping into it to the wave-lapped strand.

Behind the houses on the shore side lie dense thickets of mangrove, cotton, and tamarind trees, with the occasional feathery tops of the palms, or bare white branches of dead wood projecting: a tropic bush ever presents to the eye a mingling of the seasons, where death instead of winter strips the leaves.

There is silence on the shore and in the forest, for the houses are tenantless, and the birds have gone to roost. They do not lock doors when they go out in New Guinea, and their dogs are too sociable to stay behind their masters, so, fortunately for the travellers, they had no danger to apprehend from the village through which they had to pass. Danger might lurk amongst the mangroves when darkness came on, yet even here they felt comparatively safe, guarded as they were by the fears of the natives for their speaking-tubes, joined to their horror of the night. The natives make night-attacks on enemies but seldom, unless they have the moon to guide them: this night would be dark as pitch, and from the appearance of the sky likely to be a rough one.

The sun was a round globe of fire surrounded by dense purple fumes and overhung with swarming masses of orange and vermilion, with intersections of emerald green, and overhead, deep streaks and rivulets of intense blue, with dun-coloured clouds, like broken-up and cracked clay banks on a swampy land beginning to flood.

A livid glare fell over the shimmering waves, and lit upwards, as if by reflection those huge monstrous shapes of tossing clouds with a metal—like lustre, as if they had been copper and bronze sheets shattered by artillery. This voiceless motion of the heavens, out of all unison with the deadly quiet of the vegetable world and the lifeless stillness of the deserted huts, touched, as with a chilly hand, the hearts of those who watched the turmoil above and heard with painful distinctness the low mutterings of the three priests at that primitive altar.

"We must rush at once for cover," cried the priest, coming to the door and locking it quickly as he saw the rapid weather-changes. "We are not safe here if the tribes re-form and occupy their villages in front. Come, I will lead you a short cut."

No sound as yet from the coming storm as they started at a run along the grey beach and through the black jungle, only a few disturbed cockatoos, who rose chattering from their roost to seek a more distant shelter. Helter-skelter all went through the grass again, tumbling over one another, yet guided by the sounds in front; they had about a mile to get over before they could get free from those stinging, twining reeds, and in their hurry they no longer took note of outside sounds, while the darkness gathered down like a black tissue, fold upon fold, with appalling rapidity.

Out, at last, to the open, where they can see the little mission-station upon the promontory, with the sky behind showing ghastly illumined, reflected clouds on a cold steel background, with a dusky blackness over against them in the west. The house and outstanding huts startlingly silhouetted against those electric and brilliant, but light-absorbing, rolling mountains of clouds. Out at last, with panting chests and steaming bodies, for the heat is terrific, and the travellers are as thoroughly drenched with perspiration as if they had plunged through a river.

"Let us rest for a moment," panted Bowman and Danby with one breath, while the burly old captain, rolling heavily through the brakes, tripped over a stump and fell, without an effort to rise again—too much exhausted even to blaspheme.

Father Ambrose turned with parted lips to take a handkerchief from his pocket with his usual quietness, while his companions leaned without speaking upon the barrels of their rusty fowling-pieces, passing at intervals their shrunken hands over their brows and scattering the thickly-gathering beads of sweat as they started out.

"This is very good for us after the fever," observed the priest, when he had recovered his voice, "we do not often get such a bath."

"That may be," grunted out the prostrate captain huskily, "but I'm d——blowed if it seems good for me."

"Yes, you do look considerably blowed at present, commodore," responded the ever-ready Danby, who, being the slenderest of the company, had soonest recovered. "But if you don't want to be drowned as well as blowed, I think you had best be shifting your camp."

A blaze of wild-fire broke from the ghostly mass behind the

mission—house as Danby spoke, and seemed to envelop it and lick it out of sight as it brought out objects with deadly precision near at hand, lighting up the Frenchman's clear features and the swollen visage of the horrified skipper at his feet, who greeted it with a more than ordinary shriek of fear or agony.

The blaze, though not lasting more than a second, permitted them to see besides the forms of friends, even the most minute details, and even the individual blades of reeds; it also showed them the dark faces and mop-like heads of over a score of antagonists with up-lifted spears; and then it was darkness more intense than ever, while the captain's shrill yell of pain mingled with their fierce yelling of vengeance.

"Are you wounded, friend?" anxiously asked the priest, stooping down; while flash, flash, from two barrels, with following reports, mixed up the cries.

"Yes," groaned the poor skipper, rolling about in the darkness, and uttering oaths while he did so.

"Keep silent, friends, and move out quickly; let us get to the house if we can. Let me lift you up, my poor friend."

After much wriggling about and vain groping, the captain was got up; and, between Bowman and the priest, urged up the hill, even while the downpour of rain came upon them without seemingly the customary few large drops which act as the prelude to tropic showers.

Were they a group of spectres which that flash had revealed, or were the yells imaginary? Nothing seemed to follow those two revolver reports as they dashed up the steep, slipping sides of the mound through that deluge, or they were all in too great a state of excitement to pay attention to any outside sound in their frantic desire to get under cover. There was no time to know who followed, and they could not see one another, or know whether it was a friend or an enemy which they struck against as they slid backwards; and not until they were inside the house with the door barred could they pause to find out whether they were all there or not.

Courage is a splendid quality, and easy to practise in theory; even in daylight it is not so difficult to brace up to an emergency, but in such a sightless darkness it becomes like the weight of a nightmare; to fly is the first impulse then from the evil which we cannot see. A fight in the dark is decidedly demoralizing.

They had all run recklessly, even the wounded captain after the first start required little urging on; it was a regular stampede, with the feeling in each back as we used to feel as boys, when running down a dark stair. Perhaps two minutes elapsed between the first flash at the foot of the hill and the next flash, as the priest was fumbling about to get his matchbox inside the mission-house, yet what an eternity of horrors for all.

Possibly the sudden blaze of wild-fire which revealed each party to the other had done more to frighten away the natives than the aimless shots from the revolvers, for beside heaven's ordnance man's paltry fireworks are less than farthing rushlights beside electric flames. When the matches had been found and ignited and the candle set alight, it revealed the company intact, and not any further sign of disturbance outside than the rushing of waters from roof and sky.

The first thought of the hosts, after looking after the fastening of doors and windows, was to see to the injuries sustained by the captain, who now squatted on the floor with rather a perplexed and uneasy expression on his burly features.

"Where were you wounded, my friend?" asked the priest, bending tenderly over him.

"That is just what I cannot tell you, for I don't know myself now, that rush up the hill seems to have driven out all recollection from me."

"Ah!" the priest smiled, "then it is not so serious as I thought."

Captain MacAndrews ruefully scratched his Achilles-like head and looked over to where his tormentor Danby stood, but that young gentleman was too seriously engaged in attending to his own comfort to pay much heed to anything else. He, with Bowman, had taken off their shirts, and were hard at work wringing out much of the moisture; his roasting might come later, but at present he was safe, so in a surly fashion he slowly began to exert himself and follow their wise example, while the three missionaries, without heeding their own dripping garments, set about the task of making their guests comfortable by lighting a fire and bringing out the cognac, both of which were eagerly greeted by all now that the rain had cooled the air, and their drenching inwardly and outwardly made them the more susceptible to the change.

A little quinine, about the proportion of six grains to each, was also accepted as a preventive against this fever, which is so insidious in its approach and so easy to get, particularly in such condition as they all were then; after this they could afford to look about them and talk.

If the Europeans could go about, like the natives, in the dress which nature alone provides, I doubt if there would be many cases of fever in tropical countries, a waistband, which protects the liver and kidneys, being all that is required by way of covering; for it is the chill which comes on by the contact of damp clothes, and clothes are always wet in countries where the least exertion causes the moisture to start out in dense beads on every portion of the body, wherein the danger lies, and to this may be attributed the dying out of native tribes who come into contact with the white men and ape their customs, even more than to the fire-water that they introduce.

"I could have sworn I was wounded somewhere when that flash o' lightning showed me up the niggers with their spears, but where it can be I have no more notion than Moses."

Thus muttered the honest if imaginative skipper, as he turned his wet shirt about before wringing it like the others, preparatory to drying it at the now blazing log fire. A picturesque group of half-naked albinoes they looked as they held their sole upper garments to the flames. The three missionaries had proffered them a change; but in the tropics to go without clothes for a while, is not much of a hardship, so, as they were anxious to get once more on board, they preferred to stand as they were and wait on the drying, particularly as they knew to borrow a change meant depriving the Fathers of their own comfort, as the clergymen were all too modest to bare themselves before their visitors—a feeling of shyness the others did not experience for a second. Instead then of accepting the too generous offer, they all united in persuading the Fathers to retire and guard themselves from a relapse of the dreaded malaria not yet out of their systems.

Silence outside still, with a most refreshing sense of coolness, for now that the rain had ceased to pour with the same abruptness with which it began, the suffocating heat had been succeeded by the grateful freshness which rain-soaked soil ever produces.

The mosquitoes also swarmed in countless hordes, ravenous and large, with sonorous trumpets—from the damp mangroves they came, where they are bred, to the exposed white men, whom, no doubt, they scented for miles away. They were not so numerous as they had been, the good Frenchman mentioned while setting the supper dishes.

"Then I don't wonder that you look thin," answered Bowman, stifling about a myriad of them with the volume of smoke he puffed from his lips against the phalanx as he spoke. "We are pretty well used to mosquitoes in Thursday Island, but you beat us hollow with your Yule Island fellows, Father."

"Yes, they are very strong, and assertive of their own notions of right of way," replied the missionary, pouring into a tin flat dish stew made from preserved mutton, yams, and onions, with a few of the native herbs, which now filled the room with a most appetizing odour.

"I guess it was one of those tiger-fellows who progged you with his proboscis, captain, when you thought you were wounded with the spear to-night; they are always worse close to the ground."

Captain MacAndrews pretended not to hear this sally of the ever—buoyant Danby.

"By the way, have you found the locality of that hurt yet?"

"If you don't shut up, perhaps you'll know where your hurt is presently, youngster," growled the skipper, angrily.

"Let us sit, gentlemen, while it is warm," observed the pacific priest, anxious to prevent a scene.

"By Jove, it smells delicious," cried Bowman, sniffing up the aroma with great gusto.

"We French are all cooks, as you know," replied the priest, "if we have anything to cook."

"How do you manage?"

"It is an instinct, like painting or poetry, and when it guides you rightly the result is always satisfactory. Already we have begun to grow our own onions, and in another year, if spared, we expect to glean a splendid harvest. With a very small piece of beef or mutton, and what we can pick up in the fields, it is not difficult to make a simple dish, though we sometimes run short of salt, and we find it difficult to overcome that necessity; yet I venture to assert that any one may become a fair cook who will condescend to devote as much attention to his pot as he might do over any other composition, for it is in the firing chiefly that the dish is spoilt and the flavour lost. The pan, when once on the fire, should not be lost sight of for a single second, while the fire for stews and dishes of that description cannot be too fierce; indeed, I may say that when I am cooking a dish I have no time even for prayer until it is dished, which reminds us, gentlemen, to thank God now for the supper which He has been good enough to permit us to live to cook, and, I trust, all enjoy."

The missionary, as he said this, bent his head in silence, leaving them each to offer their thanks as they felt inclined, according to their own views on this subject, after which they all fell to with that avidity which hungry men can, and very soon showed their appreciation of his culinary skill by leaving clean platters.

"You will stay to-night with me, gentlemen?"

"Not unless you dread an attack, Father."

"Not for my sake would I ask you to stay, but for your own. They will not harm us; indeed, I expect it was owing to their uncertainty in the darkness as to whom they might strike which prevented them flinging their spears to-night."

"Then we must go very soon, as our men must be warned, otherwise the steamer may be in danger from the canoes."

"Very true; then we will go at once."

"You are not coming, Father, surely?"

"Surely I shall come and see you safely from our island. We shall take lanterns so that they will know we are with you, and since you will not be my guests I shall be yours to-night, and to-morrow will be able to quiet their suspicions. I pray to God that you may not have shot any one to-night."

"I think not," responded Bowman, "I aimed over their heads."

"And I couldn't have hit them, however much I tried," added Danby. "It isn't in me to hit anything less than an elephant, and then only if he balanced the barrel with his tusks."

"Then all will be well," replied the priest. "Let us go, if you are ready."

"Quite ready." And looking once more to their weapons, withdrawing the cartridges already in and putting in fresh ones, they all prepared once more to go into the risky darkness.

The two assistant priests went out first, and shortly returned, reporting all as quiet. When the party reached the mound, they could see over by the villages the dusky reflection amongst the deep midnight space which betokened large fires burning on the beach.

"I think all is well," muttered Father Ambrose, "but we will walk as quietly as possible with our lamps shining toward the sea. Antone will walk behind with his light covered, but ready for use if anything suspicious occurs, while I will go a little way ahead; but, gentlemen, don't use your pistols, unless at the last emergency. Remember that life is as precious to savage as to Christian."

No more words passed as they went in single file down through the fields and into the mangrove thicket, where they had left their dingey in the afternoon. Pedro, the second assistant, followed after the leader, with Bowman next, and the captain in the centre, much against his will, since he had Danby behind him, who at intervals made him leap with a prick in the ribs when least expected, forcing him at the same time to smother the exclamation of horror as he fancied each touch to be a native spear. The method of silencing him he adopted was to put his hand suddenly over his mouth and whisper in his ear, "Hush, for God's sake! do you hear nothing?" A momentous march without incident, except these torturing moments for the poor unwieldy old skipper, who rolled along with ice—cold drops dripping down his back, and a blending of impotent rage and fear choking him, while his tormentor never ceased his game until at the water's edge, when, by an adroit push, he sent him into the water, and afterwards added to his injuries the worse one of pretending to have saved his life by lugging him out again all dripping, like a Newfoundland dog.

"Sharks bad hereabouts I should say, Father?" asked Danby innocently, as he took his place behind the poor old captain.

"Yes, they are," replied Father Vincent, taking his seat.

"Another narrow squeak, for you, admiral. I expect a bottle of whisky at the least out of you for this last good action."

"You'll get it, too, my boy," responded the captain, fervently, taking an oar and pushing the dingey from the rocks. "Thank God, that's the last of Yule Island for me!—a regular nest of pirates."

Chapter XXIV
Toto as a Defender

SOMETIMES about the very worst luck which can befall a man is to gain an advantage over his adversary.

Our feelings may be outraged, or our contempt and indignation roused, until we rise up in our righteous wrath and strike out from the shoulder, and what is the result?—satisfaction? Yes, a brief instant of satisfaction, trailing behind it years of regret. We prate of our wrongs and no one listens, or if they do, it is only in order to mock us, or else betray us when our backs are turned. We avenge our injuries, and straightway rises up from the deed, misery or self-contempt in our hearts; the object of our wrath is invested with a halo of pathetic reproach the instant our stroke of justice has descended, because our humanity prevents us from being implacable, as stern justice must be; or else the object is too insignificant for the blow we have given to it, and so the blow recoils directly with double force upon our own heads.

Again, no injury can be repaired by the injurer, repentance will not do it; no ocean of tears can ever wipe out the damaged spot; we are haunted for ever by another ghost who joins a vast regiment, the ghastly army of deeds, to chase us through life; it is much easier, in reality, to bear a blow of adversity than to have become the cause of another's ruin.

Kamo, for a moment or two, as he stalked away with much majesty into the deep shadows past the tamarind-tree, felt very well satisfied with his promptitude and brave display of courage; so, also, did Rea, when she beheld her splendid young hero, with the firelight playing over his satin-like limbs, so easily overthrow and make ridiculous this very contemptible pretender to her hand; but I doubt if either of this foolish self-congratulatory young couple felt half the satisfaction that Toto did, as he picked himself up and adjusted his raumma about this same very ridiculous part which he had been brought to play in the magic ceremony.

A thorough philosopher, he cared no more about a kick, unless when it hurt very much, than he did about any other insult, so long as it touched no more than his honour. This kick had not hurt him beyond a passing sting, whereas it placed his enemy in his merciless grasp, for by that interruption in this sacred ceremony, Kamo had broken tapu, the punishment of which was death, unless the one injured chose to interfere, the punishment and mode being entirely at his option.

A magnificent kick for fortune-favoured Toto, who showed his ugly fangs in a more decided leer than ever as he looked towards the still animated countenance of Rea, while he turned with a hypocritical air of pity towards where the father, mother, and sisters stood, paralyzed with horror at the madness of their audacious and irreligious son and brother.

Half a dozen steps into the blackness of the croton shadows and the truth burst upon him with the suddenness of the doom of Cain.

"Lost, lost for ever! oh, fool! fool!! fool!!!" and, with a howl like a wild beast, he plunged his hand into his carefully-frizzed, orange-dyed hair, tearing out handfuls, as he fled frantically towards the mountains.

Rea woke up next to the utter helplessness of her position, the folly of her budding hopes, the destruction of her love. Not a child of the company who could speak at all but knew what Kamo's kick meant inside that circle sanctified by the sacred spell of the spirit-seers, or that until his or other blood washed away the evil luck, nothing but misfortune would come to the tribe. Kamo was doomed without a chance, for what pity could any one expect from laughing Toto; and as this truth broke upon her, she laid her poor head right amongst the sand and ashes, and wept as if her little heart would have burst.

Fortunately for the present personal safety of Kamo, the New Guinea native will not move in any matter without a great amount of discussion and tall talking, and it takes them, as a rule, like all livers in the open air, some little time to grasp a situation, otherwise the offender might have been at once secured, instead of being permitted to stalk away as he had done in full presence of the outraged assembled tribe, driving, as it were, the affronted prophetic spirits sheer out of the field.

But now that the ghost performance was over for the present occasion, the next thing to do was to dismiss the women to bed, while the men assembled in the Dobu, or grand house of the village, to discuss the grave question, and pass judgment upon the culprit; therefore, the chief and father of Rea, Mavaraiko, gravely rising up, gave what might be termed the benediction to that meeting. At this potent signal of dismissal, against which there could be no protest, much as the women were listened to generally, Putitai, the unmarried sister of Kamo, and friend to Rea, passed over, and lifting up the afflicted girl, led her away to her father's hut.

Meantime a guard of the youngest men left amongst them was hastily extemporized and ordered to prowl round the outskirts of the village, and watch in case of invasion from their old enemies the mountain tribes, from whom vague rumours had floated of a contemplated raid. This, indeed, had been one of the reasons why the present spirit-meeting had been convened, and now that the spirits had been driven off before they had time to come to this important portion of their warning, these simple children of nature expected nothing less than an immediate assault, all the greater reason for execrating the impious name of Kamo.

Large fires were speedily lighted up at different portions of the village, and one in front of the Dobu, until the whole place stood out in glaring relief in the midst of the general darkness of the forest, while the women concealed themselves inside their houses, and peered out with large frightened eyes from between the crevices at the hurrying figures of their lords and masters, as they hastily armed themselves and gathered before the platform upon which Mavaraiko stood leaning upon a large black palm spear, with his shield-bearer by his side, and the spirit professor behind him; where, also, the injured Toto had been promoted, now once more adorned with his yellow and red-spotted pijamas, with his broad straw hat tilted over his left ear, in all the grandeur of his civilized garb, the personation of triumphant innocence.

The Dubo House stood in the centre of the village, and was the only house dignified with a spire, which rose to a height of about sixty feet, with projecting poles of bamboo with fluttering grasses and palm—ribbons. The first floor was raised about six feet from the sand on many strong cotton and gum-tree posts, with a wide strong platform of tough undressed logs overlaid with coarse planks; how they ever managed to cut those planks being one of the wonders of their native ironless craft.

Above this platform, at about eight feet, another projected, forming a second flat and a verandah-like roof for the first platform, to reach both of which rude moveable ladders were placed against the posts; this verandah was fringed, as were the eaves of the palm-thatched roof, with bleached skulls and other human remains, sombre relics of departed friends and murdered enemies; tame cockatoos and parrots swung themselves by day upon these ghastly trophies, and roosted upon them at night.

Inside all was in deepest shadow, one large under-chamber, with the walls lined with weapons of warfare, and a small upper chamber, with funnel-like roof, reaching to the height of the spire.

Outside, where the male portion of the assembly were squatting or standing according to pleasure while waiting on the chief to open parliament, wandered droves of pet pigs with preternaturally long snouts, rubbing up against naked legs to attract notice or get scratched by their fond owners, grunting with delight, or breaking the silence with shrill squeaks, as the likewise limitless cluster of native dogs jealously snapped at their wriggling tails when they saw that the pigs were more taken notice of than themselves.

The leaping flames from the different fires mixed up the lights most fantastically, and threw black shadows, which seemed strangely animated, into the open space within the assembled motionless circle and up the knarled supports of the platform, so that the shadows seemed to be alive, and the waiting warriors to be carven fiends only; a weird and vivid golden effect of light burnished up the whole village, and to ships passing outside the barrier reef, far in the gulf, must have seemed ominous in the extreme in a land where fires of this extent denote carnage, intensified in horror by the awful after-effects of cannibalism.

A short pause after the crowd had settled themselves and then Mavaraiko opened the debate with the usual highly-coloured eloquence of the savage, be he white or copper-tinted, who only recognizes the laws of self-gratification and the lust of revenge.

He biased the court with his first words like a modern magistrate, and carried on in the same vein to the finale, demanding the one punishment—"death," which was recognized by his hearers as the punishment for almost every offence, great or trivial; in the code of the savage there are no gradations in crime, except in the case of theft, which is venal, and to be condoned by restitution.

Kamo's crime was of greater magnitude than a single murder, for by this act of interruption he was regarded as endangering the lives of all his friends and relations; even his father could say nothing by way of extenuation; he must be slain by all the laws of procedure, and Toto should have the right of being avenger.

It was at this juncture that Toto shone forth with

extraordinary brilliancy, and proved the benefit which he had received from his communication with the civilized races. Rising gracefully to his feet, he silenced, with a gentle and oratorical wave of his hand, the very hubbub of tongues which had now broken loose, and when peace was once more restored, addressed them as follows:—

"My friends and supporters, you all know me as well as I do myself, and what I have done for you since I was born. You know that I have brought much property amongst you, and made you all so greatly respected by other tribes by being so very rich; our Kavana is the great man, but am I not the rich one?"

Yells of applause and cries from one and all that he was, but a slightly lowering expression on the heavy brows of Mavaraiko gathered instantly, noticing which the adroit orator resumed.

"But what is property compared to great deeds and noble birth; is not our Kavana a mighty man?"

Signs of clearing up of the noble visage.

"What have I done in all my life compared to one of his fighting days? Who has done more to fill up the line of skulls which now fringe our Dobu roof?"

Toto pointed above him, while the chief gently patted him on the shoulder—

"You are a good boy, Toto, and are my son."

"You all hear what our father has to-night promised me," cried Toto, exultantly.

"You shall have my daughter Rea, directly you bring me the head of Kamo to hang up on that empty place."

The slobbing under-lip of Toto fell limply at this condition, but recovering himself he continued,—

"You all know how I love Rea, and also that her little heart has gone out for the present after that wicked Kamo. If I kill him, will she not hate me for ever after, and who would marry a woman to be hated?"

Toto paused to watch the effect of his wily suggestions, but saw only contemptuous shrugs of the shoulders from his hearers; his reasons were too fine drawn for their broad comprehensions, observing which, he hastily continued in a vaunting tone,—

"I do not fear Kamo, for I know how to kill with the white man's tube, but I want the heart of Rea, and this is the way I am going to get it. I would spare the life of Kamo, and only banish him from the tribe, which, if he ever comes near again, then I will take my man-trap and slay him, without mercy."

The broken-hearted father of Kamo here sprang up to the platform, and with his two arms embraced the pijama-covered limbs of the merciful Toto in an ecstasy of gratitude.

"You all see how I have pleased the father, will it not also please my wife when she hears of it?"

Signs of bewilderment in the audience; perhaps after all, the rich Toto was a better fellow than they had hitherto considered him to be. He went on more loudly than ever,—

"The white man taught me to be merciful when my enemy is in my power, but I can be brave also, as you will find when the time comes. Place me in the front when the common enemy comes, and you shall see how I can fight—"

At this moment there seemed to be a wild commotion from the outskirts of the village, which made the brave man pause in his boasting and look anxiously over the heads of his audience. The next instant three of the young men sent as sentinels, were seen to burst through the undergrowth with great force, and rush towards them with loud cries.

"Quick! to arms, the enemy is upon us."

As the men leaped to their feet with one impulse, and Mavaraiko vaulted amongst them from his lofty position, the brave defender, Toto, rolled backwards along the platform, like an highly-coloured india—rubber ball, and vanished into the dark shadows of the huts nearest the sea.

Chapter XXV
Kamo to the Fore

THROUGH the forest, towards the mountain, rushed Kamo, blind to everything except his own utter misery. Tumbling over twigs and fallen limbs of dead trees, mile after mile he ran on, until at last Nature triumphed over misery, and he sank exhausted at the foot of a gigantic tamarind.

He had gone in a direct line instinctively, taking the native track to the interior, and where he now lay panting, he was nearly midway between his own village and the village with which they were at enmity, much nearer than he would have dared to venture by day, alone and unarmed as he was.

Of course he knew every mile of the way, and with the sure instinct of the savage, discovered his locality, as soon as his first giddiness of exhaustion had passed; then, with the same instinct, caution commenced to assert itself in his breast, and he began to consider his position, and think if there could be any way out of it, anything he could do to repair his mistake and regain his place with his tribe.

Yes! it was a desperate plan, but he was in a desperate plight—blood alone could wash out his iniquity, and raise him in the estimation of his people. If he could, unarmed, take a life or two, and bring back some heads, then he would become a real hero, and they would forgive him, and he would once more work his way in with Mavaraiko and regain his love.

He would do it, or die in the attempt; to go back empty-handed meant a death as cruel as the death in front, to steal forward might mean life and love, and could at the worst only be death.

Extremity is the finest goad to exertion.

Motionlessly he now listened before he rose up, then hearing all the forest seemingly deserted, he stole, with careful feet, onwards towards the mountain village.

The upper foliage was too dense for any moonlight to penetrate, and from bush to bush he managed to glide and hide without a chance of being seen, and only the faintest chance of being heard when a twig crackled under his feet.

A deadly quiet walk through an almost Egyptian darkness, with barriers checking him, and tendrils clinging about him at every step, through a lavish labyrinth of flowers, leaves and creepers, such as only a savage could find or force a passage without waking the surrounding echoes of the night.

"Hark!" what was that?

Kamo dissolved into the intricacies of an evergreen, without seemingly disturbing a leaf, and listened with starting eyes to the sound in front.

Nothing to break the repose of the windless forest to any ears, save those of an untamed son of Nature, but enough to signify to him that a body of natives were gliding towards him, with just a little less than their usual caution, for they were still too far off their goal to care how they trod.

On the war-trail, for their spears were disturbing the leaves as they passed by his lair, and he could hear the rubbing of their poisoned arrows against their shields at times.

Up to two hundred Kamo counted as they glided past him in single file, without a word, for it is unlucky to break silence when going to the hunt. A mighty raid they intended with that number, and going towards his tribe.

It meant extermination, for they had not more than sixty fighting men ready if not warned; bad enough even then.

Was he yet destined to retrieve his fault by a mighty deed which would save his tribe? If not, he could die for and with them.

Out of the shrubby ambush, as the last man passed, Kamo

glided, without any plan, only determined to follow and take his chance.

Two hundred and one men are now upon the war-path, walking single file; but the second last man has no suspicion that there is another behind.

The warrior last but one is the youngest man of the tribe; he is now going on his first raid with his full accoutrements on; indeed, an extra supply of everything, as young men will begin life with when they can.

Has he tripped over a stone and fallen? It must be so, for he makes no sign to the one in front, so that he doesn't wait on him, but glides along, leaving the young brave to come up when he rises. A moment more and he rejoins the man in front, gliding on voiceless.

Pitch darkness in the forest where they walk, with a headless body lying bleeding in the forest, which that chance fall had given to Kamo, his first head, which now dangles at his waist-belt, the warm fluid running down his left leg, and growing chilly in the night air.

"Ugh!" a heavy breath from the next man as Kamo piths him from behind with the sharp bone-blade which the headless youth supplied him with, and he too is laid noiselessly in the path with a split heart. There is no time to take this head, but he can find it if he ever comes back that way. There are now only one hundred and ninety-eight, with one enemy, on the war-trail now.

A game of treachery? Yes, an all-round New Guinea game, like the one Judith played to save her people.

On, on through the darkness, while the men in front get angry at the want of caution from those behind; they will gasp now and again where there is no need, but as yet no one has actually broken the strictly—observed silence, only the last man but one did not die instantly, and Kamo had to hold his mouth with all his might while he felt about for the heart. This made the twigs under foot to break too loudly, and much disturbed and annoyed the chief in front; but now they are going on all right, and have got within about a mile of the village doomed to destruction.

Kamo has succeeded beyond his desires; twenty men lie bleeding on the war-path out of that two hundred, and four of them are without their heads, a heavy load for Kamo to carry from his waist-belt; but he will be honoured now even if he dies.

Half a mile and the glare from the fires begin to dart between the leaves and light up little projections like fire-flies. Kamo now knows that his friends are partly prepared, and makes up his mind to go. There is a side cutting which he knows, and which only lately has been cleared, close at hand; this will lead him quicker to the village, if the light doesn't stream through it, and betray it to the enemy.

The fire-fly flashes have now taken on the proportion and colour of butterflies in the full sun. A few more yards and they will see one another distinctly. Now is the time. They have passed the lane which is faithful in its darkness, and offers the retreat after he has potted his twenty-first man. No need for caution now; it must be a race for life.

Kamo hangs back a moment in deep shadow, so as to get better purchase with his borrowed man trap, which he dare not use before in case he missed,—just a moment while the warrior in front plunges past a bar of fire-light which crosses the foot-path. They are near to the village gardens, and with a few more steps they will be full in the light of the thinning forest-trees.

"Whish!" the bamboo man-trap, with its pithing spear, is over the warrior's head, and catches him under the chin, jerking the spinal column full against the prong, then, with a yell of triumph, Kamo let go the handle and bounds backwards into the deep shelter of that trusty cutting.

Chapter XXVI
A Night Raid

DISCOVERED! With their intended victims in front and behind. How many? Ah! the inability to answer this question in a moment of uncertainty is how a hundred armies have been conquered before now, and battles lost.

Kamo rushed down that lane with the rapidity of a racehorse, and would have been the first to give the warning to his friends had the road been clear, for the hundred and seventy-nine men paused irresolute in the forest as they heard the death shriek of their comrade, mixed with that wild yell, which gave the alarm to the sentinels in front, not knowing whether to turn back or advance; but, unfortunately for his project, there stood another guard about the middle of the path, against whom Kamo came with such velocity that they were both spun different ways, and for a moment were completely dazed with the collision.

The guard, being a much more solidly built man than Kamo, was the first to recover wind, and when he did, without a moment longer pausing to consider matters, he plunged straight in the direction of his prostrate enemy, knife in hand, to finish up his advantage.

127

The darkness, which had befriended before it be trayed the youth, once more acted on his side, for, as the other lunged wildly forward, striking at random, Kamo also slowly recovering, by chance caught at the arm, and so together they closed with one another in a most desperate and silent hand-to-hand tussle.

Kamo felt he was in the furious grasp of an ignorant friend, much more powerful than himself, and tried with all his might to make him aware of the mistake he was labouring under, but without succeeding; as it required all his waning strength and breath to hold him back for the first few moments.

At last, when the issue was no longer doubtful, he managed, with the knife almost at his throat, to gasp out,—

"Don't kill me—Kamo!"

"Ah!" the other relaxed his embrace just in time.

"The enemy is behind!" panted the exhausted youth, huskily. "To the village and warn them, I will come when I can."

"How many?"

"One hundred and—"

It was no time to explain matters further. Up leapt the savage, and away as the words were passing Kamo's dry throat, leaving him to pick himself up as best he could, and follow with his news.

So it chanced that the three sentinels broke from their cover simultaneously at the moment when Toto demanded an opportunity of proving his valour as the defender of his country, while poor Kamo once more lost his chance of distinguishing himself, for the present at any rate, by telling of his single-handed action.

Mavaraiko, an old and tried warrior, at once drew his men into the shadow side of the Dubo, where he promptly questioned the outposts.

The two first could only speak of their alarm at the yell and death—shriek, so the third had it his own way. He briefly recounted his contact and struggle with Kamo.

"How many did the boy say?" asked the chief.

"One hundred, oh Kavana!" answered the sentinel promptly.

It was as well for the pluck of the invaded that Kamo had not been permitted to finish his sentence.

"And we are sixty, counting the old men!" muttered the chief. "But where are they that they do not come?"

"Perhaps they do not know our force, and the fires have frightened them," replied Ila, the old father of Kamo.

"That must be it," said the chief, pondering deeply for a moment, while his followers watched the thicket with anxious eyes.

"We will beat them, and get many heads, for they must be afraid. Ila go round the huts and raise the women, they must help us, this must help us to-night; give them drums and the war-horns, and take four men and ten women round by the east end of the forest. Kupa, take the same number and go by the west; when you get equal distances from each other, and when you think you are behind them, make the women beat upon their drums and blow their horns, that will cause them to think our allies are joining us. Take only the young women, for they can blow hard on the conch shells, and see that Rea is of the number chosen. You, Heni, are old, and can be spared tonight;—gather the old women together on to the beach, and take all the canoes, put them in, and let them go half a mile from the shore, when that distance make all the noise you can, they will by that means think the Kerepuni men are coming to help us,—go quickly."

The three men glided off like shadows without reply.

"Toto!"

No reply.

"Where is Toto?"

Ay, where was the gallant Toto, now that the moment of action had arrived?

One of the spectators at last replied how he had seen the defender roll off the platform. A general grim laugh followed this revelation.

"No matter," replied the chief, "we can do without him; I never saw him fight, yet ye know what Kamo can do, and I wish he was with us."

"Kamo is here, oh Kavana," replied that youth with becoming modesty, rising up from the shadows beside the chief.

"Welcome, my son, as you fight to-night, so will we judge your fault to-morrow, but what have you got there?"

One of the heads had touched against the nude skin of Mavaraiko, as Kamo rubbed against him.

"Four heads for the Dubo house," replied Kamo, pitching them down so that they rolled a little way into the fire-glare.

"Good boy, you are a warrior, and have already wiped away your bad luck; how many have you killed?"

"Twenty-one dead men lie on the mountain-track, whom I have killed to-night."

Exclamations of wonder and delight broke from the assembled men when Kamo told his adventures, while the chief by a low whisper stopped him when he was about to tell of the number left.

"Hush, Kamo, how many?"

"Two hundred went before me, oh Kavana," whispered

Kamo back again; "one hundred and seventy-nine are waiting in the forest close to the gardens."

"Do not speak of it, my son," replied the chief in a low voice, and then raising his tones, he said,—

"Kamo is a boy, and has slain twenty-one men; he went to meet them without a weapon, and comes back armed with spears; we must do no less, for we are men and have our spears; come, my braves, we will meet them in the forest and drive them into the light where we can kill them as we like;—guide us, Kamo, to where they are."

Along the shadows, behind the houses, they all crept towards the cutting, leaving the fire burning brightly in the deserted village, with only the pigs to look after them, for the dogs, accustomed to the hunt, went with their masters.

Meantime the one hundred and seventy-nine mountain men were still in about the same place as Kamo had left them, the silence around them being profound, and therefore, as they felt from experience, pregnant of treachery. The fires glittered through the intersections of palm fronds, palisades and forest leaves, and flickered upon odd portions of their bodies as they instinctively gathered closely about their chief, weapons in grasp, all ready for the sudden surprise, which they had come prepared to give, but now expected to receive instead.

Was the enemy behind, in front, or had the allies joined and surrounded them, luring them into a trap and cutting off their retreat? No man dared to move or speak as they stood and listened intently.

The chief himself was at a loss—he was old and not so quick either with his hand or his brain—and so he only stood, helpless, waiting upon the inspiration which would not come.

Now, also, for the first time, they missed their twenty-one companions, at least, the twenty, for the last man slain lay a few yards away, with the man-trap still about his neck, the cane handle bent and twisted under him where he had fallen backwards upon it, and that broad bar of fire-light dancing slant-ways over his body, and gleaming upon the under half of one cheek, and this sight before their eyes, with the mysterious disappearance of the other twenty men, filled each breast with anticipated horror and superstitious chills, which seemed to freeze up their hearts, and pluck the courage from them, and the strength from their arms, their muscles seemed paralyzed, and their brains to be benumbed.

Time passed on without a change in their position—quarter of an hour, half an hour, still that appalling silence of treachery around, the uncertain flickering and dancing of those dusky lights, fluttering like bronze-winged butterflies amongst the black shadows. That single bar of copper glow, moving and shifting slant-ways over the dead body so near to them, with the motion which a sleeper's breathing causes, and at times darting from the under part of the cheek to the one glistening, protruding eye, with a red sparkle, horrible to look at.

"Ha! they are behind us," cried the chief at last, as the faint wind, breathing westward, bore the first distant blast of the conch shells from Ila's company of women, "they have got the Hood Bay men to help them."

Another burst answered the first from the west, at which the men answered, "And the tribes from Round Head, let us get home."

With one impulse they turned on their track to fly backwards, when suddenly the forest seemed alive with yells, as Mavaraiko and his party burst upon them from the cutting.

"To the beach," shouted the old chief, suddenly waking up; "let us die in the open."

And leading the way, he rushed towards the gardens, with the Hulu warriors spearing and man-trapping them as they fled.

Through the native gardens they all rushed, without order or discrimination, smashing down the palisades of bamboo, knocking against banana, palm, and Mammy trunks, tripped up by disorderly confusion on the ground of yams and sharded fronds, squashing amongst the lushness of decaying vegetable matter, and splashing up the mud from the watering pools, while their hunters, knowing the ground thoroughly and the necessity of action before reaching the light, where their disparity of numbers would be revealed, pursued them ruthlessly, with savage cries scattering them as much as possible, while they plunged their spears into them, leaving them where they stuck, pinned to the moist soil; man-trapping them when the spears were used up, casting man and trap away with force, to finish up the battle in the open with their flint-loaded clubs and axes.

Through the gardens, and down the lanes, with the fires growing less and redder in their glaring, the hill-men went in broken up, disorganized masses, hardly even looking behind them, eager only to get into open space and light. The old chief, borne along in front of the impetuous rush and charge, the air filled now with sounds enough, shrieking of the dying and stabbed, nearer blowing of the conch-shells and beating of the drums, as the loud sounds of the battle attracted the now united bands of girls who came on close to the yelling hunters, with their lanes and gardens trampled down, and sprinkled with dead and wounded men, implements of war, bare and broken-down banana-trees.

As yet the panic had been so complete on the part of the

mountain tribe, that not a man of the sixty followers of Mavaraiko had received a wound, but now, as they rushed into the dimly-lighted square, for the fires were getting low, with this half-hour of neglect, the crisis had come when fair fighting would have to decide the question of victory.

Into the centre of the village, scattering the pigs right and left, the old chief dashed with about ninety men left out of his hundred and seventy—nine, and most of these more or less wounded. With a rush and a rapid wheel round they gathered themselves about the old warrior with their faces towards their pursuers: those foremost had the advantage of a few seconds to form this impromptu circle, for slaughtering is slower work than flying, and as the wounded came on they were, with the characteristic trait of savages, made to stand on the outside and act as barricades for those unwounded inside.

Ninety men in the full light, with sixty men forming themselves like a pack of hungry wolves in the shadow.

Ninety men who did not know the force opposed to them in that darkness, and sixty men who knew exactly where they were.

Ninety men in a decided trap, more or less wounded, and sixty out in the open, and still fresh.

The chances were not much in favour of the majority, in this New Guinea game of "poker" for life and death.

Toto bounded from the platform with the agility of an acrobat, and found himself in a few more seconds dragging away at one of the numerous small canoes which were lying well drawn up on the sea—shore, with all the strength which his frantic fear inspired him with.

These small canoes are mostly used by the children and girls of Hula for fishing purposes or to carry water; they are capable of conveying with safety a dozen or more, for with their outriggers they can hardly either sink or capsize, no matter how heavily laden they may be, while, on the other hand, they can be quite easily handled by one, as they are lightly made and narrow, so not at all difficult to drag along the dry smooth sands.

Seizing a couple of small paddles from many which were lying loosely about the shore, Toto quickly got his canoe afloat, and for the next five minutes paddled with all his energy in a direct line seaward; then he paused to rest himself, and look backwards towards the village which he had fled from.

The fires were still blazing away brightly, and casting long glittering reflections down the many ripples of the coral-protected waters, while the houses built upon the sands stood out strongly in dark relief upon their piles, through which the golden firelight became the more intensified. Over within the bay eastward of him he could see the houses of refuge, raised from the waves, and about half-a-mile from shore.

It was getting on towards morning, and the horned moon which had lighted up their spirit-meeting in the early portion of the evening had long since set over towards Round Head—the darkest hour of the night, yet the stars were very lustrous in the dome above and around.

Out towards the stormy gulf he could hear the unceasing rushing and beating of the surf against the great coral walls, but on shore all was silence, with only the merry fires blazing as a sign of life.

Toto began to think that he had been a little premature in his desertion of his friends, and began to east about in his mind how he could explain away his absence if, after all, it had been a false alarm. There could be no battle without noise, and as yet there was none from the shore.

Had he not better get back before he was missed? No, there might be fighting yet, and he could always depend upon his own ingenuity to tell an easy lie, if required. Besides, he did not care much what they thought about his courage, so that he did nothing foolish enough to turn the father of Rea against his suit, and now that he had his public promise he felt pretty safe on that score, so he decided it to be wiser to wait where he was until he saw how things were likely to turn out.

"I can always pretend that I went out to look after the enemy when I am sure they are not there; but I had best be sure first, and then I can pull quietly ashore and slip among them with a big story, which I can easily make them believe."

So he consoled himself, and sat at his ease, looking towards the fires.

By-and-by he saw the shadows of figures dragging at the boats, as he had done, and quickly putting out towards him, at which again he took alarm, and began pulling in the direction of Round Head.

"What is that on the water?" exclaimed the old man Heni, as he paused to rest on his paddle, with his flotilla about him, and looked towards Round Head Point. "My sight is not good; look for me, Kupatele, for your eyes are sharp."

Kupatele, a strong young matron of about twenty-one summers, rose upright in her canoe, and, shading her eyes from the distant fire-glare, looked long and searchingly into the star-lit distance.

"I see nothing, Heni," she said at last, sitting down again and taking up her steering paddle.

"Do you hear nothing?"

A moment or two of anxious listening, after which the woman laid her ear alongside the edge of the canoe.

"Whirr! whirr! whirr!" very faintly and in the distance, but decidedly different from the monotonous sounds of the surf against the barrier; it was the vibrating sound of a steam propeller thrashing and churning the waves, miles away and going very leisurely. Sounds carry very far on the waters in those latitudes during this season of the year.

Without a word, and regardless of sharks being about, Kupatele slipped her raumma down from her waist and slid over the side of the canoe into the shallow waters, which reached up to her breasts, then stooped her head forward till her eyes were on a level with the surface.

"Puff! puff! Beretana smoking-boat coming, and little canoe going to meet it," whispered the woman, as she once more clambered into her place.

"Ha! they will help our friends. Let some of you go and meet them, and catch up the little boat if you can, Kupatele, and see who has run away from the danger to-night," said Heni, settling himself back to look on the shore.

"I think it must be Toto," observed one of the other youngest women, "for I saw him, through the cracks, jump from the Dubo House and run down towards the beach when the boys came from the forest crying."

"And you ought to know Toto pretty well, Hankowa, not to make a mistake in the man," replied Kupatele, in a jeering voice.

"Not more than Kupatele," retorted the other. "You were often enough at his place with your shells when the Beretana sailors came to smoke the bau-bau."

"Be quiet," commanded Heni, sternly, "or I shall tell both your husbands what you say. Go at once, and bring the white fellows quickly, if you want to see them again."

"If it is Toto, I shall soon catch him," cried out Kupatele as she darted off, "for he is too fat and lazy to go fast."

On shore the fires were getting low, though still blazing, only the reflections were more vermilion than golden, and the columns of smoke which before blotted out the stars as they floated amongst them now spread out transparently, blurring them only, and causing them to shake and quiver with split-up rays.

As Kupatele and the women deputed to accompany her darted off on their mission, Heni and those left behind heard the faint sounds of the conch-shells blown by the bands of girls ashore, with the beating of the drums, and at once responded to them with all their might, making such a din on the waters that Toto, by this time almost used up with his unexpected exertions, thought the enemy had discovered him, and were making all this row for his special benefit, and became so paralyzed with the horror of the idea that he dropped one of his two paddles over the side, and nearly tumbled in himself in his frantic efforts to get it again.

Meantime the women were coming rapidly hand over hand, while poor Toto dashed the water about him aimlessly in his endeavour to get away with the one paddle.

He splashed and dashed about with his canoe, making no headway, while he lost his head so completely that he seemed to forget the sea—craft which every child on the coast knows even before he can well walk, and which Toto had learnt as a child like the others, striking at the water blindly and frantically.

"Caught!" cried Kupatele, coming up the first, and running her canoe prow against his with a bang which made it almost capsize, and sent the unfortunate pandarus overboard head foremost. Toto gave a shrick of mortal horror, which was checked before full delivery by the splashing waters.

A faint gleam from the fires gave Kupatele and her companions a rapid glimpse of the vanishing pijamas before they were swallowed up, so that she exclaimed with a laugh,—

"What a funny fish that was! Let us dive for him, and take him home to supper."

Chapter XXVII
The 'Thunder' to the Rescue

WATER is a second native element to the Papuan, men, women, and infants are all brought up to it, amongst the coast tribes, and such a danger as drowning would never enter into the imagination of any fond mother there.

Also, although at parts where the openings are wide enough and the water is deep enough, the ocean inside the reefs literally swarms with sharks, yet they seem to have a profound respect for these bold divers and swimmers, as I have never heard any of the natives speak of death or injury done to their friends that way.

We will leave Ila with his conch-blowing flock of sirens to watch the progress of the battle, while Kupatele, with her own charming disregard of prudery, sets the bold example of diving after the recreant Toto. After they had caught him, they handled him with the delicacy peculiar to their sex when they have a victim whom they properly despise entirely at their mercy.

Kupatele and Hankowa must not be judged by the ordinary

standard of civilized ladies, or considered heartless because they could laugh and make fun while their husbands were ashore risking their lives. In New Guinea life is too slight a possession to create much anxiety when it is risked as it is almost daily. When it is lost the grief is wild and deep enough. People who have been born on the crust of a volcano do not tremble because the earth chances to shake. Besides, Toto had cured the ladies of Hula of much of the rigid notions and finer feelings which still hedged round the women of the other tribes, not yet blessed with Totos.

We will hurry on board the Thunder once more, for this was the Beretana puffpuff-boat whose propeller had been heard by the canoes on the waters of Hula, during this momentous night.

The Thunder, after leaving Yule Island, had gone without loss of time to Port Moresby, where they delivered their cargo and letters to the Mission House on the hill, to the Governor in his bungalow, and to the solitary Store-House belonging to that enterprising firm of Burns, Philip, and Co., who seem determined to plant their standard wherever the foot of white man dare venture. They delivered letters also to the survey party who were at the time planning out a Colonial draughtboard-shaped city in this home of the untamed savage.

Here they picked up the bold Flagcroucher, and out of consideration for the feelings of the genial old Governor (who had enjoyed the distinguished warrior's company for a couple of months), they offered him a free passage eastward, which he promptly accepted; they had also as passenger on the same terms, one of those highly refined explorers who are sometimes to be met further abroad than the geographical chambers, and in general are much loved by rough and honest traders.

The Governor at Port Moresby having heard concerning the exploits of Toto, and the Christianizing influence which he was extending amongst his own people, so much desired to meet him that he had expressly commissioned Bowman to go for him, and on no account to leave him behind at Hula. So that the lucky Toto had unconsciously been on the way to meet the very people who were sent after him, when Kupatele frightened the poor fellow so much.

To Hula from Basilisk Bay the passage is pretty plainly denoted on the charts, and, what is better, the places jotted down as safe are actually comparatively free from shoals, so that they were going along pretty easily on the night in question.

In the cabin they had partaken of a plentiful feast, for the last sheep left aboard had been slaughtered that day and the Chinese cook was pretty good at dressing it.

They were now assembled in the saloon discussing the

merits of a stone jar of Scotch whisky with "Tappit Hen" marked upon it. They had their pipes—those at least who smoked. The scientific explorer was too delicate to indulge in anything short of Château Lafite in the drinking, or Egyptian cigarettes in the smoking way, which exploration necessities the Singalese steward had inconsiderately overlooked in his stock taking before he left port.

The General held the chair; he had voted himself into it, and in spite of all protest constituted himself the single speaker; it was a Flagcroucher solo, with futile interruptions from the others, promptly checked off by the trumpet-tones of the military hero.

The scientific explorer had vainly tried to assert his superiority by a few of those drawing-room airs and funny sneers, or milky sarcasms which are effective sometimes when swallow-tails are in the majority; but what are headless fun-darts when directed against such a hide? Besides, they were too irresolutely delivered, and the General had a ferocious bloodshot glaring eye, and a moustache of noble proportions which intimidated the explorer, so that while displaying his disgust as often as he could he did it so sneakingly and so evidently with the intention of hiding it from the object, while making it plain to the rest of the audience, that he lost the sympathy which he might otherwise have obtained had he smoked and drank fairly and given his opinion in a less refined and subtle style and more like a man.

Sailors are in general a most tolerant race, and will excuse a man who declines to join the social glass or pipe if it is principle which makes him object, but they abhor the namby-pamby gentleman who sits amongst them because he has nowhere else to sit, and gives as his reasons for abstaining that their fare is not of the quality to which he has been accustomed: they will endure a man even if he be a bully and braggadocio much longer than a sneering poltroon, therefore on the present occasion they, without objection, yielded to the iron dominion of the General, and sent the scientific gentleman into Coventry.

"When I was under the Brazilian Government, gentlemen," began the self-constituted chairman.

"You told us that one at Moresby, General," observed the undaunted Danby, puffing out some tobacco-smoke from the bau-bau he had learnt the use of within the last few days; "tell us about some other government."

"Sir! do you know that you are insulting a gentleman who has fought under every flag which has a nation left on the face of the globe—powerful enough to own such a thing as an insignia?"

"The black flag also, I suppose," irreverently put in Danby.

"No, sir, not the black flag, I make an exception of that and

137

also the German ensign; you are but a boy, sir, and it does not become a gentleman of my rank and fame to quarrel with a mere boy—pooh; yet, sir, had it been a man, ah, had it only been a man!"

The General poured himself out a large glass of whisky, looking at the same time unutterable things in the way of ferociousness.

"I suppose he would have been as largely multiplied by this time as the flags you have served under?" replied Danby calmly.

"He would, sir; I am glad that you know my nature so well; but, speaking of the Germans, no man of spirit could serve under that flag. I remember once when Prince Bismarck wrote offering me a commission, I replied—"

"Have you not got the letter about with you? I'd like to see the old man's autograph?"

"My solicitor has it along with the others which I received from the European heads of government."

"A great pity isn't it, General?"

"No, boy, General Flagcroucher requires no introduction to recommend him when he goes amongst strangers, his sword is enough."

"Warranted not to damage, I suppose," retorted Danby. "But what did you say to Bismarck?"

"It was just before the gates of Paris were closed that he asked me to lend my aid, finishing his epistle something after these words:—'The fame of your marvellous faculty of preserving your valuable life and looking so successfully after your bodily safety, through dangers which would extinguish most men, has reached me. Serving as you have done with such singular success under the different powers of Europe and abroad, have you never thought of placing Germany under a similar obligation? If the idea has not occurred to you, pray let me place it under your notice, with the addition that there is at present a vacancy near to ourselves in the army for the wielder of such a sword as yours.'"

"Very characteristic of the Prince," murmured the scientific explorer from his corner.

"Ah, I see you know the old man's style, brief and to the point, always to the point. I replied, with dignity, in a short note which I think was not unworthy of a military man as well as a gentleman: 'Sir, I have served under many flags, it is true, and I think with acknowledged success, but the causes in which I have distinguished were freedom and honour, not tyranny and usurpation.'"

"A very gentlemanly reply, I must say," answered the explorer.

"I think so, sir, without being an egotist."

"And after that, I suppose you defended the walls of Paris?"

"I did, sir. You have not, I dare say, before this had the honour of a real general drinking amongst you, but I like to be affable, it is always the mark of true greatness."

"Doubtless, General; but that is my glass you are taking up, your own is the one nearest to you, and empty," replied Danby, gently.

"The more honour I was about to confer upon you, my lad."

"I rather prefer the liquor, thank you, General."

Captain MacAndrews and Bowman were on deck, except when they paid a flying visit down to consult the charts: at this instant they both appeared for another observation.

"Where are we now, Captain?" inquired the General.

"Close to Round Head, I should say, General," replied the Captain. "Are you not thinking of turning in? it is late, and we are about to anchor if we can find a place."

"I'll have a breath of air first," responded the General, getting up and stretching his lank, six feet of consequence preparatory to moving.

"I'll join you in that proposal," said Danby, as he laid down his bau-bau and followed the General, while the explorer, glad to get to bed, complained of a splitting headache and sat where he was.

On deck, the air felt grateful after the lamp-heated and smoke-stuffed saloon, so they relighted their pipes and leaned against the taffrail enjoying that final smoke before bed.

"Are you not afraid of an attack here, Bowman," inquired Danby.

"Attack? certainly not, the natives are well used to white people about these parts," replied Bowman.

"Attack?" echoed the General, "who would care about a few savages when I am with you—Ha! by heavens, we are surrounded." And with these words the General made for the saloon steps with rather more speed than seemed warranted under the occasion.

"Hold on, General," said Danby, "don't leave us at this time, we look to you as our protector."

"Let me go, sir, I tell you, we must get under cover, these savages have poisoned spears," and with these words he wrenched his coat sleeves from Danby's grasp, and promptly darted below.

"Shut the doors at once, steward, the savages are out in force," they heard him cry from below, as they turned to where the canoes were coming.

It was Kupatele and her attendant, who, having recovered the recreant Toto, were now approaching in their canoes.

Bowman, seeing only two small canoes coming, replaced his revolver in his belt and hailed them.

"Hallo! there!"

"Beretana!" replied the clear voice of the merry Kupatele, as she drew alongside.

"Women," said Bowman. "It strikes me our hero of a hundred battles isn't much to be depended upon in an emergency."

"A tarnation coward," growled the skipper.

Meantime a rope was lowered, up which the women clambered, with the dripping wet Toto after them, and now stood on deck.

"What do you want?" asked Bowman, singling out Toto from his dress, as the most likely one to understand English.

"Tell him, Toto, that we require his help ashore," rapidly said Kupatele in the native tongue.

Toto saw his chance, and took advantage of it instantly: here was the excuse for his coming out in the canoe alone.

"The mountain tribes are down fighting the men of Hula, and they have sent me to ask your protection."

"How far are we off?"

"A little way past that point, in another moment you will see the fires."

"Can you pilot us to Hula?" asked Bowman.

"Yes!" said Toto.

"Then let us on at once; return and say we are coming."

Toto interpreted to Kupatele, and added, "I knew they were coming, and that was why you saw me before you."

"I know, Toto," replied Kupatele. "Bring them quickly, and I'll not tell how frightened you were when we caught you, oh! cunning fish that you are."

With these words they once more scrambled over the side of the vessel, and darted away in front.

The General, hearing no signs of battle, now once more appeared with his historical sword girt to his waist-belt, and a brace of revolvers in his hand.

"Tactics of war, gentlemen," he observed, as he came towards them. "I went down to prepare myself—have you beaten off the enemy?"

"Yes!" replied Bowman. "So I suppose you are now prepared?"

"Thoroughly!"

"That is well, for we shall have some sharp fighting before long, I expect."

"What do you mean?"

"They are fighting ashore at Hula, and we are going to help

140

them," replied Bowman. "So you will have a good chance of distinguishing yourself."

"By God! I'll do nothing of the sort, sir, I have not come this length to sacrifice my life for a set of dirty savages."

"As you like; then you can stay on board and defend the ship."

"In the cabin, of course?" put in Danby.

"No, sir, we shall not go near the fight, you have no right, captain, to risk this steamer or endanger the lives of your passengers, and I forbid you to budge from where we are," replied the General, with great energy.

"When you are skipper here, you may do as you like, but at present I command on board the Thunder," retorted the old captain hotly, "and go we will, whether you like to fight or shut yourself in, and if you don't like these terms, by the Holy Moses, I'll lend you the dingey, and you can pull yourself back to Moresby."

"I refuse to go in such an unsafe boat as the dingey, let me have four of your men and the use of the whale boat, and I'll go at once."

"Go to the devil as you are," said MacAndrews, angrily turning away.

"You shall answer for this, sir, when we get ashore."

"When you like, and with what you like."

The skipper walked to the wheel, and the General to his former position of defence in the saloon, while the German engineer, with his usual snarl, put on the steam full speed.

All was now commotion on board, the Malay seamen got out their guns and cutlasses, Bowman and Danby went below to get out more cartridges, and prepare the explorer.

"Will you join us, or keep the General company?" Bowman asked him shortly.

"If my headache is gone, I'll join you."

"All right," and the two friends went once more on deck.

On, at the furious rate of about eight knots an hour, the "little hummer's" very fastest pace, the steamer ploughed and turned up the white forth behind her, filled with electric sparkles, while the female—propelled canoes flew in front, and very soon disappeared into the darkness. The captain was at the wheel, working under the guidance of Toto, who now felt quite reassured amongst the white fellow, and no longer doubtful about his return. So he stood calmly waving in the direction he wished them to take, and where he knew there was a deep passage between the shoals.

Round Head Point looked up dimly as they skirted it, and then the village fires became visible. They were lower than when

Toto saw them last, and objects in the distance were not so distinct. The houses with their piles looked softer and blended more into the general ruddy effect; from the canoes on the waters between them and the shore, the faint sounds of conch-shells, and beating of drums were wafted.

Nearer, and the figures in the canoes could be discerned, while the din became louder, preventing them from hearing anything from the shore.

Shrieks and wild cries of welcome from the women as the canoes darted right and left to permit the Thunder to pass, while that one which held Hena kept up with them, while a rope was thrown for him to catch, by which they were towed alongside while he got on board.

On shore the clamour could now be heard distinctly, and a wild tossing of dark figures could be seen in front of the fires, while yells and shrieks uprose above the shrill tones of the women who had laid down their drums and conch-shells to keep up with the steamer.

"Heave to and anchor here," said Toto, "you must row the rest of the way."

"Out with the long-boat!" and as the anchor touched ground, Bowman, Danby, the two engineers, and four of the sailors had leaped in and taken up the oars. As they were about to cast off, the explorer came on deck with his revolvers.

"Are you coming?" cried Bowman.

"Of course," replied the explorer, getting in.

"Where is the General?"

"Sulking or skulking in the cabin."

"Umph!"

"Hold hard a moment," bawled out the captain, scrambling over the side and heavily dropping down upon Danby, nearly squashing that fragile young gentleman.

"You hold hard, old hippopotamus," gasped the youth, struggling from beneath him.

"Saved my old bones a second time," grunted the captain, settling himself on the stern.

Hena had gone over into his canoe before the anchor dropped, and was now yards in advance.

"Pull away, lads, and a cheer for old England," shouted the captain, and with a ringing British cheer they went at it with their backs to the fray, as their oars drove the yielding waters tuggingly aside.

A sudden blackness falls over the scene, they have replenished the fires on shore, and the wood has not yet caught fire.

The women are coming on with a wild clamour of shrieks, so that the yells on shore are drowned to the ears of the excited sailors.

Light again burst out like brilliant sunshine, as the boat is run aground.

"We can now see what we are about," cried the old skipper, as with an axe in his clenched fist, he plunged into the shallow waters. "No fighting in the dark for me, as at Yule Island."

They were all floundering up to the knees by this time, with their faces to the fight, rushing as fast as they could to the dry land.

The battle was evidently over as they touched dry land, whoever had conquered, for a handful of men were flying towards them with empty hands, with the conquerors behind them, braining them as they caught them up.

"Fire in the air," cried Bowman, and a volley belched out, which brought both pursued and pursuers to a sudden halt.

Then the unarmed handful of about a dozen came on, and with the abjectness of despair, flung themselves on the sands, face downwards, at the feet of the Thunder party, and lay waiting their doom.

It was the last remnant of the marauding hill-tribe.

Chapter XXVIII
A Boat Voyage

HECTOR and Collins were, after all, fated to get their vessel towed into the river as they had hoped, not an easy task in this land of cruel surprises, when, for all they knew to the contrary, their landing may have been watched by unseen crafty eyes; however, as far as their short survey entitled them to judge, this portion of the river was a low-lying, swampy, fever-infested, but uninhabited jungle.

Mud was the most plentiful provision of nature—mud, black and slimy—from which the scrubby mangroves cropped up and swarmed about in a serpentine fashion, with a barren level behind, devoid of any larger tree than low, unwholesome-looking bushes.

During this survey they started a drove of small kangaroo-rats, a few of which they secured while the rest scuttled away; also, as they wandered along the banks, at distant points they could see the unwieldy form of the alligator as he rose from his soft mud lair in the sun and flopped quickly out of sight into the deep water-hole; they could not get near enough to shoot, for these animals are very shy of human beings when in numbers, but they saw no snakes although it seemed just the place for them to be, nor did any bush-birds rise on the wing;—a deserted, silent, and forsaken shore; not any noise producer.

By sundown they had the vessel towed to the cove which they designed as a harbour, and made fast, both by her anchors and with strong wire ropes, to stumps on either side of the river. Of course they could not hide her, even if they desired such a thing, but as they had resolved to risk her during their absence to whoso chanced to come that way, they only took ordinary precaution against the wind or tide carrying her away, and left the rest in the hands of Providence.

An anxious night passed, but without incident; all through it they were buried in the midst of a dense white, bone-chilling river fog, which made them glad to see the sun when at last it broke through and scattered the mist, although it took a good hour of hard exertion to get the blood warmed up.

At mid-day they were ready to start on their journey, having put up what provisions they could carry into separate packs, so much to each man, after which they made their observations, and, as far as they could judge from the sextant and chart, fixed their locality.

They had drifted considerably west of Mai-Kassa, in one of the smaller outlets of the Fly River, as yet unnoted on their chart.

"I tell you what, old chap," observed Hector, "we cannot do better than stick to our small boat and pull up as far as we can, it looks pretty clear, as far as we can judge, and from its course should take us into the Fly about Ellengowan Island."

"Right you are, mate; I'd have proposed the same thing; it is easier to travel that way, and we can stow a deal more away."

So in about half an hour all were ready, and after a hasty dinner of what was left on board, they started on their journey.

"I reckon the natives won't find much to steal on board, even if they do visit this part," said Hector, as they pulled round a bend of the river and saw the last of their little craft as the bushes covered her up.

The estuary which they had now entered seemed to be one of many mouths of a considerable-sized river, for after rowing along for an hour or two with little change of scenery, the mangroves began to grow thinner on the banks, with interspaces through which they had glimpses of country beyond.

Flat stretches of uneven country, with sand diversified with scrubby—grey patches of grass, or oily-looking swampy places, where the stagnant water was constantly evaporating under that blazing sun, and sending forth noisome gases which crept over the surface of the river unseen except for the quivering of the atmosphere by day, and gathering into those miasma vapours during the night.

Both Hector and Collins were well inured to the coast fever of these undrained shores, while the coloured boys with them do not seem to be so quickly inoculated by fever germs as Europeans; still that all felt the deadly and insidious influence more or less the apathetic strokes of the oars proved.

While the mangrove forests lasted this lazy feeling seemed harder to resist, while to continue conversation or even reply to questions seemed to be too great an effort for the tongue to make; they lighted their pipes only to let them go out again, and worked their oars as if they were playing with the water instead of pushing against it.

Still they made progress, for at this point the sea tide seemed much stronger than the river current, and it was on the rise as they started; so that it would have floated them inland even if they had rested entirely. As it was they aided the tide a little, while it did the rest to help them along.

Past those twisted and bare roots like snakes of various sizes coiled about one another, amongst that oozing inky mud which stained the briny greenish water which glided up after them to meet the sluggish fresh current; sun-bleached roots of the shade of those sea-snakes to be seen so often floating in the gulf when the seas are calm and clear met their gaze, with the turn they had rounded, and at the next bend blue like indigo and indefinite with the broad vagueness of that vaporous scumbling.

Past that deadly slime with the deep shadows behind cast by that raw green and blue black, amongst which large droves of rats scampered as they rushed dripping out of the brackish water, and made long ruts in their passage. At times also they rowed very near to the saurian monsters who were caught napping, and who woke up to see the uncommon sight just in time to be able to hobble down with awkward rollings, but in terrible consternation and haste, and with a wild splashing into the friendly tide, raising for yards about them foul stains of stirred-up mud, and leaving on the banks from where they had been disturbed a deep imprint in reverse of their mail-clad bodies.

Above them the sky was blue and cloudless, with the sun white and passionate in its intensity, but casting little colour upon the banks of rhizophora; the spot where it seemed specially to concentrate its full effulgence being the dingey in which they languidly moved their arms, and which appeared to float like a white splash upon the green-grey surface. Their line of vision was very circumscribed, they could see only a straight line of discoloured water, edged with mauve-like banks of purple slime, broken up with distorted limbs and ropes of exposed roots, which crossed and recrossed amongst the mud banks and unreflecting waters, and terminated in that wilderness of unkempt greenery.

No wind came to fan their throbbing heads now that they were shut in from the sea, while perfect clouds of insect life—tiger mosquitoes, and gnats—hung around them, dinning into their ears their savage war—cries, and biting till the blood came, even through their thick flannel shirts.

"I wouldn't mind much to be out of this, Collins," observed Hector, taking off his hat to strike a circle of his tormentors.

"They do bite," replied Collins, striking upon his cheek with his open hand; "make us active whether we will or not, but I fancy another half—hour will clear us of this jungle."

"It is clearing; make way, lads, before the tide turns," he added, addressing the rowers.

A little more energy was here put into the oarstrokes, and they moved faster round the bend and into an open space.

Hitherto the estuary had been turning left and right alternately, yet still tending north-easterly in its general direction, with narrow and shaded creeks leading from it, amongst the mangroves. But now they were approaching a large basin, round which the bushes grew very scarce and undersized, leaving large tracks of mud and sand between, the mud clinging mostly about its favourite roots.

A shallow basin of spreading, mud-disturbed water, in which the dingey continually struck against stumps, or ran aground and had to be pushed off again into the central stream, which they could not always see to follow.

Here they could look down upon the mangrove fringe which hid the ocean from them, and breathe more freely, as across the flats they got the benefit of the ocean breeze, before which the ruthless hordes of mosquitoes were driven back to their twilight haunts, although a few daring ones still clung swinging on their long thin legs to the sheltered sides of hats and shirts.

In this basin they rested to ascertain which was the true river, for the tide here evidently met the current on equal terms. All round about them were wide openings, some distinctly leading to the ocean, while others tended inland, to meet the river further up.

After a few experiments with some pieces of wood, which they floated to find out which estuary had the strongest inland current, they decided upon the one verging the most westward as being the true one, almost at random.

"It cannot go far west," cried Collins, "it must back on its course and join the Fly somewhere." So westward they rowed with a fresh breeze behind them and banks growing firmer and more sloping as they advanced.

Soon the sun went down full in the backs of the rowers, and dead in the face of Collins, who was steering;—a golden orb, which sank behind distant trees, the purple tops of which only they saw beyond the banks, which were every mile becoming higher, and more diversified in their character; in parts leading off into large tracts of dense forest-land, while at others they had a clear outline of sky behind, with an occasional gum or cotton-tree stretching out bare limbs.

At dark they brought up against the first sign of natives, namely about a dozen deserted hut-graves, which had been built on a flat portion of the banks—silent huts standing up grimly against the twilight, and slowly going to pieces on their piles. Scarcely a roof but was broken in parts, with the frame-work showing under the dropping thatch, proving that they had not been used since before the last rains.

A background of sombre forest stretched out behind a clearing of about half-a-mile of grass-covered plain, the grass being green and rank like rushes growing over a swamp, and here and there were traces of what had once been gardens, but the old banana-trees had all been destroyed so that only young shoots were springing up, not yet the length for bearing fruit.

"A big fight has been here at one time," said Collins, looking round, "and one tribe the less in New Guinea! I think we'll be safe enough to roost here for the night."

They made their boat fast to one of the posts of an old landing-place, and all got out, glad enough to stretch their cramped arms and legs, the Malay boys carrying the provisions, and the two leaders going about examining the houses in order to fix upon the most habitable one for sleeping-quarters. At last they decided upon one a trifle less dilapidated than the others, and set to work clearing it out from its present tenants, the fire-dried mummies of a family of five, the mother and four children evidently, with the remains of what might have been the grandmother; but the father evidently had been killed in the open, and his carcase utilized another way, as they saw no trace of him about.

With little ceremony they cleared out these relics of humanity, pitching them carelessly from the platform where they lay half sticking out from the dank grass, like pieces of charred logs. The cooking utensils, spears, and decaying pieces of matting they huddled into a corner, spreading out their own blankets instead.

After these preparations were complete they went down to their boat, and dragging it amongst the long grasses further to shore, covered it up so that it would not be easily seen from the opposite bank—at this space a distance of about thirty feet.

After a brief discussion, it was thought best not to light a fire, in case in the darkness—now gathering fast—enemies might be about and see it; so they contented themselves for the night with filling their billies from the river and qualifying their drink with a little of the rum which they had brought; this, with ship biscuit and a tin of preserved meat, constituted their supper, after which each lit his pipe and laid himself down on his blanket, puffing in silence, with the exception of one of the coloured boys, who had been appointed to the first watch.

Hector and Collins were old and good friends, but they were both quietly inclined, not much given to speaking at the best of times, but thoroughly appreciating and understanding each other's qualities, and the good faith which was between them; they knew one another's stories, and having no fresh plans to air, lay in a harmonic silence, looking through the rugged doorway towards the darkly clear sky, from which the crescent moon—a thin half-ring—was now shining with her attendant star, with the sleepy contentment of the smokers. Outside, by the corner of the platform, the Malay sailor squatted listening and watching.

"Whirr!" A flying fox darted past his broad nose and startled the watcher. It had come from the forest on the other side of the river, and was going to old haunts in the destroyed native garden.

The night was warm as yet, but before long the sea-breeze died away and the night-air sighed amongst the bushes and brought on its wings the valley-fogs, which sailed down the river's breast and spread over the banks until the land was veiled in white and the posts of the platform seemed to be rising out of water.

A low snorting and moving about at the foot of the posts startled him once more into wakefulness.

"Boss Collins, some one outside," he whispered, creeping inside on all fours and putting his mouth close to the ear of his master.

Collins raised himself up on his elbow to listen.

"Wild pigs grubbing after the corpses. Take one of the spears over there in the corner and let drive in the direction of the grunts, you may kill something for breakfast; but whether you strike or miss, don't shoot."

And the skipper lay down once more on his back, sucking away at his dead pipe.

The watcher passed over to the corner and groped about till his hand encountered a bundle of spears which had been left to guard the mummies, from which he selected three, and creeping out silently, sat down to listen spear in hand.

The snorting and snuffing still continued at the foot of the posts, so taking as fair aim as he can judge from the locality of the sounds, he pitches his three spears in quick succession, the action at once followed by a chorus of unearthly shrieks and a stampede of many cleft hoofs in the direction of the forest, the chorus growing fainter as they reach it, while at the foot of the posts he can hear a sound like an asthmatic fat woman gasping for breath.

He has evidently wounded more than one of the herd by those chance javelin-throws, and wounded one to the death.

Collins hears the sound also, and comes to the door stretching himself lazily.

"There snorts our breakfast if I don't much mistake. Get me some more of the spears, lad, and let's finish him."

The Malay gets a couple more from the inside, the others never stirring, although he treads over them as he passes and half crushes an arm under his naked foot. Sailors wake only when their watch is up, or when they are called to face a danger.

Armed with the spears, Collins feels his way down the ladder and over to where the sounds are still continuing.

When he thinks himself near enough he lunges out, going wide of the mark the first and second stabs, but being rewarded by a gurgling shriek the third, upon which he draws back his barbed spear and plunges again and again without any response; the snorting is no longer heard.

"Come down and help me, Jack," he says, as he stumbles forward and gropes about for his victim. He feels along the spear to where it is still sticking till he comes to the object.

"Ugh!" His hand touches the shrivelled-up breast of the dead woman, in which the point of his spear is sticking, so with that exclamation of disgust he feels more towards the left.

"Here it is, Jack," as his hand rests against the warm skin of the wild pig. "A fine young fellow, and just heavy enough to be tender. Catch hold of his leg behind there and haul away; he can bleed from the platform, where the ants won't get at him before morning."

They drag the limp carcase up the ladder and lay it out across the planks, after which Collins goes back to his blanket, wiping his wet hands against his trousers, while the Malay boy squats once more to watch beside the pig and keeps himself awake by counting the drops of blood as they drip from the platform spaces with distinct splashes into the pools which they are making on the ground below.

Chapter XXIX
A Tribe of Butchers

THE next morning our explorers lit a fire while the heavy mists still hung about, and cutting some chops from their prize, roasted them on the embers and made a hearty breakfast, after which they carefully extinguished the fires by pouring water over and then scattering the ashes; which done, they lay about on the logs smoking and waiting on the clearing up.

"I wonder how much further west the river means to go!" remarked Hector, in his quiet way, as he watched his pipe-wreaths curl up and get lost amongst the silver mist which the sun was now making luminous.

"Not much longer, else I won't follow it; half a day longer will decide," responded Collins. "But let us all get under shelter before the mist clears; who knows what we may be able to see once it rises."

It was prudent advice, which they all followed. When sitting inside the shadow of the hut they were able to command all sides of them from the doorway or the log aperture.

The sky above, meanwhile, seemed shot with gleams of rose and faint turquoise blue, while pale yellow rays began to pierce through the gauze curtain, which seemed to be lifting up layer by layer.

Butterflies in many varieties fluttered about and caught the sun-rays; they came from and dashed again into that silvery vagueness, with river—flies on long, transparent wings, which glistened with prismatic flashes as they darted about—a scene of fairyland luminous with light and teeming with insect life and joyance.

The grass at their feet first became visible for yards round them, spreading with the fresh greenness of early spring as the billows of light seemed to race after the mist-wreaths and drive them up amongst the clouds.

Then they saw the landing-place, where lay their boat concealed, and next the river, like quicksilver, from which columns of steam seemed to be curling and rolling along.

The opposite banks come into view, and then the forest,

hazy and fresh, looms upon the sight, and they may resume their journey whenever they please.

"Hold on, boys, don't go out," said Collins, in as soft a voice as he can get his shrill pipe to emit, as he looks through a crevice towards the inland bush. "Do you see the devils?"

Hector applies his eyes to the side Collins is looking from, as do the others, and all watch intently the sight which meets their gaze.

Three natives have broken from the forest and are flying along the further edge of the swamp, while behind them follow about a dozen of their enemies, armed with that terrible weapon, the man-trap.

It is a short run across that open space, yet the hunters are too much for the hunted. Tall men are those who pursue, and darker in colour than the men who run in front.

A second or two of excitement for those who are watching, and then it is over; the man-traps are thrown outward with unerring aim, and with one shriek, which seems prolonged, the victims are down, and the hunters surround them, hacking them up as they kneel down to finish off their gruesome work.

"Do you know them?" whispers Hector huskily.

"Of course, we have both met them afore, though never so far west. The Butcher tribe of New Guinea."

From the forest now appeared about thirty or forty fighting-men, with skins glittering in the distance like polished ebony, and enormous tufts of hair adorned with the beak of the horn-bill, their shields on their backs, and with spears and man-traps over their shoulders; some of them walked in single file, carrying, slung from long poles, huge baskets. They were all above the average size of men, while the leader appeared to be a gigantic fellow.

These are the professional butchers of New Guinea, who have no fixed abode, but hunt men as sportsmen do game, as a regular occupation. They have no partiality, but take all that they can catch, cutting up the victims and disposing them amongst the different tribes for barter.

"They appear to have a good stock in their baskets," remarked Hector, as the party reached the first group, and called a halt.

"Yes," murmured Collins, watching them intently. "By the Lord, they are going to breakfast on fresh beef!"

Firewood had been collected by this time, and lighted, for the large columns of smoke rose up from the group squatting round, tired out evidently with their morning walk, while they could see the bau-baus or native pipes handed round amongst those who were not occupied with cutting up the victims or cooking. No one amongst them seemed to glance towards these huts; probably they knew all about what they had hitherto contained, and felt more disposed for fresh than dried beef.

As the sailors gazed, they could see the huge pieces flung upon the glowing and blazing embers, while the cooks watched them broiling, turning them about with their spear-points, and, when ready, lifting them out, and falling to the feast with teeth and nails sans cérémonie.

The gigantic chief seemed to have no precedence beyond what his superior strength gave him. He made a grab at what appeared to be a breast-piece, knocking the native who had taken it up over on his back, and, without appearing to take any other notice of him, bent his massive head like a dog and commenced to devour.

"Now is our time to get away," whispered Collins. "Let us slide quietly while they are busy."

"I wish we were near enough to get a shot at the beasts," said Hector savagely, as he seized one of the bundles of provisions, slipped his revolver back into his belt and prepared to go.

"Not I; the deed is done, and we might be the next, although they don't much relish white flesh," responded Collins. "You slip down with the boys, and get out the boat, while I watch."

"All right."

"Gently does it, boys; don't stir the reeds more than you can help."

Very softly each of the men dropped over the platform, and crept on all-fours through the long grass towards the boat, dragging their provisions after them, while Collins kept his eyes at the log crevice, turning now and then to mark their progress.

The boat is got safely out, and all are seated before Collins leaves his post; then, with a last look at the unconscious cannibals, he slips out and takes his place.

Between them and the next group of bushes lie only a few yards of open space; but the grass is long, so they traverse the distance safely, and then draw a long breath of relief as they straighten up their backs and pull softly, but with steady, strong strokes, on their way.

"Keep well under the bushes, lads; for we don't know who may be on the other side."

Along the stream they glided, with the morning beams slanting down upon the pallid faces of the frightened Malays as they drew their long oars firmly through the waters, which glanced and sparkled about the stern of the boat. Being well-trained sailors they made no crabs or splashing, but feathered the blades as they drew them back without raising them above the surface.

Silently they glided, with the river behind glowing like a molten furnace, and in front softly subdued into tones of delicious grey. They were passing a reach which the flowering trees overhung and where rushes and floating leaves lined the shores, while tendrils hung down in green showers, clustering with coral-tinted blossoms, and rare orchids whose exquisite perfume filled the rarefied atmosphere.

They turned over lilies with their near oars, and tore up threads of plant-roots, which floated behind them like tresses of golden and red hair, while the river flies of all sizes, from minute white-winged, ant-like insects to the great dragon-fly, hovered about them in myriads. Wings and buds of all the hues which aesthetic painters love to blend, crossed one another and intermixed in chastest harmony, while the sailors glided on into a phantasmagoria of loveliness and peace, yet bearing with them the horror of that awful carnage behind.

Before them, through this arch of loveliness, they can see a long vista of dreamy haze banks rising, with sloping sides in portions where land—slips have taken place, gleaming white and red, with the under-bed of clay or sandstone, and a confusion of weeds, flowers, and stony boulders lying about. The river banks change gradually as they advance, and appear, as far as they can see, to be inclining towards the right.

They had now got about a couple of miles from the huts, and would soon emerge once more into the open.

"Hold hard a spell!" said Collins at this stage. "We had better land here and prospect a bit before we venture outside."

They drew their boat under the bushes, where they were unseen, and remained for a little time in quietness, with ears on the alert for noises in front or behind.

All seemed peace except the sound of insect wings, or the flutter amongst the dense leafage overhead of uneasy birds, as they drew into the shelter.

The droning peace of a tropic morning with beauty and destruction on the wing.

Then all at once that gentle quiet is shattered by the one discordancy which over breaks upon the harmony of Nature—the frantic howling and yelling of man, enraged and thirsting to do evil.

Distant sounds of warfare from the place which they have left.

"What is up now, I wonder?" uttered the matter-of-fact Collins. "Has their grub disagreed with the devils?"

"More likely another tribe come across them resting, and

paying them out for their own darned treachery," replied Hector, as he bent his head in the direction of the turmoil.

"Yes, that is it," he resumed. "By Jove, I'd give five pounds to see the sport!"

"Let us see it, then," answered his friend. "We can get near enough to see it before they wind up, I daresay, without being noticed in their excitement."

"Done. Take two or three of the dynamite bombs; they may come in handy to decide the question."

The Malays, frightened though they were, could not be persuaded to stay behind their leaders; so, fastening the dingey and blazing a tree trunk to mark the locality, they all stole out, Collins carrying his Winchester and brace of revolvers, and Hector, besides his arms, a small—sized bomb charged with dynamite, while the boys followed with some more charges.

They did not find much trouble in working their way along the banks, as the foliage, although in parts closely knitted, was of a parasitical nature, and easy to break through, while they went cautiously, but straight for the scene of action, guided by the cries and yells which every foot of ground grew stronger as they approached.

The tempest of carnage had evidently caused a great excitement amongst the feathered denizens of the upper branches; for, every few moments, as the men pressed onwards, the swift whirl of the paradise bird or flapping of the wood-pigeon, could be heard as they broke from their cover and sought more secluded places on the further shore. Once or twice the men caught a passing glimpse of the gorgeous plumage and sweeping red-brown tails as the birds crossed the open interspaces above. Once or twice also they saw the glimmer of a large snake gliding out of their way, and the ungainly rolling of an iguana amongst the snapping twigs and undergrowth, while hordes of ants fell upon them, resenting their intrusion on that virgin domain, causing even the mild Hector to grind out a low oath between his clenched teeth.

"Some one has won the day," said Collins, as much of the fury died out of the din, but the clamour was succeeded by a great crushing in the not very far distance, as of a head of cattle breaking through the brushwork.

"By the Lord, they are coming this way! To cover, lads, as best you can!"

Collins set a very rapid example by seizing hold of a strong tendril near to his hand, and drawing himself up amongst the leafage with the dextrous celerity of a sailor, an example which the others did not fail to follow as best they could, leaving their bombs on the ground.

They had hardly concealed themselves before the branches were forced aside, and five or six natives similar to the three before noticed broke through in a panic of fear, with about an equal number of the black—skinned Butchers behind.

"Shoot the devils down!" shouted out Collins, forgetting his caution, as he covered his prey, and at the word from both sides belched forth the deadly fire, and four of the hunters fell to the ground, while the others stood with gaping mouths at this fire from heaven, both hunted and hunters.

Then the two remaining black-skins recovering first with a bound leapt back into the shelter of the woods, while the others, now with odds in their favour, plucking up courage, once more reversed positions, and plucking the spears from the dead men's grasp, made again after the flying pair, never pausing to see who had befriended them, but intent on vengeance only.

"Nothing like gratitude," said Collins, leaping from his perch. "Let us go after them and see the finale; pick up the bombs, we may need them yet."

The track was wide enough now for the explorers to follow, so two abreast they dashed along, and in a few more seconds had reached the outer belt of trees, with the swamp in front, and the scene of battle spreading out.

"Gently, now, or we may fall into the trap ourselves," observed Collins, halting under the trees, and going cautiously forward to where he could see without being seen.

"Hallo! there lie the two who escaped our bullets," he said, as he held aside the branch and peered out, "stabbed in the back. But where can our late friends have got to?"

The two blackskins had been caught just at the open, and had fallen face forwards on to the plain, and now lay with both hands clutching at the grass-roots, with gaping spear-wounds behind, but not a sign of the five natives who had killed them.

Over between the fire and where they stood the ground was covered with dead bodies, lying about in all directions and in all positions, black and brown, while half-way to the fire had gathered the remainder of the Butchers, about twenty, surrounding what appeared to be some prisoners.

"Surely the fools have not been caught already," remarked Collins, as he looked over the scene. "However, we must help them out of the mess, if we can, now we are here. What say you, old man?"

"Of course, old man; we can't leave the poor wretches now to be cut up, so let's steal round the bush a bit till we are nearer them."

It was perilous work to get near to them without being

heard or seen, yet the two men felt that they could not now forsake those unlucky natives, whom they had already, at the risk of their lives, befriended, so, with cautious steps, they crept round the forest edge, looking out at the natives every time the leafage was clear enough to see through.

Four of the five natives were now left in the midst of their enemies, bound in the arms by strong withes. They were being driven forward toward the fire by the others with harsh cries and heavy blows, the blood staining their brown skins in several places.

The Butchers also seemed to be all more or less wounded, so that it must have been a savage and pretty evenly-matched battle at the beginning, and dearly won, although now the blacks had come off victors some of them trailed their limbs along the ground painfully, and seemed with difficulty to be able to raise their arms to strike the captives; yet that did not make them any the less vengeful in their efforts.

"Boss Collins, let us go back; black fellow all same. Going to roast brown fellow, you see."

Yes, it seemed that such was the atrocious intention of the Butchers, for as Collins and Hector got nearly opposite to the fire, they saw some of the savages busily engaged roping their prisoners to the bleached trunk of a dead gum-tree, which stood with forked branches on the margin of the swamp, while the others were busily scattered about gathering firewood.

Some of the wood-collectors came very close to where the party stood watching them, while they stood ready to fire, but none came near enough to discover them, so that they were allowed to take back their load.

"Had we not better make our rush now and free the poor fellows," said Hector, who seemed impatient to begin the fray.

"No," replied Collins. "Let them all be together, then our shots will take more effect. We must let none of the demons escape to alarm the country now that we are in for it."

"So, so," remarked Hector. "You give the word of command, only I hope we won't kill our friends as well as our enemies."

"That will just have to be as it happens," replied Collins, grimly.

"Are the bombs handy?"

"Here they are."

"Be ready to light one, Jack, and when I give the word the rest pick out his man, aiming from the eastern edge of the crowd inwards as you stand; that will make those we don't hit start in a body from the stake. Then, before they have time to spread, pitch it clear amongst them, and the game is our own."

"Right, mate."

"Now, Jack, light the fuse."

Jack obeyed with silent and methodical unconcern, as if it was a pipe of tobacco he had been asked to light, and now stood with the bomb in his hand blowing on the fizzing match.

"Fire, boys!"

Four well-aimed shots blazed forth with almost one report, and for an instant the smoke prevented them seeing the result. When the white puffs cleared from before their eyes they saw four prostrate figures, with the others skurrying panic-stricken in a huddled mass westward, with the prisoners left alone bound to the tree.

"Hand me that lighted bomb, and set another going quick."

It was nearly burnt down as Collins seized it, and with all his might sent it spinning in the direction of the flying crowd.

A moment it spun through the air like a tennis-ball, then it dropped about ten yards on the other side of the running group now beginning to scatter.

"The other one!"

Again the lighted ball went through the air, landing between the stake and the Butchers.

A second as the band hurried on towards the first ball, then the sound as of a rock blasting as they seemed to be beaten back by a dense volume of smoke which quickly hid them from sight.

Another explosion, as the second bomb burst, made the earth tremble under their feet, while bits of clay and dead wood seemed to be flying about, and a blinding shower of mud came pattering down upon their faces, while the field was rolling with white clouds, and only cries of affright or agony could be heard from its midst.

"That will about do the trick, I fancy," said Collins, putting another charge into his Winchester. "When this smoke clears we'll polish off the rest, if there are any left; when the time comes to kill it is the worst policy to leave one to peach."

The smoke rolling westward revealed the gum-tree first, with the four prisoners struggling madly to release themselves from their bondage, and apparently almost frantic with horror at this awful visitation. They were unhurt by the explosion, although spattered with slush from the swamp, which had been cast up high into the air and rained down again; but the old tree had suffered severely in its top branches.

As the air cleared about the scene of the disaster it could be seen that Collins had done his work of destruction with expedience and method, for only scattered remnants of humanity covered the field, while the ground presented the aspect of an earthquake. Not one of the Butcher tribe was left to carry the wonderful news about, and not a few were as completely dismembered as if some of their own craft had been at work.

A sickening picture, with the black earth sucking in the hot red blood, and the fierce mid-ray licking up the rank fumes.

As they broke from their cover, yellow flames burst from the pile of wood gathered around the captives—the blacks had fired the wood before the first shots had chased them to their doom.

To draw out their sheath-knives and rush towards the tree was the first impulse of Collins and Hector. Another moment and the prisoners were dragged through the smoke and flames, and laid dazed and helpless, but not otherwise hurt, beyond a slight scorching and a mighty fright.

"What can we do with these poor devils?" said Collins, ruefully looking down at their prostrate figures. "I don't like to kill defenceless men, and yet it would be the best way of squaring matters both for ourselves and them."

"Let us take them with us," replied Hector; "they may show us our road to the Fly."

"Perhaps, yet they are none of them to be trusted, although we must not let them loose till we are safe ourselves."

So it was settled, and again tying up their arms behind their backs, they raised them to their feet, and, pointing to the forest, pushed them along.

Both men knew some native words, but the captives were either too much stunned with their late adventures or else belonged to some inland tribe with a totally different language, for they did not reply, or seem to comprehend what was said to them, but limped along painfully in the direction indicated with that apathetic air which signifies the resignation of hope in a native breast.

As they left the field of death they observed the first of nature's scavengers, in the form of a large vulture, swoop down from the blue space above, while away in the far distance was a line of dark specks rapidly becoming larger.

Through the broken-down pathway of the forest they retraced their steps, and soon reached their boat, into which they pushed their apathetic prisoners, and then, shoving out from the drooping branches, swiftly pulled past the forest and into open country once more.

The natives sat where they had been placed, never looking up or showing interest in any action from those on board.

After an hour of hard rowing they all laid to, being thoroughly fagged out and ready for dinner; so at a sign from Collins they put in to shore, and, landing, set about lighting a fire to boil their billies.

An open country, still flat or only slightly hilly, but grass covered, with here and there a solitary tree—a good part for game, such as kangaroos, but without a sign of habitations.

But the river was decidedly tending towards the west; a turn to the cast now and again filled them with hope, to be again disappointed as they could not but observe its general direction.

"What are we to do next, captain?" observed Hector, looking up, while they were drinking their tea Australian fashion, with their biscuit and tinned mutton.

"I think, while the boys rest a bit, you and I will go and hunt for an hour against to-night's supper, after which we'll keep on till dark as we are, and consider the matter then."

The natives by this time had somewhat recovered themselves, and were eating the pieces of biscuit handed to them. They spoke in a language unknown to the explorers as they ate, and seemed to be fairly contented with their present position, their hands being now freed to show that they were guests rather than prisoners.

Thus while the Malays rested, and having given them minute instructions to watch closely the opposite shore, now not much more than fifteen feet distant, and not lose sight of their captives, the two friends went out on their hunt.

After an hour or two of hunting they came back fairly successful, having bagged a cassowary and a couple of small kangaroos.

The natives expressed great delight at their success, and proved themselves useful by skilfully skinning the game. They laughed loudly as they divided the feathers of the cassowary amongst them, tying each bundle up, and slinging them over their backs, showing no desire to run away as they once more took their places in the boat.

Undersized men they all were, of a pale bronze tint, with smooth faces and somewhat delicate features, but their dark eyes were deep-set and close together.

After a time the Malays, growing tired, handed their oars to the natives, and by signs taught them how to use them. They were by this time great friends with one another, and took to their work with great cheerfulness, learning in a surprisingly short time to use them fairly well.

A burst of laughter rose from them when one of them made a crab and went backwards, head over heels, letting go his oar, which began to float down the river.

A laugh in which the unfortunate one joined heartily himself, until he saw his oar in the stream, on which, without a pause, he plunged over the side, quickly recovering it, and swimming back again to his place.

As he climbed over the side, the long snout and dull eye of a large crocodile popped up, and, evidently satisfied that his intended supper had escaped him, disappeared again under the surface before they could get a stroke at him.

"Let us stop for the night," cried out Collins, as the shadows were growing purple, "I've had about enough of this stream."

They brought up to the bank at a point where it seemed composed of stones and dried-up shrubs, and gathering enough firewood to start their fire, set themselves to work cooking the cassowary.

A look round the country from the top of the bank convinced them that all was clear; away to the west appeared a range of far-distant hills lying faintly blue at the end of a vast plain, with hardly a tree to be seen; the opposite shore also was stone and grass-covered as far as they could see, with a spreading campaign all round.

The river had no connection with the Fly, for it was gradually growing less. It had shallow parts from which stones and boulders protruded, but still was deep enough to float the boat. It had a more rapid current, which made it harder work to pull the boat. It was clearly a distinct river, as yet unnamed, and fed from those distant ranges.

"By Jove, Collins, this beats the Fly; what say you to following it up?"

"I wouldn't mind if we were better prepared; it would be some news to take back to Thursday Island."

"Let's christen it, at all events, for it is our discovery."

"What shall we call it?"

"Oh, after you, old man, of course, hand you down to posterity. Call it 'The Collins River.'"

Collins demurred with becoming modesty; but Hector carried the question, the Malays agreeing to whatever they agreed, and the natives laughing and showing their betel-blackened teeth at the fun which they saw going on about them.

A pleasant evening, in which all were boisterously inclined, while the rum circulated, the natives turning with wry faces when it was offered, but lovingly patting the backs of their new-found friends, as they gravely puffed out of their borrowed pipes.

At last the "Collins River" was duly marked down on their charts and named, and setting himself to the first watch while the rest laid themselves down on the ground to sleep, Collins filled his pipe afresh and prepared himself for a good two hours' reflection.

It is a pleasant thing to have a book dedicated to one, or a river named after one. Captain Collins felt it so, and thoroughly pleased with himself as he sat down and puffed at his pipe, watching the stars come out one by one, and the crescent moon lift up like a boat floating upon a deep green sea.

"By the Lord, but I have been asleep," exclaimed Collins, rubbing his eyes as he started up with a shiver, to see the midnight stars serenely shining from the blackness, and hear only the sucking sound of the current as it swept round the stones.

"Hector, are you all right, mate?"

"All right, mate," said Hector, getting out of his blanket and stretching himself. "Hullo, the devil! Where are the natives?"

Ay, where? Jack and the other Malay boys roused up and looked about them stupidly while their leader flew round.

"Damn the ongrateful scoundrels, they have stolen the boat," cried Collins, savagely, from the river side. "I knew we ought to have potted them with the other niggers."

"Well, that settles our minds as to exploring the Collins River," replied Hector. "We shall now have to strike across country."

"With only a single round of cartridges and our revolver, our provisions and rifles were in the boat?"

"Might have been worse if they had brained us," retorted Hector. "Turn in, old man, till morning; time enough to growl then."

Chapter XXX
The Coming Home of the Fleet

"IF an apology will serve, General, here's my hand, and I beg your pardon and grant your grace."

"No, sir, apology won't do, you have insulted me on your own deck and served me a shabby trick, leaving me behind—a confoundedly savage trick, and what is an apology?"

"I am sorry, General, but—"

"Sorry be——"

And the General glared over at the half-tipsy skipper, as he brought his hand with a military smash down on the frail table in the house of Toto, making the glasses spin again, and the table to stagger like a drunken man.

It was the afternoon after the entry into Hula, and the General, in high dudgeon, had been paddled ashore by Ila. His honour had been outraged and himself made of little consequence, having had to breakfast with the engineer's assistant

161

only, all the others being ashore, where they had stopped after landing.

The General panted for the blood of a foe, having been disappointed the night previously, and now he bore down in full war panoply upon the poor old skipper, who, having been freely passing about cups, felt amiably inclined towards all men.

The remainder of the hill-tribe were now confined in Toto's house, which had been transformed for the present into a prison, where they were waiting to be moved on board the Thunder and taken to Moresby, to be tried according to Colonial law for their attempted raid.

Toto had come out much better from the affair than even he had dared, volatile though he was, to hope; through the dark hours of morning he sat in the saloon with the General, drinking bottled stout and whisky with him, each one capping the other's account of daring adventures with some tale more wonderful, until at last, when day dawned, it revealed the General lying on his back on the cabin floor, snoring profoundly, and dreaming doubtless of noble actions, while the gentle steward picked up the bottles and counted them carefully over. There being no one on board left to contradict him, he marks down on his slips some extra bottles; which done, he arranges his slips of paper and waits patiently on the waking of the great man, in order to present him with them and so render him happy.

It is this opportune moment which Toto takes for slipping into one of the canoes alongside and paddling himself ashore.

He avoids the groups of natives, male and female, who are busily engaged clearing the street from the dead, carrying those who have been friends into their own houses to wait the burial, and hustling the despised carcases of foemen up to the Dobu House to be dealt with afterwards as the chief and his white brothers will decide.

Meeting Kupatele, he gleans all the news from her, how Mavaraiko, the chief, and Kamo have both been severely wounded, and now lie together, nursed by Rea.

"But Kamo is an outlaw?"

"Oh, no; Kamo is the general favourite and hero of the hour; he has wiped out his faults with many lives. Ah! he is a big man now, my little Toto."

"Indeed!" sneers Toto.

"Yes; indeed, the Kavanah loves him as much as Rea does. You ought to have seen him fight last night, while you were running away; like an old warrior's, his club spun round, he saved the life of our chief when he would have been slain, taking the blow upon his own arm, poor fellow, but he is badly hurt, and it will take

Rea her full month of waiting before they marry, nursing him round."

"But what about me in all this?"

"Ah, you, they all laugh too much when the name of Toto is mentioned."

"Kupatele," cried Toto, seizing her arm, "you have told upon me."

"No, Toto, there were other eyes besides mine."

"Ah, true, then all my chances are gone?"

"Go away for a while, Toto, the great white Kavana of Moresby has heard of you and wants to see you, so the Beretana say."

"You would like me to go, Kupatele, wouldn't you?" said Toto with a leer of suspicion.

"No, Toto," faltered poor Kupatele.

"You fear lest I might tell your husband how you got the beads, Kupatele?"

"No, Toto, you would not."

"But I might, you know, if I was not a good fellow."

"But you are a good fellow, Toto."

"Kupatele, will you do what I ask you, if I promise to go away, and never come back?"

"Yes, Toto," eagerly replied the young woman.

"Then come to my house to-night, and I will give you something to rub on Kamo's wound to make it better."

Kupatele started back with a sudden horror in her usually laughing eyes, while Toto watched her with a sinister grin which revealed all his discoloured fangs.

"I shall look out for you, at the time you used to come, after the sun has gone down."

"No, Toto—not that."

"If you are not with me by the time the moon rises, I will come to your house and see your husband."

"I will come."

Kupatele had a stern, white face as she said the last words, and turned away without another word, walking steadily up the village, while Toto, with a long look after her, went in the direction of his own house.

Kupatele went on straight until she came upon a group of native women who were gathered about the well discussing the events of the night before. There were one or two amongst them whom she had in former days met in Toto's house of call.

"Have you seen Honkowa?" she asked of them.

"Poor Honkowa, she is down in her hut weeping for her man who was killed last night."

Kupatele went over to the hut owned by Honkowa, and entering, sat down to weep.

"Honkowa, we are friends?"

"Yes, Kupatele, but you know how we acted towards him who lies dead," and the poor widow covered her head and sobbed bitterly.

"It was Toto who made us what we are."

"Ay, always Toto, yet he is alive and unwounded."

"Would it not be well if Toto was dead?"

The women look earnestly on one another, then they fall to whispering quickly.

"Will they not all help us if we do it?"

"All the women who know him as we do, will," replied Hankowa.

"You get them together when they come to weep, and tell them what I have said, and bring them down to where the stream runs into the sea; I'll lure him out."

The widow returns to her task of weeping over her husband, while Kupatele goes back home with her filled water-can.

Toto finds his house occupied by the white party of the Thunder, and exerts himself with great success to play the host; from a secret hiding—place he produces some bottles of fiery gin, the Torres Straits special brand beloved of divers, and getting a few young cocoa-nuts, busied himself making grog for the company and ingratiating himself in their good graces.

"They say you can sing Kanaka hymns, Toto?" asked Bowman.

"Yes, sir, anything you like."

"Sing us a hymn," cries the Captain, and Toto gravely takes his well—thumbed hymn-book, and seating himself cross-legs on the floor, sings to them "The happy land."

"You are a sad blackguard, Toto," says Bowman.

"I think so, sir, very fair, all that same."

"And a great coward, Toto."

"Not a coward, sir, me very brave, like—like—"

Toto cannot hit upon a fair example all of a moment, Danby helps him.

"Like the Captain over there, eh?"

"No, sir," said Toto, making a droll face, and pointing over to where the Thunder lay moored, "like the General!"

A universal burst of laughter followed this sally of Toto, and he was at once established as a favourite.

They all sat drinking and talking until about midday, at which hour the gallant soldier made his appearance, sullen and disdainful.

"Have a tot, General?" asked Bowman, pushing the bottle towards him as he entered, but the General made no direct answer, stalking proudly over to the broad bamboo couch, upon which he flung himself with a force which made the wall shake, muttering under his moustache something about "low-bred cads."

"He is angry with you, Captain," remarked Danby; "I think you ought to apologise."

The skipper, now more than half-seas over, cocked his bleary blue eye in the direction of the couch, and stammered,—

"Cartainly, if it is necessary. I say, old cock of the walk, if so be as I have offended you in any way, tip us your fin, and say that score's wiped out, and a drink, and make friends."

The General rose from his couch, and walking over to the table, said sternly,—

"Captain MacAndrews, you have offended me."

"Holy Moses, what more can a man do except say he is sorry after he has asked your pardon, ye stiff-necked old rebel; will ye take my hand?"

And the Captain put forth a horny and not overclean paw.

"No, sir, I will not take your hand."

"Then, if it is fighting you want, I am your Moses; name your place and weapons, General—pistols, swords, Gatling-guns or scissors, I won't say no, only one condition I ask, which is, that this is to be none of your Frenchified sham battles."

The General stared upon him till his small grey orbs seemed to be starting from his head, while the old tar kept two lobster eyes rolling and blinking at him in return.

"Captain MacAndrews—"

"Ay, you may stare with your military goggles, and so can I. Look on, my hearty, but hear my conditions; let us fix a spot, to-morrow, or now if you like, I'm willing, only two of us must not come back, it's a chopping up job, and no blamed nonsense."

"Captain MacAndrews," continued the General in set tones, "I do not know whether you are in jest or in earnest—"

"Dead earnest, by Moses," hiccuped the Captain.

"If in jest, let me tell you, sir, that it is in very bad taste—damned bad taste—on your part to joke on such a subject with a man of my experience, but if in earnest—I say—if in earnest—"

The General paused and paled visibly, as he hastily turned away.

"But I don't think you can be in earnest, so I shall let the matter drop, and say no more about it."

The company smiled broadly at this characteristic termination of the quarrel, and poured out a fresh supply of gin and cocoa-nut, to conceal their mouths, while the Captain sank back on his seat and went on to inform Danby of a challenge he once had in South America, the result of which had been to him six months in a Mexican jail.

Inside the chief's house was a picture of mingled pleasure and sorrow, for Kamo and the father of his love lay helpless on the one mat, while Rea and Putitai were kept busy running under the direction of some of the wise old women of the tribe, who were pounding and boiling, and chewing at the healing herbs.

Rea no longer capricious and wayward, but moving about with soft feet, touching where she could with gentle fingers the hot skin of the fevered Kamo, and silently crying, hardly knowing whether misery at his danger, or happiness at having him near her filled her the most, for Toto seemed now like an evil dream which had passed away and left no trace behind.

A subdued light filled the inside of the hut, and where the wounded men lay the air from the sea stole in at the back and out from the front like a gentle sigh; while in the centre, where the old women squatted, were the earthenware pots ranged about a low wood fire; an aromatic smell pervaded the apartment, the perfume peculiar to native houses and articles.

In some of the other huts throughout the village, the same scene is taking place, men lying passive on the mats and old women nursing them.

In others the matting is drawn before the doorways where death has come upon them, while the processions of young women are going from house to house to take their allotted time of lamentation in each abode of desolation.

The men who have escaped are also hard at work, digging graves in the sand in front of each of the closed doorways. We know all who have lost a relation from the black and grease which they have just bedaubed themselves with, and few are free from these sombre suits of mourning.

Weeping inside the houses where the graves are dug or being dug, and inside one a group of women who have been misled, and who are now shedding bitterly repentant tears, and between the tears plotting vengeance against their destroyer.

The afternoon shadows are getting very long from the posts of the houses, when the Captain, affectionately leaning on the arm of the complacent Toto, with the General bringing up the rear, staggered out upon the beach to enjoy the cooling westerly breeze, and see the burials, which will soon take place.

Kupatele coming along at that moment attracts the Captain's amorous eye, and he makes a lunge towards her, which she laughingly evades, sending him full butt against the son of Mars. Both reel for a moment, then sink down on the soft sands face downwards across each other, making of themselves a fair sign of Christianity in that pagan land.

As Kupatele glides past Toto, he says, "Remember—"

To which she replies with the smile still upon her face, from the ridiculous downfall she has witnessed, "I will not forget, Toto."

And so she passes into the full glare of the setting sun, seeming to grow enlarged as she walks from him along the beach, and resembling a dark phantom in front of a background of crimson and gold.

"The Lakatois are coming!" Toto hears a boy shouting as he speeds past him at this moment with his welcome tidings towards the village, and, leaving his prostrate white friends to lie where they have fallen, he runs down to the water's edge, and leaping into a small catamaran, pulls out to the open sea to meet the fleet.

Joy in the midst of lamentation, for all know that upon this advent all their future mouths depend. "Have they been successful?" is the shout from all, as the dead are forgotten by all except those most nearly bereaved, while the shores are lined with rushing figures of men, women, and children, seeking their own individual canoes, and pushing forth to meet the bold traders who have been to distant fields west.

A golden ocean, dotted over with black spots, as the catamarans shoot out to meet the larger vessels.

"They are coming! they are coming!" are the distant cries which reach Danby, Bowman, and the explorer, and force them to the platform to see what causes the excitement.

Past Round Head they drive with their brown, double swallow-tail—shaped sails nearly bent cross-ways, and looking purple in that golden distance—twenty large sailing-vessels have joined in that daring venture from different villages of the east.

Nearer they come with their pennons flying wildly, and the laden decks swarming with figures. Like Greek galleys they look as they bulge out russet and madder purple against those western flames.

A successful passage. The small canoes are crowding round the two Lakatois belonging to Hula, and the dark figures are bending over to help up the forms of sisters, wives, and mothers, as they speed along with their shoal of small empty fry towing behind.

Bird-like they enter the bay, their allies following in their wake, sheathing their huge sails as they gracefully bring up to anchor beside the dark hull of the less decorated steamship Thunder.

Then a mighty shout goes up from the shore and from the sea, which seems to rend the heavens, as the fierce bloodshot eye of day sinks behind the dark blue line of waters, leaving the sky crowded with strange shapes, like clawing dragons and monsters of scarlet, orange and smoky russet, with an upper space of gold and silver wings floating over an immensity of deepening azure.

The dead lie unburied that night in the huts, for the living have come again after a separation which has seemed like death, and their wants must be attended to.

To-night they must all rejoice over their victory on shore and successful undertakings at sea—all except the widows, perhaps, who do not intrude upon the general joy, but shut themselves more closely in with their unwelcome dead.

To-morrow all will join in the lamenting, as to-night they join in the feast and song.

Toto makes a capital jailor as well as host; his kind generally excel in the social arts; they know how valuable it is from a business point of view, and have not sufficient sensitiveness or intensity of character to be otherwise than plausible at all times.

He looked after his prisoners according to their necessities, and gave them with their food comfort to digest it, not knowing when he might want them as friends.

"The Beretana Kavana like brave men, and you are brave, never fear, me see you all right with him, he great friend of mine, and will soon send you back, if I ask him, with lots of presents to your wives."

Toto passed from his captives like an angel of light, leaving behind him a radiance of hope. Of course it was all lies, but it pleased them and made them think kindly of Toto, and he liked to please all men when he could, without hurting himself.

As a host he was equally successful, adroit in keeping peace all round; he kept even the General in a genial mood, consenting to be his butt and buffoon, while at the droll faces he made the others laugh with him and turned the coarse, blunt jokes of the General against himself. The skipper needed no finesse, for he was slumbering since they had brought him in, with the unconscious calmness of a baby.

Adroit also in knowing just where to stop with his filthy inuendoes, he had said to Danby, seeing him young, and thinking him vicious, "I show you fine girl if you like, to-night," when, seeing a cold shade gather over the brow of that young gentleman, hastened at once to correct himself by adding—"She come to sell bau-bau, by-and-by."

The General was expatiating as usual, when in his cups, on the injustice done him by governments in general, and the Colonial Government in particular, while the rest were sitting sipping their grog after supper and smoking, taking without remark the

General's abuse, while Toto hovered about like a ministering angel, ready and plastic to agree with all, when the back door opened quietly and the dark colourless face of Kupatele showed itself for a moment to Toto, and vanished back again to the night.

Toto looked swiftly round, and seeing that no one had noticed this incident, quietly slipped through the half-open door and drew it gently behind him.

An hour afterwards they were still sitting as Toto had left them—the others silent and hazy, and the General braying out his political tirade—when once more the door opened to admit the gentle face and tall thin form of the Kanaka teacher who had replaced Toto at Hula after the latter's flagrant misdemeanour. This poor man had only recovered from a severe attack of fever, his wife at present lying very sick, and was now on his way to ask the white men for medicine, as he was short of it. He came forward to the light with a frightened air and said,—

"White fellow lying dead in the stream outside."

All jumped to their feet except the sleeping Captain. The explorer had left them early in the evening to go aboard; could it be he?

Without a word they all followed after the frightened teacher to where the stream emptied itself into the sea; a dirty, muddy little stream, sluggishly crawling down through the sands a few yards from the house, ankle deep, which any one could have jumped over without wetting his feet.

The young moon was up still, but it did not cast enough light to distinguish white man from brown, but the clothing on that prostrate figure lying with face upwards was that of a European. The teacher had turned him over as he passed.

Danby took the legs and Bowman and the teacher the shoulders, and together they bore it to the chamber in which they had been drinking. Down by the village they were holding their feast and sending back sounds of rejoicing.

Into the light, and then they saw who it was.

"Toto!"

The comic man and general favourite, with staring, lacklustre eyes and gaping mouth chock full of the slime and mud of that shallow stream.

Chapter XXXI

"Help"

"IT may be gold, mate, it looks greasy enough and dirty enough and heavy enough to be gold, I ain't agoing to dispute that matter wi' ye, but what is the good o' gold when we hain't got grub in this yer wilderness?"

It was Collins who groaned out the foregoing, as he lay on his blanket in the hollow of a small cone-shaped hill rising out of a desolate and swampy plain. He was lying prostrate with spear-wounds and fever, and had been so for days, helpless and peevish, without the chance of getting relief by the artificial means of quinine or any other medicament, and he was speaking to Hector, who sat beside him, gaunt and hollow-eyed, but eagerly showing him something which he had just found.

"It is gold," cried Hector, nervously, "and I tell you what, mate, there's a fortune in this same little hill for both of us."

"A grave, more likely, if you don't have better luck to-day than you had yesterday."

"Forgive me, old chum, I forgot in my excitement that we were both hungry, though it's the first time this week past that you've complained of that trouble."

"Yes, I do feel as if I could do a picking just now if I had it, but I daresay it is only fancy, the sight of it generally turns me up when I am this way."

"I'll get you some fresh water—thank Heaven, we have that, at least—and make you a bit comfortable before I leave you, and then I'll go off once more on the hunt. Had I only a round of cartridges it would be easy enough; but perhaps the boys will be back to-day with help; we cannot be more than thirty miles from Ellengowan."

"Not so much, I would say, as the crow flies, if they can find a straight track. How many days have they gone?"

"This makes the fourth; and I reckon they can get over twenty miles a day."

Hector left his friend's side with the billy in his hand, and went from under the shelter of the boulder which overhung their quarters and scrambled up the loose calcined sides of the crater-like hollow.

"There goes enough to keep a fellow comfortable for many a day," he muttered to himself, as he sent down rolling at every step loose masses of cobble-like conglomerate and glittering quartz amongst the light dusty pummice and heavy lava flints. "Gold; yes, I shouldn't wonder if this turned out to be another Mount Morgan."

He stuffed his specimen pieces into his trousers pocket and went edgeways down the sloping outer sides of the hill to where the swamp glittered in patches and threads under the early rays; when at one of the widest of these he stopped and filled his can with pure clear water, which appeared to flow from some spring.

170

Ten dreary days had passed since we left them at the river after discovering the treachery of the natives and their loss; days of hardship and trouble, both from unfriendly natives and want of food; times when they had to go out of their course to avoid native villages and wandering tribes; sudden surprises, in which they had wasted the cartridges which might otherwise have procured food; journeys painful though short, owing to the bad ground— sometimes marshy and filled with treacherous bogs and slime pits which threatened to engulf them, and in the crossing of which there were many hours lost retracing steps and seeking outlets.

At other portions of their journey they penetrated bush-land, sharp thorns tearing their clothes to tatters and lacerating their flesh; venomous pricks, which would not heal, but festered and swelled until the poor fellows were only able to hobble along with great difficulty and infinite torture.

The ants tormented them by day, the mosquitoes day and night. Nature seemed merciless, denying them shelter when they mostly required it—in the open—confusing them when under shadow and making them lose their way with her intricacies, tantalizing them constantly with sight of food on the plains and in the trees, but beyond their reach now that their cartridge-pouches were empty.

No, not quite so merciless as man, for she kept them alive, and might have done more had they studied her more; there were berries which they found at times which when sucked allayed their hunger for a time, and that wonderful medicine-tree, the eucalyptus, the leaves of which, when chewed, stimulated them like draughts of wine, and which, when gathered and bound round their wounds or laid upon their throbbing heads, cooled and eased them.

They had all been wounded in their skirmishes with natives, Hector in both legs, and Collins the most seriously, so much so that for the past two days before they reached their present quarters the faithful Malays had been compelled to carry him by turns, wounded and overcome by fever.

Here they had left their leader, with his friend to look after him, while they set off towards the Fly River to see if they could get and bring back help. They knew that a mission-station had been established at Ellengowan Island, and hoped to find the Kanaka teachers—if they had not been murdered—and on this prospect the two friends waited as best they could.

Four trying days for Hector, with his friend part of the time raving and the rest despairing and irritable.

Each morning he left him as he did now, crawling painfully along the side of the swamp, seeking for food for himself, for

Collins had been hitherto unable to retain even the water which his fever made him drink.

A rat caught in the moonlight lasted the second day, while a small iguana supplied him with food the third day; now with his stick as he hobbled along, if lucky, he might manage to knock down a snake or iguana; but they did not seem very plentiful about this dismal region. Still he went on, thinking upon his discovery of gold and buoyed up by the thought of future riches even in the midst of this craving for something to eat and the dull throbbing of his festering spear-wounds, which at times made him reel in a sick stupor, while objects whirled about him or grew dark.

He had been idly amusing himself that morning practising throwing at a distant boulder with the smaller stones at his feet, when a piece of quartz heavier than the rest attracted his notice and caused him to examine it, to find it thickly impregnated with spots of what he believed to be gold.

Neither Collins nor himself had much knowledge of geology, yet this seemed plain enough.

Then he began to poke with his stick amongst the loose dark earth and sand, and found to his delight that it was sparkling with minute yellow specks as he turned it over.

In a flash he remembered Mount Morgan of Rockhampton, the mountain which, against all precedent of digger and geological experiences, was found to be a quarry of the precious ore.

Collins did not fire up as Hector expected at the discovery. After six days of food-abstinence he had wakened up that morning with the conviction that he might be able to enjoy a meal, if he had it, and not having it while the languid craving was upon him made him indifferent to aught else, present necessity being of much greater importance in his eyes than only probable future luxury.

Once more up the hill-side and into the crater with his billy filled, where, after making his sick friend more comfortable by wetting his bandages, and after hanging up over the face of the boulders his own blanket, so as to form an awning from the afternoon sun in case he might be delayed, he once more went out on his weary quest after the one thing at present needful.

"Might almost as well be in London as here, seeking for grub," he muttered, as he shaded his eyes with his hands and took a long look in the direction from which he expected help to come.

A scorching day, with a monotonous and dreary waste before him, a vast spread of low tones and reaches of madder brown and dull greens drifting away to vapoury blue hazes with intersections and specks like quicksilver.

Here and there the unvarying flat line was broken up by bare stumps or ungainly branches of trees, dead or in stages of decay, with detached clumps of leafage upon the bleached limbs.

Also in parts rose grass-trees, like worn brooms with their handles stuck in the mud; all desolation and gloomy silence, which even that translucent sky and fiercely-glowing sun failed to lighten or make cheerful.

The glare seemed to concentrate on the hill-side upon which the lonely watcher stood until it glowed again in the middle of its dull surroundings, the dried-up grass glistening like thin steel blades amongst the prismatic pieces of lava, snowy flashing quartz, and ash-grey pummice cinders.

His blue eyes were violet-tinted with the appalling heat—violet flames in the centre of scarlet whites, while his soft boyish skin was like a raw beef-steak, blistered in parts and with the skin from previous burnings peeling off and hanging in white shards, like the casting bark of a gum trunk.

A tattered spectacle as to dress, with red flannel shirt split up and wanting the sleeves, buttonless at the blistered breast, and hardly to be thought of as a protection; the trousers held together by the rushes which he had twisted round each leg to keep the wounds covered, a gleam of dirty white showing above the withered bandages.

His legs had swollen to a tremendous size, so that they bulged out the upper part of the pants till they seemed like bursting, while the lower portions looked shapeless with the bandages. His feet were bootless, and looked like gaunt stumps or blown out bladders with the accumulation of water under the skin, while at parts deep cancerous sores seemed to be eating their way into the bones.

On his blonde head he wore a white pith helmet with green under—edges, battered almost out of all original shape.

"In London a man might hobble till he drops down dead; here, I suppose, it is the same. No, by Jove, I'd rather be here than there, for no one can look on my misery only the sun, which also joins in with the hundred thousand cold eyes who stare on him pitilessly over there; cold eyes and a cold sun. Here, at any rate, the sun is not cold, and it is the only eye, besides that of heaven, to watch what happens next."

No sign of the help he was expecting, so, with a deep groan, he tottered down the hill towards the swamp, pausing every now and then to rest upon his stick, while he panted heavily, or gave a sharp sob when an extra twitch came from his dull and constantly throbbing wounds.

By the side of the swamp he sat down in a kind of dreamy

stupor, with the white glare darting from the glistening waters to his blinded eyes.

They had smoked the last of their tobacco, and he had not even that consolation in this hour of despair, yet he did not feel too wretched as he sat; he was past all thought, and now only looked, without any emotion, having only the uncertain sensation of hunger and pain blent so together that he could not separate them in his mind.

As he sat in this deep stupor of silence and stillness, across the white reflection before his eyes slid an interruption which woke him up into acute consciousness.

A marsh snake, of the tint of green slime, leisurely trailing its eight feet of cold life almost over his dropsical feet.

His stick was in his hand, so he just let it clear the track and get to the distance where he could strike fair, then swiftly raising it, and letting it drop, the slow movement of grace was transformed in an instant into a writhing confusion of active lines, almost impossible, for the first few moments, to follow with the eye as the water about it dashed and shimmered.

"Dinner for this day," said Hector, with a shrug of his shoulders, as he watched the motions diminishing in speed; "cheap, and not over nice when one has to eat it raw."

And lifting up the now twitching and jerking but limp body of the reptile by the tail, he slowly retraced his way to where he had left Collins.

A sorry meal as they had no fire, and all the efforts made by Hector to make a light, by rubbing sticks together after the native fashion, or striking flints against each other failed. Collins' tardy and feeble appetite failed at the sight of the feast offered, while a terrible nausea overcame him as he watched Hector, much less particular, gnawing at the flabby, eel-like body.

And yet snake, properly roasted, is very good and nourishing.

A long afternoon, with nothing to relieve the monotony excepting the regular wetting of his own and his friend's bandages, hobbling over the hill to replenish the water-can, or watch for the eagerly longed for succour.

But the sun went down as he had risen, changing the quicksilver gleams into molten gold, and nothing altered the general aspect of the landscape.

Silence, where even the cry of a vulture would have been welcome.

Night came, with the moon now growing in size, stealing softly up and over their heads, while from the swamps came the croaking of the frogs.

A chorus which started off at the deepest bass and passed up to the shrillest treble, unvarying in tune and constant until dawn.

The insect marauders also drove up in their myriads, singing about their cars and dashing against the exposed parts, where they swung and fed, leaving behind as payment for their fare only poison-stings.

Over head a wonderful plain of glowing worlds, golden, red, and purely white, through which that barge-like moon seemed to be steering from the east to a haven in the west.

And down the hill-sides and over the treacherous swamp myriads of flashes of intensely brilliant green and electric blue, the countless fire—flies with their lighted lamps.

Then over the land crept that pallid veil, which gathered about the two miserable wretches like a chilly shroud, making them creep close together, and shiver even in their torpid sleep.

Morning once more comes up, cool and virginal, like a merry maiden clad in white muslin, to find Hector lying beside his friend unable to move a limb.

"I am fairly done, old man," he mutters drowsily; "we'll just have to wait where we are until they find us."

"Or our carcases," replied Collins.

"It don't much matter," wearily responded Hector, painfully turning his back upon his friend, and gazing down upon the centre of the hollow.

Hour after hour they lay without a word, with the water-can empty beside them, and the sun's rays gradually coming round till they shot over the pair, making the pain of their wounds and sores more acute under the hard pressure of their dry bandages, while a newly-developed thirst was added to their former miseries.

They were both parching, without the power to go to where the water lay so close at hand.

Over the distant plain, not yet in sight of that coneshaped land-mark, the faithful Malay boys are guiding the two South Sea Island Teachers, with a dozen of their New Guinea disciples, to the rescue of their masters.

The natives carry a large bamboo litter well laden with provisions, boat-like wooden platters of cooked yams, with clusters of bananas and cocoa-nuts, and beside them the large, generous mammy apples.

A couple of large kangaroos lie swinging over the sides, caught that day, and to be cooked when they have reached the hill.

They all pace out with confident feet, for they know their way back, although it has cost them many a weary détour in the coming.

Over the dry grass plain they pass, and approach to the margin of the swampy land.

Yes, there is the hill, blue and dark against the mellow afternoon sky; they will easily reach it before sundown.

Over the swamp, zigzaging, and in a line of two abreast as the firmer parts gave them room to walk, sinking at times, by false steps, up to the thighs, and being dragged out by their companions who had reached safer ground, feeling every step in advance, although, profiting by their former experience, hurrying as fast as possible so as to reach dry land before darkness.

They had reached the hill with the last gleam of daylight, and without a pause scrambled up over the ridge with loud shouts which their leaders do not respond to, although they can hear their voices down beneath the shelter of the boulder.

Hector is singing in his sweet tenor voice, "The Harp that once through Tara's Halls," while Collins is talking in his shrill, piping voice, as if to a third party, and paying no heed to the song, although it is rendered with much expression.

They rush down towards them in a body, to see them lying upon their backs with flaming eyes.

"Plenty much fever here, teacher," observed Jack, kneeling down and feeling the burning foreheads of his masters.

"Light big fire to-night, and give them plenty sweat," replied the head—teacher, and at the order the natives rush about to gather up the dried-up briars and parasites lying about, and soon after the crater is lighted up as with a second eruption, while the Malays and teachers cover up the unconscious men with their shirts.

The kangaroos are skinned and portions cooked for the hungry company, while the skins are also heaped over the invalids, as the fires are kept up throughout the night by constant supplies of firewood.

Hector goes through his entire répertoire, and begins again as if he had been encored by an appreciative audience, gradually singing in a more drone-like way until at last he seemingly sings himself to sleep. Collins has talked himself speechless long before Hector is half-way through, but now both are breathing calmly, with the large beads of perspiration rolling like rain-drops down their cheeks, and making the soil moist around the bed.

"They will know us to-morrow." observes the teacher, as he turns away and flings himself by the side of the fires.

Soon all are sound asleep excepting the natives who move about the sides of the crater gathering firewood and feeding the flames and casting up the concave sides of the hollow long shadows which grow vaster as they recede until they appear like great-headed gnomes with crouching backs flitting about.

"Hallo!" said Hector, as he awoke next morning, "I feel as if I had lost a couple of hundredweight from my bones, and a ton lighter."

"Better, sah?" observed the teacher, smiling mildly as he bent over him.

"So you have come at last, thank God! thank God!"

"Yes, sah! it is well to thank the Lord for all His goodness; we came last night."

"Wait till I get up, I feel fresh as new paint, though decidedly weak." Hector had tried to rise, but sank back again wearily.

"Have some kangaroo steak first, and a cup of tea, breakfast is just ready."

"Breakfast," echoed Collins, opening his eyes at the sound; "say, stranger, have you such a thing about you as a fill of 'baccy."

The fever had been sweated out, and now the craving for tobacco came upon him first.

A pipe was charged and lighted for him by his faithful man, Jack, after which Collins lay puffing in quiet ecstasy his first pipe for eight days, exhibiting no curiosity about anything going on about him.

After a strong dose each of quinine mixed with spirits, and a fair breakfast, the party got up, laying the two men upon the litter, and prepared for the homeward journey.

Hector, as he got on to his feet, looked with amazement at his lower limbs, from which the bandages hung loosely.

"By Jove, lads, here is a reduction; last night I had a pair of thighs to be proud about, but now where are they?"

"Helping to water the next crop of grass, I expect, Boss," responded Jack, wringing out the wet blanket, which had been under Hector and Collins.

All day they travelled rapidly, changing hands at the litter, and feeding, when hungry, from the fruit which they had brought with them, and resting only for an hour at sundown until the moon rose, then on again, over a dry and grass-covered, undulating country, until, about day-break, they reached the banks of a shallow and slow-flowing stream.

"Halt and rest," said the teacher; "we are now only eight miles from the station; let us have breakfast."

The natives scattered with their spears and bows, while the Malays lighted the fires;—they soon appeared again with another kangaroo, a brace of bush turkeys, and some cowled pigeons, gesticulating as they drew near, and shouting out in their own language to the teachers.

"What is the matter?" asked Hector, sitting up.

"There has been fighting since we left, at Ellengowan; they have seen the remnant of a tribe, hostile to us, hurrying off south, as if in a panic. Pray heaven our families may be safe."

The teachers had anxious faces as they set about getting breakfast ready, and appeared eager to get it past and proceed with all haste.

Through a country becoming more thickly wooded as they drew nearer to their destination all pushed forward, all preparing against emergencies as the miles grew less, and sending scouts out in front, into the forest, where a native path had been made, and which leads to the river.

There it is at last, broadly flowing between its leafy banks, and the next turn will show them the mission-station.

Over the trees between them and it they noticed floating vapours like the blue smoke from burning wood, and an ominous silence sinks upon the group as they rush eagerly forward.

Ellengowan Island comes into the view as they dash round the point, and where the mission cabins had been the night before is a clear space filled with charred ashes, from which the thin wreaths of vapour are rising and floating amongst the trees.

"By the Lord, there is the Sunflower!" cried Hector and Collins, as the two masts and hull of the schooner project above the landing-place.

"Yes, yes," says the teacher impatiently, "Captain Niggeree with Professor Killmann passed up the river a week ago; they must have recovered his little steamer, for there she is alongside, but what of our wives and children?"

A loud shout uttered in various tones—men's, women's, and children's voices uniting—came from the decks of the two vessels now lying alongside each other, replying to the teacher's sharp words, and proving that the shore party had been observed by those on board, while they could see as they advanced two boats lowered and filling with people.

Another moment and they can recognize one another; the wives and children all safe, stretching out their arms to their fathers as the boats are shooting across the stream, with the piratical-looking Niggeree and pale—faced Professor steering their individual boats.

"Hallo! Collins and Hector, who would think of seeing you here. Where is your boat?"

"Wrecked on the coast, Nig," laconically replied Collins, shaking his former mate by the hand and nodding to the Professor whom he had met before; while the teachers and their wives went through extravagant pantomimes of reunion, and the natives and Malay boys flung themselves upon the grass to rest.

"What's been going on here, mate?" asked Hector, looking at the burning ruins before him.

"A little mill last night—natives attacking the squaws. We arrived in time to save the crew and send half of the enemy to eternal blazes; but come on board and have a drain."

Chapter XXXII
Port Moresby

THE Thunder anchors once more in Basilisk Bay, and the prisoners from Hula have been removed to the new wooden structure, which has just been finished as a jail over in the township, as yet with only this house upon it.

A small guard of Hannabada young men act with great importance and satisfaction the part of jailors and patrols over this batch of legal captives, while from behind the iron bars, the dark faces peer out at the bright sunlit sea-shore with very dejected and pensive eyes.

General Flagcroucher has been invited in kind but firm tones, by the Governor's secretary, to go on board the Government sloop, and accompany his Excellency back to Thursday Island, where he purposes landing him and leaving him to relate to credulous audiences throughout the colonies and at home, the story of his marvellous and hair-breadth escapes in New Guinea, and to speak in terms of praise or censure about the hospitality he met with there.

The Governor is an easy-going man, and does not mind what the General may say about him, more than he minds a few extra mosquitoes of an evening, having by this time become well used to both nuisances.

He steps on board to shake hands with Bowman and Danby before leaving.

"Good-bye, gentlemen, I hope you have enjoyed your visit to Hula?"

"First rate, Sir John!"

"Use the bungalow while at Moresby. I have left instructions with the Captain about that job I want you to do, if you have time. We can give you a couple more weeks. That ought to do; see if you can open up the Aird River a little more, or find something fresh about that part of the coast. Your leader, Mr. Brown, is an able man, and has done good work before, he will be with you shortly—and, I say, try if you can hear anything of Killmann, we are getting uneasy at his long silence."

"We will do what we can, your Excellency!"

"Good-bye again; I'll meet you at Thursday Island on your return."

His Excellency shakes hands all round, and getting into his boat is rowed on board the Government sloop, which in a short time has lifted anchor and shaken out her sails.

The Thunder fires her gun in honour of the occasions, and yells shrilly on her steam whistle, which the Governor responds to; a waving of pith helmets, and New Guinea has seen the last of that leader of armies, the General.

As they are still watching the departure, a boat from the shore joins on to them, with three or four white gentlemen on board; with nimble steps they leap on to the deck.

"How do you do, Bowman?"

"How are you, Brown? How are you, Graham?" &c., &c., as they all shake hands, and go down below to try the "tappit hen."

"You know the instructions from headquarters, I suppose, Bowman?"

"So I hear you are boss of the show, Brown; when do we start?"

"As soon as we can take in water and overhaul our provisions. Graham will go over the list with us, and make us right where we are short."

"Oh, we have loads to last us another month; however, I will show you the list, and what we have used up."

And the three men, with the Captain and the steward, were in a moment hard at work stock-taking.

Mr. Brown was a determined-looking, sharp-speaking young fellow of about thirty-five; he was free and off-hand in his general manner and very quickly settled business and returned once more to his pipe and glass.

"That will do for one day, Captain. Have you begun to take in water?"

"The niggers are hard at it now."

"Then we will start at daybreak to-morrow. Steward, have you any cham?"

"Yes, sah, one case only."

"Well, we don't want it on our journey, so what say you to a little party to-night, gentlemen? There are the war-sloop party of

180

officers, the Rev. Mr. and Mrs. Lang, for respectability, the surveyor, and Captain Maunville, of the Bungalow."

"Not a bad idea, if they will come."

"Oh, they'll come fast enough. I wonder when any of them tasted champagne last!"

"But how are we to hold them?"

"We'll manage, don't fret, old man."

"Best take the store for the occasion," observed Graham slowly.

Mr. Graham never was long free of fever, and just now was languid from a recent attack, yet his faith in and love for New Guinea never died out. It was his own land, much of it by right of discovery, and in it he meant to leave his bones.

"Take your place, and have our throats cut by your mad cook! not for this child."

"He is all right to-night."

"Yes, but how about this afternoon? Why, gentlemen, if I hadn't dropped by accident into the place, and separated them, you would have had the old man's head to take back as a curiosity. Sambo was busy with a chopping-axe upon his master."

It appeared that Mr. Graham's body-servant was given to what his master kindly called fits, and while these were on him his weakness consisted in murderous proclivities. He was a native of Moresby, and a favourite with his employer, who always excused these paroxysms.

"Drink up, lads, and let us go round with our invitations; we'll know, then, who are coming. Steward, tell the cook to do his best against six o'clock; and, Captain, try to comb out your hair for once."

After the glasses were empty, they all pulled ashore, and made for the mission headquarters, where Mr. and Mrs. Lang were now staying; it was a prettily situated house on the face of an eminence, overlooking the village of Elevire, with the lofty Mount Pullen rising up behind. The school-house stood close at hand, where, under their supervision, and with the assistance of South-sea teachers, over a hundred native boys and girls were learning to read and write, with such other accomplishments as the native mind could grasp.

As they passed along the beach they came upon a group of youngsters, some of very tender years, practising spear-throwing—making it a game, as our children might play with dolls.

The eldest set up a stick as a target, and they all took turns with a number of toy spears, trying to get nearest the mark, and striving to ascertain who could pitch farthest.

They observed that the elder children were very particular

in making the younger ones take the correct pose of the body when aiming, also in the position of their fingers as they grasped the spear.

It was also astonishing to notice the strength and art with which they made the fling, by a peculiar motion of the wrist, without the hand seeming to move; they observed the weapon to quiver for a few seconds, then it was sent straight on its mission.

Few even of the youngest fell far short of the mark. Some of the children could not have been older than two years of age.

Going up the winding steps to the mission-house they met a couple of the teachers' wives coming down with their babies in their arms—graceful Kanaka girls, who bent their heads modestly as they passed, with their simple blue and white-spotted robes falling from their sloping shoulders, like the fashionable afternoon tea-gowns; lovely-faced women with blue-black, long straight tresses and large, tender and melancholy eyes.

Up at the house they were kindly received by the missionary and his wife, who spoke with sorrow about the tragedy at Hula, and seemed at a loss to know how to deal with the culprits.

"What they have done is no wrong according to their old creed. This particular tribe are amongst those who did not send representatives to confirm the annexing ceremony, so I don't suppose they recognize our authority or right to interfere with their private action; besides, I think they have been punished enough already. I expect we shall have to let them go in a day or two."

"Regarding Toto?"

"No one ought to regret his death, whoever caused it, for he has demoralized Hula, and yet he was one of our aptest scholars here."

"A little too apt, perhaps," responded Bowman.

They saw the school, and the children learning from the black board and listened to them singing one or two school-board songs. They were all, nearly without exception, bright, intelligent specimens of boy and girlhood, and made merry over their tasks.

"There grows the future New Guinea, gentlemen, and a prosperous future it must be if we can keep back the taste of fire-water; as yet, with the exception of Toto, no New Guinea native has taken kindly to it; they all regard it as a very nasty medicine."

They were learning to read and write at Moresby, and some had already learnt the necessity of wearing a shirt to cover themselves with, as did our first parents when they had partaken of the apple of knowledge. How long will the cocoanuts and yams content them? At present, with their one banana-tree, they are wealthy, because they have enough, but with the Western problem of progress put before them, how long will they be able to keep poverty back?

The other day I heard a school-teacher wondering which foreign mission would be the most profitable, in a Christian sense, to endow with the savings of his pupils. It was a cold, miserable day in London, and the unemployed workmen were starving to death in the streets and East-end dens by thousands. I did not like to suggest New Guinea, with its warm sunshine and utter absence of want or privation, as our English savages understand the words, simply because I had travelled through those lands.

Cannibalism is much more frightful to contemplate than starvation, when we stand back and view them both from a safe distance; but when close enough to the two evils I am inclined to lean in the matter of opinion towards starvation as the bigger horror. Murder, of course, is rampant all over the world, and not a whit more revolting as to detail in New Guinea than it is in Christian England. Starvation thrives in this land of fogs and ice, and cannibalism in that atmosphere of warmth and quick passion.

Mr. and Mrs. Lang had just returned from a visit round the coast, and reported all to be orderly and quiet where they had visited.

They all left the mission-house much impressed by the kindness of the missionary, and his evident sincerity and faith in the cause for which he and his wife had left the comforts of social intercourse and friends at home to risk their lives in the work of raising the natives of an, as yet, unwholesome country. They both appeared, like the naturalist Graham, to be much debilitated by old attacks of fever, yet, like him, hopeful, enthusiastic, and devoted to their adopted land.

Their next call was at the store, where they saw the native cook in his hammock; he was lying exhausted from his afternoon attack, and regarded them with dull, expressionless eyes.

"Some day he will polish you off," observed Brown.

"No fear of that," responded the naturalist. He had lived in such a constant atmosphere of death and violence for the past ten years that he took these incidents coolly.

As they were looking over some birds of paradise and native shields for sale, some young girls appeared at the door, looking in with mischievous faces.

"Now then, get out of that!" shouted Graham, harshly, making a rush at them, upon which they all ran away with merry bursts of laughter. "Never saw such wanton hussies!" he muttered angrily, coming back.

"The girls of Moresby are the same as all their sex; they

know the old man to be a regular woman-hater, and won't leave him alone," explained Brown to the others.

"Does he always treat the women that way?" asked Danby.

"Always; that's why he can go all over the land in perfect safety; he is well known amongst the tribes, and the men can trust him anywhere with their wives and daughters."

As they left the store-house one of the twin brothers Hawley rode up on a white horse. They had lately imported a few horses to Moresby, and they were taking kindly to the land, although the natives viewed them with great awe and wonderment, and flocked out to see them whenever they passed.

"Will you join us to-night, Mr. Hawley, with your brother?" asked Brown.

"With pleasure, Mr. Brown; who are coming?"

"We are only going on the round with our invitations, and you are the second, so I am glad you can come, for Mr. and Mrs. Lang have declined, afraid to damp the party, I suppose, Mrs. Lang being the only white lady in Moresby."

"Are you going to invite any of her Majesty's men?"

"Of course."

"All right, I'll take your invite as I am going on board shortly on business."

"Thanks."

Through the village of Hanuabada they all went to the survey camp at the other end; here they met Mr. C——and his party, just come in from a hard day's work amongst the ants and underbush. Three of the surveyors were down with fever, and the others burnt almost black with the sun, and mopping their grimy wet faces and exposed chests. The leader paused before giving his consent for the night.

"Remember, boys, you must be up at four o'clock to-morrow morning, and we can't excuse headaches, now we are so short-handed."

"Let's go for an hour."

"All right, I'll come with you to see you all safe home."

Captain Mannville, like Mr. Lang, excused himself on the plea of hard work, so together they made for the steamer once more.

On board they found the old skipper and Hans, the engineer, busy washing old clothes, to make themselves respectable against the occasion. They squatted on the deck, facing one another, with a bucket of fresh water between them, scrubbing away at their greasy trousers and shirts, and helping one another to wring them out.

In the cabin the steward and seamen were hard at work

hanging up old bunting and nailing croton-branches, making it as like a conservatory as they could, while the upper decks were being mopped down for the first time since leaving port.

The outside was lined with canoes and natives filling up the water—barrels, &c. They brought their supply in old rusty tanks from the native wells ashore and handed it up in buckets; slow work, but rendered a little faster by the multitude of workers. Their wages were to be a stick of tobacco per day.

"Hello! what's the matter now?" yelled out the skipper from his seat on the deck.

A sudden stoppage amongst the natives produced this query.

"They want part of their wages before they go on," replied the Irish mate.

"Holy Moses! Why, they have only done half a day's work."

"And want their half-stick of tobacco," replied the mate.

It was a strike. The skipper got up with wild gestures and loud words, but the natives stood in their canoes quietly, but obstinate, with the tank half-emptied, refusing to work without being paid for what they had done.

"There's no use bullying them," said Mr. Brown, "they have made up their minds and nothing will make them move, except yielding to their demands; your rag-tag appearance must have raised their suspicions."

The poor old persecuted skipper sat down to his washing-tub with the air of a martyr, while the steward brought out a bundle of tobacco sticks, and went about dividing it amongst them, after which they resumed their work as before.

"They will take these no trust fits occasionally," explained Brown, "and then it is the very devil if you havn't got the wherewithal to meet their demands. I remember once being left in the lurch the same way amongst the Astrolabes, because I refused to give way, thinking firmness was the best, and had to trudge back to the coast alone and leave my baggage behind."

"Jolly awkward for an explorer."

"It is one of the difficulties with which we and all future explorers will have to contend with in the discovery of this locked land. A man has more chance with his gun and alone, without provisions, than with a crowd. There is the Rev. James Chalmers, for instance; he would set out on a voyage of discovery with three oars and a single banana for provisions, trusting all the rest to Providence or good luck, and is ready any day to do a three-hundred-mile tramp up the country with only his walking-stick and a pouch of tobacco, and I'll go bail that if any man is able to cross this dark island, he is the one, with all his recklessness and happy-go-lucky want of fore-thought."

Night comes, and the guests assemble. The warsloop is represented by two junior officers, who come polite and stiff in full tropic dress, and behave themselves as if in church for the honour of the service. The days are gone by when junior officers were larky and filled with monkey tricks; they are all now good boys and well-behaved, with an eager eye after the main chances in life and a thirst to study carefully all the byeways to promotion.

The survey party came like schoolboys let loose for an hour, boisterous and much inclined for practical jokes. Their leader let them do as they liked, while the champagne circulated, but put his veto on the whisky, and told them to remember the morrow.

The Captain astonished all by appearing in a clean white shirt which he had borrowed from Hans, and looking mightily unhappy in it.

"Never thought you could look so much like a gentleman, old man," said Danby in a complimentary way, making room for the Captain beside him at the table.

The one brother Hawley came before the other, and after dinner and while Bowman was telling him something, he excused himself for a moment and went outside. While still out the other entered, dressed the same way, and sat down on the vacant seat, while Bowman continued his story.

"But I don't quite comprehend."

"You know what I was telling you when you went out just now."

At this moment the right brother entered again, saying, "I say, brother, you have taken my seat, make room. Yes, Bowman, and how did you get on?"

Bowman had made the usual mistake, for the twins were exactly alike.

It was a source of constant fun, like the "Comedy of Errors," with the two brothers, and the party was a merry one before they broke up.

The surveyors left first and much against their will, but their leader was firm—business before pleasure. "Let us get the Laroke road made and you can enjoy yourselves as much as you like," he said.

The rest sat till daybreak, at which time the steam was put on and the anchor weighed; the Captain had got rid of his uncomfortable shirt, and now was once more in his element, turning round with loud oaths in an old pair of pants and a buttonless under-flannel.

"Success to the Thunder."

186

The last toast is drunk, and they shake hands all round, while the steam-whistle yells out for the third time; then natives skurry back to their canoes and the shore-dwellers to their boats, as the stars are getting dim in the growing light.

And out of the bay the little Hummer puffs, in her own peculiar style, leaving the stifling huts and calm waters and silver-grey hills behind them as they steer on their adventurous course to unknown places in the west.

Chapter XXXIII
A New River

Discovered by Mr. Tendin Beven, 1887.

THE Nora, Professor Killmann's little steam yacht, lies at anchor, close to a shore where the banks are vast precipices towering fifteen hundred feet over her masts and funnel, with vast forests of gigantic trees growing on the tops.

The river is deep, wide, and rapidly flowing, so that where they anchor they require strong chains to hold her stationary.

They have anchored early that afternoon because daylight is quickly lost in these gloomy gorges, and they are ascending a river never penetrated before by white people, so that they have to go cautiously and feel their way as they go.

Professor Killmann is busy to-night amongst his specimens, with his spirit-bottles ranged out on one side and his diary on the other, in which he makes his entries from time to time when he has any fresh remarks to make upon the natural specimens which he is preserving.

At present he is engaged upon the skinning of a rare bird and has his arsenic paste ready to his hand. A dirty job it is which has made him take off his alpaca coat and roll up his shirt-sleeves.

On the couch near at hand are sitting Hector and Collins, engaged in polishing up the steel work of their rifles and revolvers; they are greatly recovered since leaving Ellangowan, and can both walk about with only a slight limp. Niggeree is on deck taking charge of the first watch and looking out for enemies.

"My friends, this new river is of much more importance than the Fly, and I should not be astonished if it leads us right into the centre of the country. Already we must be over a hundred miles from the sea, and there seems no diminishing."

"How far up do you intend to go, Professor?" inquires Hector.

"Until the Nora can draw no more water."

"But our provisions are getting low."

"Then we must all have a day or two of hunting to replenish the larder and increase my stock of specimens. What a blessing that the natives, when in possession, left my bottles alone; they must have thought them to be exploding machines."

"What do you think of the specimen which I showed you yesterday, have you tried it yet?"

"Ah, yes, but it is not good. There is a little gold in it, but iron is the principal ingredient, yet we will mark on my map the latitude and longitude of your route after you left the river, as I may visit the place some time; meantime I shall put your stone amongst my specimens of minerals."

"No, Professor, with your leave, I'll stick to my bit of quartz, it will do to remind me of our suffering."

"As you will, friend; I will let you have it when you like."

"Any time will do for that before we separate."

"You will have it—when we separate, my young friend."

Hector and Collins shortly after join their friend, Niggeree, leaving the Professor to his preparing and classifying.

He makes some curious contortions of his face as he bends over his bird, while the lamp lights it up, handling his knife with the apparent delight of a vivisector, giving some demoniacal side-glares now at his spirit bottles and now at his diary, while he mutters to himself as he works,—

"Gold! yes, I would think the fool ought to have known it without asking any one, but I must not let him tell any one else about his discovery. Ah, I shall go over that swamp myself when I am rid of them all."

He has finished his bird-curing, and now directs his attention to some insects caught that day. They have been long enough immersed in the spirits, and he now goes to work with his fine pins fixing them to the empty frame. He stabs at them as they lie before him with a grin of delight, which fairly twists his mouth under his long black and silky beard.

A handsome man is the Professor, in spite of his sickly pallor, with dark curly hair growing bare about the temples, full dark and soft beard and moustache, a fine aquiline nose, and rich brown eyes.

But he has a manner of moving his mouth and puckering his eyes when he is interested in his task which is apt to make an onlooker shudder.

"The explorer is a fool who would allow any white man to

return with him and share the honour of his discoveries. I shall have discovered this river and found the gold when I reach civilization, and these three friends of mine will have to stay behind, but at present they are all useful. Well, Niggeree, how goes the night?"

"All quiet," said Niggeree, as he entered. "We have not had the trouble on this river as yet that we had on the Fly."

"Not as yet."

"It's a bit tame, don't you think, sailing up, day after day, without a change?"

"Change, Niggeree! What more would you have? We have discovered a river never known to have had existence by white men; we have fathomed the Aird, supposed to be a river hitherto, and have proved it to be only one of many mouths of this grand fresh-water passage hitherto unsuspected; but what of the Fly now when we look on this, and think upon the scenery which we have already witnessed, besides what may be in front—the splendid country we have passed through, rich in soil, the sport we have had with our guns, the gigantic forests, and the capital health we have all enjoyed since entering upon this earthly paradise?"

"All that is good enough, but we have not seen a native yet, and my Winchester is growing rusty."

"Ah! Niggeree, still the love of the big game. But surely you had enough up the Fly this time. How you made them hop about at Snake Point! I wager they have not often seen such an illumination about that part as the night we got back our Nora. They will not forget us this next monsoon."

"There ain't much left to remember us about that part of the Alice."

"Enough to warn the rest for forty miles up the river to give us a wide berth; but, Niggeree, you want some more excitement?"

"Yes, Professor, I'd like something of a change."

"So you shall, my friend. To-morrow, at the next gully we come to, or cleft inland of this wall, I intend to land and explore it a bit, but I want you and I to go alone."

"Why you and I?" asked Niggeree, in a suspicious tone—he had not too much faith in his friend.

"Why? Look at this, my friend, first."

The Professor went over to his small chest of drawers which stood in a corner, where he kept his chemicals and medicines, and returning with the specimen of quartz which Hector had given him to test, placed it in Niggeree's hand, watching him while he examined it by the lamp-light.

"Three parts gold, by the great Harry! This was not found in New Guinea?"

"Hector says be found it in the hill where the Malays left him and Collins."

"Loose?"

"Yes, and only one piece of many."

"Then what the devil are we doing here when the gold lies over there?"

"Gently, my friend; we know where to find it when we want it over there—you and I—but we need not bring all Queensland upon our trail."

"Ah! you want to get rid of them first?"

"That is it, and you will help me. Besides, if it has been found there, may it not be also here—this here is a likely country."

"The same thought has struck me once or twice to day; the rocks do look gold-bearing."

"It is in the gullies we must look, friend; but say nothing. We will go on our collecting expedition together, and leave them behind on guard."

As Niggeree left the cabin he said to himself, "Yes, my smooth—tongued chum, and I'll take good care not to let you get behind me when we are on that ere expedition."

Professor Killmann looked after him with an indulgent smile, and muttered softly, "He is going upstairs to find out all that he can about the locality of that mountain from Hector, so that he may go alone after that gold. Ah! well, he is welcome to all the knowledge he is able to glean to—night, but he is very innocent for a native of the sunny isles of Greece."

This is the twelfth day since the Nora picked up Hector and Collins at Ellengowan.

They had only stayed long enough to assist the poor missionaries to erect a shelter for their families, which, with the help of the natives, they were not long in doing; then they gave them what they could spare in the shape of provisions—a couple of bags of flour, one bag of rice, some tins of preserved beef, tea and sugar, over which they made loud demonstrations of gratitude.

Collins and Hector promised to send them more when they got their vessel to Sabai, if they found it had not been molested meantime by unfriendly visitors.

"Poor fellows!" he said, as they sailed away. "Their ideas of religion may be right or wrong, but there is no question about the sacrifices they make. They are allowed twenty pounds a year, and have no notion of the value of money, so that they order all sorts of rubbish and spend it in a month or so, and often would starve if it was not for the kindness and charity of their countrymen, the divers of Torres Straits—reckless devils they are, these Kanaka divers: but I know of more than one of my own lads who have handed me over forty pounds at a time out of their wages to send over to their starving missionary brothers in New Guinea; damn fools, they call them, to go over there to die on starvation wages. But they come here to die, and seem to glory in it, for they have always fresh recruits eager to fill the places of the murdered men from the South Seas."

They passed down the river with the ordinary incidents— hostile natives showing up and being frightened away, a little relaxation ashore with the gun getting game, sultry days and watchful nights.

At Kiwai Island Niggeree left the Sunflower, in care of one or two of his boys, with orders to take it on to Moresby and wait his coming when the monsoon changed to the west.

Then they went in the Nora to the mouth of the river named after Collins, and, luckily, found the Coral Seas as they had left her. The Professor made a chart of the river from their directions, after which they towed her back to Kiwai, where the lads were left to patch up her helm, and take her also back to Moresby with the Sunflower.

"I'll try the mouth of the Collins for shells by-and-by," observed the master of the Coral Seas.

"I'll join you in that," said Niggeree.

They coasted round from Mibu, keeping close to the shore, until they got to the mouth of the Aird River, as marked in the chart.

"There's a good broad channel here," observed Killmann. "What say you, friends, if we try it up a little?"

All on board agreed, time being of little object to any of them, so they put in without pausing.

They lost about three days dodging backward and forward, trying different channels and finding no apparent passage inland, or getting grounded on mud-banks.

At last, when they were about to despair of being able to penetrate it, they almost accidentally struck the right mouth of the main river, and found it a most magnificent stream, over half a mile broad, with a steady tide and plenty of bottom, up which they boldly steamed straight on to the mountain ranges.

They passed banks such as they had never witnessed before for fertility and richness of soil, without meeting either natives or mosquitoes. It was a wholesome and dry land, and seemed specially adapted for future colonists, so that their health improved almost every hour; the water was fresh and pure, and the place seemed unoccupied by man, for the game were very plentiful and tame, proving that they had not been much hunted.

Then, after the fallow agricalatural flats, they came to

mountain ranges, a most magnificent vista of highlands densely covered with forests of mighty cedar and other trees—in the far distance great peaks towering up, blue and picturesque, towards which they steamed swiftly with many a twist and curve, yet still going easterly and northward.

Then they got into the mountain chain, the river still cleaving its way, smooth and rapid, between vast chasms; a constant changing of earth's features as the mighty panorama grew vaster about them and grander. They passed beetling cliffs with great rifts and gullies, down which the roaring waters rushed to feed this river, gleaming white and tumultuous as the sunshafts slid down the mountain sides and struck upon them.

They could see great distances away, when the landscape at times opened up, showing lofty peaks, towering above the dense forests all blue against the ambient sky; they beheld the fresh-green tints of the nearer ranges, and got glimpses of fairy-like valleys, plentifully watered, and which served as sheltered homes for countless herds of kangaroos and cassowaries, as the forests were the thronged mansions of the birds.

Not a shower had yet fallen over this land of unused plenty, yet the torrents flowed ceaselessly over the crags and past the roots of clustering parasites and gigantic tree roots: these waters, with the rivers, made the air cool even in the fierce mid-day heat, while at times they passed through an unbroken twilight of balmy shadow, where the walls of rocks rose hundreds of feet above their heads, with the great branches and umbrella-like leaves spreading far beyond the tops and highest of all ran narrow lanes of deep blue sky.

It was a region of delicious surprises.

Chapter XXXIV
A Prospecting Expedition

AT daybreak next morning the Nora was once more under way, and before very long they had come abreast of one of the many natural rifts or gullies which split, in a zigzag fashion, the mountain through which they were penetrating. These gullies were doubtless the effect of a series of eruptions and earthquakes in the unknown past, rounded off by countless centuries of water-wearing. A mighty crack this rift looked like from the deck of the Nora, with huge strata exposed in irregular confusion like the blasted sides of a long-disused quarry, covered up in parts by vegetation where the layers or accumulations of débris allowed vegetation to take root and flourish in that prolific warmth of atmosphere.

In the valley of this gorge a vast assemblage of great boulders and stones were scattered about, making a series of waterfalls and foam swirlings as the stream leapt over the high places or twisted about the separate rocks and stones, glittering snow-like where the forenoon sun—rays fell down upon them, and looking cool grey in the violet shadow.

They could look up this glen for about half a mile only, by reason of its turnings. The morning haze still hung, gauze-like, over it, and gave to it a fairy-like look of light, particularly as from every bough and division of leafage seemingly hung thick hammock clusters of spider-webs, swinging from glistening threads like glass-blown fibres stretched out and interlaced in the open spaces.

A soft, suggestive picture all this, after the first framing of boulders and greenage in the direct foreground! The scene melted away into light tones of purple and warm greys, with the dew-hung webs like filigree—work done in frosted silver and with polished edges; the whole seemed alight with blazing diamonds.

The Professor had in a way explained his intentions to Hector and Collins, appointing them to guard the vessel during his absence ashore; and as it was quite a customary thing for some one or other to take these occasional excursions, they felt no surprise now.

Niggeree came up from his berth with his customary complement of war implements at his belt, a brace of Colt's revolvers, with a bag of spare cartridges, a small cutlass, and, slung over his back, his fifteen chambered Winchester; he was going ashore with his friend and seemingly thought it well to be prepared against the occasion.

"Don't you think, friend, that you are somewhat heavily equipped, considering the hard climbing before us?" said the Professor, who contented himself with a single revolver and a small sheath dagger. He carried in his hand a light geological hammer.

"So long as I don't grumble at the weight of my baggage, you needn't," responded Niggeree in a surly tone.

Another moment, and they stepped ashore a few yards from the mouth of the stream, and had begun their march.

The Professor went first, with Niggeree a few yards behind. With his usual politeness he had offered to the Greek the precedence, which, however, the other declined, and so they passed on their way into the haze, wending round the boulders where they could, and climbing over others which they could not avoid.

For the first few yards, owing to the intense sultriness of this breathless hour of day, a frightful sense of oppression weighed upon their limbs, the veins rose upon their arms, and their heads throbbed as if they would burst, while their skin burned with a dry fever and seemed to be distended and prickling all over—a moment or so of intensest agony, then instant relief as the perspiration broke from every pore, saturating their light flannels; they could now toil on with ease and comfort.

A fatiguing journey from the beginning, even while the defile was open enough to allow them room for climbing along its margin, but increasing in difficulty as they advanced, for the stream rushed close to the sides of abrupt cliffs and wall-like precipices, so that it became a constant struggle, either with the current, which, although shallow, swirled about their legs with a force almost enough to draw their feet from under them, or else with the rough rocks which they clung to as they clambered over the many different leaps which the torrent took in its tumultuous passage down.

They could not speak much to one another as they struggled on, the noise of rushing water filling their ears; besides there was the necessity of saving their breath for the labour of climbing.

"Tough work!" observed the Professor, getting astride a large stone and resting for a moment.

"Rather!" responded Niggeree, taking a perch on another mass of rock close by, and wiping his brow with the back of his hand.

They had reached a part of the ravine where the Nora was shut out by a turn of the overhanging cliffs. Above rose walls some hundred feet in air, with trees at the summit meeting from both sides and shutting out the sky. Before them lay nearly sixty yards of comparatively level stream, with another small cataract of about six or eight feet, terminating their line of sight with the same rugged background of broken up rock and bush.

At their feet lay a deep sleeping pool of bistretinted water, protected from the general rushing current by some immense basaltic boulders which had fallen over one another and made a kind of bay. It would require an energetic spring to get from their present rest to the next mass close to the stream.

As they sat silently resting and looking down they could see yards below the surface, but not far enough to reach the bottom.

"A good spot for a bath, friend, don't you think?" said the Professor.

194

"If there is nothing besides water there;—let's try," replied Niggeree, and, suiting the action to the word, he broke off a small piece of dry wood near at hand and cast it downwards.

Instantly a commotion took place in the pool, at which Niggeree brought his rifle to the point.

"I thought so," he observed, firing off quickly a couple of charges as the long snout of an immense alligator darted up; "I have spoilt that fellow's idea of fun."

The still water became in a moment like a whirlpool, dashing up against the sides of the rock and becoming stained with a ruddy tint, shortly to subside as the great body slowly rose to the surface and floated belly upwards, with the short legs and claws outstretched and bent.

"Not the safest bath in the world, Professor!"

As they still looked upon the carcass two great jaws appeared by its side, gaping and closing with a snap upon the dead body, and in another instant it was dragged below the surface.

"That's the proper way to use a dead mate;—it's the old boy's wife, I expect, taking him down for the young one's dinner."

"Nature is very merciless," responded the Professor gravely.

"Nature don't like anything to be wasted, you mean," retorted the Greek. "He's no more good in the way o' love, but he isn't bad to eat, so good luck to the female who can make the most of her husband while she has anything of him."

On again they went, scrambling through the water and up the sides of stones, until after about an hour they had reached a part where occurred another diverse rift which seemed to stretch into the heart of the mountains to the right, while the stream led onward towards the left.

Between them and this aperture rose a sheer wall of rock of about twenty feet in height, cracked and ridged in all directions.

"I should like to see what lies beyond this wall if we can get over it," said the Professor. So, after taking a breath, they at once began to climb.

A much harder task than any they had yet attempted this proved to be, for, at the best, they could only insert their toes and fingers between the crevices, and had to feel for the next crack while clinging on with all their strength.

It was a task which only determined men and good climbers would attempt. Both got out their knives, digging them in where they could, and holding on while with their feet they frantically and blindly struggled for a footing, with their muscles straining and veins starting out with the effort.

A few feet would be gained, then the knives would give way,

195

and back they would fall against the boulders which were scattered about the bottom.

Niggeree was the surest footed, and, after many a slip, managed to reach the top, and clutch hold of an overhanging branch with which he drew himself up, even as the Professor made his fifth slip and now lay on his back looking up helplessly.

"Chuck me up your belt, Professor, and I'll fasten it to mine and be able to reach you," cried Niggeree from the top.

The Professor unfastened his leather belt, and pitched it up, with which Niggeree hooking the two together, and holding on to the branch leaned over, reaching to within four feet of where he now stood.

Another scramble up, and he catches hold of the end dangling near him, and then slowly works his way up to where the Greek lay.

"A stern pull, friend, and I hope we have no more of that work."

"So do I," panted Niggeree, as he unfastened the belts, and put his on again.

They were now inside a dried-up watercourse, composed of loose sand and brownish-looking basaltic boulders of all sizes and shapes, some lying detached and rounded, while others were piled against each other like rounded castle-walls.

The sides of the mountain were of the same character, great walls split up as if by earthquakes, with dark fissures opening up, half concealed by dense masses of foliage, knarled trunks, and roots wreathed about the stones like vast snakes.

The sunlight poured over the place where they stood, but further on the beetling cliffs seemed to meet over-head, and to close in the passage.

The gully led upwards towards this dark vista at a steep incline, so that as they stood they reckoned themselves to be over three hundred feet above the river.

"Friend Niggeree, if there is gold to be found in this land it ought to be here, let us pause and examine."

The Professor bent down, and passing his hand amongst the sand raked it up; as he turned over the first few handfuls, the Greek watched them filtering down.

As it ran between his fingers the sunshine, streaming over it, flashed on a number of minute specks.

"I thought so, my friend, it is here for the washing; let us follow up the course, and see where it has been sent from."

They went along slowly after this, turning over stones out of which scrambled many a strange insect monster—centipedes, white and deadly-looking, scorpions, which waddled away like crabs; they paid little heed to the alteration of scenery in their eager watching of the ground.

At times the Professor became diverted in his gold searching when some new species of the insect world was exposed; at these times he got out his case from his knapsack and paused to secure the prize, Niggeree going on it front.

At one of these pauses, he looked up to see the other a good way ahead; an evil gleam came into his dark eyes as he saw this, while he muttered,—

"Ah! you are eager to find the gold for me, my friend; the alligator is a good precedent."

Niggeree had swooped suddenly down at that instant, picking something up, and with a half-glance behind, stuffed it hurriedly into his pocket.

"What have you found?"

"Nothing," replied Niggeree, going on, and kicking at the stones as he went.

They had now come to a part of the gully where the rocks seemed to close a couple of hundred feet above them, shutting out the daylight, and leaving before them a vast, cavern-like aperture.

A gloomy, Dantesque scene, with columns—masses of rock piled up—and long rope-like roots of trees dangling down from the crevices above and running along the ground until they found a hole in the earth below.

They seemed to face one of the gateways to the Inferno.

The daylight penetrated for some yards inside over the rugged sides of the walls and the confused masses all around. Beyond that, deep impenetrable blackness lead into the centre of the mountain.

"We must get a light."

Niggeree with his knife cut off a length or two of the dry roots, and gathering some of the scrubby, sun-bleached bushes which clustered about their feet, carried them into the cavern mouth.

Then he bent down and struck a match, and set the wood on fire.

"What was that?"

He started back as he spoke, and looked into the darkness, as a loud hissing broke on the silence.

"Snakes!"

Along the floor glided an enormous serpent, not less than twenty feet.

As it rose to face them Niggeree fired his Winchester, blowing the head right off and raising a thousand echoes, which vibrated along for about five minutes until lost in extreme

197

distance, while at the report a perfect cloud of bats and flying-foxes hurried out, with dazed eyes, and casting down an avalanche of dust, which drove the two explorers into the open, coughing and choking.

"Are you going any further?" asked the Greek, as he recovered himself.

"Certainly, my friend, this looks like an adventure."

"And tastes like one also," replied the other, spitting on the ground.

The firewood was blazing up inside by this time, and glaring up the sides of the walls, while they could hear the sounds of legions of bats retreating backwards.

As the Professor spoke Niggeree went forward and held his links of roots to the flames, where they quickly caught fire, and sputtered as he held them.

"There's your torch for you; let us cut some more down and go on."

Each secured a bundle of root-ends, and holding the lighted one, pushed forward.

"I hope there is no more of that chap's family about," said Niggeree, as they went on.

"Try to get the next one whole if you can," replied the Professor, thinking more upon his specimens than the danger.

Onward through the blackness, only dimly lighted up, they went, tripping over stones and running against bigger masses, sometimes having to leap across ugly fissures which yawned across their path, yet never thinking about the going back, impelled by the curiosity natural to explorers to see what lay in front.

The upper portion was lost in darkness, as the links only served to illuminate a few yards round them.

They have lighted fresh links, which are resinous and easily kept alight.

For about a mile and a half they went on, when all at once the ground took a sudden dip, into which they stumbled before they were aware and dropped simultaneously upon their knees, groping eagerly in the darkness for their links, which had both fallen from their hands and lay sputtering amongst the sand.

"Quick, the matches," cried the Professor, in an impressive voice. And Niggeree strikes a match and once more sets fire to the torches.

"Ah! gold at last."

Yes, it was there unmistakably, in dust and water-worn nuggets, as much as they could wallow amongst, washed into this natural pocket or depression of the ground by some far-distant watercourse, and cleaned from the débris, which had been driven further down.

A natural cradle in some mighty past. The accumulations of ages had been forced into it from the earth above and swirled about by the dashing water until the heavy lumps and grains had been deposited clean at the bottom, while the flood bore the lighter dirt out of the water-worn basin; it lay clean and to their hand, to lift and carry away as they could.

The two men for the first few moments looked at the treasure with stupified eyes, oblivious to one another and all around them; they seemed as if they were alone in that place and unconscious of each other.

Round them the great blackness hung, which the two torches, now stuck upright amongst that glittering dust, hardly lighted, the two men stood with flaming cheeks and lips apart.

Gold more than enough for twenty men, more than they could carry away in forty journeys!

And out of the darkness in front came a dull roaring, which neither of them heard in their excitement, the roaring of water falling from a great height and into a vast depth; the muffled roar of a subterranean waterfall.

With a gasp Niggeree awoke, and began to stuff his trousers pockets and inside his shirt with the precious rubbish.

"Hold!" cried the Professor, darting forward and seizing him. "It is my discovery—it is all mine!"

"What! you cursed thief, ain't I to have my share?" And Niggeree caught the Professor by the throat.

"No, only one can claim this prize."

"Then I'm the prize-holder," cried the Greek; and in a frenzy they both closed with one another.

They were both powerful men, well matched, and both for the time madmen.

It is no uncommon frenzy, this gold fever. Once a friend of mine coming to England had as a fellow-passenger a lucky miner. He had converted his pile into sovereigns, which he wore constantly round his body in a belt; sleeping and waking he never took it off. One day, near the tropics, they saw him come on deck and take his belt off, which he opened, and deliberately poured the contents overboard, afterwards jumping after them.

Another digger, one of three who had been working a hole for months, drew to the surface a large nugget; he looked at it a moment, and then dived down the hole, breaking his neck at the bottom.

They were both well matched as far as strength lay, but Niggeree was hampered by his Winchester and his weight of gold-dust, which got into his way and tripped him up as they wrestled and fought together.

Now up, now down, rolling amongst the riches, they had fallen over the links and stamped them out, so that it was a battle in the dark.

Out of the gold vein and backward they struggled towards that sound of roaring water, with their ears filled with curses as they hit at one another and rolled about.

Niggeree is under now, and the Professor has got him by the throat—closer—he is gasping for breath, and his hands slightly relax.

With an effort they are both on their feet, but the Professor has not relaxed his mastiff grip.

"Ha!" The Professor gives his enemy a sudden pitch forward and he is free, standing waiting on the next attack from his unseen enemy.

But Niggeree does not come again, and the Professor collects himself and listens intently. Niggeree has the matches with him, so that the Professor cannot strike a light.

Then he hears that sound of rushing waters, and a great horror comes over him as he listens.

What is it? He drops on his hands and knees and goes forward in that fashion, feeling carefully one hand before another as he creeps.

Three hand-lengths it is a solid and smooth water-worn rock, inclining slightly upwards from the gold bed; but at the fourth stretch his hand suddenly dips down into vacancy, while upward float cold spray—vapours, which chill his very soul as they damp his tangled hair and soft beard.

Chapter XXXV
Return of the Professor

HECTOR and Collins, from the deck of the Nora, watched the forms of the two excursionists as they passed up the glen and disappeared into the hazy atmosphere; then with a look up and down the river, settled themselves for a comfortable forenoon smoke and talk together.

They did not anticipate much danger from natives, as they had nearly persuaded themselves by this time that this portion of the land was uninhabited, as they had not seen hitherto the slightest indication of human life—no vestige of smoke or gardens, not a single banana leaf breaking upon the general tree-covered hills, always the signal of natives.

The men on board had all been imported from the two schooners, Killmann's original crew having entirely disappeared. The Chinaman, who acted as cook, came from the galley of the Sunflower, while the others were Malays and South-Sea Islanders, Malays mostly, and all familiar with and attached to their temporary masters.

They did not, however, relax in vigilance, although free from anxiety, every man having his loaded weapon to his hand if wanted, and as they swung their legs over the gunwale it was seldom that an instant passed without some glance sweeping their surroundings.

From the galley wafted apetizing perfumes of roasting flesh, while from the engine-room rose occasionally an aroma of machine-oil not quite so agreeable.

"I tell you what, mate," observed Collins slowly between his whiffs, "I don't much mind when this exploring of the Professor's comes to an end, and we get once more back to our own diving operations. I don't care much for either of the two gone together up that ere gully, but of the two I'd rather have Nig."

"They are both bad nuts."

"None worse, when they get a fair show; but of the two, Nig is most to be trusted. He don't muddle amongst them poison pastes and undrinkable spirits, he's rougher and more like his trade, and you know pretty well when he's on the job; but the other, with his friendship here and friendship there, puts me always in mind of Lucretia Borger."

"Oh, we are pretty safe, he has no call to get us out of his way," replied Hector.

"I ain't so sure o' that, mate, with that discovery o' yours over there."

"He tells me it's useless."

"If he tells ye that, believe the direct opposite. By the Lord, Hector, I never thought you had found gold until this moment, now I do."

"So do I, in spite of his telling me the contrary."

"Whar's your specimen?"

"The Professor has it, but promises to give it me when we part company."

"Did he offer it ye, or did you ask for it?"

"I asked him for it; he wanted to put it amongst his curios."

"Then see that ye get it, mate; and take my tip, look alive again parting time; we hain't said good-bye yet to the Professor."

"We must both look up to time, I reckon, then. This new river discovery is worse for us than the gold finding, the Professor don't like to share his finds with white people."

"Tell you the truth, mate, only that they gave us a hand, and that I would not do a mean action, I'd up steam and cut now, while they are ashore, I would if it wasn't for that and old friendship for Nig."

"No! we must stick to our post whatever happens, only we'll watch his movements. Besides, we are always three to one, for Nig will side with us, and the boys are all our own on board; he'd try the lot of us if he tried one," said Hector.

"Still, I'm almost afeard he may dose us."

"No fear, Johnny will see to that, he is the man most afraid on board, of the Professor; he knows how the last Chinaman went, and don't sleep much when the other is awake."

"Carolina Joe now is a mate worth calling a mate. I reckon him true as yourself, Hector, when he gives a mate his paw."

"Yes, he is as white a man as we have in these seas, but Nig will do, so long as ye don't go dead agin him."

The Chinaman glided forward at this moment.

"Dinireb, skippels, am on de tably."

"All right, Johnny, and we can do it."

"Skippels, me hear de Plofesshy man muttat to himself muchly last night and lookly uncommon ugly when no on nealey."

"And what do you 'spect, John."

"Niggly no come back to-day, and den Plofesshy go for you."

"We'll look out for that, John, boy."

"Me lookly uncommon libely also."

They both rose and went into the cabin, the Chinaman following after to act as steward.

"Fishly belly good, me caught him last night."

The fish was discussed and found excellent.

Some blue pigeons came after, dressed à la Chinois, that is chopped up bones and all, after which they had some roast wild pig.

"Me no cookly the paladisely bild Plofesshy skinned last night, me nclel cook what Plofesshy skin, chuck him ovleybold unless Plofesshy want to eat him himself."

"You are mighty suspicious, John, about the Professor."

"John know Plofesshy, dat all 'bout it."

Both men laughed at John's conclusion, and rose to get their pipes.

"Canoes coming round bend," laconically shouted out Jack the Malay from his place on deck, which made them both dart to the door.

202

Yes, at last they were to see what they had almost given up.

Three, fishing canoes apparently, two with women inside, and the third containing a couple of natives and half a dozen of boys.

"Oh, we needn't bother much about that lot," said Collins indifferently, going back for his pipe.

The natives had not at first seen the Nora as they floated down the stream, but now the appalling sight burst upon them when they were nearly opposite it, and with loud exclamations of surprise and fear they paused on their paddles.

Yet, on the whole, they seemed much less shy when viewing white men for the first time than many natives whom the two friends had been amongst, and after shouting the Moresby dialect to them, "Mai! Mai!" several times they appeared to comprehend that the strangers were friends and meant "peace," for the canoe with the men came very close and waited for the next advance.

Eventually, after proffering several articles, such as beads, gaudy bits of cotton, sticks of tobacco (it was like luring on a bird that you wish to capture) the men handed the wares over the ship's sides, which were taken by the male natives and given over on the blades of their paddles to the women who took possession of them. The full act of friendship was consummated when Collins passed over a handful of salt; the men tasted, first doubtfully, then eagerly, handing over a very small share to the women, who no sooner tasted it than they at once impulsively paddled over to the side with pleased grimaces, holding up their hands for the rope which was cast to them to lift them aboard.

The day is waning before the treaty is quite concluded, but now they are all squatted on deck telling the two friends, in a language from which they can distinguish as nearly approaching the Motu dialect, that their village is near at hand up in a valley about four miles from where they are anchored, and that they are not so numerous as they were owing to a very powerful and savage tribe which occupy the mountains.

"Are they also near at hand?" inquired Collins.

"Oh no, they live several days' march distant, but come down sometimes on a marauding expedition, and then we have to fly."

"You like Kiki?" asked Collins, pointing to his own arm as he spoke.

"No! no!" with motions of disgust. "The hill fellows kill and eat."

As they are still conversing, a distant shot fired in the gully attracts their notice.

"By Jove, that is our party, and in danger. Quick, boys, let us go ashore and help them."

Hector decides to stay on board to look after the ship, so Collins, taking his revolver and guns, while the two natives offer to accompany him and three of the Malays, row over to the water-edge and leap ashore.

"Keep the boat ready here when we come back," says Collins to one of the boys, while the four others follow him as he rushes up the glen.

Two more revolver reports, nearer at hand, greet their ears as they approach the bend of the rocks and then they are round it, and can see the Professor staggering towards them with his shirt torn from his back, hatless and ghastly.

Is this the same man who left them that morning, whom they rush forward to lift up? He has stumbled forward on his face, and they can see a couple of arrows protruding from his back.

His curly hair looks bleached and grey, and when Collins lifts him up, the face is pinched like the face of an old man.

"Killmann! Rouse up, old fellow."

The Professor opens his lids for a moment, staring wildly at Collins, then, even as he tries to speak, falls back in a swoon.

"Look out, Boss," cries one of the Malays, and Collins is on his feet once more to see a dark band of savage-looking gigantic men swarming over the rocks.

"Fire, boys, steady," cries the leader, and the three rifles pour out their deadly contents, bringing down an equal number of the advancing crowd, and causing the others to fall back for a moment, while the two friendly natives bend their heads and put their fingers into their ears.

Collins beckons to the natives to lift the prostrate man and carry him on before them, and both being tall fellows stoop and pick him up at once, and between them begin the retreat towards the boat, while the three armed men once more face the enemy and cover the others, as they struggle over the uneven ground.

The two friendly natives were tall fellows, with good-tempered faces and light-coloured skins, differing in this respect from the enemy who were more like negroes than the ordinary type of Papuans. As they stooped to lift up the unconscious Professor, they gently took hold of the arrow ends between their fingers, and broke them off near to the wounds, but did not attempt to pull them out.

Although expressing great fear of their enemies when they first appeared, as they saw the effect of the shots they lost all sense of apprehension, and went along intent only upon their burden, without looking behind and evincing an utter trust in the master

204

white man to have power to protect them, when he had such tremendous powers at his command to destroy.

How numerous the opposing forces were, they had no means of calculating, as only a few of the foremost had as yet fully appeared over the rocks, but before they sank from sight they had a view of the topknots from many a woolly mop for a considerable distance up the glen, as they hurried down to join their comrades in the front.

A few moments of silence followed after the first volley, during which pause the natives managed to get their burden round the corner, then Collins, with a parting volley, aimed at whatever the rocks did not cover, turned quickly to follow.

A shower of arrows at once whistled from behind the rocks, falling far short of the men retreating.

When they reached the bend they could see that the two natives were striding along half-way to the boat in which the Malay waited.

"Hold firm here till they get him down, then make a run for it."

The savages seeing them run had made a rush after them, but upon this sudden halt they shrank back, and seemed inclined to turn tail. However, when they had paused irresolute the ground was comparatively clear, so that those in front could find no shelter to get behind, while the others in the rear were pressing on, and unable to retreat.

The Papuan will run when he can, but if that is impossible, he will fight as desperately as the bravest: it is in moments of emergency such as this that the brute courage seems to rise superior to his natural timidity at this strange mode of warfare.

The rifle was a mystery to him, and mystery ever demoralizes mankind.

But now that there was no escape, their irresolution was only momentary, and with a blood-curdling yell they came on again at a run, the rocks behind seeming to disgorge dark figures, which swarmed over their tops and leaped down into the rushing stream.

"Fire as fast as you can and bolt, they have reached the boat."

Thirteen shots from the Winchester at Collins' shoulder, and two from the Malay double barrels surrounded them with a veil of smoke, under which they turned and ran, loading as they did so.

Another stand and volley half-way down, as through the clearing vapours they could see the indistinct figures, and hear the appalling yells and shrieks. Then the next run brought them to the boat, into which they all sprang, and pushed off.

"Fire from the deck," shouted Collins to Hector, as they pulled round the stern, so as to place the Nora between them and the enemy till they could get on board.

"Aim anywhere, you're sure to hit something, for they are as thick as gooseberries."

Hector and the boys on board blazed away as directed, while Collins clambered up the sides and bent over to help up the wounded man.

"Up with the anchor, and draw off a bit," ordered Hector, as he loaded once more, and watched the smoke clearing.

The anchor is up, and they draw across the stream with their stern towards the gully.

"Pitch a charge from the big gun into them."

A blind aim was directed straight inwards, and fired with a thundrous din, which caused the friendly natives, male and female, to fall flat on their faces, and lie there trembling till the smoke had rolled away.

Then they saw the savages who were not shot, gathered about the water's edge, gesticulating wildly and impotently towards them, while further in were dark figures lying in all positions still, or trying vainly to raise themselves from the ground and the dashing shallow stream, which flowed over them as they lay.

Chapter XXXVI
White Gods

"ARROWS poisoned, and too far in; white man will not live."

This was the verdict given by three of the elder women as they rose up after examining the Professor, whom they had laid upon the aft-deck with his hair mattress under him, while the younger females and children stood round with sympathetic faces.

"Take out the arrows, and let us try what we can do."

"No, he will die at once if the arrows are pulled out; him live till to—morrow this time if they are left in."

They were slowly steaming up the river while this consultation was going on, the natives completely at their ease with their white friends, and eager to carry the surprising news of a victory over their old enemies home, along with the great strangers who had come to help them.

Killmann they had not seen before, and regarded him as an outsider. It was towards Collins and Hector that their hero-worship was extended, whom they regarded with their repeating rifles to be invincible.

There are no gods in New Guinea, yet here was something which came as nearly up to their ideal of what the immortals should be as their materialistic instincts permitted them to entertain.

The savages in the gully they had left behind still leaping about the water's edge and shouting out their blind impotent rage, the arrows which they sent off striking harmlessly against the plated sides or falling short of their mark into the stream.

"Plofesley no bling back Nigley," observed John, gliding up to the group and speaking softly over the heads of the girls.

"By Jove, you are right, John," said Hector with a start, as they remembered, for the first time, the Greek.

"Where is Niggeree?"

The Professor opened his languid eyes at this moment, and gasped out, "Water!"

They ran for a pannikin of water from the cabin, and, adding a few drops of brandy, brought it and held it to his lips, which, after he had drunk, seemed to revive him.

"Niggeree!" he murmured.

"Yes, where is he?"

"Dead."

A silence fell over the group, then the Professor continued in a low whisper, with many a pause,—

"We went up the gully till we came to a vast cavern, into which we penetrated. It was pitch dark, so that we had to carry lighted sticks—a gloomy cavern of vast circumference, and seemingly without a termination, filled, as we advanced, with noxious gases, which made us feel as if intoxicated. Niggeree had the only box of vestas with him, and went on in front. After going about half a mile we both fell over a ridge where the ground seemed to recede under our feet, and our lights were knocked from our hands and all was blackness.

"I shouted to Niggeree to give us another light, but he did not answer me, and for a few moments I lay on the ground listening and waiting for him to speak. Then, in front of me, I heard the muffled rumbling and roaring of a mighty cataract, which seemed to have its termination far underground.

"At last I could bear no more suspense, but crept forward, feeling in front of me with my hands; then all in a moment I found myself half hanging over the edge of a precipice, with nothing to grasp at before me.

"It was so black that I could see nothing, only feel the cold damp mist floating up from that vast abyss, with a deadly feeling as if millions of tons of water were gliding silently before me—how far off I could not say—millions of tons, sinking pronely down, down, thousands of feet into that everlasting darkness.

"A mighty horror chained me to that spot, so that I could not draw myself back, but lay feeling as if years had passed away since last I saw the daylight, and that eventually I must be sucked into that awful gulf, and no one ever know more of my doom than I did of Niggeree's.

"My mind, also, even while thrilled with the horror, seemed to be hard at work forming a hypothesis of the cause of this gulf and the former depressions in the rock over which I had stumbled, so that while I was lying in all this hell of icy fear I seemed, also, to be travelling over the countless centuries which had already passed, and to feel the water rolling over me as I lay at the bottom of the dried-up basin into which I had first fallen—a period when the rocks above projected over where I was lying, and the torrent rushed into the cavern from the mountains above and formed an outlet down the valley.

"Then the upper ledge becoming thinner by the constant wear, and finally breaking off, or by an internal convulsion being split along with the earth in front of me, shifting the position of the fall while it swallowed it up, leaving the cavern and gully outside dry.

"At last I seemed to wake up from my frozen stupor to a burning desire to escape; or was it that I felt myself drawn back by strong hairy claws, with which I fought, and at length threw from me? I cannot say, for my mind seemed utterly unstrung as I madly sprang back in the direction we had taken, and fled with a thousand horrors behind and around me.

"There were some fissures which crossed our path in the coming, but I did not think upon them as I rushed along, and somehow chance aided me in my leaps, for I must have crossed them by accident.

"I panted as I ran, and it must have been my own hot breath returning upon me from the near proximity of the rocks, which I at times struck against, but it seemed to my excited imagination as if I was pursued by demoniac figures, who blew their steaming breath against me, while clutches were made at my shirt and hair from behind as I ran.

"At length I saw daylight filtering grim and grey as it reflected upon the sides of the rocks nearest, and much of my fear departed—my foes also, if there were any, seemed to drift back into their congenial darkness and leave me alone. Another turn, and the gully spread before my eyes bathed in the ever-blessed sunshine of God, through a framework of rocks and rope-like roots which dropped from above.

"I was free, and a great flood of gratitude filled my burning brain like rose-coloured flames, as, beside the headless body of a great snake which Niggeree had shot at the entrance, now growing putrid, I flung myself down and gabbled out loudly my incoherent thanks."

The Professor's cheeks glowed with fever spots, and his dark eyes blazed, as he recited his weird experiences, so that he seemed to forget his weakness, as the words came with fewer pauses and louder as he went on; but now he made a longer pause, and seemed unable to go on.

"So that's the wind up of Nig the bold, is it?" observed Collins, holding up the pannikin to the dying man's lips.

Killmann slowly nodded assent as he drank.

"It is good for you that you could remember some prayers up there."

"Why so?" retorted the Professor.

"Because it always becomes a man to be thankful for benefits received, and I hope ye didn't forget to put in a word or two while at it for our poor mate, who had no time to do the job himself."

The Professor did not reply, but shut his eyes as if tired out.

"Where did ye meet the savages?"

"Not far from the mouth of the gully. I had come out of the dry watercourse and was wading through the stream, when my first intimation was this arrow in my left shoulder—my shirt had been torn from me in my passage through the cave. I turned about to see a vast number sliding down the steep sides of the hill, and holding on to limbs of trees, and ran on, shooting backwards as I went. It was just before I met you that I received the second one into me; then I can remember no more."

"Bad wounds they are, Professor," said Collins still wishing to prepare the wounded man for his end.

"Not so bad—not fatal."

"I don't like to say much, Professor."

"But I feel easier now—bah, I have been wounded before as seriously."

"Not when your blood was in such a heat; hardly so deep, and I doubt if ever by the same kind of weapon."

"Ah, now I know; are they poisoned?"

Collins only looked down without replying.

"My God! am I to die like a poisoned rat, and with none of my work in order—hardly begun?" shrieked out the wounded man, in an agonized tone, while the women looked on with pitiful eyes.

"But, sir, there are some still left alive amongst my destroyers. Where is my revolver?" and he pointed savagely at the group of friendly natives with one hand, while he felt about his empty belt with the other.

As he snarled out the words, they all turned about as if to leap overboard in their fear, when Collins stopped them.

"Hold hard, friends, he can't hurt you, for he has no weapon; and you, sir, if you want to die easy, keep still, as they have been good friends to you."

"No dark skin can be a friend of white men."

"Can't they though, keep your mind easy, we have punished your enemies pretty well, and these people are taking us home out of kindness."

Killmann breathed hard as he lay back, but said nothing more on the subject, and in a few moments afterwards permitted one of the women to come over and sit beside him.

They had reached a portion of the river where it made a sharp turn, and ran through a long valley with sloping banks and broad green grass—fields.

Native pathways led through the fields and down to the waterside over to a thick plantation, where at last they could see the welcome tops of banana-trees.

"Let me go on shore and tell my people that the strangers are our friends," said one of the natives, as the anchor was dropped over the bows. So giving him some presents to take to his chief, they sent him off, the women and children still staying with them.

In a short time they heard the loud sounds of drums, while from the plantation came a band of men, women, and children, following the chief, who strode on in front unarmed, and displaying lively symptoms of joy; their friends had been singing the praises of their great deeds of daring and the victory which they had won.

Hector and Collins met them on the banks, and made the usual signs of friendship observed throughout the west; then the chief took their hands and welcomed them as benefactors.

"Welcome, great white strangers, with your fire bamboos. Stay and help us to kill all our enemies."

They all went through the gardens and villages, finding little difference between the arrangement of houses there and those upon the Fly River; only that they were mostly new, and some as yet unfinished, as they had lately returned to this part of the country, having been driven away the former season by the hill-tribe, and the old place destroyed.

That night there was a great feast, celebrated with a native dance, and many impromptu songs delivered in honour of the White Gods who had come amongst them. The fires were lighted on the banks of the river so that the Nora shone out brightly, on the deck of which they sat with the chief and looked on at the performers, as they danced in their feathered head-dresses and sang.

One of the young girls who had come aboard in the afternoon still hovered about near to Hector, with whom she had made great friends; a pretty young maiden of about sixteen, who showed her preference with the open candour of a widow of forty-five.

In the shadow of the galley they both sat together and talked, while Collins and the old chief smoked gravely on the open deck full in the warm firelight.

Some of the wise women of the village had taken the Professor under their charge, and were now busy upon him with their soothing herbs, and muttering charms.

Before they went to sleep, they had arranged a grand walloby hunt for the next day.

Professor Killmann had been deeper struck than even they at first feared, and that night kept them all awake with his ravings.

His body was swelling rapidly before they came to anchor, and the old chief no sooner saw him than he said calmly, "He will die before the sun comes up," and went on to discuss the arrangements for the morrow as if that matter was settled and need no longer be talked about.

All through the night the fires were kept up on shore, while the natives kept coming and going, sometimes with messages from the old women who acted as death-bed attendants, or moving about the deck and engine—house, touching things out of curiosity.

Collins sat smoking or dozing off close to the mattress on which the dying man was laid, while Hector, tired out with his courting and unaccustomed gallantry, had laid himself down on the cabin sofa where he now lay sound asleep, while his dusky inammorata took her place calmly on the floor beside him, to look after and watch the awakening of her own special white god.

"Blast me, if that err wench won't make another Joe of my mate, if he don't look out; none of them ever bother me."

Collins had come in to mix himself some grog, when he saw this picture of connubial-like repose.

When he reached the deck the Professor was re-acting the scenes of the day which had so fatal a termination.

"Hands off, you thief," he shouted. "It's all mine—gold—

gold! No, I will not give you a penny-weight. Ah! you will have it?—where is he?—God, what a gulf."

"Strikes me, somehow, the Professor hasn't given us his yarn quite complete," murmured Collins, stroking his jaws with his hand as he meditatively stood looking down and puffing slowly.

"I guess he knows more about Nig's death than he is willing to say. No odds, his score will be all wiped off the slate soon now. I wish I could remember something suitable for the occasion, even a grace might do for want of anything better."

But Collins could not recollect even a grace to do service over this dying sinner.

A picture of pathetic gloom, this man of culture and scientific enthusiasm dying like a dog, without being able to command a prayer at this last dark hour. On the deck he lies, raving out suggestions of past blood-guiltiness, with classical reminiscences of old college days, or formerly built up arguments for his theories, ever and anon coming back to that hour of gold lust and the after-time of horror.

The crowd of natives squat or lounge about with perfect indifference to his recollection or wealth of words, and only Collins tries to pick out some thread of information regarding the fate of Niggeree.

Hector woke up next morning as the daylight began to dawn, and cast rather a sheepish eye upon his companion, who quietly rose as he stirred and prepared to accompany him on deck.

"Pletty comfortably last night, skippel?" blandly inquires the Chinese cook and steward, as he glides about, putting things to right. "Bely pletty wifely you hab got now; me get mallied also befole we leab."

"How is the Professor to-day?" inquired Hector, ignoring the other's inuendo.

"He jist about finishly up his plofessleyship. Will you hab yurl bathly firstly or your coffee?"

"I'll take coffee, and go up to see him; bring it to me?"

"All right, skippel; Misely Hector will help you, pelhaps, to bathly aftelwalds."

Mrs. Hector, as John described her, seemed prepared to help the young man in anything;—prepared for every extremity, in fact, except that of losing sight of him; as he went up the little companionway she glided after him like his shadow.

The dying man lay on his side, where he had been propped so that the arrows might not touch against anything; his hollow eyes wandered over the distant hills which terminated this fertile valley, through which this broad river wound about like a silver-grey ribbon. The light was pulsing up over the sky, and rapidly bringing life to this sleeping landscape as it was ebbing away from Killmann. He knew now that he was dying, and, like the brave explorer that he was, had accepted the inevitable calmly, if not with resignation.

"Bury me here, for it is the fairest spot that I have yet seen in this adopted land, and it is mine by right of discovery; you will remember that if ever dispute arises—my discovery."

"Yes, Professor," said both the men.

"Call this river the Albert River, and write over my grave, 'Discoverer of the Albert River;' you promise to do this?"

"We do."

"Thank you;—my steamer and specimens take on to Thursday Island, they are all addressed and catalogued as I went on, and my diary is pretty complete; you have only to deliver them over to Government as they are, and I leave you to tell the manner of my death——"

A long pause, as if the Professor was struggling with his feelings, and trying to brace himself up to say more. They waited patiently for his next words. At last they came, abruptly and hurriedly,—

"Good-bye, my two friends, and forgive me if you can; I would have killed you as I killed Niggeree yesterday, if I could have done it; I threw him over the precipice, although I did not know it was there, we quarrelled about—the——"

The Professor stopped, while his head suddenly fell forward on his chest as the sun lifted its upper rim over the hills.

Chapter XXXVII
A Walloby Hunt

BEYOND the ordinary feelings of gloom which follow death, there was not much regret exhibited by any one on board at the death which had just taken place. Killmann had not done a single action of kindness to any one on board, and if his manner were at times soft and his voice gentle, they were always suggestive of the tiger-cat playing with his victim; the cook, indeed, did not attempt to conceal his entire satisfaction at what he considered to be a most providential dispensation, and went about his duty of preparing breakfast with a more beaming countenance than he had shown since he had been drafted on to the Nora.

It was, therefore, with a feeling of relief that Hector hailed the appearance of the walloby hunting-party which he was to accompany, Collins having promised to stay on board and look after things.

The natives were by this time all over the ship; yet, although they touched and handled everything, they were scrupulously honest, and laid the things back, after gratifying their curiosity, as they had found them.

Amongst the party who came on board, and who were of the hunters, were the father and three brothers of "Jenny," as Hector called his lady friend. She introduced him, and gave them special charge to attend upon him during the day.

They made no inquiry as to where or how she had spent the night, evidently thinking that she could look after herself, as Hector now also began to think.

The other maidens who came on board chaffed her a good deal about her conquest, but did not offer to cut her out in any way; she received their fun with perfect calmness, and showed by her manner that she was in complete possession.

Hector did not attempt to combat this female arrogation of his free will. The tyrant was pretty and winning in her method of subduing him, and he seemed pleased with the silken fetters which she had cast about him from the first, yet it was not so much a case of love-making on his part, as of allowing himself to be adored.

"I say, mate," growled Collins, "how far do you intend this tom-fooling to go on?"

"Well, mate, I haven't quite made up my mind yet about it," replied Hector.

"She intends making it up for you, if you don't."

"Well, you see, mate, I might go further and fare worse; she's a good—looking gal, and there'll be a tidy bit of land go along with her."

"What! d'ye mean to settle down?"

"I might do worse," replied Hector, turning away.

"Ah! that's the way the wind blows; by the Lord, we might all do worse, easily."

After the party left, Collins walked about the deck, puffing at his cherry-wood pipe in a very much absorbed manner.

"Not a finer piece of ground in the whole country. A man might easily clear his pile by a few years' squatting, and do nothing himself all day long except lie on his back; Joe aint such a cussed fool after all," he thought.

The girls made themselves merry with the Malay sailors and John, who seemed to become a great favourite in a very short time. John's cooking operations in consequence were much disturbed, and for the first time a smell of burning pervaded the forenoon air, as his galley became a general reception-room; but none of the fair ones offered to approach the meditative Collins, perhaps considering him too high a dignitary to approach without feelings of awe and reverence.

On the after-deck, which none of the young women came near, sat a circle of old crones, chanting a monotonous song in dreary tones as they watched over the corpse, and kept the flies from alighting upon the wax—like, sallow features.

The natives had to cross the river before they reached their hunting—ground, and by way of preparation they came fasting to the ground, and, when they started, walking in single file, trailed their hunting-spears behind them without speaking a word.

Hector knew enough of native customs to accept his position in the ranks, walking between the brothers of Jenny, and also carrying the spear which they brought for him; yet, besides his spear, he had taken the precaution of slinging his Winchester to his back.

In the rear followed the younger men, carrying coils of native-spun nets and long poles.

He did not mention the breakfast which he had partaken of that morning to his fellow-huntsmen.

By-and-by they came to the crossing, where they found a raft lying ready made, composed of several pieces of log and crossed vines, above which a large platform had been raised. Long rattans were attached to the raft, and carried by expert swimmers across the river, the swimmers then drawing the others over.

After crossing the river, they passed along in the same order and silence until they reached a field of dry cane-grass, enclosed by steep low hills on three sides, leaving a single outlet towards the river-side.

They did not enter the field or valley, but now the younger men ran round it, enclosing it with their nets, which they fastened to the poles at different points, leaving here and there wide gaps between, at which the hunters stationed themselves.

They had chosen the hour of day when what wind there was blew from the hills down towards the river.

Then, after these arrangements were completed, they set fire to the grass at the top of the valley, and waited patiently but watchful at their gaps for the scared game to come out.

Hunting, like fishing, is a brutal and ignoble game, even at its highest and most daring aspect, gloss it over however writers may with showy descriptions and merry songs of, "We'll all go a-hunting to-day," &c. This was merely the converting of a peaceful valley into a battue and slaughter-yard. As the flames and smoke rushed downward all that had life fled towards the river, butting madly against the restraining netting, until they had discovered the treacherous gateways, and rushing, to reverse the simile, from the fire into the frying-pan.

Kangaroos, wallobies, and wild pigs came charging down and out, and as they passed were stabbed to death by the hunters.

It was all over in about half an hour, and then they could count up their victims and carry them back to their rejoicing friends. Hector did marvels with his spear, and when his arms tired of that sport he brought out his Winchester and potted the retreating game that had escaped the spear—thrusts. The wild pigs inspired no pity in his breast. There is something about a pig, wild or tame, which prompts one to kill it; a dead pig has no pathos about it: it is only suggestive of roast pork, bacon, and grovelling baseness, without a spark of sentiment to redeem it. But it was different with the kangaroos and wallobies, as they leapt forward wildly and beat against their trap nettings with the flames behind them, and their hind—like eyes meltingly expressive of horror; Hector found it much easier to hold back his spear and let them escape, than he did to stab the gentle creatures to death.

With the other hunters supper was of much greater importance than weak sentiment. Hector brought down a much greater number of wild pigs than he bagged of kangaroos.

As they returned, heavily laden, they all sang a loud paean of rejoicing over the quantity of flesh which they had secured.

Along the pathway, over the river, and towards the village they passed, dancing and singing their loud song. Here the women met them with glad cries, and took the game from them, staggering under the welcome load, while the men slackened their pace, and prepared the bamboo pipes.

Jenny came with the rest, and brought her mother along with her, so that Hector had the rare delight of a maternal embrace to refresh him. The old lady wanted to take him home, so that he might begin his month of trial at once, but waved this fine point of etiquette when she saw he would not come, and allowed him to go his own way, her daughter following instead. Still the old lady wagged her head disapprovingly as she let them go, as if it was establishing a precedent dangerous to the rights and happiness of womankind. She, however, looked narrowly after his share of the game, claiming all which bore bullet-holes, and as many as they would allow her of the others, carrying them, with the aid of the sons and husband, to her own residence to cure at her leisure.

Hector was pleased to see the maiden again, and passing his arm round her naked waist, went on with her leisurely through the fields towards the river's edge. He had committed himself now, and did not regret his betrothal, for she was very tender and soft when she was alone with him, if dignified a trifle before spectators.

They did not speak much, for they could not, as they went through the fields, but they paused often and faced one another; then the space lessened between them considerably, and Hector did not care how soon the wedding came off, as he felt her warm body against his upper pijamas, and her moist, loving lips pressed against his.

They did not require to speak much, for Jenny felt herself the mistress of the position; she had caught her hare, and she knew how to dress him, as what woman doesn't, savage or civilized.

When they came to the banks of the river she was like Venus carrying the arms of Mars, for round her slender shoulders she had the dreaded Winchester, and stuck in the waist of her raumma or grass petticoat his trusty revolvers, while he walked along at her side, with his arm loosely circling her neck.

He had made up his mind to be a Papuan farmer.

"Hallo!" said he, starting back, as his eyes rested on the river, and rubbing them with both hands to see if he was really awake; "the Thunder alongside of the Nora!"

It was so. There lay the Thunder alongside of the Nora, with the light smoke escaping from her funnel.

"Who would have thought it?" And he ran along the river-bank and up the plank towards the steamer, Jenny, faithful, never-failing Jenny, following at his heels.

There a greater surprise awaited him—the supposed to be dead Niggeree calmly smoking his pipe, in the company of Bowman, Brown, Danby, Collins, Captain MacAndrews, and Hans the engineer.

"Had good sport?" observed Niggeree, looking up with an unconcerned air.

"Well, I'm blessed!" was all Hector could ejaculate, as he dropped of a heap into the vacant deck-chair. "Could any one hand me a drink?"

Chapter XXXVIII
Hibiscus Blossoms

"WALL, you see," said the Greek, settling himself down for a tall yarn, "this is how it all happened, as nearly as I can spin it," and then he paused for some time to collect his thoughts.

They had consigned the Professor to his last home before

supper, the natives digging the grave for him on the river-bank; the grave-stone was a slab of wood, at present painted white by Collins, and on which he intended to write the dead man's last wishes after the present coat of paint had dried. It was lying up against the boiler.

Supper was over, and they were all on deck, with their glasses placed handy, and a lantern swung aloft to let them see the way to their mouths; the Singalese steward was in attendance, as John had gone ashore to stay with some of his newly-gained and admiring friends. Hector had his own special attendant, who took care never to let his glass remain long empty, so that already he began to feel as if the comforts of married life were dawning upon him.

Jenny filled his pipe—she had learned the English way of doing it—and kept his glass well replenished, in spite of the coarse jests of the others. Jenny acted as young ladies will do in the days of courting and very early honeymoon, while Hector leaned back, contented and satisfied with himself (as the male animal always is under such circumstances), thinking that this was the sort of life that ought to last for ever. It is so gratifying to be an autocrat, and have at least one faithful slave at your elbow.

"I don't want to abuse any one who is dead and gone," said Nig, "so I'll jist say that the party as has just been stowed alow ground and myself had a bit o' a racket, about what is of no consequence to any one not concarned. We froze on to one another, and raised creation, all in the dark; for, as you will obsarve, our mill took place in a cave arter our torches were kicked out."

"Wherever were you, Nig?" inquired Danby.

"Wall, you see, as they will tell you, the party as is gone and I went out on an exploring expedition, and, after going up a gully, we came to a cave, where all was black as Captain Kid's flag, barring the skull and cross-bones.

"A mighty snake warned us not to go in, but the party as was with me would do it, so I blowed the head of that ere reptile and pushed on.

"By-and-by we both fell on our noses, knocking the light out, and that I reckon raised our bile, for afore long we had holt o' one another, wrestling and kicking up the clay all round. I guess I was as much to blame as he, an' he was as much to blame as me, and that's the best I can say about it.

"Wall, as you can see, we were fighting away, not knowing whur we were putting our feet, whan all at once I felt the ground give way under me, an' I was falling, the Lord only knows whar.

"I made a wild clutch forward, and at that moment got catch

of a bit of ledge, to which I clung on like grim death, with my feet dangling down, and the devil's own darkness all about me.

"I reckon that I am a pretty fair holder-on if I once get a grip, but I held on to that rock as I never thought any man could.

"It might ha' been moments, and it might ha' been hours, that I hung on to that rock, as you might do to a trapeze, with nothing below me to touch with my feet, an' a most awful sound below, like as if it was two miles of a drop into boiling water, and all my weight upon my two arms like to tear them out of their sockets.

"I can't tell you what it was like,—like something I once read of in the 'Spanish Inquisition;' I darn't let go with that sound below me, an' I felt I must give way some time.

"An' all the time my hands and arms ached; it felt as if raining upwards, a drizzly ice-cold rain that froze and cramped me all over.

"At last I began to see things dancing afore my eyes, bloody spots and rings of yellow with blue insides, that grew from little to big, and down again to wriggling worms, and the cramp got into my aching fingers, and I felt that I must let go.

"Wall, you see, it's nothing-like to tell about it; but, Lord above, it wor something to feel.

"When would I stop dropping when I fell, and into what would I drop; would I hit anything on the road and hurt much, afore the last landing—place? My fingers were slipping, spite of me digging my nails in till they were torn off, as you ken see; then I gave way."

"You did not fall into that infernal gulf, surely," cried Hector, excited over the remembrance of the Professor's account of the place.

"Wall, no, I didn't quite fall, for it had been a ghastly sell all the time. I warn't three inches from my landing-place, yet I thought my heart had burst as I came down on my back, for as I touched the solid everything went from me, so that I knew no more for that time.

"I guess I must ha' fainted, for when I came to I found myself lying on the side of the mountain not far from the edge of a great deep hole, into which a big waterfall plunged from a high cliff over my head.

"I could see the water rushing over the rocks black and swift, like a mill-race, without a sound of water, so that it gave me the creeps to see it fall so deathly quiet."

"None of your lies, Nig; tell us how you got up?"

"That, mates, I can tell you no more about than the man o'

the moon. There I was, and that's all I can say about it—it might ha' been an angel that flew up with me, or else—"

"The devil, more like!"

"I won't be positive either way, for as I got up I saw two or three black—looking critters, not unlike the devil, skurrying up the trees, with long tails behind them."

"Had you been drinking much, before you went out on that spree?" inquired Danby, gravely.

"Not enough for what you mean, Mr. Danby," said Nig, lighting his pipe, and sucking energetically for two or three seconds.

"Well, go on," said Bowman. "How did you get down?"

"Wot's the good of telling a yarn if it's not believed?"

"Oh! I believe it," said Bowman.

"Like Gospel," added Danby.

"Come, finish it off," they all cried.

"The getting down warn't at all difficult. It got on dark not long after I started, so I lay down in the bush and had a sleep till daylight this morning, and then I got down to the gully we started from, to find the Nora gone."

"Did you see any natives?" asked Collins.

"Plenty lying about without their heads, but not one alive; so I thought, maybe, ye had had a bit of a scrimmage, and might come back to look after me, and I sat down to wait."

"Yes, we—yes, we saw him sitting without a stitch on the shore as we passed, and picked him up in the passing," observed Bowman, "and brought him on."

"That's all my yarn, mates," said the Greek. "I went into that cave with my togs on, my Winchester, colts, and cutlass around me, and summut in my pockets, and found myself on the hill-top same as if I had been born again, an' I don't ask you to believe it; I guess I wouldn't either, if any one else told it to me."

Niggeree took up his glass and drained it, and then returned to his pipe.

"What do you think the animals were that you saw?" asked Hector, from his seat.

"Monkeys—or baboons, I dunno which."

"Monkeys in New Guinea?" exclaimed Hector.

"I can't think of anything else," replied Nig, "and I don't want to bother my brains any more about it. I was down that hole, and now I am sitting here, and that is all I know about it. It is uncommon strange!"

This they all admitted, and then turned to hear the other adventures.

"What do you think of the scenery about this part of the

country, captain?" asked Collins, of MacAndrews, as they hob-nobbed together.

"Grand, sublime, just like a drop-scene which I saw in Sydney, when they were acting Micky Dhue."

The worthy old skipper meant the "Mikado."

"Yes, the Albert River beats the Fly all to fits," returned Collins, in the gratified tone which a man uses when he hears something belonging to him praised.

"Collins, old man," said Brown, at this point, "you may call it the Albert River, if you like, out of respect for the departed, when amongst your and his friends, and write the name on that slab also, as it was a dying promise; but it must be written differently on the charts, as it had been christened before ever you saw it—say, how many days is it since you sighted it?"

"This makes the sixth day—two days going down the Fly, four days back and forward from the 'Collins'—that makes six, and the other six we've been on this water, from sea-entrance to here," replied Collins.

"Ah! that just gives the Thunder two days' clear start of the Nora, which I will demonstrate to you beyond a doubt," said Brown. "Eight days ago we penetrated the Aird River, to find out as you did, but before you did by two days, that it was only one of many mouths of the present river, which we christened 'The Douglas,' and the Douglas it has to be from this time henceforth."

"Have you also christened the Collins River?" inquired Hector, quietly getting up from his chair, and coming forward towards Brown.

"No, Captain Hector; I yield to you and your friend the right to that discovery," responded Brown, frankly.

"Thank you, Mr. Brown, I only asked for information," and Hector went back once more to his shadow.

"If I had been there I would have proved it to your satisfaction, as I hope to do this. Steward, fetch my charts and diary," said Brown.

The Singalese glided off and returned with the articles required, placing them at the feet of the explorer, and while stooping whispered something in his ear.

"Oh! hang your slips of paper," said the explorer, "mark all the drinks down to me to-night."

"Thank you, sah," and the steward slid back once more to his place behind the circle.

"There you are, boys, and something more than you know already, which you can look at as I read my notes," said he, spreading open his rough chart and showing it to them. Collins and Hector both came forward and knelt down over it, while Mr.

Brown read; Niggeree, as if taking no interest in the matter, sat where he was.

"This is the 29th, isn't it?" asked Brown.

"Yes," responded the others.

"All right, now listen: 21st.—Arrived at the mouth of the Aird River, where we found a broad channel carrying three to sveen fathoms of water right into the river. After following up the Aird, we found that it was only one of many mouths of a great freshwater river coming from mountain ranges. After trying several channels we got into the main river, which we followed up for several miles in a direct line from coast, carrying good water all the way into mountain ranges."

"Right you are," say the others.

"We determined to call it the Douglas River, and returning down, as we had to go to Motu-motu, struck a fresh branch and came out in Deception Bay."

"Ah! you did, did you?" said Collins.

"We did. After finishing our business at Motu-motu, we returned, searching the coast, and discovered a magnificent new river with an entrance over three miles wide, close to Bald Head. We proceeded up this river 110 miles, passing through ranges and gorges, in places 1500 feet high, its principal trend being easterly and north easterly, and unusually serpentine. This river we called the Jubilee, while the ranges we have called what you want the river to be, viz. the Albert Ranges. There, are you satisfied, boys?"

Mr. Brown closed his diary, and clasped it as he spoke.

"Quite satisfied, Mr. Brown, and I ask your pardon," said Hector, going up with his hand outstretched.

"Don't mention it, old man," said Brown, cordially taking the other's hand. "I wish, for your sake, I could have obliged you by being last on the ground"—and he laughed heartily—"but can't afford it, you know—have to report dates, &c., to headquarters."

"It isn't for our sakes I wanted it," said Hector, "but for the poor professor, who has found a grave where he thought he had discovered a new river. He was late for the Fly, and now he is too late for this."

"It is hard lines," said Brown, "to be too late for everything, and to discover only what some one else justly claims; but it is a common destiny of mankind. At the most we can only travel along in this too-late century. The world, after New Guinea is laid open, will be used up, and ought, by the natural order of things, to burst. Still, boys, there's a lot to find out about here yet, and a deal to be made out of it, also; so let us drink, 'Success to the Land of the Hibiscus Blossom.'"

The glasses were drained to this toast, after which the explorer continued,—

"I can see it all coming about in the future—in my mind's eye, Horatio, of course—these splendid-looking savages, with their quick adaptability, blending in with us, the men of civilization, and rising in the ranks; towns rear where the villages now stand, and the acclimatized Queenslanders flocking over and growing rich when drivelling old England has lost her best blood, as she has already lost the best portion of this mighty island, through her own blind old-world stupidity."

"And the Germans will set us the example in their end," quoth Niggeree quietly. "No blank missionary there to spoil fair trade."

"I suppose you mean black traffic by fair trade, Nig," put in Danby.

"I mean what I mean," responded Nig. "The Germans will set us the example, as they always do when new ground has to be broken, when perseverance, patience, and hard labour are wanted. I don't blame them for taking what they had offered to them, though I, as a good colonist, grudge them their luck; but I do blame the man with the ass's ears and foxy tongue who, in the triumph of his blundering ignorance, gave away the birthright of Australia from his country's own daughter, because she was abroad, and not under his very nose to assert her rights."

"As for the missionaries," continued the explorer, "they are doing what they can, as they always do, to raise the races, and if they do try to keep the world as it was, or supposed to be, in the early days of Mother Eve, small blame to them, even although their work should be all in vain. As it has always been so will it be, the natural man must disappear, with his simple tastes and little wants, before the artificial man with his requirements. They may merge, but they must eventually disappear; it is all according to the law of evolution."

At this moment the Ching cook came back with a bevy of fair maidens following, and the outside of his solitary lock adorned with a wreath of hibiscus leaves and flowers, while clusters of the same ornamental shrub, intermixed with croton leaves, had been twisted about his slender form. He approached decked out like a Chinese god during high festival, surrounded by his devotees. Three of the damsels seemed to have taken him under their special charge, and now gathered forward, fondling his pig-tail tenderly, as if it was a charm against witchcraft.

"There is John, you see, setting the example in the merging question, if he can decide amongst so many."

"I hab decidedly, Messly Blown, to do my duty and not be gleedy. I am going to tuln a falmer, and only hab tlee."

"Three of them, John? Why, you are easily pleased. When is the marriage to take place?"

"In a monthly, if Skippel Negley will let me stay behindly."

"You can stay, John, till I return with the Sunflower, and I reckon by that time that you will have enough of matrimony on the large scale," graciously answered the Greek, whose frequent applications to the pannikin had made him more than ordinarily agreeable.

John thanked his master profusely, apparently thunderstruck with his unaccustomed generosity, and retired to the fore part of the vessel with his train, where the Malays were, and where shortly arose loud sounds of merriment.

"Do you intend coming back soon?" inquired Hector from his corner to Niggeree.

"Yes, I mean to explore that mountain again, and find out what lifted me up; also see if I cannot get back my Winchester again, as I prize it. You intend stopping, also, don't you?"

"Yes—I think so," returned Hector, in a hesitating tone.

"And I think you are wise, old boy," returned Brown. "If I hadn't left a Mrs. B., I might follow your example. I reckon the pair of you ought to make a fine breed for the future country, and there's a good few pots of money lying idle in these fat fields."

"I reckon there aint much gold about these fields," retorted Niggeree with undue haste.

"Not in the sense you mean, perhaps, although even about that I have my own thoughts; it is in a broader and much more profitable way that I refer to the man who can claim some of this land as a freehold to hand down to his offspring. I hope some day to be able to settle down here myself."

"Look out for a squaw for me against I get back, mate," cried out the Greek.

"Why, you old polygamous pirate, how many women do you want to claim before you are strung up?" asked Danby.

"You shut up, youngster."

"You can see that you are not born to be drowned, at any rate now, surely, after escaping that waterfall; so I don't see how else you can pass away except you are translated, you know," remarked Brown, with a laugh.

"Take my advice, and stick to the East End beauties which you have already won, Nig, down amongst the cannibals of Killerton, and leave these Western beauties alone. You would never make a good farmer."

"Talking about Killerton Island, they say that you had to hook it from there for eating two of your wives. Is that true?"

"No, it aint true, and I can go back to Killerton to-morrow if I liked," answered the badgered Greek in a surly tone.

"Then you must take me over there some time when you go," said Brown, quickly.

"When you like, mate; and I promise to bring you back safe, also, if you do come."

"All right; we'll arrange about it by-and-by. Good-night, boys; I must turn in, for we mean to be off again to-morrow. Time's about up, and we are due at Thursday Island next Saturday."

Chapter XXXIX
Bon Soir, Queen Ine

NEXT morning the Thunder and Nora turned their prows towards the sea, a regular flotilla of fishing and state canoes accompanying them for some miles upon their way.

The young braves came decked up in their gala-day ornaments, and the plantations seemed to be stripped of their glory for the occasion, as not only were the heads adorned, but the carved beaks and gunnels were glowing with scarlet and green until they looked like floating gardens.

Hector and the polygamous-inclined John were to go into regular matrimonial training-harness when the canoes returned, their month of probation to reckon from the hour they began their courtship, as the results were considered settled already and the dowry regarded as satisfactory.

John had invested his past wages as cook in bags of rice, packages of salt, and much trading tobacco, which the Malays had helped him to divide and convey to the different mansions of his brides. It was arranged that he would divide his hours equally amongst the three, while meantime they assisted him to put up his future house and palisade his different estates; for as each bride brought her own portion of land, the astute Celestial was twice wealthier than the unambitious Hector, and as he was, like all his race, by instinct a born gardener, if he could only keep his team in order, he boded fair to be the wealthiest man of the district with this superior start in life.

So far his blandness and impartial partiality seemed to keep the yellow fiend from the ground; they were all merry over their

225

prize, and regarded the pigtail with as great affection and respect as he felt for it himself.

So the warm sun gilds all nature, and there is no sign of rain about.

Niggeree went with Collins in the Nora to Port Moresby, to look after their different vessels, with a promise that they would join the Thunder soon at Thursday Island and start on fresh adventures.

Over the laughing ocean went the Thunder towards home, past the sleeping sea-snakes and flying-fish, while the dolphins gambolled in front, and all creation seemed to play.

A merry passage, in which young Danby did not torment Captain MacAndrews more than he could help.

A brief halt at Darnley and Murray Islands to take orders, and a parting glass with bluff old Joe and his tawny queen, who has forgotten her grief and grins grimly upon them as they sail away.

"Ta-ta, Prince Consort. Bon soir, Queen Ine. It is not good-bye, but only au revoir."

THE END